SEA OF BETRAYAL

MITCHELL SAM ROSSI

This novel is a work of fiction. I have tried to be as accurate as possible with historic events, times, and locations. However, as is the nature of fiction, some fanciful license was employed.

The characters and the story are solely creations of the mind. Any resemblance to persons, living or dead, is entirely coincidental. This is a revised and updated version of the author's story, *Truk Lagoon.*

No part of this book may be reproduced or transmitted in any form or by any means, electronic or mechanical, except for the purpose of review and/or reference, without explicit permission in writing from the publisher.

Cover artwork design copyright © 2024 by Sleepy Fox Studio
sleepyfoxstudio.net

Published by Paper Angel Press
paperangelpress.com

ISBN 978-1-962538-72-5 (Trade Paperback)

10 9 8 7 6 5 4 3 2 1

FIRST EDITION

For my wife and daughter,
My treasures who make every day worthwhile.

To my cousin, Stephen Moorhouse, not only for introducing me to Classic Studies, beach volleyball, and old cars, but for so much more.

And always, to my friend and mentor, Ben Masselink.
I miss our talks and our laughs.

ACKNOWLEDGMENTS

THERE ARE SO MANY PEOPLE I wish to thank it would easily take another book, but certain ones need mentioning. To Joe Infanger, for passing along details, insights, and a few rich tales about his time as a torpedoman's mate aboard the *U.S.S. Carbonero (SS-337)*. John D'Angona and Bill Erwin, two former submariners who allowed me to pick their brains. To technical scuba diving instructor Jim Eckhoff, who not only helped me sort out the aspects of technical wreck diving, but also shared his experiences diving Truk Lagoon.

To Steven Radecki, managing editor at Paper Angel Press, for believing there was a new generation of readers who would enjoy my story. To my editor, Lisa Jacob, for helping me fill the many story holes I overlooked, and to Kelley York for transforming my words into an incredible book cover.

A SPECIAL ACKNOWLEDGMENT

"Lest we forget these boats on eternal patrol."

To the 375 officers and 3131 crewmen of the 52 U.S. submarines who sacrificed their lives in World War II. The passing years have not diminished your gallantry nor lessened the gratefulness our country feels for your sacrifice.

SEA OF BETRAYAL

1

CHOUKOUTIEN, CHINA, 1929

"*HERR DOKTOR. HERR DOKTOR. Wir haben es gefunden,*" a young Chinese man emerged from the cavern's narrow entrance. It was little more than a jagged gash in the side of the parched, crumbling hillside. He pressed his hands to the sweltering yellow-brown dust, lifted a knee to the edge, and crawled out.

In his rush down the path, the man missed his footing over the unforgiving limestone pebbles and dirt. He bounced once across the ground and rolled to his shoulder with a grunt. He stood without pause as his excitement deferred all pain until evening.

"*Herr Doktor!*" He called again to the row of rectangular tents pitched against the canyon's southern wall. The natural barrier gave the camp shade and respite from the burning glare of the sun and the bite of the arid wind.

Hearing Pei's high voice clatter about the rocks, Doctor Otto Zdansky stepped from the breakfast tent. The paleontologist shaded his eyes from the midmorning sun with an overturned palm.

He saw his soft-faced assistant standing at the crest of the footpath. "*Ich habe es grunden!*" he called, his accent making the German words sound comical.

Zdansky snatched his straw hat from the tea cart, slipped it over his thinning red hair, and started the steep climb up Dragon Bone Hill.

This was the thousandth time he mounted the path. Perhaps the hundredth of the season. He was not exactly certain. The true number of times he had squeezed through the dusty mouth of the dragon was irrelevant. All that mattered would be the last time.

Zdansky reached his assistant. "Wohin?"

"In the small alcove off the main chamber. In the lower level," Pei gulped. "It's what we've been looking for. This time. This time I'm certain."

Zdansky nodded solemnly. His zeal had risen and fallen so often that he was numb to anything but certainty.

Following his assistant, the doctor squirmed into the crevice. They crouched until their fingertips hung beside their boots, then pushed forward with their shoulders cocked awkwardly along the stone wall. Twenty meters in the fissure opened, allowing them full stance. From there, a string of flickering lanterns hung like glowing trumpet flowers urging them downward.

The air temperature dropped, causing the sweat-soaked shirts to chill their skin. Another fifty meters, the walls diverged into a high, vaulted chamber. Fists of lanterns now encircled them like cathedral chandeliers.

Descending a series of bamboo ladders, the men reached the lowest of the cave's four chambers. The first three were now considered complete, while they had only exposed this last chamber in the previous two years.

Zdansky made his way past a crew of hunched Chinese men scraping at the soil. He greeted each with a pat on the back and a nod. Their names were a mystery to him. "*Nî hāo,*" he mumbled. "Good day."

In return, they rattled back in an incomprehensible dialect and presented him with slivers of rock and animal bone in calloused palms, hoping for verification and praise.

The Chinese were the best workers, he thought. They dug from morning to night with more eagerness than any colleague he had ever had.

When Zdansky and Pei reached the cave bottom, the young man waved the doctor further. He moved toward a single lantern hung on the far wall. Bending low, he crawled through a fracture Zdansky had not noticed before.

With his brow arched, the doctor took a deep breath and forced himself through the gap.

The minor chamber was little more than cloakroom in size, with a low ceiling and a moist sandy floor. Three spirit-soaked torches illuminated the center dig.

There, a petite girl with a ropey braid of black hair, worked a small, soft-toothed brush along the base of a coffee-brown oddity rising from the floor. The girl glanced nervously at Zdansky.

"Here, Doctor," Pei said as he knelt beside the girl.

Zdansky drew his gold-rimmed glasses and tucked them behind his ears. He inspected the unearthed segment the girl had coaxed from hiding.

To his amazement, it looked like a fired bit of porcelain, easily mistaken for a rice bowl or teapot. But the cave was too deep in the substrate, too far into the hill to hide any artifact made by modern hands.

Zdansky fumbled at his breast pocket for the leather pouch and the dental tools he carried. A small needle, the tip flattened. He scratched at the dirt, taking care not to mar the bone.

As he cleared away more deposits, he realized this was not a fragment of bone, but rather a nearly complete cranium. Zdansky's heart punched his ribs. He stopped. Took a breath. Tried to settle his hands.

It took nine more hours, with each of them taking turns to remove the sand and rock and the millennia that held the fossil. Finally, Zdansky coaxed the treasure from its natural sarcophagus.

Wiping his glasses, he scrutinized the small globe in his hands. The supra-orbital was intact, the brow ridge highly overstated as he had theorized it would be. The braincase also fit his assumptions, as the skull was long and low. To his surprise, the occipital cap was thick, much thicker than he expected. He had not considered that possibility. It would be a topic of study for years, and that thought alone brought a chuckle.

And there, still embedded tight in the upper jaw, were teeth. Teeth. Four wretched brown molars. He heard himself laugh again.

Zdansky slowly leaned against the rock wall and lowered himself to the sandy floor. With both hands, he lifted the skull as if it were the Holy Chalice. He turned it in the torchlight, a smile growing ever wider on his face.

Turning to Pei and the young dirty-faced girl leaning over him, he nodded thankfully. "*Xièxiè,*" he whispered. "*Xièxiè.*"

After so many years, *Sinanthropus pekinensis*, the Peking Man, was finally his.

2

NORFOLK, VIRGINIA, 1986

F ROM THE GLOOMY NIGHT SKY, snow fell unseen until it passed into the tarnished light of the dockside lamp. There it became a lace curtain flowing into the rippling black waters of the harbor. Indifferent to the snowfall, the waves stroked the wooden pillars of the dock with whispers.

Commander Brian Bovan stood with his right foot on top of a huge iron docking cleat. The snow gathered on his shoulders like heavenly epaulets, pure white and glittering.

He toyed with an unlit cigarette between his lips. Finally, he tossed it into the bay and thoughtlessly wiped his palm over his face. Two days' worth of beard pulled at his wool gloves.

He turned to the enormous silhouette hovering over him. *God, she's beautiful,* he thought. The outline of the conning tower and brief section of stern deck rose above the waterline. Hidden beneath the water was another three hundred feet of the nuclear submarine. A lethal dagger resting in a black sheath.

The *John Adams* sat motionless save for a slight roll that caused the joining gangplank to moan as it slid forward and back in well-worn grooves. Against the ink sky, her shadowy hull absorbed the lights sparkling across the vast harbor.

By design, Brian thought as he envisioned her gliding at 400 meters beneath the open sea. She could be fluorescent pink at that depth; it wouldn't matter. Only on the surface did she need the special skin that made her nearly invisible to prying eyes and curious radar beams.

The heavy arm of dread spread across his shoulders as he realized he would not feel the turn of her deck again or hear his crew's response as they made ready their rise from darkness to sunlight. He would not hear the rush of water leaving her ballast tanks, nor the waves washing across her bow planes or tower.

"She is a gem." Captain Fife appeared at Brian's elbow.

Brian didn't turn. "She certainly is," he said to his commanding officer, his former commanding officer.

"Not a wild guess you'd be here." Fife was not a small man but standing beside Brian's six-foot-two frame forced him to push his cap back to see Brian's face.

"Couldn't quite sleep."

"Me either," the captain said, kicking a pile of fresh snow off the edge of the dock. "I don't know what to tell you, B."

Brian stared at the sub's dive planes and saw the snow clinging to the edge.

Fife turned up his collar and slapped his hands together. "I made a few more inquiries from the four starts down to their drivers. I wish I had something to report. Good or bad. I got nothing."

"You shouldn't be surprised," Brian said, his voice flat. "We both know how this goes."

"This should be your command, B. No fucks about it."

"You're biased, sir," Brian said. He heard Fife chuckle. "If you'll excuse me, Captain. I'm going to walk her one more time." Pivoting, Brian started down the dock toward the submarine's stern.

To Brian's dismay, his captain clung to his side. He had expected no one beyond naval security to be on the dock at 2 a.m. Especially with the snowfall.

"I gave you the highest recommendation."

It was cold out, and Fife's comments were making it colder. Brian did not want to hear what he already knew.

They stopped at the dock's edge. The two men stood silent for a time, staring at the weapon of war as if she was a lover to both of them. Then again, she had been. A steel maiden who beckoned them to release her lines and set her sails. It was the lure felt by every submariner. Unlike the modern giants that crossed the oceans with crews numbering in the thousands, a submarine was akin to the old wooden warships. One captain and one crew separate from the world until she docked in some distant port.

"It makes no sense," Fife said finally.

"Doesn't have to. It's the Navy." Brian went for humor. Neither laughed. "Does the repair crew know about the mid-deck ventilating duct?"

"Stop worrying about that crap. I am sure maintenance has it covered."

"Hard to let go," Brian admitted.

"True," Fife agreed, although neither believed it.

"I was damn lucky to be on this boat. I don't think I've thanked you for that."

"It should be yours now," Fife bit. "It wasn't your record. I've seen your jacket."

Brian gave no response. There was silence between them. A lone tugboat chugged upriver with purpose.

"This is the second time they've denied me a command. Either I take a desk job, or I'm out." Brian said, his jaw tightened at the thought.

Fife stared at his feet. He never stared at his feet. "This had to come from high up, B. Someone with a lot of brass on their shoulder and a dock cleat up their ass."

"This is all I am." Brian pushed his hands into his coat pockets. "I don't know how to steer a desk."

"I still think you should talk to Mills. It can't hurt having an admiral for a family friend."

"It's too late for that," Brian said. He opened his heavy coat and unpinned the submariners' insignia from the breast of his uniform. He juggled the pin with its distinctly stylized dolphins over the black water.

Fife glared. "Don't," he commanded. "You earned those, B. You toss them, you throw that away. And no one, admiral or not, can take that. Ever."

Brian sighed. He slipped the insignias into his pocket and re-buttoned his coat.

"A desk might not be so bad," Fife ventured.

"I don't think you've ever lied to me before, Captain. Are you starting now?"

Fife laughed. "I am just saying. It keeps you in the service."

"Land locked."

"Not something we're used to."

"I think I'll take a drive north to see my mom. Her health hasn't been the best over the last couple of months."

"Sorry to hear that," Fife said. After a moment, added, "How about we head over to Farley's? You can buy."

Brian shook his head. "Mind if we set that for another night, Captain? I am going to stand here and freeze my ass off for a little longer."

Fife understood. He brushed the snow off the top of his collar. It was melting into his shirt. He put out his hand. Brian squeezed it. "If there is anything," he offered.

Brian nodded graciously. He then watched his commanding officer return to his car on the other side of the chain link fence. He saw Fife stop and look back. Not at him, but at the warship. Next month, the captain would be living in South Dakota and fishing freshwater streams, utterly bored with retirement.

The breeze brushed against Brian's coat and dusted the docks with a fresh sweep of snow. It was time to go, to move on, and find something else.

Brian could imagine nothing else after being a submariner. There would be no more deep dives or mid-Pacific rendezvous. No more commands from the bridge. Like his captain, he was going to feel misplaced.

Sliding behind the wheel of his old Ford Bronco, he twisted the ignition key. He stomached a last glance at the *John Adams* as the reclusive vessel disappeared into the falling snow.

Brian wove his way between the naval warehouses and toward exit Gate Number Two.

When the Bronco's headlights fell on the red and white striped swing gate, he stopped the truck.

"Are you cheating this kid, Max?" he asked as he stepped into the guardhouse. Max, the Corporal of the Guard, sat across from a young Marine. Like Max, he held a spread of poker cards over a declining stack of plastic chips.

The grey-haired Marine did not turn. "Ya want in, Commander? Billy here is just about to lose half his pay grade."

The sentry sitting opposite the corporal froze as he stared at the naval commander.

"Tempting," Brian eyed Max's hand. He noted only a pair of kings. "Just not tonight."

The elder Marine set his cards face down on the table. He eyed the sentry. "Go double-check the lock on the east gate, would ya, Billy?"

The soldier stared at the corporal. Glanced at his hand. Looked at the corporal again, hesitant to set his cards on the table.

"You little shit. You think I am going to peek?"

He grabbed his rifle and coat. "Not with the Commander here, sir."

"Asshole," Max mumbled as he reached for the coffeepot brewing in the machine atop the file cabinets. "Coffee?"

Brian grabbed a thick porcelain cup. He held it out.

"So, I hear you're leaving us."

Brian nodded. "Hear anything else?"

"You know me, Commander, scuttlebutt is just a hobby. I'll tell ya, since your boat pulled in, you've been the headliner."

Brian glanced over the rim of his cup. "Lucky me."

"What I have heard, the reasons you got passed over. All manure. I know how it is. The Navy's not much different from the Marines. You didn't kiss enough ass," the old Marine said, with a smirk.

"Probably not."

"Well, it is all bullshit and politics. And I couldn't care less about any of it," he said as he sweetened his coffee with four mountainous spoons of sugar. "You drive up to my gate any time you like, Commander. I'll wave you through."

"Thanks, Max." Brian set the cup on the filing cabinet.

Max stiffened to attention and snapped a salute. "Sir. Have a good evening." The veteran of three wars, with the granite jaw and hard thin lips, had always pushed against the rules. He had a brash mouth and thought little of his superiors. Except for Commander Bovan.

Brian grinned. "Much appreciated, Corporal." He returned the salute, moved from the warmth of the guardhouse to the Bronco.

The young Marine returned a few minutes later.

"That was him, huh? That sub commander they deep-sixed." He snickered to himself.

Max ignored him. He sat at the table and lifted his cards. "Whatcha holding?"

The young Marine returned to his original position and scooped up his hand. "I heard he was fucking an admiral's daughter," he reshuffled his cards. "Bubbleheads. They all think they're better, right?"

The corporal teetered his chair back as he studied his cards. "I know you're new to my detail, son, so let's not talk about the commander," Max said.

The Marine frowned. "Just saying what I heard."

"Let me rephrase myself." Max rested his elbows on the table and glared at the younger man. "I hear ya talking crap about that particular naval officer, and I'll plant the heel of my boot at the back of your throat," he said calmly. "Understand?"

The Marine stared across the table at his corporal whose stare did not waver. He nodded nervously as he turned to his cards.

Max slid the lowest cards from his hand and dropped them on the table. "Deal me three," he said.

3

FALO ISLAND, TRUK LAGOON, 1986

CAUGHT IN THE LAST RAYS of sunlight, the scuba diver's hazy silhouette danced across the twisted deck of the massive shipwreck. Although the waters of the tropical lagoon were renowned for their clarity, the physics of light and color painted the aquatic world a willowy shade of indigo at one hundred and forty feet below the surface.

Reaching the freighter's superstructure, the diver grasped the remnants of a handrail that once encircled the pilothouse. He pulled himself, hand-over-hand, to the forward windows. The glass that once protected the crew from the elements was gone, although he could not tell if it had shattered during the American's attack or if the windows had fallen after decades of rust and decay.

With a flick of his fins, he slipped into the wreck that, forty-two years before, had been his sanctuary in a war-torn world. He had spent three years crisscrossing the South Pacific aboard the *Kuma Maru*, but he could never have imagined their reunion would be at the bottom of the sea.

Today was the sixth time he had entered the freighter in the last week. The sixth time he had motored across the lagoon, dropped his anchor off the sun-bleached islet, lowered his extra air tanks and plunged into the depths. But with each dive, he sensed he was getting closer to his prize.

Inside the bridge, the exhaust bubbles from his regulator crashed into the ceiling and, forced by the ship's odd list to starboard, skated like droplets of quicksilver into the upper corner. From there, they escaped through a jagged crack in the bulkhead.

The diver removed the Dacor diving lamp from his waistbelt and swept the expansive room with its light. The beam revealed the tapestry of life that had slowly transformed the wartime relic into an ethereal garden.

Orange sponges and purple corals dappled every surface while shy damsels and rainbow parrotfish peeked out from a myriad of cracks and crevices. The diver glanced at the cabinets that once held logbooks and binoculars, expecting to see the resident school of silvery-green jackfish that had greeted him before. But they were gone, and he wondered if his comings and goings had driven them to seek quieter lodgings.

The diver turned his light to the chart table still dominating the bridge's center. From one of its cubbyholes, a speckled green moray eel emerged. Mouthing the water as it breathed, it flashed impressively sharp teeth. The display was daring the diver to swim closer.

At the bottom of the table, just beneath the eel's lair, a human skull rested half-buried in the thick, reddish-brown silt. Where eyes had been, dark shadows stared at the intruder.

With deep reverence, the diver bowed his head. "Shimizu-san, yurushi te kudasai," he said into his regulator. It was a simple request, and he asked it of his fallen shipmate each time he entered the wreck.

He could see Lieutenant Shimizu again as he hunched over the chart table. The young junior officer with gaunt shoulders and round spectacles tucked behind his ears, his angular face etched with intensity as he calculated the best route across the southern sea.

In truth, the diver was unsure if the bones at the foot of the table were those of Shimizu. It could be Lt. Itomura or Second Officer Yokayama. It did not matter. His plea for forgiveness was meant for all of them, for all the men he had mistakenly outlived.

At the back of the pilothouse, the diver found the tied end of the yellow safety rope he had secured the day before. After so many years, and with the devastation inflicted by the American torpedoes, he was not as sure about the ship's twisted interior. Thus, the rope was his ball of thread, his lead through the twisted catacomb of steel and iron just as Theseus had used to escape the Minotaur's labyrinth.

Entering the passage, he left the last remnants of sunlight behind and entered a world of complete darkness. Here, his dive lamp became as essential as the air in his tanks.

With his hand on the rope, the diver retraced the path he had taken the day before. Gliding along the starboard bulkhead, he carefully avoided its serrated edge that opened like a monstrous gaping jaw. He could not tell if the ruptured metal was the result of a direct hit or from a secondary explosion triggered by the ammunition stores in the midship hold. Seeing the blast had torn so quickly through the heavy superstructure, he wondered how many men were obliterated by its flash of heat and flames.

He passed the officers' quarters. His cabin was two decks below as he had yet to earn the captain's permission to move upward. Ironically, Captain Kiyohara's animosity toward him had possibly saved his life.

Finally, he reached the stairway that led to the lower decks. As the diver descended into the passage, the water seemed to abate, and he saw his crew again. Ghosts in their dark blue uniforms rushed in a frenzy along the steep ladders, their voices high with excitement and fear as alarms blared and emergency lights flashed.

At the bottom of the stairs, he carefully made his way through a web of fallen cables and conduit lines drooping across the doorway. It was as if a giant sea spider had set its trap and was now waiting in the gloom. He continued deeper into the ship.

During his first dives, he had entered the forward hold, where he found the three-man HA-GO combat tank he remembered waiting to be off-loaded. Like everything else in the freighter's belly, the deadly machine never had the chance to enter the war. It was now left to surrender to time and the elements.

The stern section had also escaped damage, allowing the diver to make his way easily into the aft hold. Inside, he discovered the wooden crates that held the freighter's last delivery of munitions had broken open and become a prickly bluish carpet of decaying machine gun rounds, each a tiny time bomb ready to set off the others.

Satisfied he had searched where he could, the diver turned his attention to the midship cargo bay. He had witnessed the initial attack and always assumed that was where the freighter had first been struck. The *Kuma Maru* sunk so quickly he knew the breach was massive. Yet, the angle at which the ship lay along the bottom had blocked any entry into her holds from the outside. The only way in, he realized, was through the carnage of the superstructure.

He checked his air gauge. Twenty more minutes of air. Twenty-five if he was cautious with his efforts, although lingering too long would risk reaching the fresh set of scuba tanks waiting for him along the decompression line.

Finally, he reached the bottom of the staircase. From here, the auxiliary passage was only a few yards away. It was a secondary entry into the cargo bay, and he remembered the ship's mechanics using the network of narrow corridors to move quickly from one end of the vessel to another.

As he swam to the hatchway, he felt a sudden chill and hastily swept his light across the darkness, praying there were no more ghosts to find.

At the end of the passage, the three-foot crowbar he had left the day before was waiting for him, still perched where he had set it against the bulkhead. He had managed to pry open one of the door's four dogleg latches, but the effort had taken all his strength. He hoped the remaining levers would relinquish their grip more easily.

Wedging his finned feet against the bulkhead, the diver jabbed the crowbar into the second latch. With both hands, he gripped the bar and lifted it. The force of metal against metal sent a shrill through the water as the tool clawed into the rusted steel. Spikes of pain shot across his shoulder, and his legs began to shake from his effort. The iron bar felt red hot in his hands as he strained against forty years of corrosion.

Had he been twenty years old again or just twenty years younger, he knew he would have broken it free. But for the moment, the latch did not budge.

Gasping for breath, he stopped. He grunted into his regulator and let the heavy tool slip from his fingers. It crashed against the steel deck with a hollowed clang that shook the entire ship. The sea had not weakened the mechanism but instead welded it into a solid fist of corrosion.

He checked his pressure gauge. The needle hovered at the thousand-pound mark. His jaw tightened with frustration as he realized he had no choice. It was time to go.

As he made his way to the corridor, he began planning tomorrow's dive. He would bring the oxyacetylene torch and sever the door at its hinges. Although cutting thick steel underwater was tediously slow, it was the only way he would breach the hold. The process would add at least two dives. Two dives meant two days.

He sighed. Two more days.

She was coming in three. His daughter was flying halfway around the world to see him, and he would have nothing to show her. He had been sure he would have found the crates by now, but the *Kuma Maru* was determined to keep her secrets.

The diver's disappointment was his own, as his daughter had no idea what he was looking for or why. The war meant little to her. It was an abstraction, a nightmare she never felt or dreamt.

For him, the horror he endured had become a shadow figure standing in every corner of their lives. Like an unwelcome guest with an appetite for strife, it was a wedge that severed him from his family.

It never let him get close to his daughter. Or his son. Or his wife. Not truly. And then there was the accident. It was not his fault, but it was all his fault.

Now, he wanted to make amends. To tell his daughter of the nightmares that chased him into dark alleys from which he could never find escape. And how, even in his drunken stupors, the torment did not stop.

Of course, there were some confessions he would never share.

The Americans had killed only a fraction of the men who would die on the islands. In the months after the attack, when he and the other soldiers realized their emperor had forsaken them and their provisions were dwindling, the diver began to envy Shimizu for perishing aboard their ship. It had saved his friend from engaging in the vile atrocities needed to survive. Unforgiveable crimes the diver could never tell his daughter.

Following the rope through the serpentine passage, the diver recalled the last time he had seen her but stopped himself as the memory came. They had squared off like adversaries, slinging spiteful words and callous accusations. It was not a day he wished to relive.

Exiting the bridge, the diver bid his friend farewell, then continued out the window. He followed the arc of the hull to where he had lashed the decompression line to the freighter's stern railing.

Tied to the small skiff that had brought him across the lagoon, the line hung in the crystalline waters with two sets of air tanks. Positioned separately at different depths, the tanks designated the timed stops required for the diver to ascend safely.

The first stop was eighty feet below the surface. He would exchange the empty tanks for the new set, pause there for seven minutes, rise to fifty feet, and wait fifteen minutes more.

The last set of tanks dangled only thirty feet beneath the surface, but the diver had to remain at that depth for nearly forty-five minutes.

Although tedious, if he rose too quickly, the nitrogen molecules his body had absorbed during the dive would accumulate into microscopic bubbles that would clog his veins and rupture his organs. The diver knew that miscalculating or rushing the protocol would likely be fatal.

As he continued through the blue haze, the diver's mind wandered. What will she say when she steps from the plane? Will she smile? Grant him a hug or a kiss on the cheek? Or will there be a salvo of harsh words? He doubted their reunion would be warm, but he hoped the islands were too far for her to bring bitterness.

The diver tilted his head back. Against the shimmering surface, he saw the silhouette of the first scuba tanks above him. He checked his pressure gauge. It was leaning toward zero.

As he reached the fresh air supply, he slipped off his empty tanks and secured them to the line. He pushed the new regulator across his lips.

It took unexpected effort to retrieve the first breath. Worry seized him. Not panic, not yet.

He checked the valve at the top of the steel tanks. It was open fully. Quickly, he fumbled for the pressure gauge and saw its thin needle resting against the red zero.

He was fifty feet from the next set but chanced a third breath, filling his chest with all that remained in the regulator hose. Then, fighting against fear, he kicked upwards.

Slow. Go slow, he told himself as he remembered the rules of free ascent. Release the bubbles from your mouth. Do not hold your breath. The nitrogen is still there. It needs to be released.

His heart pounded in his throat as he pulled himself up the line. Deep within his chest, his lungs began to burn as they struggled for a breath that was not there. He envisioned himself suddenly breaking through the surface, choking, gasping, taking in the sweet, warm air. He forced the thought away, shook his head, and continued upward.

When the diver saw the next set of air tanks above him, he forgot the cautions and raced to the equipment with powerful kicks. Snatching the regulator, he crammed it into his mouth. He inhaled.

Nothing.

It was empty, altogether void of life-giving air. He could not stop himself. He spit out the regulator and swam madly toward the surface.

There was only thirty feet of liquid between him and the surface. Thirty feet of oxygen-rich water he could not use, oxygen his body could not absorb. With no breath, the distance became thirty miles.

Feeling his hands cramp, he released his weight belt with clawed fingers. His sense of speed increased, but pain blurred his vision as the nitrogen bubbles behind his eyes pushed outward.

In a cold boil, his soft organs began to inflate within him. His chest swelled twice its size, severing the nerves along his backbone.

In the last moment of life, he called out his daughter's name, but the only sound was the dull thud of his lungs exploding. A trickle of frothy blood rose from his lips as the natural buoyancy of his body continued to carry him to the surface.

4

RYE VILLAGE, NEW HAMPSHIRE, 1986

"COME CLOSE," the priest lifted his arms toward the last of the somber crowd, making their way to the gravesite. Beneath their stiff shoes, a frosted carpet of maple leaves crackled.

Easing into the first chair, Brian saw the simple spray of white roses resting on the top of the casket. Behind him, he could hear sniffles and whispers. Someone tried to muffle a cough.

In the church, under the fluorescent lights hidden in the vaulted ceiling, Catherine Bovan's chestnut brown coffin sparkled like a new car on a showroom floor. But here, a sorrowful winter sky dulled its shine.

Brian scanned the faces encircling his mother. Soft and rumpled, their eyes puffy and red. *When had his mother grown as old as her friends,* he wondered. When had her hair become thin and grey and her stride as unsure as theirs?

"Let us pray," the priest said, drawing his leather-bound book from under his black vestment. "Lord Jesus Christ," he began. "The three days you lay in the tomb, you made holy the graves of all who believe in you."

Brian felt his aunt Martha slip her arm through his. She squeezed his hand.

He could feel her frail body shiver. With her other hand, she dabbed her crocheted handkerchief to the edge of her nose. She was seven years older than Catherine, and the two had lived together since Brian's uncle had died ten years before. Now she would be alone in the old house on the river.

He would stay a few days just to make sure everything was working and in order before he had to be… Suddenly, Brian remembered he had nowhere to be.

"And even though their bodies lie in the earth, they trust that they, like you, will rise again." Warm clouds of breath rose from the priest as he spoke. "Give our sister peaceful rest in this grave until that day when you, the resurrection and the life, will raise her up in glory."

On the opposite side of the casket, a little girl, resting in her mother's arms, stared wide-eyed at the priest. Brian watched as she looked through the crowd, her curious gaze touching each bowed head. She saw Brian watching her and she snapped away as if caught her in an unforgivable act.

"Then may she see the light of your presence, Lord Jesus, in the kingdom where you live for ever and ever," the priest said.

"Amen," said the crowd together.

After a proper pause, the priest took the silver scepter from the small, neatly dressed boy beside him and sprinkled holy water over the casket. "Let us pray for our sister to our Lord, Jesus Christ, who said: I am the resurrection and the life. The man who believes in me will live even if he dies, and every living person who puts his faith in me will never suffer eternal death." The priest lifted the small brass cross from where it rested on the coffin's lid.

He sprinkled it with the water, closed both hands, and prayed. Finally, he moved to Martha and passed her the cross. He kissed her on the cheek and whispered calming words.

He turned to Brian. "God be with you."

Brian nodded with appreciation.

"Today, the Lord has taken someone very dear to us," the priest lifted his voice. "Our tears will flow today, but not for Catherine's death, for that is but a step into our Maker's arms. He has set a following of sequences for us, from birth to maturity, to wife and husband to parents. We are all here to fulfill his wishes."

Brian sensed the priest's words were meant for his mother's friends, most of them in their eighties. *This must become a common event in their lives*, Brian thought, until the funeral was their own.

"No, our tears are not for Catherine," the priest continued, "but for our loss of her presence among us. We will miss her friendship and her kindness." He lowered his head. "Lord, you wept at the death of Lazarus, your friend; comfort us in our sorrow. We ask this in faith."

"Lord, hear our prayer," everyone replied.

From the corner of his eye, Brian recognized the tall figure crossing the path. The man closed on the semi-circle of mourners, yet he did not mingle. His air of privilege and distinction was palpable. Brian knew, however, it was a false aura Rear Admiral Mills carried long before they stitched the golden stipes onto his sleeve.

Mills removed his cap, revealing the shaved dome of his head that was his hallmark. When he pocketed his wire-framed glasses, Brian saw he wore his full-dress blues.

"You raise the dead to life, give our sister eternal life. We ask this in faith."

"Lord, hear our prayer," the mourners followed.

Fifty yards away, along the frontage road of the small cemetery, a white limousine pulled quietly into the churchyard. Hidden behind tinted windows, a woman in the car's rear seat lifted a Leica camera to her eye. She found Brian through the high-powered lens. She snapped off six frames, photographing as much of his face as possible.

"Over to the left," the limousine driver pointed. "Look who came."

The woman turned the lens on Rear Admiral Mills. More quick photos. Satisfied, she sat back in the thick leather seat and waited.

The priest continued. "Our Father, who art in heaven, hallowed be Thy name, Thy kingdom come, thy will be done on earth as it is in heaven. Give us this day, our daily bread, and forgive us our trespasses as we also forgive those who trespass against us. And lead us not into temptation, but deliver us from evil. Amen."

"Amen," they finished with a single, firm voice. Somehow, the priest's words gave strength to the sad and weary. Still, Catherine's friends remained huddled about the grave, unwilling to let go.

Finally, the congregation thinned as they plodded toward the cars.

Brian helped his aunt to her feet. He kissed her cheek. "I'll be over here," he said as her friends closed in with condolences and promises of companionship.

"Your mother was an extraordinary woman, Brian. We will miss her," the priest took Brian's hand with both of his.

Brian nodded. He knew the priest meant that honestly. "I hope you'll come back to the house. There is enough food to feed the Seventh Fleet."

"Of course." He patted Brian's arm before moving to console the others who remained beside the casket.

Several more people approached Brian to express their sorrow and fondness for his mother. They were close friends and not-so-close friends, the gentle people of New Hampshire who still came to comfort neighbors even on cold winter mornings. Brian was confident that neither his mother nor his aunt had felt lonesome.

As Mills stepped in front of him, his face stoic. It was the face Brian knew well, the one from childhood birthday parties, little league baseball games and in the crowd of his high school graduation. It was the one that looked teary-eyed when watching Brian stand on the field of Annapolis Naval Academy in his formal dress whites and raised his right hand and swear to uphold the US Constitution.

"My condolences, son."

"Thank you for coming, Admiral," Brian said, although not surprised he had. "She, uh... passed in her sleep," he said, his voice catching in his throat.

"I knew Catherine before your father did," Mills said. "Her folks lived two blocks over from mine. We played hooky together and snuck off to the cinema every Wednesday."

Brian had heard all the old stories.

"You were her good news on her worst day, did you know that?" he asked as he stared at the coffin. "She found out she was pregnant the very day I had to tell her Douglas' boat wasn't coming back." He took a breath. "Did you know that?"

"I knew about the timing. I never realized you were the one who told her."

"I asked to. It was the least I could do for her," he sighed. "For him." Mills caught himself in memory, shifted and squared his shoulders. "If there is anything, you know you only have to ask."

Brian remembered Captain Fife's words, "*It can't hurt having an admiral for a family friend.*" He shook his head. "Thank you, Admiral. There's nothing."

Mills' deep-set eyes held on Brian. "You've never been a good liar. Not even as a kid."

"You were the one who taught me to always be honest," Brian pointed.

"Then why aren't you?"

"What do you want me to say? That the Navy screwed me after I gave most of my life to it? I don't think it would make much difference. Do you?"

Mills' lips stiffened.

Brian realized the admiral had probably never been spoken to as harshly. It did not matter. He was a civilian now.

"Did you tell Catherine?"

Brian glanced at the casket as he shook his head. "That would have been the last thing she needed to hear. I was happy she recognized me at all in the last days."

"It wouldn't have mattered to her."

"It would have crushed her," Brian countered.

Mills went quiet for a moment. "I made inquiries."

"I wish you hadn't."

"Do you think I'd let you lose a command and not try to find out why? Or if there was a rule I could twist, I wouldn't?"

Brian sighed. "And?"

"And not a goddamn thing," Mills snapped.

"If you can't get an answer…" Brian said with a shake of his shoulders.

"I'm sorry, son." He settled his cap square. "I tried to be here for you and your mother as much as I could, because your father would have done the same for me. But I never tried to replace him, Brian. That I couldn't do. He was too fine of a man." With that, Rear Admiral Mills walked to the deep blue sedan waiting for him.

Brian walked back to the gravesite. He settled into the same chair. Now, it was only him and his mother. Her congregation of friends had retreated either to his aunt's house or to their own.

He eyed the roses still resting on the casket and noticed, even in the cool morning, they were wilting.

Near one of the maple trees, two men in overalls stood quietly watching him. They were waiting a respectable distance away, anticipating his departure so they could lower his mother to her final place.

"Commander? Commander Bovan?" the soft voice came from behind.

Lost in thought, Brian had not heard her approach. He rose to his feet automatically.

"Commander?" She was a petite woman of Asian descent with pepper-gray hair uncommonly long for her age. Bundled in a heavy gray sweater, black scarf, and a black woolen cap tilted over her left ear, she barely reached his shoulder.

Spiderweb wrinkles etched her cheeks and pulled the corners of her mouth as she smiled at him. As if catching herself, she turned to the coffin, "I am so sorry about your mother."

"You were a friend of hers?" he asked.

The woman shook her head. "I am not sure she would have wanted my friendship."

"I don't understand," he said.

"I know," she said as she pressed something into his hand. Without warning, she rose to the tips of her toes and kissed him quickly on the cheek. "You have his eyes," she whispered. Then she was gone.

Brian could only stand there as he watched her hurry to the open door of the limousine. Her words brought a warm rush to his face. It was not until the car had disappeared onto the main road did he feel the small package in his hand. Wrapped in thin parchment paper and frayed twine, he pulled it apart easily.

An envelope slipped out. Yellowed by age, he read the faded print across the upper edge.

COMMANDER IN CHIEF OF THE U.S. FLEET PACIFIC: CINCPAC

Brian dug his fingernails into the corner and tore it open. A black leather logbook dropped into his hand. Embossed gold lettering centered the cover:

LCDR DOUGLAS BOVAN

USS MAKO

SS-360

A torpedo slammed into Brian's chest.

The *Mako*. Brian knew her. He knew her patrols; the type and tonnage of the enemy ships she had sent to the abyss, when she used her 20mm Oerlikon deck gun for a surface attack, and the names of the downed pilots she plucked from shark-infested waters.

In his senior year of high school, Brian memorized her entire crew and recited their names and hometowns at Christmas mass.

While at the Academy, he had even authored a paper plotting her last patrol, theorizing what could have happened to her and where she might still lie.

The USS *Mako*. His father's submarine.

He ran his fingers over the cover and along its edge. A breath, and he opened it slowly.

He flipped from the first page to the next, finding both pen and pencil entries dark and clear. His father's writing was distinctive, almost typewriter perfect. He had seen it in his mother's letters.

Penmanship was one of Douglas' qualities, Catherine would tell her son as she leaned over the kitchen table and watched him scribble out his homework. It took practice, but Brian finally made his father's habit his own.

> *October 5, '43. Freighter (4,200 tons) destroyed. Blackett*
> >   *Strait.*
> *October 17, '43. Cruiser, Kuma class, challenged. Night Run.*
> >   *Squall. Failed attempt.*
> *October 22, '43. Aussie pilot recovered. Dead Man's atoll.*
> >   *Transferred - USS Hornet by PBY.*
> *October 26, '43, Convoy sighted. No fish remaining. Course*
> >   *set for Pearl.*

Its pages were filled with notes for harbor repairs, suggestions for spares, a crewman's birthday, and various other reminders within the entries. He turned to the last few pages as if beckoned.

> *Oct. 30, '43. Pick Catherine up at airport. 1400 hrs.*
> >   *Party at Sammy's tomorrow. 1830 hrs.*
> *Jan. 5 '44. Take Catherine to the airport. 0700 hrs.*
> *Jan. 19, '44. Report to HQ, 0600 hrs.*

Jan. 25, '44. Reorder shaft bearing for forward motor.
Burkie shipped out. Shark preparing.
Feb. 3, '44 HQ. Pick up orders. Tomorrow.
Mid-night departure.

At the bottom of the page was another note, *Third hatch, leave locked.* With its smudged lettering, it looked as if someone else had written it in haste.

It was the date of the last entry that tore into Brian's stomach and set his nerves on fire. With his ears ringing, Brian closed the logbook and stared at the mosaic of gold and red leaves under his feet.

This is wrong, he thought. *Impossible and wrong.*

In his hand was his father's private logbook. Like other captains, Douglas kept this back-pocket notepad for reminders. He had little doubt the remaining pages were filled with birthday dates of crewmen, their wives' names, and perhaps those of their kids. There might be an entry, quick and crude notes about events aboard. Favored meals. Bad coffee. Perhaps a reflective thought about a whimsical sunset.

It was all unofficial. Any entry that needed to be, the captain would transfer daily to the ship's official heavily bound naval logbook.

But the last date. The date of their departure.

February 3rd, 1944.

The day the United States Navy confirmed the loss of the captain and crew of the USS *Mako* in the South China Sea.

5

CANTON, CHINA, 1942

CAPTAIN TAMURA PUSHED the scrubby cloth map across the cluttered desk and leaned into the leather-tufted American chair. He rubbed his scratchy eyes. Seven hours focused on the best plan to move his men north, and only now the sun was reaching the zenith of midday.

He stood. Arched his back. Stretched his arms. A steady feeling of excitement swirled within him. Today, he had set a morning execution for Ci-Yip Leu, the owner of the estate he and his soldiers now occupied.

Leu had given no resistance to Tamura's men when they arrived to turn his Colonial-style home into their province command post. The Chinese businessman had welcomed the poisonous influences of the West, flaunted his wealth and local stature, and used it for political gain.

Tamura had no misgivings about having Leu and his eldest son held in the barn, tied and gagged, and forced to witness his soldiers having their way with his wife and three daughters. There had to be rewards for men or they might not fight valiantly when needed.

Tamura's own compensation came in the form of Leu's youngest daughter. Unfortunately, in a fit of rage, he had broken the girl's neck two nights before.

He reached for the cup of sake resting on the edge of the dominating oak desk. The drink had gone cold. He finished it anyway in a quick gulp. The sharp taste lingered at the back of his throat as he wove his belt and holster around his soft waist. He set his wool field cap over short grey hair and strolled into the courtyard.

The two soldiers guarding the house entrance fell in behind him, their steps synchronized with his.

"Igawa-san," he called to his first lieutenant.

Igawa, a hardened soldier with a willowy mustache, entered the yard as if bored. He bowed with just enough respect to escape reprimand.

"Bring them," Tamura demanded.

Another dip of his shoulders and Igawa crossed to the barn. Reaching the heavy, weathered door, he slipped inside. A moment later, two more guards pulled the Chinese family into the warmth of the day.

The flabby, half-naked woman fell to the ground shaking; her dirt-caked face streaked with tears. Her eleven-year-old daughter moved quietly beside her, put a hand on her shoulder and stared blankly into the harsh sun. The older two daughters, screaming loudly, darted instinctively to their mother's side, hoping for protection she could not offer.

Their once elegant silk robes were torn and soiled from the barn floor and the abuse. Their faces were bruised, and their breasts exposed to the sunlight.

The captain glared at Leu and his son, who now stood behind the remnants of their family. The boy dropped his gaze while Leu stared defiantly at Tamura.

"We have charged you with the corruption of Asia. You have exposed your community to the Anglo demons and the lies they propagate in their pursuit to control our world," Tamura said, and Igawa translated his words into Chinese. "Death is the punishment. A sentence you alone have brought to your family."

Tamura waited. He watched Leu's eyes, but they did not turn away. The Chinese man held the captain's glare, their intensity matched.

Frustrated, Tamura extended his hand. A soldier instantly filled it with an elegant sword, its delicately arched blade glistening. It was at once a work of art and a harbinger of death.

Tamura stepped briskly toward the woman. Grasped with two hands, the sword rose. The strike was effortless. Graceful. The well-honed blade opening flesh and severing bone without hesitance.

The child made no noise as her fragmented body fell to the dirt. Showered with her warm blood, however, her sisters screamed hysterically.

Tamura felt his groin tighten at the sight of the terrified girls trying to push the corpse away.

A sweep of his arms and the screams of one girl turned into a rush of air as her head jumped off her neck and fell to the ground.

The captain could not help himself. He hardened under his uniform as he stepped to the last daughter. Leu's wife pulled the child closer, cradling her against her breasts. Leu's son dropped to his knees and vomited. The Chinese man, however, stood unmoved. His mouth almost at a smirk.

Tamura shifted his stance, squared himself over the boy. He felt the trickle of excitement again as he lifted the sword skyward.

A scream stopped his hand. From across the yard, a peasant woman bolted past his guards and towards him, yelling. She kept her hands high above her head.

Instantly, the soldiers raised their rifles. "Matte!" Igawa called, stopping them.

The woman dropped to the ground next to Leu's son. Putting her arms around him, she absorbed him as tightly as she could. She shook her head at Tamura; her face contorted with fear. She repeated what she had yelled across the yard.

Tamura turned to Igawa. "What does she say?" His lieutenant looked puzzled.

"She begs you to spare her son." he said.

"Her son?" Tamura frowned; his face reddened. "Who is she?"

Igawa repeated what his captain asked. The woman responded at length. "She is a cook's assistant. Her son was the houseboy here."

The woman spoke again, and the lieutenant translated. "They are all from the village, Captain. They were promised a share of Leu's land if they pretended to be the family until we moved out of the region."

Tamura trembled. In one motion, he drew his pistol from its side holster and stepped up to the man who he had thought was Leu.

Tamura pushed the barrel into the man's brow. Only as the hammer fell, did he finally close his eyes. The explosion echoed against the house. The body dropped as his skull and brain were scattered several feet behind him.

Tamura turned toward the boy and aimed.

The peasant woman grabbed Tamura's legs. She cried out the only Japanese word she knew, desperately trying to stop him. "Taisetsu!" she screamed. "Treasure! Treasure!"

Tamura pressed the gun against the top of her head.

The woman turned to Igawa. "Treasure. I know. I know."

"What is she saying?" Tamura asked, his finger tight on the trigger.

Igawa hesitated. "What are you saying?" Igawa asked as he grabbed her arm. "Speak quick."

"The Chinese treasure. I know where Leu hid them. I'll show you. Let my son go, and I'll show you," she reached out to the lieutenant, who took a step back. "Please, he is my only son."

Tamura turned. "Well?"

The lieutenant told him what she had said.

"Is she lying?" Tamura asked. "A desperate mother?"

"The guards can stop him on the road. And we can always shoot her later," Igawa said. "If Leu offered his land to peasants, what else might he have hidden?"

Tamura glared at the woman, shivering at the end of his pistol. He grabbed the boy's neck and pulled him from his mother's arms. He shoved him toward the front gate. The boy glanced at his mother. She nodded, and he ran as fast as his bare feet could carry him.

"Show me now," Tamura said as he lifted her by the hair. She fought back until her son had disappeared around the bend in the road.

"In the main house," she said to Igawa as she led them inside.

Before following her, Tamura ordered the bodies removed from the yard, and the remaining two women returned to the barn. He would execute them tomorrow.

The peasant woman went directly to the room Tamura had transformed into his office. She pointed to the wooden floor below the desk. "Under," she said.

Tamura called to the two men stationed at the entrance. They pulled the heavy desk to the side of the room and rolled the thick carpet away. With their knives, they stabbed the floorboards.

As they lifted the first planks, Igawa saw the stretched canvas beneath a thin layer of dirt. "Stop," he ordered.

"Put the woman in my quarters," Tamura added. "Tie her well."

Igawa yanked away the remaining sections of the floor. Feeling through the dirt, he found the corner of the canvas. Together, they pulled it back, filling the room with a cloud of gritty dust.

Beneath the tarpaulin, the Chinese had hidden two long wooden boxes. Tamura and Igawa each grabbed an end and lifted one box from the hole.

With the back of his hand, Igawa brushed the dust clear, revealing an odd insignia on the lid. It was a hand-painted globe with an eagle standing on the top and an anchor laying diagonally behind it. In the bird's beak was a banner reading: Semper Fidelis.

"Do you recognize it?" Tamura asked with impatience.

Igawa chuckled. "It is from the Americans. Their Marines."

"A trap?"

Igawa stared at the box with reserve. "Maybe. It seems too well hidden. Wouldn't they want it found if it was a trap?"

"Open it," Tamura said, sweat and dust pasted his face. The room was becoming unbearably hot.

The lieutenant used his thick-bladed knife to break the single padlock. Before lifting the lid, he glanced at the captain one more time.

"Go on," Tamura told him.

Igawa could not help himself. He held his breath as he lifted the lid. The hinges squeaked, but there was no explosive surprise.

Reaching inside, they found several packages wrapped carefully in thick paper and twine. The lieutenant tore one open. He stared in disbelief at what he found.

"What is it, Igawa-san?"

The lieutenant lifted it. "It is a skull." He passed it to him.

"Treasure," Tamura growled. "The bitch lied to us." He cocked his arm to smash the bones against the far wall.

"Captain, wait," Igawa held up his hand. He had found a letter and was reading it quickly. "I have heard of these. When I was at the university before the war."

"Of what? A pile of bones?" Tamura asked.

"They are fossils. Humanoid bones that are important to the Peking University," he said. "The letter addresses the American consulate. It asks they be kept safe and taken to the United States until the war concludes."

Tamura turned the skull toward him, face to face. "So, you were on your way to America?" the captain joked.

Igawa did not smile. He continued to read. "These might be valuable, Captain. They are to the Chinese."

Tamura leaned into the locker and poked at the other carefully wrapped packages. There were more skulls and an array of dissimilar bones he did not know could fit in a human body. "You are serious, Igawa-san?"

The lieutenant took the skull from his captain's hand and re-wrapped it. "Finding these could do well for your career." He set the parcel on the American crate.

Together, they muscled the box back into the shallow trench, returned the tarp and the floorboards. Tamura leaned against the desk as Igawa centered the rug. He drew a handkerchief from his pocket and wiped his face.

"The Chinese think of these fossils as their ancestors," Igawa said, slapping his hands clean. "They honor them as we would a Masamune sword or a Meiji banner. They are much more than relics for a museum."

Tamura rubbed his hand over his short, bristly hair. "If the peasant woman knows they are here, so must others."

Igawa nodded as they stared at the rug.

"What do you suggest, Igawa-san? You are better educated than I am in these matters."

"We took this property under your command, Captain. Anything commandeered is to your merit, of course. Still, it might be dangerous to announce them. We should secure their transport to Tokyo."

"That is probably best, Igawa-san. You always think of problems I have not considered."

"Only because I studied the enemy, Captain. They will do what they can to regain their treasure. It offers them prestige."

"Monkey bones?"

Igawa snickered. "The Chinese are not sophisticated, but they are zealous. It might be wise to send this first to Shanghai. From there, I know it will be easier to ship them quietly to Sasebo," he said.

"You can do this?" Tamura asked, suddenly aware of his lieutenant's resourcefulness.

Igawa grinned sheepishly. "I can."

•　　　•　　　•

Tamura pushed away from the woman's soft, naked body and sat up in the bed. Still wet from his gratification, the sheets clung to the peasant as she lay on her right side. It was the only position she could manage, with her right wrist so tightly bound to the brass bedpost.

The sizeable bed was the best thing Tamura found at Leu's estate. It amazed him how many objects the landowner's brother had sent from America. It was too bad he would have to burn it with the rest of the house when his troops moved on.

Tamura swept his leg from the bed, tucked himself into his cotton fudoshi cloth that roped between his legs and around his waist. He ambled to the window.

His men were doing morning calisthenics. Others marched. A few were leaning on the animal pen, cigarette smoke rising from their lips into the warming day.

From the distance, Tamura heard the growing drum of a diesel engine and saw one of his jeeps pull into the estate. In its trail was a military truck with canvas drooping over its bed.

As the captain climbed into his uniform, he noticed the woman was watching him. Her face was emotionless, her eyes dead though they followed him across the room. He finished dressing.

•　　　•　　　•

"We had engine trouble up the road, Lieutenant," said the tallest of the two soldiers was saying as he handed Igawa their papers.

When Tamura approached, all three men saluted. The lieutenant handed him the men's orders.

"They are transporting foreign weapons captured near Anqing." Igawa pointed at the last order on the paper. "To be shipped home."

Tamura looked at Igawa briefly. "You will not make Wenzhou by the time this ship sails."

"There are freighters leaving every few days," the sergeant assured him.

"The road to Wenzhou is not secure," Igawa said. "These weapons would bring a high price on the black market, Captain. Perhaps an escort? We can send them with two jeeps in the morning."

Tamura was not sure what Igawa was saying. Suddenly, he felt unease about his lieutenant's cleverness. "Yes. See that it is carried out," he said and returned to the house.

Igawa passed the papers back to the tall soldier.

•   •   •

The clear evening was pleasantly cool, with a light breeze arriving from the north. It smelled fresh, organic—a stark difference from when the wind traipsed up from the south carrying the stench of Canton's industrial sprawl.

Igawa made his rounds with extra purpose and certainty. He wanted to be sure his guards were at their appointed positions and had not slipped off a quick snooze or a few drags off a cigarette. He needed an accounting of each man for his plan to work smoothly.

Crossing the yard, he glanced toward the barn where the military truck had parked all day. The spot under the broken eaves was now empty.

With a slight bounce in his step, Igawa headed to the main house. He stopped in front of the posted guard, made drama of an unbuttoned shirt.

Inside, he moved directly to Tamura's office. The door was closed, but in the gap beneath them, he could see the room was dark. Still, he entered with caution.

He pulled the drapes and, with a firm tug, slid back the iron latch that locked the two opaque windowpanes together. Carefully, he eased one open. Against the bamboo hedge that ran along the house, Igawa could see the silhouette of the military truck.

He strolled across the room to Tamura's desk and found the escort orders he had suggested. They were signed. Folding them carefully, the lieutenant tucked them under his uniform shirt.

Igawa made his way to the steep staircase and up to the second-floor landing. In his throat, his heart pounded. With concentration, he kept his breath slow and steady.

At the bedroom doors, he listened. The rhythmic swaying of the brass bed and the gasps of a woman filled the oversized chamber. Timing the unlocked handle with the captain's brutish thrusts, he eased the door open.

In the disjointed shadows tossed by a single light, Igawa saw Tamura laying over the woman, his fists entangled in her hair, his narrow hips pumping comically into the spread of her legs.

The peasant's eyes clenched shut, her face a contortion of pain and determination. While Tamura focused only on his indulgence, the woman was working desperately to free her hand from the leather strap binding her to the bed frame.

Igawa crept to the edge of the bed. With loose fingers, he eased his long knife from its sheath. A flash of blade, and with a heavy stroke, he plunged the weapon between Tamura's shoulders.

The captain shrieked as he tried to lift himself to face his assailant. Igawa leapt on top of them, pressing his knee into the swell of Tamura's back.

To Igawa's surprise, the woman did not scream. She immediately wrapped her thick legs around the captain's waist. With her free arm, she pulled him tight into her breasts.

The captain struggled desperately as Igawa plunged the blade repeatedly into his back. It shattered his backbone and ruptured his left lung and heart. Tamura's body shook violently in spasms until, finally, it fused into her grasp.

Leaving the knife standing in the oozing flesh, Igawa stepped away. The woman, now drenched with Tamura's blood, stared at him.

He peered out the bedroom window. As he hoped, the truck was gone. His hired soldiers had completed their task and the American crates were now in the possession of his long-trusted associates.

Returning to the bedside, Igawa casually drew his sidearm. He put a finger to his lips. "Shhhhh," he motioned.

Once again, the peasant did not call out. She simply glared at the Japanese officer standing over her and his dead captain.

The bullet's impact slammed her head into the silk pillow and sent blood and bone across the Western-styled side table and brass lamp.

Holstering his gun, Igawa retrieved Tamura's identical knife from his belt lying on the dresser. He slipped it into his sheath as the guards bolted into the room.

6

WASHINGTON D.C., 1986

B RIAN DRAGGED HIMSELF out of the taxi, pushed a crumpled twenty between the headrests, and slammed the door without change.

It was 4:50 p.m. by his watch. He rolled the collar of his overcoat, switched his briefcase to his left hand, hunched his shoulders and ascended the marble steps of the Navy's Bureau of Personnel building.

A gray evening with a stabbing wind. The perfect accouterment to the chill that was cutting through Brian's veins like razor blades tumbling along an Alpine brook.

The logbook threw him into a tunnel without a light at the end. His accepted vision of the world was gone. Skewed. Off. Dive planes angled down 30 degrees. Deck tilted. It was as if someone had pointed out the earth was, in fact, square.

Brian pushed through the tall glass doors with his forearm. A guard with a dimpled chin and blue uniform stood near the elevators watching the wall clock. His shift was nearly over, the last minutes dragging into years. He barely glanced at Brian.

Brian slipped his wool gloves into his pocket as he followed the wall placards leading him to the second floor.

He found the indistinct door marked Naval Records at the end of the hall, pushed in.

A glance around the empty waiting room. "Busy today," Brian said as he moved to the black counter that split the room in half.

The young man sitting on the opposite side lifted his pen from a yellow legal pad that was filled with lonely games of tic-tac-toe. "Three-day weekend. Everyone beat it out of here by noon," he said with a smirk.

Brian took in the clerk's name. Ted Gruel. Good name for a football player. Unfortunately, the young man was a wobbly stick in a collared shirt and narrow tie.

"I'd like to look at my files and also my father's." Brian set his I.D. card on the legal pad. "My dad was Douglas Bovan. Active from 1936 until 1944."

"'44?" Ted asked with an exhale. "That'll take a few minutes. Records before 1962 aren't on computer files yet. Anything to narrow the search?"

"He was the commander of the *Mako*. A sub out of Pearl Harbor."

"Got it. Let me grab yours off the computer first." He moved to a small desk at the back wall. A cream-colored IBM computer monitor dominated the workspace. With one finger, he pecked at the keyboard.

Brian unbuttoned his tan overcoat, moved to one of the brown vinyl waiting chairs. He pinched the bridge of his nose with his index finger and thumb. Someone was kicking the base of his skull as if they were testing the tires on a used car.

He had only slept in fits over the two days since the funeral. The thick dust of his mother's attic did not help. Childhood allergies he thought he had outgrown returned as he tore through the vintage trunks and file boxes hidden under the shadowy eaves.

There was nothing for him in her treasures. At least nothing he needed now. There were the old dresses with lace hems, a collection of *Life* magazines from the 50s. A shoe box of photos and postcards and costume jewelry. He found a half-dozen cigarette tips, the glamorous holders women used for smoking. Two were made with mother-of-pearl.

Brian could not remember his mother smoking. She hated when he did, saying it ruined her cooking and made the house smell like a sweatshop.

By the time he reached the far end of the attic, a trail of tossed and pillaged boxes behind him, Brian had found nothing that revealed how the Asian woman had gotten the logbook.

At the back of the office, Ted watched green lines of symbols and numbers shuffle up the monitor screen, searching for Brian's files. He strummed his fingers in time with the dance. Finally, the screen came to life, but the readout was not what he expected.

```
BRIAN BOVAN:
COMMANDER, U.S. NAVY
INACTIVE
ALL PERSONAL AND NAVAL RECORDS SEALED.
CODE: 7-BLUE
```

Ted sat up.

7-Blue. He had never run across a 7-Blue before. He glanced at the commander. The code told him that the name he had called up was someone with top Naval clearance. It also declared that person a possible risk to national security.

The clerk cleared the screen and walked to the counter. "Mr. Bovan," he said with heavy emphasis on the mister. "I'm afraid I'm not authorized to release your files."

"Excuse me?" Brian pressed his hand to the counter.

"The computer system. The guys upstairs, they are always changing programs. I really don't know much about it," he said flatly.

"When can I get to them?" Brian could feel his headache increasing.

"No telling."

"What about my father's? You said they weren't on the computer. They were in the basement."

Ted frowned. Thinking under pressure was not his best skill. "I am sorry, sir. You'll have to speak to the records officer at the Pentagon. He'll be able to give you more information." Ted angled his watch. "Probably closed by now, though."

"You can't get them?"

The clerk shook his head. He took a half-step back from the counter. "Sorry."

Brian felt his growing anger, understood the young man's effort at self-preservation. "Is there an office manager or someone else who can help me?" Brian asked.

"Not until Tuesday."

Brian glared. Ted was lying. Before he realized it, Brian felt himself reach across the counter and grab the clerk by the arm. "Bullshit," he snapped. "Who do I talk to?"

"Man, like I said, you have to go to the Pentagon office," the clerk pulled away, breaking Brian's grip. He caught his foot on the bottom of a chair and fell to the floor.

"You fuck," Ted barked.

Brian ignored him. Outside, twilight was slipping to darkness. The wind had fallen, as had the temperature. Brian hit the sidewalk and turned north. A taxi slowed. Brian did not flag it down. He wanted to walk. He needed to walk.

Tuesday. He could not wait for Tuesday. There was one person he knew he could talk to before then.

•   •   •

"Thanks for seeing me, Admiral." Brian followed Mills through the sterile white hallway. "Sorry to interrupt your Saturday." He suddenly felt awkward in his wrinkled brown suit.

In contrast, the admiral wore starched white pants, a powder blue polo shirt and a wool V-neck sweater. *Ready for a Saturday cruise on the Potomac,* Brian thought, and wondered if that was exactly what he had pulled Mills from this morning.

They walked down corridors lined with framed photographs of modern warships and military planes as they headed towards the inner offices of the Naval wing of the huge Pentagon complex.

"You said it was urgent," Mills said as he nodded to the guard seated within a circular counter. It was the third such station they had passed after reaching the fourth floor. Each was carefully centered in the middle of converging halls, allowing the guard a clear view of anyone approaching.

"Where did you say you were staying?" Mills asked.

"The Hyatt," Brian said.

"You should have called. There is plenty of room at the house and Beth would love to see you."

"Please give her my best."

"You can tell her. Maybe dinner tomorrow?"

"Maybe," Brian said.

Finally, they walked onto the thick emerald rug of the admiral's office. Oil paintings of old galleons and other square-riggers at full sail hung on the rich wood-paneled walls. The four rows of secretaries' desk were all cleaned and polished. Each of their phones, notepads, Rolodex card files, and assorted paraphernalia sat in the same position. *Military precision*, Brian thought as he followed Mills into his private office.

"So," Mills rounded this oak desk like a chopper landing on an aircraft carrier. He motioned Brian to the red leather chair in front of him. "What can I help with?"

Brian cracked open his briefcase. Withdrawing the logbook, he stood and slid it into Mills' hands.

If years of military service had taught the admiral anything, it was the importance of control and composure. Yet at that moment, as he scanned the gold letters on the cover, Brian could see the blood rush from his face. From his smooth dome to his cheeks, he turned as white as the froth of a sea wave.

Mills opened the book and flipped each page slowly, reading every entry. Finally, he pressed the covers together. "Where did you find this?"

"It was given to me at the funeral," Brian said. "The last entry. You saw it?"

"Yes," Mills said. "This is an important heirloom, Brian. You can show it to your grandkids."

Brian read through the evasion. "The date. February 3rd. He was supposed to be in the South China Sea. This proves his sub was in Pearl," Brian said. "The records are wrong, Admiral."

"Brian," Mills raised his hands. "It was a big war. While I like to think the Navy operated with perfection, it didn't. The records are not perfect. They never are. People write them down. They make mistakes, son. That is all this is."

"I tried to pull my files. All I got were weak excuses."

"Jesus, Brian. You only left the Navy a week ago. They are probably still in the Review Board's office or en route back to the records building. You were the second in command of a nuclear attack submarine. You might never see your files."

"And my father's?" Brian asked.

Mills leaned back. "Attached to yours, I am sure."

"Why?"

"Because they go through your history, son. Yours and your family's. That is the way it is," Mills said. "They look at everything. You know that. The Navy doesn't hand out warships with nuclear capabilities like popcorn at the theater."

Brian took a breath. He felt himself sink in the buttery leather of the chair. "His records influenced mine, didn't they?"

Mills' broad shoulders, comfortable with the weight of gold admiral stars, suddenly drooped. Pushing from the desk, he opened a hidden cupboard on the bookshelf. From a crystal decanter, he poured two tumblers of Blanton's Black label. He set one in Brian's hand.

"What the hell did he do?" Brian asked.

Mills hiked a leg and sat on the corner of his desk. "The last half of 1943, we pushed the Japanese backwards. It was brutal, every day. Still, we made progress.

"The Japs, though, they had an ace. Their big navy base in the Caroline's. The way the islands are spread out and the extent of the reefs, it's a natural fortress. They had constructed five airfields, put in defensive batteries, and dug mortar lines and pillboxes into the hillsides. And manning all of it was about forty-thousand soldiers."

"Truk," Brian said. He had studied the history books.

Mills laughed. "God must have been a Navy man the way He laid out that lagoon. We all knew it would be a meat grinder for the Marines if we sent them in. So, we didn't.

"We sent the planes instead," the admiral continued his story. "Hellcats and Avenger torpedo bombers. We let them do the job."

"Not to be rude, Admiral, but I know this history. Every Navy man does."

Mills sloshed the bourbon gently. "For you, there is a bit more to it." He added more bourbon to his glass, thought to ask Brian if he wanted more, but saw he had yet to take a drink.

"A few of the Hellcats that were part of the first wave carried aerial cameras," Mills explained. Brian could almost hear him searching for the right words. "Damn. There's no way to say this easy, son. One photo showed Douglas' submarine inside. She was moored to a Japanese freighter."

Brian stared at him; not sure he was hearing the admiral correctly.

"I always held they forced her to surface and had to surrender, but there were no records of a *Gato-class* submarine being captured or taken to Truk. Hell, after the war, I even sent a few retired Navy divers back to see if they could locate her." Mills gulped his bourbon. "Nothing.

"The files say we lost the *Mako* on the 3rd of February. U.S. Official Naval records list her as being turned over to the enemy by a cooperative captain. Had he returned, he would have been charged with treason."

Brian eyed the faceted tumbler. "You don't believe that."

Another sip of bourbon. "At the time, I believed what I was told, that we had lost him and his crew on patrol. I didn't know anything different from anyone else. There was an inquiry into your father's activities at Pearl. They questioned several officers about who he knew, who his friends were, who he associated with off-base, that type of thing. We were told he was up for a Navy Cross. I felt pretty good about that," Mills smiled. "We all did. He was one of the best submariners in the corps.

"Then nothing. No medal, no announcements. Radio silence. Douglas, being my friend, I started poking around. I was just a captain still trying to make my way up," Mills admitted. "So, I got a long way to nowhere. Until finally I poked the right officer, and he showed me Doug's file from the inquiry board."

"And?"

"And that was when I found out about the photograph and the charges and how the seemingly harmless testimonies of his friends and fellow officers all built a case against him," Mills said. "Even what I had said about him drew the same conclusion."

Brian pulled the bourbon into his throat.

"He was a hell of a guy, your dad, but he had unhealthy habits. He gambled a bit, always losing to the wrong people. And no disrespect to your mother. He loved Catherine. But there were other ladies. Well, he never shied away when he should have. We were all like that. A bunch of boys in paradise trying not to think about the next day because we knew it wasn't a guarantee.

"Worse for Doug, he had an eye for the exotic girls. Blonds bored him, he'd say," Mills almost laughed. "When we thought every Asian was either the enemy or sympathizer, your dad was buying them drinks. Like I said, he had bad habits."

Brian stared at his empty glass. "Loyalty is the last stance. Isn't that what you used to tell me?" Brian set the tumbler on the center of the desk and swept up the logbook. "Thank you for your time, Admiral."

"Brian."

"You said it yourself. War records are never accurate. The Navy believed those of the enemy."

"It's forty years in the past, son. You can't change history."

Brian held up the leather-bound logbook. "Actually, this changes everything. It might be the past for you, Admiral, but not for me."

As the door closed, Mills dropped into his chair. He gulped the last of the bourbon. It was the past, and it was dead. Dead and buried. Unless someone went turning over headstones and kicking ghosts. He picked up the phone, his finger floating over the gray push buttons. His chest heaved with sadness as he poked the number of the Pentagon's secured line and made his call.

•   •   •

Jamie Powell hated his name. It was his mother's name. His father, a quiet man with a rattling stutter, had hoped to name his only son something heroic, like Clyde or Dillion. His wife, however, wanted nothing to do with such tough guy names. The nurse at the maternity ward agreed and Jamie's birth certificate was signed and filed while his father sat in the waiting room with thoughts of playing catch with a Dillion who would never be.

At twelve, right after the latest bully stole his treasured Eddie Cicotte baseball card, and with his father's consent, Jamie joined Coulon's Gymnasium on the Southside of Chicago. Thus, Jamie became 'JP,' and the brawny gym pug who carried a respectable right-hook and notorious hatred for tough guys.

Now, the boxing ring was years behind him, and JP had a new way of dealing with thugs. Sitting at the window of a vacant office on the seventh floor of a Washington D.C. high-rise, Central Intelligence Agent

JP pressed his Bushnell binoculars to his slightly crooked nose and watched the ebb and flow of the traffic below.

A line of taxis pulled through the Hyatt's circular driveway like a conveyor belt. They emptied their passengers, returning from tours of the Lincoln Memorial, the Washington Monument, the Smithsonian. JP imagined waves of parents, exhausted from miles of history, dragging themselves into the hotel with limp children in their arms.

JP was pleased. His team was in place in under an hour. Not a record, but it showed the up-and-coming agents what experience could do. There were shortcuts to take when time was a factor, and he knew all of them. Even invented a few. Yes, he was pleased with his team.

Only one thing bothered him. JP hated the Hyatt Hotel. Of all the hotels in D.C., it was the worst for surveillance. Its bulbous facade stretched out over the driveway, blocking any clear view of the hotel's entrance. There wasn't a single point where both the front doors and the rooms could be watched.

The hotel forced him to place someone on the street, and he didn't like that. It called for more personnel, and it put them in the open. That created margins for mistakes, and JP did not accept mistakes.

He swung the binoculars to the black Dodge van parked kitty-corner near the office building. It was across the street from the Hyatt's main entrance.

"Karen. Anything?" JP spoke into the thin tube that ran along the side of his cheek. A third of the surveillance team was inside the van, hidden by ink-black windows.

"Nada," she whispered into his earphone.

JP glanced at Beckman behind him. "Still nothing," he said, repeating what he knew Beckman had heard over his own earphone.

Beckman did not turn from the one-inch screen of his mini television set. He nodded, glanced at his wristwatch, and returned to the *I Love Lucy* rerun that was playing.

"Doesn't that thing give you a headache?"

Beckman was a large man with thin oily yellow hair and a habit of scratching his groin with disregard. Vulgar habits aside, he was an excellent agent and always JP's first choice when he needed an electronics man.

"Nope," he said.

JP scrutinized the watermelon-sized mound under Beckman's maroon plaid shirt. He judged his own rounding physique. They were dinosaurs, he lamented. Forsaken to gloomy rooms so they could watch the world through binoculars while the young, aggressive agents like Karen tackled the villains.

"You have anything?" JP asked him.

Beckman made a gesture of putting his hand up to his earphone. He listened. "It's quiet. There was a handyman in the room for a few minutes. He's gone. I checked him through the scope. A huge son of a bitch. He didn't bother the bug. I still got a green light on the panel." Beckman said, pointing to the electrical array of tape recorders and microphone receivers mounted in the two silver Halliburton cases. "I still don't get why we're here."

"Someone called in a favor."

"We will not get in hot water? Even lukewarm water?" Beckman asked once again. "I just don't enjoy setting up inland." Inland was his term for domestic work. If anything was pounded into their collective minds at the Farm was that the Central Intelligence Agency did not spy on U.S. citizens. That was the FBI's job. They were the assholes of overreaching government. The Agency was always the international hero.

"We're good," JP assured him. "Look at this as field practice. We're just brushing up on our surveillance skills," he said as he spied the hotel room directly across from them. It was empty. Quiet and empty, and it was almost 8 p.m. *Where the hell could he be*, JP wondered. He hated waiting for the first contact. Always had.

"Got him!" Karen snapped into his ear. He could hear the adrenaline in her voice.

Beckman flipped on the recorders.

"Tan overcoat, brown suit, no vest, striped tie. Brown briefcase. He's alone and proceeding to the hotel entrance," Karen spoke clearly. "Follow?"

"Just to the lobby."

"Roger," she responded.

With no view of the entrance, JP instead focused on his ground agent as she stepped from the van. At five-foot-eight, she was a big woman with a mane of black curly hair. Still, she somehow blended into a crowd.

JP would use her as often as he could, knowing it wouldn't be long before she would vault up the Agency's ladder.

"You'd better call this in. Contact, Bovan. Time, 8:07 p.m.," JP told Beckman. "The old man will want to know that he finally showed up."

Beckman switched off his television and picked up the phone from inside one of the suitcases. It dialed automatically. On the second ring, someone picked up. "K-team. We got our target on location at 8:07 p.m. Continuing surveillance."

"Confirmed," the woman's voice said. "Will transfer the message."

He hung up and swiveled his chair to a more comfortable position. Adjusting one knob, Beckman increased the microphone's sensitivity near the hotel room door. "Green and waiting," he said.

JP said nothing. He hunched over the binoculars.

•　　　•　　　•

"Room 755, please," Brian said to the young female clerk.

She flashed the Hyatt smile, pushed her oddly thick glasses up her nose and retrieved the key from the under the registration counter. "No messages, Mr. Bovan," she passed the key and its cumbersome number plate.

The first elevator to open expelled a family of seven on their way to dinner. They scrambled across the marble floor as if it were a hockey rink.

Brian stepped in and punched the button for the seventh floor. To his relief, it was a direct flight. Reaching his door, he slid the key into the lock.

The man who slid in behind him arrived silently and with such speed that Brian had no chance. All he felt was the colossal arm as it wrapped around his chest and lifted him off the floor. Yet, it wasn't a violent assault; it was as if Brian was simply in his way and was being moved aside.

With a massive hand, the man gently closed the hotel room door, relocked it, and handed Brian the key.

Across the street, in the vacant office, Beckman turned sharply toward JP. "I heard the key and the door open. Now, nothing."

"Did he go inside?"

Beckman concentrated on the earpiece. "Dead quiet."

JP did not move at first. "Where did he go?"

Beckman shook his head.

"Karen," JP heard himself shriek. "Get up there. Find out what the hell happened to him."

7

HONOLULU, HAWAII, 1944

DOUGLAS SLOUCHED in the dining booth with a Pabst beer between laced fingers. The inevitable was coming. For four nights in a row, the two men seated across the table had slammed their knuckles into the hardwood. Twice spilling his drink.

"Christ," Burk grunted, his face was red and contorted. Sweat droplets pebbled on his forehead.

"Come on, Burkie. You can do better," Walrus taunted his opponent.

Walrus' massive right hand encased Captain Burk's with 50mm shell-sized fingers.

Douglas watched with mild interest. The outcome was always the same. Walrus collecting Burk's money, Burk rubbing his hand while cursing.

A glance around the room confirmed what Walrus had warned. A fresh group of ships had arrived in Pearl and their officers were eager to scout the local watering holes. Through the haze of cigarette smoke, Douglas casually scanned the unfamiliar faces. All smiles, slightly drunk on warm beer, each hoping for companionship before heading further west.

The joke floating around the base was there would be so many ships in Pearl by mid-February that Admiral Kimmel could walk across the harbor without getting his socks wet.

Douglas glanced at his two friends. For once, he'd like to see Burk torque Walrus' wrist into the tabletop. It would not happen.

Captain Walton P. Corton, or The Walrus as his buddies called him because of his large coffee-brown mustache and less than trim physique, outweighed Burk by an easy forty-five pounds.

James Burk stared at their clenched fists, trying to will Walrus' hand to the table. He might be the youngest submarine captain in the Pacific, but with his gray beard, mustache and thick wash of white hair, he looked like Neptune himself.

The first night of their matches had brought most of the patrons in the club around the table hollering and hooting. After three consecutive losses, the crowd had given up on the David-Goliath struggle.

Burk was a better captain than an arm-wrestler. Initial concerns about his age and experience were scuttlebutt for weeks. That ended after his second patrol sent 170,000 tons worth of Japanese armament to the bottom. It was a record for any CINCPAC sub, yet he only mentioned it when his age or height came into the conversation.

"Finished?" Walrus said, reaching with his left hand for his beer. "Be careful, Burkie, you're going to snap your own wrist, you push much harder."

"Screw you, fat man," Burk grumbled through wrenched lips.

"Now, don't need to get personal, kid."

It was amazing how long the Walrus could hold his arm at a 45-degree angle over the table. That was his strategy. Let his opponent push him so far and then no more. After a few minutes, they would not only tire physically, but mentally as well. As soon as their efforts faltered, he would attack with a full spread of torpedoes.

Walrus dug his cigarette pack from his breast pocket. He shook out a Camel stick like salt and grabbed it with his mustache and lower lip. He opened his cranky Zippo lighter and snapped the striker.

The instant he tried to light his cigarette; Burk mounted his assault. The young captain pumped his arm hard against Walrus' oak-like forearm.

Walrus drew in his smoke, glanced over his hand at Burk. "Enough," he announced, and swiftly reversed Burk's efforts with a grunt. Knuckles crashed, and the table bounced.

"Shit," Burk screamed as he rubbed his hand. "Shit, shit, shit."

Walrus' eyebrows danced as he laughed. "What do you expect, kid? You're out of your league." A drag on the Camel and a fog bank between them. "You wanted double or nothing, right? So, that's forty bucks you owe me."

"Fuck," Burk said. "Why don't we talk about some real money? Something all three of us can get in on."

"Real money?" Walrus sat back and crossed his arms.

"You in Douglas?" Burk asked. "You're the gambler."

"Gambling is for fools," Douglas replied. "I bet on the sure thing."

"Right," Burk sneered. "A week's pay to whoever gets the most kills on the next patrol."

Douglas laughed. "You're letting your luck go to your head," he said.

Walrus called over the clamor of the bar for beers. "Not an even bet. Any one of us could get stuck escorting a tugboat, while the others are out hunting," he said to Burk.

Douglas leaned in. "I'll do you better. Not a week's pay, a month's? Whoever drops the most iron collects."

"Hang on," Walrus waved his massive hand. "Let's be clear, are we talking tonnage or individual ships? And just fish or the deck gun, too?"

"Either or. Torpedoes or the cannon. Anything counts as long as it's official," Burk said.

Douglas saw Walrus' grin fade.

"You in?" Burk pressed.

Douglas clasped Burk's hand. They turned to Walrus.

"A month's pay?" he twisted the end of his mustache. "You bastards," Walrus said as he shook their hands.

Burk slapped Walrus on the shoulder as he stood up. "Don't worry, old man, it's only money," he assured him. "I'll see you knaves in the morning."

The two captains watched as Burk weaved his way through the couples swaying to Frank Sinatra's "Night and Day." Ol' Blue Eyes was doing his best from an overplayed record under the worn needle of a Victrola player. As the young captain slipped out the door, a cluster of nurses arrived.

"You're an asshole," Walrus said, slouching. "I'm still paying the bets from that cockfight you dragged me to."

"I didn't drag you," Douglas said.

"You think that little bastard just conned us?"

Douglas shook his head. "He just thinks his periscope is the biggest in the fleet."

The Walrus did not get the joke. "He's seeing that ginger-haired girl in HQ. Jenny or Georgia or something like that. Maybe he already knows his patrol orders."

"She's a civilian, Walton. I think she is in bookkeeping."

"She couldn't get a peek at his orders?" he pressed.

Douglas stared. "No. No way."

Walrus frowned. He was about to raise a new point when someone caught his attention. He sat up. "Margaret," he called over the music, his arm waving.

Douglas did not see her but knew who could inject this much energy into the big man. Plus, she was the only Margaret on the base and the one person Douglas was sure hated him.

Brash and headstrong, Margaret O'Tullie could talk for hours about nothing in such a high-pitched voice that it reminded Douglas of a bad shaft bearing.

"Mind if we join you?" Margaret plopped her slender, almost frail, body into the booth. She pushed herself against the Walrus.

"You kidding?" Walrus moved over.

It took Douglas a moment to realize Margaret had not come alone. Another woman was standing beside the booth, waiting politely for him.

"Jesus, Douglas. Where are your manners?" Margaret quipped. "Move over."

He stood, apologizing awkwardly, which got a laugh from both Margaret and Walton. As Douglas stepped from the booth, he saw the young woman was not one of Margaret's usual office cohorts.

She was small, barely reaching his chin even though her ink-black hair was styled high with loose curls. A sidelong glance came with an honest apple-red smile. The line of her cheeks carried a whisper of blush, and her chocolate brown eyes looked almost black in the dim bar lights. Douglas felt as if the floor had shifted.

"Thank you, Commander," she said, her voice boyishly soft. She glided across the bench seat, her black silk dress outlining every curve of her.

"This is Lai Ming," Margaret introduced. "Douglas. Walton."

"Please. It's just Mimi," she said as she set a delicate hand in each man's rough palm.

"Mimi?" Douglas said, his gaze not wavering from her.

The woman laughed and it sounded like wind chimes on a warm breeze. "A childhood nickname."

"She's with the Chinese delegation," Margaret said with excitement. "She's flying to Washington to meet the President."

"The President?" The Walrus whistled.

"Isn't that something?"

"I won't meet him," Mimi said, slightly embarrassed. "Ambassador Wei will. I'm only one of his translators and not the best."

"Don't listen to her. She's an excellent translator," Margaret told them. "Her English is better than mine. The ambassador will pick you," she persisted.

Douglas caught only fragments of the conversation as he watched Mimi through the corner of his eye. He watched as she sipped vermouth without ice. How she giggled into her palm at Walrus' crude jokes, the way she twirled the tips of her hair between long fingers.

He listened as she spoke about the war, the Japanese and their imperialistic government and how she was certain the attack on Pearl revealed desperation and not strength.

As the Chinese woman spoke, Douglas noted the perfection of her translucent skin above the sea-green collar of her silk Cheongsam blouse and how its woven buttons trailed downward across the rise of her chest. When the local population was doing what they could to conceal their Asian kinship because of the resentment it might draw, she embraced it.

She was, of course, part of an official Chinese delegation on a mission to meet the president of the United States. Still, she seemed to disregard any constraints on her dress or appearance. Maybe she did not realize that only one out of the fifty sailors drinking in the bar knew the difference between being a Jap and a Chinese citizen. And the one who did, did not care. The enemy was the enemy, and they looked like she did.

Or perhaps her bravado had to do with the company she was keeping. Margaret was Admiral Kimmel's secretary, after all. And Walrus, well, The Walrus could send a mouth-full of teeth down a wise-ass sailor's throat before a halfwit could finish his sass.

Douglas realized it was none of that. This Chinese woman would not stand behind The Walrus for protection. Not that she had a right hook to dislocate anyone's jaw. She was a pixie of a woman, a waif. Yet there was something about her that he could not define.

After a time, Mimi turned to him. "Are you always this quiet, Commander?"

"I'm not. I'm just enjoying listening."

"I talk too much, maybe?" she joked.

"No. Not at all," Douglas said, feeling suddenly awkward.

"My family were farmers. My mother tried to raise me as a proper Chinese girl. Always sit quiet, do not listen to the men, do not speak up. They were lessons that never stuck."

"I am glad they didn't," he said, honestly.

"You are in the silent service. I shouldn't be surprised if your guard is always up. Especially one who looks like me," she said with a bit of a smile.

"I, uh…" Douglas fumbled for a clever response. Nothing came quick enough.

She squeezed his forearm. "Don't worry, Commander. I have the same orders." She laughed, and Douglas felt a surge in his chest he could not explain.

The Chinese woman interrupted Margaret and Walrus, who were now wrapped in their own conversation. "Margaret. I think we should get back."

Margaret twisted Walrus' wrist to see the face of his watch. It was half-past ten. She signed. "I suppose."

"Dance with me first?" Douglas asked.

Mimi studied his face as if assessing his intentions. "One dance," she agreed.

She followed him to the small square of open floor just steps from the bar. Two other couples were already swaying to the scratchy disk spinning about the Victrola.

Douglas slid his arm around her boyish waist and carefully led her across the floor. The gentle fragrance of lilies rose from her hair.

She leaned her head back. "Margaret said to be careful of you."

He laughed. "Did she say anything about the Walrus?"

"Walton? Yes. He's loud, but always fun."

"I'm not fun?" He turned her, with Bing Crosby's voice leading their steps.

"Your eyes scare her," she said.

Douglas glanced at the booth. Margaret and Walton were watching them. "I hope they don't scare you."

"They intrigue me," she said, her chin up, watching him. The music stopped. Neither of them let go of the other.

Someone exchanged records, and "I'll Never Smile Again" started. Without a word, they fit themselves together again.

"Margaret mentioned you and Walrus are leaving on patrols soon. Do you know where you'll go?"

"She told you that?" he said, surprised that the naval secretary would trust anyone with such information. "We usually don't know our orders until we're underway."

"Must be terrifying under there," she said. She pressed her cheek to his chest. "The Japs hunting you. You hunting them. It is all so foolish, isn't it?"

"I never thought it foolish," Douglas said. "Just doing my job. Going out and getting my men back."

"The Japanese murdered my parents when they came through our village. They shot them because they helped the British years before," she said. "I was studying in Peking and didn't hear they were dead until six months later."

"My folks are in Virginia. Pretty far from the war."

"I thought the same," she said.

They continued. One couple sat down. Two others joined them. They did not notice.

That was the purpose of the club. It was a place where officers came to drink and laugh. To talk of anything other than war. If they were lucky, or charming enough, they might even find a moment of female companionship after months on patrol. Or a last night of tenderness before setting sail again.

Finally, Mimi eased herself away. "Thank you for the dance, Commander."

Douglas followed her to the booth.

"Margaret, we need to get back," she said.

Margaret pursed her mouth. "Why are you so punctual?" She frowned, then kissed Walrus on the cheek. "Good night, boys."

Douglas helped Mimi into her sweater, covering her graceful shoulders. "I am sorry about your family," he whispered.

"Me too." She patted his chest. "Good night, Commander," she said and followed Margaret to the front door.

Douglas fell into the booth.

"What do you think?" Walrus asked, leaning across the table.

"I think you are asking for trouble with Kimmel."

"Not about Margaret. Her friend?"

"What's to think?"

Walrus laughed with a snort. "You can't bullshit me, Bovan. I know you. She's not one of your likey-likey island women. This one has class and brains. Probably too much for you?"

"No doubt."

"And a looker. Lots to that little package," he noted.

Douglas shifted himself toward the bar, hoping to catch another round of Pabst.

"Glad you think so," Walrus told him. "We're having lunch with them tomorrow. Margaret's putting together a picnic."

"Picnic? I don't have time for a picnic. I got torpedoes to load."

"Make the time, buddy. Odds being, we won't get a chance to share potato salad with two lovely females again. Not in paradise."

Unfortunately, Douglas knew Walrus was right.

•　　　•　　　•

It was hot by 11 a.m. Tropical hot and Walrus' khaki shirt already revealed his body's moist reaction to it. He saddled the gangplank of the *Mako*, stepped on the deck and yelled to Douglas above. "Permission to come aboard?"

Douglas glanced down from the sub's tower. "Not granted," he told him. "I'll be right there." He finished giving his XO, Lieutenant Mike Alberts, his instructions. "Get Charlie to help Clancy on the number two engine. She's got to be a hundred percent before the mooring lines drop."

"Aye, Skipper," Alberts said. As he was about to drop below, he glanced towards the docks. "Holy cow, would you look at that?"

A Packard roadster as brilliant yellow as the breast feathers of a Hawaiian 'anianiau, pulled briskly to the edge of the dock, its massive hood dipping as it stopped. Mimi was behind the wheel with Margaret beside her, her hands pressed to the dashboard in an effort not to slide into the footwell.

Both women wore bright sundresses, Margaret in sky blue, Mimi in white with green. They waved in unison.

Douglas shoved his clipboard at Alberts. "I want us seaworthy by the time I get back."

"You got it, Skipper," he said, his gaze not turning from the ladies.

Douglas slid smoothly down the ladder to the sub's aft deck and crossed the gangplank.

"What a beauty," Walrus ran his hand over the Packard's swooping fender.

Margaret grabbed Walrus by the wrist. "Look, look," she pulled him excitedly to the rear of the car. "It has a rumble seat." She reached over the arching hump and yanked the discrete hatch. It revealed an upholstered clam shell that was hardly big enough for a child, let alone Walrus and Margaret. "Isn't it cute?"

"Who's supposed to fit in there?" Walrus asked with a frown.

"Us, silly," she laughed. She stepped on the bumper pad and pulled him aboard.

Douglas leaned on the passenger door. "You can tell who commands that crew," he said.

Mimi set her arm across the seat back. "I am glad you are coming. I was worried I'd be playing chaperone all day."

Douglas felt the car shift as Walrus tried to maneuver into the rumble seat. A battleship squeezing into a pond. Packed into the tiny space, he wondered how many ribs Margaret would crack on the ride to the beach.

"All ready," she said, her voice a gasp.

Douglas slid next to Mimi.

Mimi eyed them in the rearview mirror. "Here we go."

Walrus huffed. "I can't feel my left leg."

Mimi and Douglas laughed as the Packard eased forward. She weaved around the crates and military trucks that lined the submarine docks.

At the main gate, he lifted a hand to the Marine guard. Mimi drove briskly off the base and onto the narrow street that lead them toward the green peak of Diamond Head.

"It is the Ambassador's car," she said, anticipating his questions. "His cousin's car, actually. They live above Honolulu."

Under the arching Hawaiian sky, the warming sun, and steady breeze, they drove through the hustle of town and beyond, where the road narrowed and cut behind the dead volcano.

Douglas could not hear Margaret and Walrus over the wind as it whipped across the convertible but could see their heads pressed together as they talked.

Mimi's hair flirted with the convertible's speed, whispers of it tugged and swirled about her cheek and around the rim of her sunglasses.

"How long have you been in Hawaii?" he asked her, his voice raised.

"A week. I came first to make the arrangements," she said, adding. "I like the island."

Along the road where the asphalt fell into a gravel trough, soft palms hung like the thick eyelashes of a sleepy green giant. On the opposite side, a calm sea stretched to the end of the world. There was no war out there. No battles being fought, no submarines running deep and silent. Just gentle Pacific swells topped with cake frosting.

Descending the back side of Diamond Head, only a handful of vehicles passed in the opposite direction. As the Ambassador's young niece had instructed, Mimi watched for a grouping of three thatched huts. Just beyond, she would see a dirt patch and a narrow half-road that dropped steeply to Thukkie Beach. Only the locals went to Thukkie, but it was worth the walk, the niece said. It was a lovely slice of shore with clean sand edged by a thick grove of mango shrubs. The ocean was shallow and always calm.

Mimi spotted the huts. Her exit from the road was sudden and jolting. She stood on the brakes, driving the car into the red dirt patch. Douglas braced himself.

Parked at the edge of the sandy trail, Walrus lifted the wicker basket from the luggage rack. "Jesus, what did you women bring?" He shouldered the basket and made his way along the shaded path.

Douglas followed, carrying four bottles of Hamm's beer and a smaller basket that Mimi insisted he keep horizontal.

Once on the sand, the women took the lead. They wanted a shady spot away from the bugs that always came with trees. They wanted it cool, but not windy. After four locations, completely acceptable to Douglas and Walrus, they found a patch of sugar sand guarded by two tall palms. Walrus raised concerns about possibly being killed if a coconut fell.

Spreading out a thin red and white checkered blanket, Margaret opened the basket and handed Mimi plates and silverware.

"We've got fried chicken, potato salad, cheese, and fresh pineapple and mango slices," she said.

"Can there be anything better than fried chicken?" Walrus said, lowering himself onto the blanket.

"Walton," Margaret said with exasperation. "Mimi made sweets. Real Chinese pastries."

"You cook?" Douglas asked, realizing he sounded more surprised than he meant to.

"Bake," she corrected. "And yes, I can bake and cook."

"I just meant..." Douglas fumbled.

Walrus laughed. "Put your foot in that, didn't you, Commander?"

Douglas felt himself redden. The women laughed.

"Well, don't have high expectations. They should be warm. I am sure they are cold by now."

"They'll be wonderful," Margaret said. She spooned a generous portion of salad onto a plate and passed it with a chicken wing to Walrus.

Douglas snapped the caps off the beer bottles and passed them to his left.

"A toast, someone?" Margaret asked.

Douglas lifted his. "To warm afternoons in paradise."

"To friends, old and new," Walrus said.

"To killing our enemies," Mimi added quickly.

Douglas and Walrus glanced at each other.

"Amen to that," Walrus leaned in, and they clanged the bottles.

Certain Walrus was content, Margaret started another plate. "Douglas?"

"In a minute," he said, standing. "I'm going to take a walk down the beach."

"Mind if I come along?" Mimi asked, her hand arched over her eyes to block out the sun.

"Not at all," he said, switching his beer and helping her with his left hand.

"Don't hurry back," Walrus called. Margaret slapped him playfully on the shoulder. He put a massive arm around over her shoulder and pulled her into the blanket, potato salad flying.

"They're funny," Mimi said as they walked over the crisp sand between a mango grove and the high-tide rush of the waves.

"Like goofy high school kids," he agreed. "I hope Walrus knows what he's getting into."

"What do you mean? Margaret has been just sweet to me," Mimi said.

"She's great for Walton. It's just if they get too tight, she's going to be left waiting."

"Is that why your wife went home?" Mimi asked. She took comically long steps to keep with him.

She caught Douglas off guard, although he should have expected Margaret would mention Catherine.

"Mostly," he said. To himself it sounded less than convincing.

"Well, today, there is no war for them," she said. She stopped and plopped onto the warm sand.

Douglas sat down. "And for you? No war today?"

Mimi looked out where the sea washed across an unseen reef. "It is here every day for me. For every minute."

He sipped his beer. "When do you fly to Washington?"

"Friday."

"Can you be free for dinner Wednesday?" he asked slowly.

"I have a party to attend with the ambassador."

"Right. I probably shouldn't have asked." He took another swig.

"Would you be my date? If you don't mind mingling with a lot of pompous old men?" She tilted her head and smiled the type of smile sailors pin above their bunks.

"I'm not so sure you want a measly lieutenant commander as a date. Sounds like there will be a lot of brass at this party," he said.

"And many ribbons and gold stripes. A few stuffy diplomats and boring politicians too," she acknowledged. She eased herself into the sand and threw an arm behind her head. "But I will be the only girl there with a submarine commander for a dance partner."

Douglas thumbed the neck of the beer bottle and stared at the blue horizon where a line of paper clouds tumbled.

"You like being a captain, don't you?"

"I could have signed up as a surface dweller, I guess. But this way, I don't have to answer every radio call that comes through." He stabbed the bottle into the sand next to her narrow hip and stretched himself out.

Through the crook of her arm, she asked. "What were you before?"

"Not much," he admitted. "I married my high school sweetheart and was just trying to get my feet under me when the war broke. I guess the Japanese decided for me," he shrugged. "And you?"

"You'll laugh."

"Probably," he teased.

"I was studying to be a scientist."

"You mean like looking through microscopes and cutting up little animals?"

"Not exactly. I was going to be an anthropologist."

"That is…?" he hesitated.

"The study of human evolution."

"Just what I was going to say," he lied. He heard her laugh and it caused him to smile.

Turning on his side, he angled his head into his hand and focused on her perfectly manicured fingernails stabbing the sand. He watched her stomach rise and fall slowly, as if she had just fallen into a Snow White slumber.

Under the soft blue tropical sky, he studied the smoothness of her skin and the way her sundress gathered under her breast and cascaded away. Something about this woman pulled at him, made him want to know more of her. Inside and out.

He had felt this way only once before. This tug in his chest and tightening of his throat. He was a teenager watching a fine figured girl cross the library while reading from a thick green book with a loose spine and worn cover.

That was how he fell in love with Catherine. A teenager not knowing better. By the time he fell out, it was too late. Their celebrated romance had become the plans of other people. Of their parents and siblings and friends.

He knew it was the wrong decision. So did Catherine. She just refused to admit it.

Douglas pushed the thoughts out of his mind, turned to the Hawaiian sunlight, and followed Mimi's lead. He set his forearm over his eyes and let sleep take him.

•   •   •

"Douglas," Mimi jabbed his ribs with the beer bottle. "Douglas."

He cracked an eye slowly.

She leaned over him, one hand on each side of his chest. "Hello, sailor," she joked in a childlike voice. "Are you going to wake up, or do I have to carry you back?"

He sat up, catching her in his arms. "That is going to be difficult from this angle."

"Ah," she put her hands on his chest. She did not push away. "We should get back," she said.

He scanned the beach as if on patrol. "We should," he agreed, as he gathered her close and could feel her breath rise and fall with his.

Mimi swept a wave of brown hair from his brow. She shook her head. "Trouble in the making," she whispered.

"Only a little," he said, easing away.

Before he could, she slipped her hand to his neck and pulled herself to him. She kissed him long and hard. No hesitation, no penance. He tasted her lipstick and his heart raced.

As they walked back along the beach, he shifted close and slipped his hand into hers.

8

WASHINGTON D.C., 1986

"COMMANDER," SHE WHISPERED from the edge of the open doorway. "Please."

Brian saw the Asian woman who had appeared at his mother's funeral and slipped his father's logbook into his hand.

The huge man, who had lifted Brian off the floor, now stared at him with a whimsical grin. A former lineman, Brian assumed, or sumo champion.

The man eased the leather satchel from Brian's shoulder and took the coat bag from his hand. Gingerly, he set them inside the woman's room and motioned Brian inside with his massive hand.

The woman crossed the tan carpet to a small coffee table and chairs poised in front of floor-to-ceiling windows. Beyond, the Capitol Building was bathed with landscape lighting. "Sugar or cream, Commander?" she asked filling a porcelain cup from a stainless-steel carafe left by room service. "Both?"

"I'd rather pass on the pleasantries and find out how you got my father's logbook?"

"Fair question," she said as she finished pouring a second cup and sat in the wing-backed chair. "But I do insist on a bit of civility."

Brian surrendered and sat down.

"And introductions," she said with a smile. "Lai Ming, but Mimi will do." She hung her small, elderly hand over the table. It was a translucent parchment of age, a tablet where the weave of her veins charted her life's long, hard journey.

He took it gently. "I am guessing there's no need to introduce myself."

Her laugh was light and airy and oddly casual for the circumstances. "I don't know everything about you, Commander. Only what is official and maybe a little more."

"You knew who my dad was and when I'd be burying my mother," Brian said, his voice piercing in the quiet room.

"True. I have been keeping an eye on you."

"Why?"

"To return the book," she said as she drew her cup to her lips. "When the time was right."

"Someone gave it to you?"

"Douglas gave it to me," she said. A smile formed at the edge of her mouth. "I don't think he meant to, but…"

"I'm sorry, what?" Brian stared at her with confusion.

"He left the book in my car."

"By mistake?" Brian's brow deepened. "Then why the secrecy? Why did Godzilla have to grab me?"

"Oh, Tarō. He is as harmless as a puppy."

"A rottweiler."

"Your room, Commander, is sprinkled with little microphones. Men are also watching from across the street and there is a woman in the lobby." She sipped her coffee again.

"Because of the book?"

"Because of what is in it. You've seen the dates."

"And these people watching me, they are…?"

"The Central Intelligence Agency, of course."

"Of course."

"They could be Naval Intelligence," she told him. "I don't have the connections I once did, so that is possible."

"Or the FBI." Brian felt like he was the target of a practical joke, and she was about to laugh at him.

"Not FBI," she said and waved her hand dismissingly. "They would never understand the implications of locating the *Mako*."

He frowned. "That's not possible."

Mimi looked at him and grinned. "Trust me, Commander, you can find anything if you know where to look. Even a splinter in a mountainside."

"*If* you know where to look."

"But you have a starting point. The admiral gave you that."

Brian chewed the inside of his lip, wondering if there was anything this woman did not know. "They marked my father for treason."

The elderly woman with the kind face and long, salted black hair instantly melted into a snarling demon. "A lie," she spat, her face darkening. "A lie to protect others."

"Who?"

"If I told you, you would dismiss me as a crazy old woman." She shook her head. "You need to find out for yourself. It is the only way you will believe me."

"Did he set sail on February 3rd? Was that the date?"

"Yes." The harshness in her face faded as quickly as it appeared. "I drove him to the dock," she began. "I still remember the white glow of the moon. It made me so mad. Like the sky was pointing them out to the enemy with a giant lamplight," she smirked. "I also remember the smell of engine fumes and all the god-awful clanging inside that machine. It looked so small and fragile compared to the other ships."

She turned to the hotel room window. "We were late, and he dashed out of the car, barely grabbing his coat. That's how I came to have the book. It simply fell out of his pocket."

"Why wait so long to give it to me?"

"Because you would have seen the dates which would have made you question everything about your father. It would have ruined your career."

"You might have noticed I don't have a career."

"You became a naval commander of a United States nuclear submarine. Do you think you would have gotten that far had I given you that book before now?" she asked. "The Navy is a strange club. They have an odd tradition of putting honor before their men. You weren't denied a promotion because of your record, Commander. You were passed over because of your father's," she said plainly. "Clearing his name, clears yours."

Brian felt his throat tighten. "Mills said they have proof."

She shook her head, turned to the window, and stared at the night sky. "Douglas did not surrender to the enemy," she said softly. "He surrendered to me."

Brian sat back as realization set in. "You were the bait."

"Think what you want, Commander. I was a soldier of war. I might not have carried a rifle against my shoulder, but I also had orders."

"A spy?"

She smiled at him, a whimsical grim. "Do spies fall in love?"

Brian studied her for a moment. He tried to imagine her as a younger woman, a beautiful, vibrant young woman swept into the turmoil of war. It was clear she had known his father intimately, but regardless of how he felt about their affair, Brian could not blame her. "I'm sorry," he said.

"Me too," she said, feigning a smile.

"I still don't understand why he was sent into Truk."

"Have some more coffee, Commander, and I will tell you about a little girl hired to dig in the caves near her parents' farm." Mimi poured the last of the brown liquid into his cup.

"It was in the spring of '27 when a group of foreigners came to my village. I remember they had pointy faces and light eyes. And thick beards and mustaches like I had never seen before. They were so ugly that my mother would hide when they walked by.

"They came to explore the caves that littered the mountains near my home. I didn't understand why. My brothers and I had been through them a hundred times, but the men knew what they were after."

She smiled at the memory. "They paid my father a few Fens, just pennies, for me to work for them. I was twelve, but small for my age but that is why they wanted me. They would tie a rope to my wrist, give me a small oil lamp, and send me into the tightest fissures.

"It took two years to find the first skull. Just a yucky clump of bones," Mimi laughed. "But you would have thought it was Egyptian gold the way they acted."

"They were paleontologists?" Brian finally sipped his coffee. It was cold.

"I lived in the province west of Peking. They named their discovery after the city."

"The Peking Man," Brian said under his breath.

Mimi sat up, surprised. "You know of them?"

"From something I read somewhere. *National Geographic,* maybe. I remember they were lost during the war."

Mimi set her cup on the table's edge. "I was doing my dissertation at the university. It was on the very fossils I helped uncover.

"We knew the Japanese were coming. The soldiers had been raiding the museums and temples for artwork and religious pieces for months. It was only a matter of time until they came to the university."

"You didn't try to escape?"

"Not until I knew the fossils were safe. You must understand, Commander, the Peking Man fossils were a national treasure. I could only think to send them to the U.S. Marines in Canton. It was a mistake. Three days later, the Japanese captured their base."

"The same day as Pearl Harbor," he remembered.

"I thought they would be safe with the Americans," she said with a sigh. "Instead, they disappeared."

"Until?" Brian asked.

"Two years later, the Chinese ambassador in Chongqing was contacted by someone who dealt in the black market. Luckily, the soldiers who stole the fossils were not honorable men, but they knew what they had. The ambassador was able to strike a deal. Five million dollars in uncut diamonds for my Peking Man."

Brian's eyebrows lifted.

"Your father knew it was an illegal mission. At first, he refused to go until I explained the importance."

"Someone else had to know. Someone on the chain of command. Submarines and their crews aren't sent on patrol without proper orders."

"He was given falsified orders and charts that lead him into the lagoon. We knew where the freighter would be anchored, its name, and captain. It was all planned."

Brian felt his chest tighten. It was a suicide mission. "Even if I found his sub, it won't clear him."

"It will if you find the diamonds aboard."

"After forty years?" Brian shook his head.

"Without proof, the logbook is little more than a keepsake."

"You want the fossils."

"Since the day the Japanese stole them from your Marines," she admitted. "But I also want Douglas' record cleared. And those of his men."

Brian slipped the logbook from his satchel. He stared at the aged leather and fading cover. "My mom thought he was a saint. You knew a different man."

"He was what I expected of an American captain. Composed, rational, and intent on doing right for his men. He was also what I did not expect. Kind and compassionate. We only had a few days together, but hardly an hour goes by that I don't think about him."

From her purse, she retrieved an airline ticket. "Pan Am to Honolulu. Tomorrow, 10:30 a.m."

"I haven't agreed."

"The *Mako* will haunt you as she does me. One day, you will have to look for her. It might as well be tomorrow." She pushed the ticket into his hand. "There is also a flight to Boston leaving at the same time. I suggest you make those reservations as well."

"You seriously think I am being watched?"

"You will see," she said as she slipped her purse over her shoulder. Stepping close, she touched Brian's cheek and smiled. "Oh, those eyes," she sighed, then slipped out the door.

Brian looked across the Washington skyline, knowing she was right. The *Mako* had always haunted him and would now more than ever.

•   •   •

Brian let the hot water stream through his hair and down his back. The combination of sweat and steam beaded on his face. After a time, he cranked the shower valve from hot to cold and let the jolting chill run across his body.

The bedside radio continued filling the hotel room as he wrapped a towel around his waist and searched his satchel for his overnight kit.

He had seen it in a James Bond movie. Blasting music across the room was the perfect way to overwhelm hidden microphones. It was silly. He was not about to talk to himself. Still, it gave Brian a bit of satisfaction if, in fact, the woman's paranoia was true.

"Bond, James Bond." He snickered.

He had shuttered the hotel's heavy curtains before the shower, which now, in the late evening, threw the room into a shadowy gloom illuminated only by the red LED light of the radio dial.

Brian found comfort in the clandestine. He was a submariner. A member of an elite selection of military men whose chosen battlefield was a thousand meters beneath the sea where the darkness was total, the silence complete, and the pressure instantly lethal.

He had performed most of his training blind. Drill after drill, he had functioned without a flicker of light until he could instinctively find any lever, switch, or button amongst the thousands that filled the world's most advanced warship.

Enemy attacks, electrical failures, fires, reactor meltdowns, and missile malfunctions were all practiced a hundred times over in the blackness of a titanium hull.

Having heard enough punk rock for a lifetime, Brian spun the radio until he found a rock-and-roll channel. Jimmy Buffett's "Margaritaville" came on. *Close enough,* he thought, rolling the volume higher.

Ironically, he almost did not hear the knock at the door.

•   •   •

"I've got someone at the door," Beckman said, increasing the sensitivity of microphone number three and decreasing the others. "I'm telling you, he knows we're in there. No one listens to this fuckin' music. Not even my kids."

"Can you get the voice outside the door," JP said, watching his partner's face. *Where the hell had he been?* JP wondered. Thirty-five minutes from when Bovan stepped from the elevator, he finally entered his room. The gap was killing the CIA man. He simply found it impossible to believe a Naval officer could suddenly become a threat to national security.

•   •   •

Two quick strides put Brian against the door. He stayed away from the peephole, knowing his shadow might be seen.

Another two knocks. Quick and firm.

Brian peered at the illuminated dial of his Seiko Diver's watch. 10:45 p.m. He had given room service his suit, but even with a rush request and an extra ten dollars on the side, the hotel's cleaners said it would not be ready until midnight.

The knock returned.

"Yes?"

"Commander Bovan, sir?"

"Yes."

"I have a delivery. From Admiral Mills, sir."

Brian unlatched the door slowly, leaving the six-inch chain attached. He saw the three stripes and insignia of a first-class yeoman. The uniform fit on the young red-haired man perfectly.

"What is it?" Brian whispered, unsure if his voice was transmitted to some far-off location.

"A package, sir. And a message directly from the admiral," the yeoman said, moving his head back and forth, trying to make sure of the man's identity.

"What's the message?"

"I am to impress upon you that once you have reviewed the contents, they are to be returned directly to me, sir. And only to me," the yeoman said.

Brian released the door chain. He took the thick envelope from the man. "There's a restaurant in the lobby. Get yourself something to eat," he told the yeoman. "Charge it to my room. I'll bring this down when I am finished."

"Yes, sir. And thank you, sir," the yeoman said, and between the door and its frame, Brian saw the man snap into a salute.

Brian closed the door and replaced the chain. He moved to the table near the window and shifted the lamp so it would shine against them. Another cinema lesson, no silhouettes for the eyes across the street.

He pulled open the outer envelope and slid the official file from inside. He uncoiled the figure-eight of red string that secured the flap.

Methodically, he removed the contents of Douglas Bovan's jacket, his naval file. In the early years, he found entries for when his dad served aboard the *Skipjack* and the *Marlin*. A half a dozen commendations from three different commanding officers.

His progression up the ranks was steady yet unremarkable. A thoughtful and dedicated submariner, the letters said. A few had handwritten notes along the bottom. Highly recommended. Men respect him. By the book on duty but tends to freewheel while on leave. The last one made Brian laugh.

He found Douglas' transfer from New London to Pearl Harbor and onto the *Mako* in '42. Brian had seen most of these records or copies of them. Fragments of the past were deliberately given to a young boy who believed his father was a war hero.

Beneath those records, however, were files and photographs he had never seen before.

The first was an undated black-and-white picture of the *Mako* running along the surface off Waikiki Beach with Diamond Head's shark fin peak rising in the background. The stack contained a few more photos of the sub at the dock and a loose collection of scribbled orders for supplies and repairs.

Finally, he came to the thick, hard-covered binder that filled most of the envelope. Its label was simple:

THE USS MAKO INVESTIGATION. PACIFIC FLEET HEADQUARTERS.
BOARD OF INQUIRY. MARCH 1, 1947.

Brian stared at it. Being handed his father's logbook was a jolt. But this was the Navy's official inquiry into his father's actions. Whether or not he believed their findings, what was inside was going to crush him.

He opened the binder.

As he expected, the Navy investigation was filled with detailed transcripts from personal interviews. Brian recognized most of the names. His father's wartime buddies were probably surprised by the inquisition.

He shuffled the pages until he found Mills' interview. Dissecting each sentence, he found nothing surprising. The admiral defended his friend across the battlefield of an interviewer's notepad.

He pulled the next section of the report and read the title.

OFFICE OF STRATEGIC SERVICES
November 10, 1946
From: William J. Donovan, Director,
Pearl Harbor Office of OSS
To: The Officer-in-Charge, Board of Inquiry
Subject: Loss of USS Mako

Lt. Cmdr. Douglas Bovan

Enclosure: Summary of personal observation records

(NOTE: Observations of military personnel are part of standard OSS procedure.)

Observations began October 1, 1942, with the subject's transfer to CINCPAC.

Questionable activity started on August 22, 1943. Subject sighted participating in a gambling event at a private ranch near Kapolei, Hawaii. Local police suspect the involvement of criminal elements. Most participants of local Hawaiian heritage. Some U.S. Military participants. Further interviews by police reveal debts for several U.S. personnel, including Lt. Cmdr. Bovan. Debt amount could not be established.

Not a good mark on your career, Dad, Brian thought. The report continued highlighting his father's gambling habits. There were reports of his activities with women, something that was uncomfortable to read.

But it was the last paragraph of the report that Brian read several times over.

Lt. Cmdr. Douglas Bovan was sighted numerous times in the company of one Lai Ming, assistant to the visiting ambassador to the Republic of China. On the day of the Mako's departure, Bovan was seen leaving the Naval base with the woman in question.

Brian remembered Mimi's words. "He left the book in my car."

At the back of the report, he found the 8x10-inch photograph Mills had told him about. A snapshot of war. A two-dimensional memory of one of America's most decisive attacks against the Japanese base.

The image was a harsh, black-and-white photo blurred by the shudder of the Hellcat F6F amid a nosedive attack, its massive 2,000 hp Pratt & Whitney engine driving it into battle at nearly 350 mph.

The belly-mounted camera of the fighter plane captured a line of toy ships floating off a narrow, crescent-shaped beach. The surrounding water, turquoise blue in life, looked dusky and dull. A fan of white specks compromised the lens. It took Brian a moment to realize it was incoming anti-aircraft fire frozen by the shutter.

A ship in the lower corner had just taken a direct hit. An ink-black plume billowed from its decks, telling of the horror. The other, the large freighter in the foreground, was still untouched by the onslaught.

White ink arrows scribbled across the photo highlighted an irregular shadow against the freighter's hull. Brian immediately recognized the distinct silhouette of a Gato-class submarine moored alongside the ship's starboard side.

A second picture was stapled to the first. It was a crude enlargement, the image grossly out of focus, yet the submarine's presence was undeniable.

He turned the photograph over and read the handwritten note. 'USS *Mako* moored to the freighter, *Kuma Maru.*'

Brian set it on the table and caught his breath. He could see how the inquiry board could come to their conclusion. Proof in black and white. Then he thought about what Mills had told him. *"Records aren't perfect. People write them down. They make mistakes, son."*

Brian found a pen and the hotel's customary stationery in the bottom drawer of the nightstand.

Placing the thin paper over the photograph, he traced the images of the two ships and the smooth curve of the shoreline.

He folded the paper in half, then rolled it tightly until it was the size of a cigarette. In the bathroom, he slipped the tiny tube into his toothbrush holder and tucked it into his overnight kit.

He gathered the photographs and slipped them back into the envelope. Climbing into his extra shirt and slacks, he headed downstairs.

Wary of the large lobby, he crossed the open field of polished marble, conscious of everyone around him. A young couple, newly in love, stood at the check-in desk. In the gift shop, a lone customer was browsing the magazine rack.

He found the red-headed yeoman sitting in the center of the restaurant's main dining room. A few other hotel guests were enjoying late-night coffee and dessert. Brian tried to make a mental note of them.

Before the yeoman recognized him, Brian set the package beside his slice of pumpkin pie. "How was dinner?"

"Sir," the young man scrambled to his feet.

"Don't salute. Please."

The yeoman caught himself. "Yes, sir," he said, easing his arm down.

"Express my gratitude to the admiral."

"Sir, I was instructed to ask you to join Admiral Mills for lunch tomorrow. A suitable time for you, sir?"

Brian saw the tall woman walk slowly past the restaurant out of the corner of his eye. She scanned the menu board next to the entrance, but before moving away, she stared a bit too long in their direction.

"My flight home isn't until the afternoon," Brian said purposely. "I'll be at his office at noon."

"Yes, sir. And thank you for dinner," the yeoman said.

Brian could see the pain in his face as he tried not to salute an officer. *An ex-officer*, Brian thought as he withdrew from the restaurant. He picked up his suit at the cleaners' window next to the gift shop, saving the teenage attendant a trip up to the seventh floor.

•   •   •

"I got tagged," Karen whispered into the radio. "Not a hundred percent sure, but maybe."

In the office across the street, JP was feeling tired. This was supposed to be an easy twelve hours. "Okay. Get back to the vehicle. We'll reassess," he said. He stretched his legs across the floor.

Beckman fussed over his equipment. "The old man won't be happy about all this."

"No shit," JP sighed. "Pass me the damn phone," he said, knowing this was another call he did not want to make.

•   •   •

In the hotel room, Brian cranked the radio up again. He piled the bed pillows against the headboard, switched off the lights, and lit a cigarette. He stretched himself over the bed cover and studied the glowing amber floating over his fingers.

It was clear Mills had sent the records to dissuade him from pursuing his questions. It was the fog of war. Let it go. Let the dead rest. That was what the admiral was telling him.

But sending classified records with a yeoman was not like his family friend. Nor was the twitch at the corner of the admiral's mouth when Brian showed him the logbook. Though Mills tried to hide his reaction, he had played it too casually.

Either the Chinese woman was lying, or Mills was. *The woman had her reasons but what were the admiral's?* Brian wondered.

Whatever they were, Mimi Ling was right. He had to find out for himself.

9

HONOMU, HAWAII, 1986

WITH WATERY EYES, Retired Full Admiral Joe Tendrey watched the distant aqua-blue sea roll shoreward. Rising, curling, raging across the reef. He could no longer hear its anger, even though the reef was only a mile away. His hearing had weakened to the point even the thumb-sized electronic aids hanging behind his ears could not bring him the symphony he loved.

So, he watched the Pacific's mood swings from the grand house's open-air lanai, hoping the breeze would come to his aid and deliver the smell of salt and foam. Hour after hour, he stared across the trimmed lawn, the football field of green carpet that fell down the hill from the red, koa wood deck, to the volcanic stone walls of his estate.

The admiral didn't care about the land inside the wall. He enjoyed the acres he owned beyond it. The thick, natural grove of palm trees and vines that continuously threatened his ocean view.

The groundkeepers wanted to cut it back and trim it down, but he would not allow it. He enjoyed the wildness. The jungle sense of it. The palms reminded him of the Philippines, of Iwo Jima. Sometimes he would turn from the waves and stare at the green vegetation and remember.

"Admiral," a voice rose from behind him. A sweet voice of comfort and admiration, a youthful voice filled with eagerness to please. "Admiral," the woman called as she walked towards him.

Tendrey winced. *What the hell did she want now?* he wondered. He judged the sun's angle and knew it was only 1530. He had another hour, and he was fine where he was.

She would not move him, not today. Not until it was time. It was a beautiful day, blue and bright and warm, and he was fine where he was. *Damn it, go away*, he thought.

"Admiral," Miss Swanson touched his shoulder lightly as she circled his wheelchair with her bubbly smile.

She was almost blinding in her spotless white nurse's uniform and her short bleached-blond hair. "You have a phone call from the mainland," she said, pulling out the antenna of the cordless phone.

"Oh," he said, letting a rare grin form at the edges of his mouth. It caused the soft wrinkles of his face to tighten. He took the handset, cleared the gravel from his throat. "Yes."

"Afternoon, Joe," the voice from the mainland said.

"Just a minute," the admiral covered the receiver with his palm. "Thank you, Miss Swanson," he said to her with a nod. "That will be all."

"Can I get you anything else, Admiral? A glass of iced tea? Some yogurt? A hat? Here, let me pull you into the shade. It's so hot out here," she said, reaching for the brake release on his wheelchair.

"No. I'm fine," he said, parrying her attack.

"I don't think you should be in the heat for so long," she pressed. "It's not good for you."

"Ice coffee? Can you get me a glass? With cream. Please?"

"You know you can't have coffee. How about tea?"

"Yes, that'll be splendid," he surrendered.

She sparkled with success. "Very good. I'll be right back."

As she hurried toward the kitchen, Tendrey remembered why he kept her around at all. God, she made his pulse jump. Her breasts were massive for her slight frame. Such a young, firm frame, alive and tan. If he was only sixty years younger.

"Sorry," he said into the phone. "Go on."

"It's done," the voice said.

Tendrey eased a sigh of relief. "Did it go easy."

"Of course. I'll wait a few days and then make sure I find the body."

"Did you have the chance to find anything, anything aboard his boat."

"There was no time," the man said. "I will search the house again, but does it matter?"

"Yes," Tendrey said. "He might have found something."

"I'll look," the man promised.

"There will be another transfer to your account."

"That is very good to hear, Admiral," the man said as he ended the call.

10

HONOLULU, HAWAII, 1986

D ROPLETS OF SWEAT gathered slowly until they formed a limpid
pearl that defied the microscopic imperfections of her skin and
rolled toward the center of her stomach. At the rise of her hipbone, it
veered inward, crashing into the cotton string of her swimsuit. Fibers
absorbed the perspiration like the tentacles of a feeding anemone.

The sun was scorching as she had never felt it before. It was intent
on baking her, searing her flesh where the three triangular blades of her
bikini did not cover.

Without opening her eyes, Leslie Maetani reached for the small
spray bottle she had set at the top of her beach towel. She floated it over
her face and pumped the trigger releasing a cool mist of water and baby
oil that drifted onto her cheeks and across her forehead where the line
of her dark hair was brushed back and away.

She dropped the bottle into Waikiki's coral sand and resettled herself
over the towel. This was not New York City. Not even Central Park on the
best day of a summer heat wave. The noise was different, the laughter of
children was brighter, and the street traffic was muffled by the barricade of

high-rise hotels behind her. At her feet, there was the crash of the waves. *This, I could get used to*, she thought.

Eric, of course, would never enjoy this. Too much relaxation, too much of nothing to do. Her former boyfriend did not know how to enjoy life unless someone or something in his orbit was in crisis and needed his immediate attention. His advertising firm, his family, his country club, his college alumni association, his West Village condominium's HOA. Something going off the rails that required him to engineer a solution.

He joined the clubs, she realized, to push his way up the ranks for that very reason. So that he was necessary. The cure-all for everyone. What he did not join was her.

He never managed to attend her engagements. As one of Tish Hospital's youngest staff doctors, her presence was mandatory. An obligation that was never stated but understood. The director's award ceremonies, the holiday banquets, the fundraising, and charity events. They could be boring, she would admit, but they were important to her and her career.

In contrast, she was his. The elegant swan with brains. One who had once trained as a dancer but became a surgeon instead. Weekends were filled with his dinner parties at the Ritz, corporate getaways in the Hamptons. There always seemed to be another vital cocktail party where he could sell the two of them as the perfect couple, the young entrepreneur, and his elegant girlfriend with a medical degree.

His clients' wives loved her. She was an exotic princess with an angelic face and magical powers to heal.

"You're more like Beauty and the Beast," Leslie's long-time friend, Terry, would say of them. Deep down, Leslie knew she was right, and it gnawed at her just below her ribcage. A mouse nibbling at the bars of its enclosure.

It took eighteen months for Leslie to end it with Eric. Then another three months of ignored phone calls and erased messages until he understood she was not confused or simply needed time. She knew their break was inevitable even if he did not. Still, it felt like death. Leslie's own version of flatlining.

Terry hired a moving van. She double-parked it out front, made the doorman promise to watch their stuff and bore half of Leslie's hastily packed boxes out of the high-rise, and three hours later, into her spare bedroom.

Leslie hardly had time to unpack her shoes when the telegram somehow found her. Collapsing into Terry's sectional couch, she opened it warily. "It's from my dad," she said, with exhausted surprise. She read it twice. "I don't believe it. He wants me to visit."

"Why is that a surprise?" Terry was in the bathroom, running a brush wildly through her platinum hair. Her new pixie cut gave her a boyish flare she loved.

"Because I haven't seen him in…" Leslie glared at her friend, their eyes meeting in the reflection of the bathroom wall mirror. "You?"

Terry brow rose with false innocence. "You said he lives on the other side of the world. It's not the other side. It's just Hawaii."

She waved the telegram at her. "I'm not going."

Terry laughed. "Too late. The reservations are non-refundable."

"What?"

"Day after tomorrow," Terry marched from the bathroom, swept her purse from the arm of the couch. "Come on, let's get Indian."

"Terry." Leslie felt herself disoriented. "It isn't about distance. I haven't talked to my dad in years."

"Sounds like distance to me." Her new roommate pushed Leslie's clutch into her hands. "What do you think? Panna Garden or Nirvana on Lexington?" She pulled her from the couch. "Tonight, we celebrate your new freedom with dinner. Tomorrow, we celebrate with shopping."

And keeping to her word, the next day they were in the Village and Terry was dangling clothes between Leslie and a full-length mirror.

"I really can't go," Leslie told her. "I've got patients. And Friday, I have four surgeries scheduled."

"Taken care of," Terry said simply. "How about this?" She held up a blue halter top.

"You can just make a phone call and change my schedule?"

"Sure can and sure did?"

"Terry," Leslie wrinkled her nose.

"Whose dad is friends with the hospital's director? And who gives them lots of money?"

"That is so wrong," Leslie glared over the top of a circular rack.

"Les, you haven't had a vacation in two years. You are stressed, you just broke up with your fiancé and you are thinking about quitting medicine all together."

"I am not," she shot. "And Eric was not my fiancé."

"The director doesn't know that. And my dad said the director respects your work and doesn't want to lose you. So, you now have a ten-day vacation," she beamed.

"Oh, Christ."

"Stop worrying, would you? People take time off, Les. Even surgeons."

"To be honest, maybe a break will be good."

Terry froze. "Really?"

"It's just working at a giant city hospital. I thought it would be different." She brushed a curtain of blouses across the rack.

Terry's brows lifted. "Hold on. I connived a vacation. I don't want you quitting medicine. You are a brilliant doctor. It's like a calling."

"It's not that," she assured her friend. "It's just, I don't know," she pressed her lips. "It feels like I am working an assembly line. Patients come in, I repair the damage, they go out. Beyond a few consolations, I don't know any of them. They're just paperwork."

"That is just modern medicine," Terry dismissed. "It's the same at my dad's law firm. People aren't the job anymore." She returned to her shopping.

Leslie sighed. "I guess so."

"This?" Terry found a red string bikini that was more string than bikini. She held it against her friend.

"I couldn't wear that," Leslie told her.

"Yeah. Too much." She switched to a plum-purple version from the same designer. "Better?"

"You don't know my father."

"Believe me, Les, this isn't for your dad. You're in Waikiki for three days first. And for three days, this is all you wear."

"How am I going to pay you back for this?"

"You don't have to. Remember, I am a spoiled trust fund baby." Terry stepped in front of the mirror, held the same bikini to herself, and frowned. "I have the bod of a pre-pubescent boy."

"You have a great figure."

"If I wasn't five-foot-two and looked twelve."

Leslie laughed.

"Now that is what I like to hear. My new roommate laughing. I am telling you, Les, this is going to be good for you."

"I feel like I'm sneaking out of town just before my college finals," Leslie said. She circled the small boutique that catered to Manhattan wives with houses on the Vineyard or along the Cape.

"Your father asked you to come, right?"

"After you wrote him."

"I just passed along your new address. I didn't know you hated each other."

"It's not like that," Leslie admitted.

"Trust me, you'll love Honolulu. It's more than just Florida with culture." Terry cruised the back racks displaying lacy slips, camisoles, and silk pajamas. She lifted a pink teddy from the wall hook. It was adorned with long, thin ribbons and elegant bows. She held it at arm's length.

Leslie wrinkled her nose with disdain. "Pink?"

"You're right. Black is more me."

Leslie passed the array of delicate lingerie without a glance. *No Eric, no need*, she thought, although her dressing to undress never enticed him much.

"So, this thing with your dad?"

Leslie gag-laughed. "Direct questions?"

"Just curious. I mean, you honestly sound worried."

"It's that obvious?"

Terry rolled her eyes. "Not at all."

"It was an argument neither of us knew how to stop. I said things I shouldn't have. When I came to New York for med school, the phone calls just got shorter and shorter until it wasn't worth dialing."

"He didn't want a doctor in the family?"

"He wanted grandchildren."

"Ouch," Terry said, sweeping through the blue jeans rack.

"It was just the two of us. You know, after my mom and brother…" she said.

"Oh god," Terry's hand went to her lips. "I forgot."

"It is okay," Leslie shrugged off her concern. "I was seven, so I don't remember anything about the accident. My dad wasn't much of a doting father to begin with. Afterwards?" she frowned. "How do you heal from that?"

"Can you?"

"I don't know but he had no idea what to do with a little girl. I went from helpless, to demanding, to bitch by the time I was sixteen," she chuckled. "Poor guy."

"I think that was my timeline, too. But I skipped the helpless part."

They laughed.

"I still don't like the idea of leaving my work."

"Sometimes you have to be the patient," Terry said. She took the bikini and shorts from Leslie and circled to the cash register. "Come on, I'm buying these."

"No."

"Yes. Only way you'll wear them is if you feel guilty."

"All set, ladies?" the teenaged boy working the counter was too young to be trusted. Chubby cheeks and baby fuzz. He leered at them as if he knew their secrets.

"What else is bothering you?" Terry asked.

"Nothing."

"Something," Terry persisted in a big sister tone.

"He lives in Honolulu. Why couldn't we meet there? Why do I have to go halfway to Australia?"

"Maybe it's nicer than Hawaii?"

The doctor laced her arms and leaned against the register. "It's his research," she said, almost to herself. "He's testing me. Seeing if I'll make the effort."

"Is that so bad?" Terry asked. She handed the teenager her Gold AMEX card without bothering with the sales' total. "It's probably paradise, right?"

"Sure."

•   •   •

"Doctor Maetani, ma'am?"

Leslie rose from the towel, a palm over her eyes. "Yes?"

It was Jimmy, the young beach attendant from the Moana Hotel. Since her arrival and first day on the sand, he had been especially attentive to Leslie. Towel? Umbrella? Lounge chair? He'd be sure to save her the best spot, close to the water and away from the other hotel guests.

He smiled at her with sparkling braces. "Sorry to bother you, Doctor," he said. "You wanted to know if there were any messages? I saw a telegram at the front desk, ma'am."

"Thank you, Jimmy." She swept herself into a crochet cover up, collected the spray bottle and towel, and rolled them into the large straw bag she had bought that morning. The shop in the Moana's lobby was exactly as Terry had told her. Forget anything at home, the Moana would have it. Want something for the beach, check the Moana shop. Need a paperback to read, a straw visor, a miniature statue of King Kamehameha, or a box of chocolates? The Moana gift shop.

As Leslie stepped from the hot sand to the hotel's stone path, she dropped her new flip-flop sandals–today's gift shop special, 30% off— in front of her toes. With perfect balance, she brushed the bottom of each foot, then worked them under the plastic straps.

The walkway rose from the beach and flowed into the half-acre of hibiscus hedges, palm trees and iron patio tables. The crystal-blue swimming pool, the terrace's chief attraction, was foaming with hysterical children and inflatable inner tubes.

Just beyond, tucked against the hotel, was the Moana's tiki bar. It was a similar crowd to the pool. They were much older, but no less rambunctious. Instead of chlorinated water, they were splashing colorful, umbrella-topped drinks. Vacation was playtime for everyone.

Entering the cool, dim interior of the Moana was a leap back in time. The hotel was the first on Waikiki Beach, rising out of the sand at the turn of the century. Somehow, while Honolulu grew into a misplaced metropolis with every defining asset from freeway traffic to seedy alleys, the Moana kept its colonial charm. Although Leslie's father once said, colonial times were not charming for everyone.

Mahogany floors with cream-washed walls, peacock wicker chairs hidden behind behemoth potted palms, slow turning ceiling fans with dried palm fronds overhead, and a staff dressed in white slacks and blue Hawaiian shirts with stiff collars. The Moana was old-world elegance draped with a tropical flair. All that was missing from this movie set was Bogart and Bacall.

As Leslie approached the polished bamboo front desk that stretched half the lobby, she felt her chest tighten. Leslie hesitated to draw the attention of the concierge, who had his head down, busily sorting postcards.

She had sent her father a brief letter with her travel plans. Her flights, stay overs, the number of days she planned in Honolulu, and when she would arrive at his distant outpost.

She also made sure he knew Terry had made all the reservations and he would have to use her name if he wanted to call the hotel.

Now, as she stood in front of the reservation desk, she realized she did not expect him to contact her. What if he had changed his mind? What if he had decided too much time had passed, and they honestly had nothing to discuss? Could he think that? Maybe. Suddenly, she did not want to see the telegram.

She pivoted and found Jimmy directly behind her.

His face exploded with happiness. "Your message? I can get it," the teenager told her. He swooped around the desk, his fingers dragging the countertop as if setting an anchor point. He reached into the pigeon boxes beneath and pulled her key and an envelope with the hotel letterhead. "Here you go," he said. He slid them together.

"Thanks." She lifted the key, and with unease Jimmy may or may not have noticed, pinched the envelope off the counter. She retreated, then remembered. "Oh." She dug to the bottom of her beach bag for her wallet.

The teenager flashed his palms. "I did nothing."

"Next time," she promised, pinning a note inside her head to tip Jimmy well.

She settled into a solitary wicker chair as far across the lobby as she could find. It hid her from guest traffic by two potted Areca palm trees. Dropping the beach bag between her ankles, she studied the sealed envelope.

She stiffened her jaw, snapped the short end off and slipped the tri-folded piece of pink paper into her fingers. Leslie glanced at the return address. The stress in her shoulders dissolved. It was from Terry.

Heya Les,

Guess who I found praying for a cab at the airport after dropping you off? Stephen!! Was I shocked! He was shocked! He got a free ride. I'm hoping for the same. We're getting together for drinks on Friday.

Last thing, Eric called. Guess he wants to play kissy-kissy and make up. Don't do it. We're going to have fun roomie. Don't worry, I didn't tell him where you went.

Just take care and enjoy. Worry about nothing. Just reconnect with your pop.

Love ya, Terr

She was glad to hear from Terry, glad she had come across her ex from three boyfriends back. She could picture Stephen, the actor who could not sing or dance. Dark eyes, dark brows, dimpled chin and dark mood. He could be nice, but it was not consistent. She hoped Terry remembered why she left him.

As she crossed to the elevators, Leslie slipped the letter into its envelope and dropped it into the bottom of her bag. She would see her father soon enough, she told herself.

She had come too far to turn around. He was her father and she, his only child. They were all they had. Her mother had passed so long ago, Leslie could not remember her voice and the only mental picture she held she gleaned from an 8mm home movie. A tall, thin woman in a sundress with a pudgy child hoisted onto her hip and one standing at her knee.

They stood at the entrance of the Los Angeles Zoo. The camera angle low to get the arched sign behind them. Leslie had bowl-cut bangs with a blue bow over her ear. Her mother wore thick, cat-eyed glasses and was shooing the cameraman, her husband, to hurry. He was embarrassing them.

Tomorrow, Leslie would strap herself into an airplane seat, jet across the Pacific, and reconnect with that cameraman. She would not leave her memories of him to old celluloid.

As for Eric? Those memories she could do without.

11

BRIAN SAT HUNCHED in the stiff plastic chair, his elbows on his thighs, the morning edition of the *Post* spread between them. His fingers were black from turning the long, floppy pages. His gaze, however, was not on the lead story or the weather or the jump line.

They were slicing across the paper's scalloped top as they roamed the airport lounge, leaping from face to face. What had the Asian woman said? There was a woman in the hotel lobby? Had he seen her? Would he recognize her again? Or was he being paranoid?

That was certainly possible. No one was giving him a second glance. They were all, at some level, nervously waiting to step inside a steel tube with dubious wings because statistics and the airlines told them it was safe.

He was a businessman, climbing on to his morning hopper back to New York or Chicago. A lobbyist taking good news back to his custom suit investors. Just a man, like hundreds of other men and women milling around Dulles waiting for their escape.

"United's Flight 23 to Los Angeles, now boarding at Gate 13," the female voice sounded like it was echoing from deep inside a Folger's coffee can. Brian forced himself not to react. He side-glanced at the people and felt both suspicious and silly.

After a natural amount of time, he glanced at his wristwatch. 10:32 a.m. Someone would soon announce the flight to Boston out of Gate 11.

He stretched his back, casually eyeing Gate 13. The crowd was still large as well-wishers said goodbye to family and friends.

The experienced travelers were making their move to the head of the line. Elbows in, carryon tucked, like fullbacks lining up for the snap. The first ones to their seats earned a coveted spot in the overhead.

"Commuter Flight 6 to Logan International, now boarding Gate 11," a different female voice called out. It held a pleasant tone saying don't rush but please hurry.

Brian folded the newspaper and tucked it into the side pouch of his flight bag. He stretched his arms. Another casual scan of his fellow passengers.

It was then he caught her eyes on him. The tall woman with the auburn hair in a loose bun standing at the entrance to the airport bar. He recognized her. From where? As suddenly as she appeared, she stepped back into the mock tavern.

Was she watching him or waiting for her husband's arrival? His mind was playing tricks, seeing what it was expecting to see. He had not noticed if there was a drink in her hand.

He knew he had seen her before. Where? Think! Where had she been? The front of the airport. She had walked past him as he got out of his cab at the curb. He had glimpsed her from behind. Her hair was combed out, but it was the same tailored burgundy suit.

There was somewhere else. Spoons dug deep into his head, trying to reach the hippocampus. Where else?

The Hyatt. In the lobby. Different clothes. Glasses. Hair braided. Did he see her? He was not sure.

This is ridiculous, he thought. He was becoming paranoid. It was the Chinese woman who said he was being followed and that there were microphones in his room. He searched and found nothing. No one was following him. It was crazy.

Brian thought about walking past the bar when the second call for the Boston flight crackled across the ceiling.

Threading his arm through the flight bag's strap, he pulled it to his left shoulder. He grabbed his briefcase with the same hand and sauntered toward Gate 11.

At Gate 13, the last dozen passengers were moving measuredly past the United boarding steward. He checked each ticket with a gleeful nod as he sent them onward to paradise.

At Gate 11, the crowd swelled with exhausted families and solo fliers. Brian mingled at the back.

Another quick glance across the airport. Gate 13 was empty now, the steward standing at the door browsing his boarding list. Brian saw him check the enormous clock designed into the airport wall. Stabbing his pen into a breast pocket, the steward tugged at the door's aluminum handle, releasing it from the metal peg in the carpet.

Finally, the double doors leading to an MD-80 jetliner opened from inside. A flight attendant gave the steward a thumbs-up and disappeared into the boarding ramp.

As if on cue, the passengers heading to Boston surged forward with lemming-like determination. The steward rushed to take tickets.

Brian did not follow. As they moved forward, he pivoted, squeezed through the crowd, and darted for Gate 13. "Wait," he called to the United steward. "Sorry, I almost climbed on the wrong plane," Brian said, forcing a laugh.

"That doesn't happen very often," the steward grinned. "Flight 23?"

"To L.A." Brian nodded as he drew his airline ticket from his coat.

As the steward verified the flight, Brian glanced over his shoulder. The line at Gate 11 was rapidly thinning. He looked toward the airport bar. The woman was not there.

"There you are, Mr. Bovan," the steward was saying. His clipboard had appeared from nowhere. "First class. Seat four near the window." He held open the door. "I think Toni, your attendant, has a package for you."

"A package?" Brian pushed the ticket into his pocket and stepped onto the ramp. "Great. Another package," he mumbled.

•　　　•　　　•

"Are you sure?"

"One hundred percent. United Flight 23 non-stop to Los Angeles," Karen said, her voice heavy with frustration.

"You didn't check the flight to Logan?"

"You know damn well I did," Karen growled. She did not like being second guessed, even if she deserved it, even if it was from the boss. "I checked the manifest. He should be sitting in 41B, eating salted peanuts and drinking a Coke."

"What the hell is in Los Angeles?" JP was still in shock. Easy. This was going to be an easy surveillance job. That's what he had told himself twenty-seven hours ago.

"He might not be going to Los Angeles," the agent said. Her voice shifted from frustration to concern. "The flight continues on to Honolulu."

"Christ," JP clenched the phone receiver. "Has the plane left?" he asked, knowing there was nothing he could do to stop Bovan. The authorization to do that would take several minutes.

"No, but the doors have been closed. He was the last to board."

"There is no way you can get on?"

"No," Karen retorted.

"Pack it up and come home. I'll put in a call to Los Angeles and have someone hook him there," the CIA man said.

JP dropped the phone into the receiver, thinking. There was nothing else to do. He knew his team had not failed. He had.

Lieutenant Commander Bovan. Second-in-command of a nuclear attack submarine. He was schooled in deception as much as Karen or himself. Maybe on a larger stage with a much more potent weapon, but the game was the same.

Hide and seek in the open. Lurk in the shadows. Blend in. Stand still and gather. Sit back and watch. Trust no one. It was the same methodology. JP and his crew work hotel rooms and government buildings. Bovan ran his operations a thousand feet under the sea. It was all the same.

JP's fingers danced lightly over the back of the phone's receiver. Why Hawaii? In those missing minutes between his elevator rise from the lobby until he stepped into his room, Bovan had spoken to someone. They had tipped him off to their surveillance, or, at least, warned him to take precautions.

Why Hawaii? The package from Admiral Mills? The old family friend. That was how the CIA's data analyst in rainy Virginia described him. Was that sending the Commander west? A suggestion from a friend?

Maybe. Maybe not. Maybe Bovan took a sudden vacation. It was possible.

There was a feeling of heat on the back of his neck. That burning discomfort JP got when assignments were compromised. And this one, he realized, was jeopardized before first contact.

One thing was certain, JP thought as he pressed the phone to his ear and dialed. *Admiral Tendrey would not be pleased with his report.*

●　　　●　　　●

"We almost shut the door on you," the slender woman said as she showed Brian to his seat. She was right off an airline advertisement poster. Pearlescent skin, wedge-cut blond hair, perfect teeth. Her face said girl-next-door. "I'm Toni and I'll be your hostess to Honolulu."

"I almost walked onto the wrong plane," Brian said. He slipped out of his coat. "The guy at the door said you had a package?"

"Your assistant dropped it at the front counter."

"My assistant?"

"As soon as the captain turns off the seatbelt sign, I'll bring it. Would you like a drink before we back away from the gate?"

"Rum and coke?"

"Of course." There was that smile again.

Toni hung his coat in the curtained closet and disappeared behind the wall of the service station.

Only half the first-class seats were filled. Brian swept the cabin quickly and saw no one had given his arrival much notice. That was the promise of first class, he guessed. Passengers did not bother fellow passengers. You could stretch out your feet and lean back as if you were in your favorite leather chair at home.

The huge Boeing 747 swayed gently as it taxied from the terminal to the runway. A comfortable, familiar motion for Brian. He felt the plane pivot, settle itself for a moment, as its four turbofan jet engines began swallowing massive amounts of air with a growing roar that shook the overhead cabinets. A heartbeat of hesitation and the airliner lunged toward the end of the long strip of concrete.

It lifted, defying gravity, its long shimmering wings reaching into the morning mist that lingered above urban Washington. Not unlike the rolling deck of a submarine, the 747 banked to starboard and headed toward the Atlantic. With a mechanical rumble, the claws of the bird retracted into its belly.

The pilot twisted the yoke and turned north. Brian could see the brown shimmering waters of Chesapeake outside his window.

A few minutes later, the seatbelt sign clicked off, and Toni appeared. "Here you are, Mr. Bovan." Toni handed him a small manila envelope and a glass tumbler swirling with ice and asphalt black liquid.

When Toni moved on to her other wards, Brian settled himself into his seat. He sipped his rum and coke. Fingered the magazines in the seatback pocket at his knees.

Then, casually, carelessly, with feigned indifference, he retrieved the envelope. His name and seat number were across the front. Handwritten.

A glance down the aisle assured him Toni was giving the other first-class passengers her first-class attention.

Unlacing the waxed string from the red paper buttons, he released the contents into his lap. Three thick stacks of American bills slid out, 100s, 50s, and 20-dollar bills, bound by rubber bands. His heart stopped. He shoved them back inside.

A pair of shiny car keys on a simple ring, another airline ticket, and a folded piece of paper remained on his lap.

Dear Commander,

Please do not be offended by the contents of the package. It is merely a loan. I made you leave in such a hurry I assume you had no time to gather necessities. This is for accommodations and dining.

It is best if you do not use your credit cards. They can easily trace your location.

The keys are to a white Chevrolet Camaro. It is parked in the furthest corner of the second level of the east parking structure at Honolulu International. License plate number DML 301.

In the car's trunk is a suitcase with clothes and odds and ends of a vacationer traveling to an exotic island. I hope you will not mind my taste in men's clothes.

Your flight to Truk departs at 6:20 a.m. tomorrow. Relax and enjoy Honolulu while you are there. It is a beautiful city.

Mimi

Brian returned everything to the envelope and pushed it into his briefcase next to his feet. 'Relax and enjoy.' *That's a joke, right?* He thought. *This is crazy. She was crazy.* He squeezed the bridge of his nose with his index finger and thumb. She was crazy at a clinical level. But she was also efficient and was not wasting any time getting him to Truk.

• • •

"Kornic, it's JP," the CIA man muttered. He was tired and not looking forward to what he knew was coming.

Edwin Kornic was a by-the-book man. A man from Duke. Top of his class. No humor, no imagination. Belt and suspenders. Bow tie kind-of guy.

He and JP had gone through the Farm together. They had unique styles in their approach and resolution to the same drill, yet at the end, their scores were only a tick or two from each other. It annoyed Kornic and tickled JP.

JP was aware Kornic did not like his loose tactics. He did not like his use of women on top priority jobs, did not like the way he gathered his teams and let them run free. Mostly, he simply did not like JP.

"Well, this is a surprise," Kornic said. "I didn't get the memo about Satan's icebergs."

"I need a favor," JP continued.

"A favor? From an agent you wouldn't work with unless hell froze over?"

"That was alcohol talk. I didn't mean it."

There was a grunt on the other end of the line.

"A subject is heading into your sector. I just need surveillance until my people can get there." JP waited. The line felt dead, like a fishing lure that had lost its bait. He continued. "United, Flight 23. Arrives 12:35 p.m. your time. He'll have to..."

"Where's clearance for this?" Kornic cut in. "Authorization?"

JP expected that. "It's need-to-know."

Kornic's laughter came harshly across three time zones.

"I'm asking for surveillance, Kornic, not a fucking Dallas." Claws pinching the back of his neck. They were on a secure phone line, but his reference to an assassination was careless. He had to hold back his anger, otherwise Kornic would dig his heels into cement. "This is bottom level. For a friend."

"Just a simple surveillance job which your people screwed up. You had a green target, and they still lost him," the Pacific agent crooned. "I'll bet you had one of your girls working him, didn't you?" Laughter over the line. "You never learn."

Now the anger took hold. "Kornic, my guy lands at L.A.X. in three hours, twenty minutes. I want a man on that plane for the rest of the flight, and I want his kneecaps glued to the back of my guy's legs until I tell you otherwise. You understand me?"

"Fuck you. Your sector doesn't reach out here, JP. You can't ask for help without authorization."

"You're right, Eddie, I can't. But I am close to the people who can. The people who watch us both and okay our 401s. I bet I can bend more ears in my favor than you can, because I go to their kid's birthday parties, we golf together, we drink Budweiser from bottles and talk shit about our wives. By the time I get out there, Kornic, I'll have my authorization, and I'll have your balls in my back pocket as well."

There was silence on the phone in Los Angeles.

"How does the next five years planted behind a desk in Albania sound, Kornic? Paperwork to your eyebrows?"

"You're an asshole."

"I am," JP agreed.

"You got a photo and a file?" Kornic's voice was horse.

"Teletext in ten minutes."

"I don't know whose ass you kiss to keep your job, but they must love it."

"That's the best you can do, Eddie? You're losing your touch," JP said in the happiest voice he could muster. "As always, good working with you, my friend."

•　　　•　　　•

The runway at LAX greeted the 747 with a jolt. It was touchdown after two attempts. The city was having its worst storm in seven years and unknown to the passengers; the tower had suggested the captain try landing at Burbank Airport or Orange County if he could not manage this time around.

He had managed, and they taxied to the terminal, locked in the covered walkway, and shut down the engines. The steel skin of the plane glistened in the rain and the airport's flood lights.

Brian watched through his window as two tarmac attendants drove a string of luggage containers alongside the plane. As if orchestrated into a dance, luggage came off for passengers debarking while luggage came on for those heading to America's tropical state.

As Toni had suggested, Brian remained aboard. There was nothing that was worth seeing near the terminal gate, she explained, and as they were departing in under 30 minutes, there was little time to wander far.

He was watching the suitcases pass between the attendants like circus juggler spinning bowling pins when someone touched his shoulder.

"Excuse me." A small man hunched at the right shoulder draped in a winter coat and far-too-wide tie stood beside the empty seat next to Brian. He clutched his ticket and scratched at his grey mustache with his thumb. "54F?" He pointed at the empty seat.

Before Brian could answer the gentleman, Toni swooped.

"May I help you?" she asked, angling her body to keep him from stepping further into her first-class realm.

"I think I am here. 54F." He studied the seat numbers over Brian's head.

"Oh no," she peeked at his ticket. "Further back. Mister… Mr. Cranken." She stretched out her arm as stiff as a guardrail.

Brian heard her pass the man to the economy class attendant and pull the royal blue curtains that separated first-class from the rest of the plane, a barrier between them from us.

It took three more attendants to help Mr. Cranken find his seat. As he half-expected, 54F placed him in the last row. He knew the rear of airplanes. Knew them more intimately than he liked to remember.

It was in the radar navigator's seat of a B-52 bomber that he had watched much of Vietnam's lush green countryside sweep by.

Cranken slipped a small notepad from his breast pocket and scribbled,

Bovan. First class. Seat, 6. Light brown slacks. White shirt. Black briefcase.

The small man with the slight hitch to his shoulder pushed the pad into his pocket. He depressed the button in the arm rest and leaned his seatback as far as it would go, closed his eyes, and let sleep take him.

12

PEARL HARBOR, HAWAII, 1944

THE FULL MOON ATTEMPTED to cast its brilliance onto the slick, inky highway that wove through the mountain valley. But the clouds edging the hillside were defiant. Thick and heavy with rain, they packed themselves tight into the lush tropical forest and sporadically released their torrent in cold sheets.

Douglas held the Packard closer to the center of the narrow road than to the right, where the edge dropped steeply toward the sea.

He shifted the car into first gear as they approached another back-bending turn. The road climbed so steeply he worried the front bumper would catch the asphalt. The large headlight beams swept the Loulo palms that waved their fronds like bystanders at a Macy's parade.

Mimi sat close to him, her left hand resting on the top of his thigh, her perfume filling the interior of the car.

"Jesus, where is this place?" Douglas asked. They had driven most of the way in silence. He sensed something was bothering her.

"It shouldn't be much further," Mimi said. "There's a gate before you get onto the grounds."

Douglas managed several more turns, the Packard's massive in-line eight-cylinder motor pulling them to the mountain's crest.

"I'm glad you came tonight," she whispered.

"I'll try not to embarrass you. Although arriving with a submariner, it might be too late."

She sat up and kissed his cheek. "You are funny."

It started to rain again, gently at first, then heavier, cutting the distance the headlights reached by half. The trees and hanging vines closed in, creating a tunnel over the road.

Moments later, they rounded another steep crook in the road and, as Douglas navigated the turn, found the pavement split in two. The right fork continued up the mountain, while the left lead them directly to a forbidding iron gate. The gate's black pickets stood like spears of a Roman army ready to march. In the center of the barricade, two brass letters glistened in the Packard's headlights. R.C.

Parked off to the side was a military police Jeep. Two MPs stood in waxed-coated ponchos, their M1 carbines leaning against their shoulders. A third MP stepped to the car as Douglas edged it forward.

"Good evening, sir," the MP said as Douglas slid the side window down a few inches. The humidity outside blew into the car with the night breeze.

The rain was now a tropical downpour, and it pummeled the MP's poncho-covered hat. Behind him, the slit opening of the Jeep's headlamps cast him with an eerie halo. "Invitation?"

Mimi leaned across Douglas. He felt her hand purposely hold the inside of his thigh.

"Lai Ming, assistant to Ambassador Wei Tao-ming," she said in a voice loud enough for the soldier to hear above the drumbeat on the convertible top.

"Yes, ma'am." The MP stepped back without hesitation. He waved to the other MP, and the gate was pushed open. "Have a nice evening, ma'am."

"Either you have a lot of pull or they are terrified of you," Douglas said as he drove forward.

"A little of both, I hope."

The jungle fell away, revealing thick lawns, clipped trees and sculpted bushes decorating both sides of a volcanic gravel driveway. At the top of the mile-long path, a white colonial-style mansion from Hawaii's past rose out of the hilltop.

Every window of the three-story structure glowed with an inviting warmth. At the entrance, the front double-doors stood wide, allowing the brightest welcome to roll out into the storm.

Douglas pulled the car under a broad canvas tent at the foot of the stone steps leading into the home. It shielded arriving guests from the evening showers that often came to this side of the mountain. As he stepped from the Packard, he eyed several cars lined like library books on the far side of the house.

A young native boy appeared at Mimi's door. Dressed in pleated red pants and a red coat stained to brown by the rain, he opened the car for her.

A second boy, another islander with an alligator wide mouth of crooked teeth, came from nowhere and welcomed Douglas. The boy slipped into the driver's seat, and though barely able to reach the pedals, maneuvered the big car toward the others.

Mimi straightened her silver-white silk dress with red stitching and silk buttons that snaked along her shoulder. "Remember," she whispered as Douglas moved beside her. "Please don't hold this against me." She laced her arm through his and they headed up the covered stairs.

"Just give me a heading toward the bar. I'll be fine." He brushed down the pocket flaps of his uniform whites.

She paused at the top of the stairs. "Promise me something, Douglas," she said, her voice suddenly desperate.

"Anything."

"That after the party, you'll stay with me tonight. No matter what. No matter what they say or what's decided."

"Decided?"

"Promise me," she said with the urgency of a child. "Please."

"Okay," he nodded. "Promise."

As they walked in through the doorway, the roar of the rain on the tarp gave way to chirps of laughter and the wash of conversation. The crowd inside filled the ground floor like the tide swelling through a reef. They spilled from the white-marbled entry hall into the grand room with its brass ceiling fans, into the library with its shelves of oak imported from Maine and lined with leather-bound tomes, into the secondary study and several smaller alcoves behind narrow doorways.

Few people noticed their arrival and of those who did, their stares turned to Mimi. Everyone knew the Chinese ambassador was in Honolulu, and some had heard about his beautiful assistant, but when she entered the hall wrapped in her shimmering silk dress and her raven-black hair falling over svelte shoulders; they realized how true the talk had been.

From an interior balcony overlooking the guests, another set of eyes watched the latest arrivals. They did not, however, focus on Mimi. They were interested in her escort and every movement the formally dressed submarine commander made as he passed through the crowd.

"You are too eager," Ambassador Wei said as he stepped up beside the Naval man on the balcony. He pointed the stem of his tobacco pipe at Douglas and Mimi. "Let them enjoy themselves. Miss Ming will let us know when it is time."

The man continued to watch Douglas as the ambassador patted him on the shoulder and moved away.

•　　•　　•

Douglas felt Mimi release his arm and turn from him. She stretched out her arms and met the elderly woman head on as they rushed together. "Auntie Violet!"

"Good heavens. Look at you," Violet Seymour held Mimi at arm's length. She swept Mimi into her arms. "What happened to the boney girl with the dirty palms I left in Peking? You are beautiful, my dear."

"How are you?" Mimi asked.

"Still standing. Can't ask for much more."

Mimi laughed. "And Uncle Horace?"

"Somewhere. He is a good ambassador, but a terrible host." Mrs. Seymour finally saw Douglas. "And who is this you've snagged?"

Mimi put her arm around the woman's frail shoulder. "Someone I very much want you to meet." Douglas could see Mimi's eyes sparkling. "This is Commander Douglas Bovan. Douglas, Mrs. Violet Seymour, Ambassador Seymour's wife."

"His better half," she quipped. "How do you do, Commander?" she set an impossibly frail hand in his. "You are lucky to be with such a charming woman tonight."

"That, I am realizing more each minute, Mrs. Seymour," Douglas said, a quick look to Mimi.

"Did you know, we found this one working in the basement of the Peking University," Mrs. Seymour squeezed Mimi's shoulder. "Down in the shadows like a little pack rat, she was. We sort of adopted her as our own," she said, remembering. "My husband was in the foreign office. A million years ago. Now, the world has gone to hell."

"They forced Ambassador Wei to hire me," Mimi said.

"We did not. We only introduced you to the proper people and did our best to stop you from playing with those skeletons."

Douglas laughed. "With dirty hands."

"Oh, Commander, let me tell you, she was terrible. Always digging into something. Even after we left and she had a good government position, our friends were constantly telling us she was still spending half her time in the countryside or at the University," Mrs. Seymour confided.

"No need to tell him everything, Auntie," Mimi said.

Mrs. Seymour laughed. "Tell me, Commander, what type of ship are you assigned to?"

"A submarine, ma'am," Douglas said proudly.

"Oh my, how exciting," she said as she hooked her arm through his. "Come, I have so many people for you to meet." She turned to Mimi, who followed behind them as they weaved through the crowd and said, "Maybe we can find him an aircraft carrier to command. They are much safer."

Douglas glanced at Mimi, who was holding back her laughter.

Mrs. Seymour led Douglas to several groups in the room. She introduced him to captains, commanders, full admirals, rear admirals, and their wives. He met statesmen and ambassadors and dozens of liaisons.

To his surprise, the admirals were pleased to see him. The true fighting men, the men with guts, one had said about the submarine corps.

Douglas was relieved to see Mimi remaining close as he was paraded about the house. She had a way about her, a casual way she greeted the other guests, set her hand in theirs, and made small talk. Between polite introductions and nods of agreement, she would glance over and hold him with her eyes.

Mrs. Seymour led Douglas to a fist of men at the library door. They were cradling whisky and cigars. "Commander?" Mrs. Seymour tapped the shoulder blade of an officer. He was a big man, broad in the back and with short blond hair, making an atoll around his head. "I would like you to meet Lieutenant Commander Bovan."

Full Commander Thomas Mills pivoted with the grace of a tugboat. His head cocked, gave Douglas the up and down, and burst into laughter. "Goddamn, they'll let anyone in here."

Douglas grabbed Mills by the shoulders and pulled him in. "How the hell are you, Tom?"

"Good. Real good. And you?" Mills grinned.

"No complaints," Douglas said.

"Seems you two have met," Mrs. Seymour said.

"We go back a long way," Mills said.

Douglas drew Mimi in. "Tom, this is Lai Ming."

Mills reached out and shook her hand. "Do I need to warn you about him or have you already heard?" he asked.

"Oh, I have heard," she smiled. "Did you know each other before the war?"

Mills laughed. A deep baritone chuckle that radiated out of his barreled chest. "Before we wore britches."

"Not quite," Douglas countered. "I think you were nine when your family moved into town."

"Remember, we used to sneak into the movie house to watch Mae West movies?"

"And I remember you stealing pies from the back door of the bakery for us to eat during the show."

Mills stuttered an excuse, his face reddening, as the two women laughed.

Mrs. Seymour saved him. "Let's leave these two to their reunion." She took Mimi's hand. "We'll find Horace. I know he'll be furious if I don't take you to him directly. If you gentlemen will excuse us?"

"I'll just be a few minutes," Mimi promised. "Commander, it was nice to meet you."

"My pleasure. Miss Ming," Mills said. As she slipped away, he leaned into his friend. "You haven't changed, have you, Doug? Still playing the field. And with a Jap, no less."

"She's Chinese," Douglas said flatly.

"There's a difference?" Mills stopped a butler with a silver tray. He lifted two champagne flutes and passed one to Douglas. "How's Cath?"

Douglas' head dropped slightly, burdened. "She was here for Christmas."

"Nothing resolved?"

"She's not interested in resolve."

"How's the boat?" Mills changed the subject.

"I've got a good crew. My second needs a bit of watching over, but he'll come around. I thought they had you banging around the Atlantic."

"To everyone's surprise, the Brits are finally doing a decent job of it. So, they shipped the lot of us West," Mills sipped his drink as he eyed the guests. "I hear it'll be over soon enough."

"Not soon enough," Douglas said.

"How's the side action? Find any profitable distractions?"

Douglas lowered his voice. "The locals aren't card players, but there are some games around to keep your interest. Just don't expect anything like the old neighborhood."

"Everybody likes the cards."

"Trust me, they have just as many angles going as we did. Out here, they're better at it. I am still licking my wounds."

"I don't believe it. You're never down."

"Well," he shrugged.

"Maybe too many distractions."

"We'll blame the war."

"What did they give you for command?"

"A *Gato-class* boat. The *Mako*. She's already gotten us out of some scraps and held together," Douglas said.

"Commander Bovan," a slender man called with a streaky voice. He had thick-lensed wire glasses on a sharp nose, curly gray-blond hair and he wore the distinct uniform of a full naval captain. Apologizing his way through a circle of elderly women, he crossed the library.

Douglas and Mills instinctively stiffened their backs. "Sir," they said in unison.

"None of that here, gentlemen," the captain said. "Ronald Tucker." He introduced himself as he grasped their hands. He turned to Douglas.

"Someone mentioned you were here, Commander. I wanted to say thank you and shake your hand."

"Thank me, sir?"

"You picked up a pilot off Dead Man's atoll in November," Tucker said. "My son-in-law. So, thanks to you, he's back in the States."

"I'll pass that along to the crew, sir. They'll be glad he is doing well," Douglas said. He felt someone move behind him. Petite fingers slipped into his. Mimi had returned.

"Please, let them know they made this old man's daughter very happy." He squeezed Douglas' shoulder. "Perhaps we can talk again later," he said. He melted back into the party.

"That was nice of him," Mimi said.

"Sounds like you're on your way to making admiral," Mills joked.

"Douglas, I have someone who wants to speak with you," Mimi said. "If you don't mind, Commander?"

"Not at all," Mills said. "I should mingle. Maybe my commanding officer-to-be is here. Doug, any idea when you sail again?"

"We got a few more repairs to button up."

"Well, plan on a few beers before you head out."

"Absolutely," he agreed. He slapped his friend on the shoulder and followed Mimi through the grand hall. "Who am I parading for?" he whispered.

"Ambassador Wei. But this isn't a social greeting," she said.

Douglas suddenly realized her cheer had vanished. She led him out of the hall, through the dining room, and into a hallway that circled the rear of the mansion. Away from the party, the house became oddly quiet.

"Is something wrong?" Douglas asked. There was not time for her answer as they stepped into the secondary study where two men were waiting. "What...?" Douglas stopped at the door.

He felt Mimi tug at him slightly. "Please," she said. She pulled at him again.

"A bit surprised, Commander?" Rear Admiral Tendrey said in his molasses drawl. He was a tall man with narrow shoulders and narrow hips and feminine hands. His brown hair was razor-cut short.

"Sir," Douglas said, intending not to sound respectful. But his naval training took over and his body lifted to the proper pose.

"No need for formalities tonight, Doug," Tendrey said as he tapped a Lucky Strike from the carton. "I don't think you've met Ambassador Wei."

The second man was compact, heavy just above the beltline. Jet black hair greased back. He nodded abruptly. "How do you do, Commander Bovan? I have been looking forward to this meeting."

"A drink, Doug?" Tendrey sauntered to the bar wedged on the opposite side of a poker table with chip pockets and a clean felt top. Four red leather-backed chairs surrounded it.

"No, sir," Douglas clipped. He felt Mimi leave his side and out of the corner of his eye, watched her retreat to one of the large windows overlooking a garden. It was still raining, tearing down the windowpane.

"Ease the hostilities, Bovan," he said sharply. "You and I don't see eye-to-eye, that's a certainty. But we're playing in the same band."

"Are we, Admiral? I don't remember my friends selling faulty torpedoes to the Navy."

Tendrey glared at Douglas. The Admiral's association with military contractors who had had supplied defective torpedo triggers was well known. It had caused him a lot of public embarrassment but had cost the Navy more.

The ambassador laughed again. "You were right, Admiral. He's fearless. Even of you."

Douglas had not stepped completely into the room. He knew the smartest thing to do was turn and leave, but he saw Mimi staring at him.

"Perfect for what?" Douglas asked harshly.

"Come inside, son, and we'll explain." The admiral waved his unlit cigarette.

Douglas saw Mimi was watching him now, her face tight with concern. As he moved inside the room, he knew this would be a night he would regret.

"Want that drink now?"

"I am still good."

"Suit yourself. I am going to have a whisky. Miss Ming, join me? I know the ambassador will." Tendrey poured three tumblers and handed them out. "Find a chair, Commander."

"I'll stand."

"This is the only order of the night. Sit down."

Douglas dragged a leather chair across a blue Persian rug with blanched tassels and eased into it.

"We've got a proposition for you," Tendrey continued.

Douglas glanced at Mimi again. She had turned to the window and was watching the rain gather on the pane. "Not interested," he said.

"You haven't heard it."

"I don't need to," Douglas said. "Not if you're involved."

Tendrey smirked. "I know you are a bit of a gambler." He hoisted his hip on to the edge of the study's pedestal desk. "I have a friend. A captain in the military police. He does me a few favors, I do a few for him." He sipped the whisky. Sucked it through his teeth like a Texan. "It is a good working relationship. Odd thing about this MP, he keeps tabs on the local gambling games. You know, the roulette, craps, those sickening cockfights the natives hoot about. He even knows who bets on the kids' baseball games. But he doesn't arrest anyone. He just keeps names in a notebook."

Douglas stared at Tendrey as he spoke. He wanted to look into Mimi's face, into her eyes and understand why she had brought him into a viper's den.

With the tumbler in hand, the admiral pointed at Douglas. "Your name is on those pages," he said, his voice low and emotionless. "How much do they have you for? Ten-grand? Twenty? Probably a bit more, right?"

Douglas glared; his fingers making dents in the arms of the chair. Tendrey had more on him than rank.

"Your interest piqued now, son?"

"Not in the least." He rose from the chair.

Mimi quickly crossed the room. "Please Douglas. Hear them out. For me."

How easily she had reeled him in, he thought. *Hook, line, sinker, and topped with sultry bait.* In barely a day and a half, he had become so enthralled it was impossible to break the leader and run. Douglas sat back down.

"It is quite simple, Commander," the ambassador said. "We need someone who will go to the Caroline Islands and make a delivery."

"You need my sub," Douglas said.

The ambassador nodded. "We are forced to deal with elements of the Japanese black market. They acquired something that belongs to my government. I am responsible for its return."

"Maybe no one has mentioned it, but the Carolines are under Japanese control," Douglas said, his tone hard and direct. "You know, the guys we are at war with."

"And the Republic of China, Commander, is our ally."

"We are not addressing this in an official capacity," Wei stressed. "My government would never admit to dealing with the enemy in any form and the Imperial Navy, if they knew what they had, would never return them."

"This isn't a delivery. It's a swap." Douglas knew he was right by the drop of Wei's face. "What is it?"

The ambassador glanced toward Mimi, silently passing her the argument. "Fossils," she said. "Fossils of the Peking Man. They are one of China's most sacred treasures."

Douglas remembered what Mrs. Seymour had said earlier. '*We found this one working in the basement of the Peking University.*'

"You're asking me to risk my boat and crew?"

"Oh, if that shakes your boots, you'll love the details," Tendrey said as he gulped his whisky.

Douglas shifted in his chair. "And you are offering them what?"

"Five million dollars in uncut diamonds," the ambassador told him.

Unintentionally, Douglas' eyebrows rose. "For bones."

The ambassador dragged one of the leather chairs from the card table, angled it close, his knees almost touching Douglas. "Tell me, Commander, what would you do to retrieve the Liberty Bell or the Declaration of Independence?" he asked. "Or do you think of them as simply a piece of old parchment and a chunk of metal? I do not think so."

Douglas did not trust Tendrey. The ambassador, however, he was still deciding. "What's to keep them from blowing my boat out of the water once they get their money? Respect thy enemy?"

"Not exactly," Tendrey said. "The diamonds will be placed in a crate wired with explosives. By the time they disarmed them, you'll be outside the harbor."

"Harbor?" Douglas felt the muscles in his neck knotting.

"A small detail," Tendrey said with a meager shrug.

"The freighter is inside Truk Lagoon," Mimi said, her voice soft.

Douglas felt his jaw slacken as he stared at her.

"It wasn't our choice," the ambassador said.

"You might as well have picked Tokyo Bay." Douglas ran his hand across his chin. "Japan's Fourth Fleet is stationed at Truk," he pressed. "Do you have any idea the defenses they have? How many anti-sub nets and sea mines they've strung around those reefs?"

The ambassador inched his chair closer. "Actually, Commander, we know exactly how many and where they are located. Our contact has given us the Imperial charts of the atoll."

Douglas laughed as he climbed to his feet. "This joke is in poor taste."

"It will work, Douglas," Mimi said. "It has to."

"It won't," he told her. He glared at Tendrey. "Any sub captain who thinks he can navigate those nets has a death wish."

"They missed the back door," Tendrey said. He drew a Zippo lighter from his pocket, snapped it open. He lit his cigarette and, through a dense cloud of smoke, explained.

"We got charts of Truk too. Most were made before the Japs moved in and installed their airfields and garrisons. Our corps have been charting the Carolines since the '20s. The islands' strategic position between here and Solomons is not a surprise, son," the admiral said.

"I put their charts against ours, and guess what?" Tendrey grinned like a jewel thief with the safe's combination in his pocket. "We found a hole. A passage big enough to run a freight train through. Or a submarine. They didn't see it because it is not a break in the reef. It's a tunnel."

"You are talking about slipping a three-hundred-foot, twenty-five-hundred-ton submarine through a keyhole."

"Not an impossible task. For the right captain."

Douglas glared, but in the back of his mind, he was already calculating. How many Japanese ships were in the massive lagoon. Fifty? A hundred? How many were freighters? Or tankers? Or possibly destroyers? Certainly, more than the number of torpedoes the *Mako* carried.

He imagined a line of enemy ships resting quietly at anchor with their captains believing they were untouchable. Just as the U.S. battleships had been at Pearl Harbor.

The old adage, *shooting fish in a barrel* could not have been more appropriate. Except, these fish shot back, and he'd be in the same barrel.

Tendrey lifted his voice. "I'll sweeten the deal. Your debts with the locals? They'll be covered. And my friend's notebook? That disappears."

"I'm not signing my men up for your suicide mission," he said and in three strides was out the door.

"Son-of-a-bitch," Tendrey said, slamming his fist into the desk.

"He has to do it if he believes you will report him," Wei said, his voice squeaked with concern. He turned to Mimi. "Don't wait. Go after him."

•   •   •

Douglas walked through the main room and into the hall entry. As he weaved through the guests—most of them swaying with a percentage of alcohol reaching their heads—they barely noticed him. He searched for Mills, but without luck. He saw Captain Tucker at the front door.

"Captain," he called out.

Tucker greeted him.

"Are you headed back to the base, sir?" Douglas asked.

"I thought you had come with that charming young woman?" he said as they walked from the house. The tropical rain had given way to a night sky shimmering with a band of diamonds from the horizon to the zenith.

"Turns out she had other plans for the rest of the night," he said with a shrug.

"I see," Tucker said. "Well, I can certainly give you a lift back, Commander." He patted Douglas on the back.

•   •   •

Mimi stood on her toes, trying to scan the room. She had seen Douglas turn the corner but lost him from there.

"Miss Ming," Mills appeared beside her. "Looking for Doug?"

"Did you see him?"

"I think he headed for the cars."

Mimi thanked him quickly as she hurried to the front door. At the threshold, the departing guests were amid their goodbyes, the men shaking hands, their wives hugging and kissing cheeks, and, to Mimi's frustration, blocking her path.

113

By the time she reached the bottom of the stairs, she caught the last glimpse of Douglas climbing into the back seat of an olive-green Chevrolet sedan. The military driver pulled briskly away from the house, leaving the elegant Chinese woman with tears swelling in the corners of her dark eyes.

13

HONOMU, HAWAII, 1986

A S THE CHAUFFEUR brought the massive car to a stop in front of the mansion's front stairs, Admiral Tendrey had his seatbelt off and the door open. With effort, he swung his legs out and tried to stand.

Luckily, Miss Swanson was waiting for them at the entry with Tendrey's wheelchair poised to swoop him up.

"Leave me alone," Tendrey shrieked as she rushed to him. "I don't need your help."

It was not true. One step away from the limousine and the elderly statesman's knees buckled. The chauffeur caught him with thick, powerful arms and lifted Tendrey into the chair.

The admiral's brow furled but before his barbed tongue could do any damage, Miss Swanson smiled brilliantly. "That was easy," she said, her voice as sweet as white hibiscus.

She exchanged a nod with the chauffeur, pivoted the wheelchair and pressed toward the ramp leading to the entryway.

With a few unintelligible words, Tendrey surrendered and dropped his hands into his lap. He was mad today. Mad at the world. On such days, his staff knew better than to linger near him too long. They each wanted to go about their business on the opposite side of the estate.

He was justified in his anger as he returned from an overnight physical at the Naval hospital. The doctors had not given him good news. Among his ailments of age, his sight was deteriorating at a rapid rate.

"Quacks!" Tendrey had roared. "Fucking quacks. You call yourselves experts? You're all a bunch of fucking quacks."

He had continued to yell anyone passing in the hall as the stoic nurse hurriedly rolled him out of the hospital and to his waiting car. He sunk into the backseat mumbling to himself while picking lint from the khaki uniform slacks.

"Admiral," his male secretary, John Marks, a handsome young man with a too-straight jaw, met them at the main hall. "Two messages while you were out, sir. Neither left a name. One left a number, and the other said he would call again."

"Take me to the study," he said to Marks as he dismissed Miss Swanson with a wave of his hand.

She hesitated to relinquish the wheelchair, knowing what the doctors had said. *The admiral would need her*, she thought. The scowl from Marks told her to move away. They had business.

"If you need me, Admiral," Miss Swanson said.

"I won't. Go lay on the sand like you do or whatever you do." He signaled Marks forward as if giving him a heading.

"I'll make sure your lunch is on time."

"You do that. Come on, John. Push already." They left Miss Swanson in the chair's wake.

Inside the study, Tendrey took over the chair as Marks closed the polished door and slipped the brass latch.

"Don't make me wait. It has been a goddamn awful morning," the admiral said as he wheeled himself to the desk.

"You know, sir, she'd kill me if she found out. She is like a mother hen with wolf's teeth," the secretary said as he moved to the high bookshelf, stood on the tips of his feet, and reached the very top shelf. Lifting a copy of *Kim* by Rudyard Kipling, he found the tiny skeleton key where he had left it. He crossed the room to the small antique chest on the far table.

"Screw Miss Swanson," the admiral said.

"I thought you were," Marks joked.

Tendrey laughed. He liked the spunk of the young man. Marks was not the brightest assistant he had ever had, but he was trustworthy. Having never served, his slips in protocol were expected. It grated on Tendrey at first, now he found it refreshing. The admiral did not realize how boring yes-men were until they were no longer serving him.

Marks cracked open the chest and retrieved a decanter of Hennessy V.S.O.P. "If you want ice, I'll have to go to the kitchen."

"Don't bother. The doctors were bastards today. All assholes. Dying. I am not fucking dying."

Marks set the cognac in front of him.

"Not one for yourself?" the admiral asked. This was the ritual. Marks would serve Tendrey his illicit drink and the old man would ask for Marks to join him. If this was an evening session, the secretary would do so happily. He might even share cigars on the lanai, watch the Milky Way rise and listen to his string of war stories. Marks liked the old guy and enjoyed their time. During the day, however, the secretary would decline his offer politely. And so it went today.

Tendrey scooped up the snifter between his fingers. "Those messages?"

The secretary pulled two scraps of paper from his pocket. "The first was at 0600 hours this morning. The caller left this number for you to reach him. I told him it wouldn't be until around noon. The second call came in right before you returned." He opened the paper. "He didn't leave a name or a number. Said he'd call back." Marks pushed the pieces across the desk.

Tendrey recognized the Washington area code. "Is this a three or an eight?"

"An eight, sir."

"Okay. That will be all for now, Marks. Be sure you put the key back. We wouldn't want Miss Swanson to find out you're forcing me to drink this sludge against my will."

The secretary laughed. "No, sir." He returned the bottle to the chest and hid the key. "Anything else?"

"No," Tendrey said as he reached for the phone and dialed. There were the usual clicks of computer links as the line was connected through. It rang.

"Red Coat bar, may I help you?" the woman's voice cheered through the receiver. In the background, he could hear the phony soundtrack of bar patrons laughing.

"Give me Powell," Tendrey said bluntly.

Karen turned to her boss, who was stretched out on the couch in the hotel room. His suit coat was folded over his eyes as he tried to nap. "JP. It's him," she said as she flipped a switch, silencing the canned noise.

The CIA man sat up quickly. "Good day, Admiral."

"Not so far. I hope to hell you are going to make it better."

JP took a deep breath. "Probably not. We lost Bovan at the Washington airport. He was scheduled for a commuter flight back to Boston. I gave him the benefit of the doubt and figured he'd be heading back to his mother's house. It was my mistake."

"And have you fixed this mistake?" the admiral's voice was dry.

"We picked him up on a stopover in LA. West Coast has a man with him."

"LA? You mean Los Angeles?"

"Yes, sir," JP swallowed. "A connection flight to Honolulu."

"Jesus. Fucking. Christ."

"I am sorry, sir. This is completely on me. I've been in touch with the Honolulu sector, and I'm booked on the next non-stop out."

Silence from Tendrey's end.

Sweat began to form in the swell of JP's back.

Unexpectedly, the admiral's tone went calm. "That won't be necessary, Agent Powell," Tendrey said. "I'll have someone take care of it from here. What's his arrival time?"

"Three-forty-five this afternoon," JP said. "That's not all, Admiral."

"Of course, there is more."

"During our initial surveillance, he was contacted by a Naval yeoman from Admiral Thomas Mills' office and given a package. We did not have the ability to assess what it was, but we've learned this Mills is a long-time friend of Bovan and his family."

There was silence for a time. Tendrey finally spoke. "Thank you for your time, Mr. Powell. That will be all, then."

"Sir, if I could…"

"There is nothing more to do except close it down. I asked for a favor from your director, you delivered the best you could. I did not have enough intel to get you up and running or prepare you. Just make sure LA closes their surveillance as well. I'll take it from here."

JP sat with the dead phone in his hand and a moon-sized crater in his stomach. He had failed, failed miserably, and he knew it.

• • •

Tendrey glanced at the brass ship's clock that hung in his study. *Three hours*, he thought. It had been three goddamn hours. He lifted his glass and took a long drink.

He knew who had phoned earlier and not left a name. The man would never leave his name or a number. Tendrey wondered if he would still be in his office. It was 1745 in D.C. He called the private line. On the third ring, it was answered.

"You called?" Tendrey said.

"Your assistant said you were at the doctors."

"He talks too much."

"Everything in order, Joe?" the man asked.

"They don't know their heads from their rectums. Why did you call?"

"To let you know I took care of your concerns."

"Oh, did you?" Tendrey said bitterly. "You mean about the young commander. You mean you took care of it by showing him his father's files?"

"Christ, you have me under surveillance, Joe?"

"Hell no. I've had Bovan under since his mother's funeral. And damn lucky I did. The old instincts still work," he said. Those doctors were fools. He was still as sharp as ever. "I knew he wouldn't leave the past alone. The son-of-a-bitch is as stubborn as his father," Tendrey said, remembering.

"What do you mean?"

"I mean he is on his way to fucking Honolulu."

"Shit." There was shock in the voice from Washington.

"Exactly. Come on out, Tom, we're having a fucking beach party."

"He's headed to Truk," the voice said in exasperation.

"Because you showed him his father's files."

There was a pause on the other end of the line. "I thought it would settle everything," Mills said. "Let him bury the past."

119

"Instead, you've set a match. Now, we need to stomp out the fuse."

Mills hesitated. "Brian told me there was a woman at his mother's funeral. The one who gave him the logbook."

"It's the woman."

"What woman?"

"The ambassador's assistant."

"Lai Ming? She's dead, Joe."

Tendrey squeezed the phone receiver until his gaunt fingers went whiter than normal. "Get out here. Get on a fucking plane and get out here," Tendrey told him.

"To do what?"

"Stop him. Stop that son-of-bitch," the old man hissed. "Or your young commander is going to end up like his father."

14

HONOLULU, HAWAII, 1986

THE PLANE BANKED GENTLY to the left, dipping a wing over the blue frosting of the Pacific, and eased its belly toward runway 8R26L of Honolulu International Airport.

Brian was still asleep when the 747's eighteen tires made landfall. It was the hellish rush of the jet's engines diverting their thrust sideways to slow the massive machine that brought him back from the abyss of slumber.

He found himself sweating, his forehead wet, his hands cold and shaking. Within his restless sleep, he was entombed in a small steel room, an aft cabin of a sinking ship, its hatchway blocked by twisted metal and a fast, rising sea.

As the water pushed in, he scrambled to the highest corner of the cabin. The doomed ship rolled to starboard, slipping from the surface. The pressure grew against his chest.

There was screaming of tearing metal, the hiss of escaping air, and the stabbing chill of the arctic sea enveloping him. The cold so painful it felt more like fire than water. Brian pressed his face into a crack in the steel bulkhead and struggled for a last breath.

"Mr. Bovan?" Toni appeared with his coat folded neatly over her arm. "We'll be at the gate in a moment. I hope you enjoyed your flight and will fly with us again."

Brian shook his nightmare away. He thanked her, took his coat and tried to find his smile. His mind was clouded with images, his nerves tense from the dream. Letting his head drop back against the seat, Brian took several slow breaths.

After twenty-five hundred miles, the 747 pilot positioned the nose wheels of his monstrous machine in precisely the same spot on the tarmac he had placed them the day before. Tomorrow a co-worker with similar skills would take his over his seat and do the same, day after day, week after week.

It was a conveyor belt of vacationers and honeymooners, a nearly endless stream of humanity slowly filling paradise. Had outbound flights ever ceased, the island would quickly become a Calhoun experiment, the rats nibbling on more than pineapples.

At the back of the plane, Cranken sat with his fake leather carry-on in his lap, staring at the seatbelt sign above him. Once it switched off, he had only a few seconds to rush to the exit before his fellow passengers rose in mass and blocked the aisles.

He needed to be out, or at least within sight of the first-class cabin before his target stepped from the plane. Otherwise, there was a good possibility he would lose Bovan in the mixing crowd of the airport.

The CIA man felt the sway of the plane as it continued toward the gate. He glanced down the row of seats, considered who might stand up quickly and who would linger. He sensed his fellow travelers were becoming restless. Mainlanders who had whittled down their lifesavings to spend a few days in Eden.

Cranken, himself, had never visited Hawaii. He had once tallied up the countries he had visited. Ninety-seven. Only two were for vacation. His ex-wife had insisted on visiting Mexico City and Canada. The rest were strictly business. He could not remember if he had ever purchased a postcard.

The wobble of the plane stopped as the pilot maneuvered to the gate. Cranken was on his feet the instant the seatbelt light flickered. His timing was perfect as long strides carried him to the middle of the fuselage before the horde rushed into the aisle.

Over bobbing heads and shifting bodies, he watched the first-class cabin empty into the passageway out of the plane. His target spoke briefly to the perky blond who had escorted him out of her precious domain with the grit of a nightclub bouncer. They were exchanging niceties without sexual overtones.

Cranken was trained to see such things from one's body language, word choice, and facial expressions. He saw none. His target was not there for a rendezvous.

By the time Bovan stepped from the footbridge between the 747 and Honolulu International, Cranken was only a family of four behind him. As the passengers poured from the gate and into the arrival hall of the multi-level airport, the CIA man slowed his pace.

He stayed twenty feet behind Bovan and to his right. Cranken had discovered a person will usually glance left if he thought he was being followed. Unless he was a Britt or an Aussie or someone from Hong Kong. They always turned to their right first. A habit gained from crossing the street as kids, he guessed.

•   •   •

Stepping from the air-conditioned building into the thick humidity of the tropics was like slipping on a woolen poncho. Brian pushed his coat through the strap of his shoulder bag and hoisted it higher on his shoulder.

He followed the unbroken line of cars and taxis as they inched their way along the arching curbside. Passengers climbed in and climbed out. Arriving and departing. A never-ending flow of an artery pumping blood cells to keep the body alive.

Brian reached the blinking yellow crosswalk signal that offered safe transit across the busy street. As the cars slowed to the line, he dashed along the phalanx of chrome bumpers and into the empty stairway of the parking structure.

The white Camaro coupe was where Mimi had promised, parked in the furthest corner of the second floor. He dug the keys from his pocket, swung open the passenger door and tossed his coat and briefcase onto the bucket seat. He carried his flight bag to the rear of the car, wiggled the key into the trunk lock and moved to open it.

Something stopped him. Something he did not hear or see, but simply told him to turn.

The man from the plane who had mistakenly entered the first-class cabin stood in the stairway staring at Brian with his mouth agape. Their eyes met for a fraction of a second before he pivoted and headed to a red sedan a few spaces away. Brian watched him, hoping he would produce a set of keys and drive off.

Instead, he made theater of searching his pockets, grunting loudly in frustration, and muttering to himself as he returned to the stairs and disappeared.

Had he forgotten his keys? Lost them on the plane or in the airport? The possibilities raced through Brian's head. No, there was no honest disgust in his face. No anger at the mistake. All that was there was the shock at being caught.

Brian yanked the key from the trunk. He snapped open the driver's door, threw his flight bag over the seat and climbed in. The eight-cylinder started with the first turn of the key.

• • •

Cranken did not panic. He never panicked, but he was certainly surprised. He should have expected the possibility of the target being helped as soon as he entered the parking structure. The guy had a car.

As he dropped two steps at a time to the ground level, the CIA man heard the blast of the Camaro's engine and the squeal of its tires.

DML 301. DML 301. Cranken kept repeating the license plate of the late model white Chevrolet sports car. When he reached the street, the agent walked as quickly as he dared to the line of taxi cabs.

Cranken snagged the second taxi as the first cab was taking in a giggling pair of retirees to their hotel. He leaned over the seat back, a twenty-dollar bill dangled from his fingers. "A white Camaro coming out of the structure. The guy's screwing my wife. I want to catch him."

The Hawaiian taxi driver with the fishbowl head and lollipop on his lip, frowned. "I'm wasting no tires for a measly dub." He stared at Cranken through the oval slit of the rearview mirror.

"Forty."

"For a fifty, I catch you a marlin."

"Just the Camaro," Cranken stated, and as the driver eased gently away from the curb, he was sorry for his choice.

Cranken might have forgone the taxi all together had he known his dash across the street had brought him into focus of two sets of expressionless eyes.

One man sat behind the wheel of a Cadillac sedan watching the traffic over the dashboard, while the other, wearing a straw fedora atop his thick black hair, stood in the jaws of the passenger door. They were watching the arrivals, although not knowing exactly who they were watching for. But when the oddly dressed man ran from the parking structure to the line of taxis, and clambered into one he had just strolled past, they knew.

The driver twisted the ignition key as the standing man with the fedora slid in beside him. As he was about to close the door, a third man rushed to the car.

Like the other two, he was thick and foreboding. "Here." He pushed a piece of paper into Fedora's hand. "It's the plate number. I'll call Marks and tell him you tak'n care of the tail." He stepped back and slapped the top of the Caddy.

The taxi was still in sight and the driver was going to keep it that way. He gunned away from the curb without regard for the oncoming traffic.

•   •   •

It was insane. All of it, Brian thought as he steered the Camaro out of the airport and onto the highway. At the last minute, he cut two lanes and exited onto Ala Moana Boulevard. The side road likely headed to Waikiki Beach and would make following him more difficult.

Following him. Jesus. Someone was actually following him. Or, he realized, they were there to stop him?

He checked the rearview mirror several times. There were dozens of cars behind him, half of them taxicabs.

Brian turned off the main street and aimed for a smaller avenue. He watched his mirror. Made two more turns and found another boulevard and continued toward Waikiki.

The number of cars behind him had dropped considerably. A slow pickup truck, its bed filled with boxes of fresh pineapples, was in the right lane just about to pass the King Street intersection.

Brian stomped the accelerator, and the Camaro jumped forward. As he blew past the truck, he cut the wheel hard to the right. The car swerved across the lanes, slipped the pickup's front bumper by inches.

Brian misjudged the intersection. His rear tire kissed the low curb, sending the Camaro sideways. A snap of the steering wheel and a stab at the gas pedal brought the Camaro in line down and away.

•   •   •

"Son-of-a-bitch," Cranken hollered as he watched Bovan's escape.

"Brah, your wife's boyfriend, he's crazy," the taxicab driver said as he swerved to avoid the skidding pickup truck and its shifting cargo.

"Go back, you're going to lose him," Cranken said, catching a glimpse of Brian's car out the rear window.

"I can't turn around for another quarter mile," the driver said, shaking his head.

"I'll give you another fifty," Cranken said.

"Not worth the ticket. I'm already rolling on a suspended license."

"Goddamnit!" The CIA man slapped the headrest. "Find me a phone. Somewhere. Anywhere." He had no choice now. He had to call the local sector and explain who he was and what had happened. With connections to the local police, they would find Bovan in minutes.

The taxi pulled into the first gas station. The pay phone was against the outside wall of the garage. Cranken found it, dropped a quarter into the slot and dialed the agency's Honolulu number. He waited for the connection.

"Take off," the man in the Hawaiian print shirt said as he leaned into the cab's window.

The cab driver pulled the lollipop from his cheek. "My fare is on the phone."

"Pau," the Hawaiian said, telling the driver he was finished. He tossed a hundred-dollar bill onto the seat.

The driver scooped it up and flashed him the locals' shaka, their thumb-n-pinky two-finger wave. "Aloha," he said as he drove away.

Cranken leaned deep into the small phone booth, trying to find as much shade as possible. The late afternoon sun was burning into the back of his pasty white neck. His verification from Los Angeles was taking minutes rather than seconds. The relaxed pace of the islands had clearly reached into its CIA station. Cranken impatiently switched the receiver from his right hand to his left.

"Excuse me," said the voice behind him.

Cranken had heard that voice a dozen times. A voice that always came from behind, from a dark stone alley in Nice, a hallway in Moscow, a crowded train in Tokyo. It was the same tone from the same type of man. A deadly man, and he was behind Cranken again. The CIA man instinctively reached for the slim dagger sheathed secretly inside his belt.

Cranken had not mistaken the voice. It was that of a killer, a professional.

The Cadillac pulled out onto the highway, leaving the CIA man's bloody body slumped in the phone booth, its receiver dangling over him.

•   •   •

Brian sat on a stacked low wall made from thousands of black volcanic stones, each bowling ball sized. Below him, the blue waters of Hanauma Bay sparkled as a handful of snorkel divers explored the bay's underwater gardens. They were the last, the stragglers trying to stretch their vacation by refusing to yield to the setting sun. The others who had swarmed the pristine beach and crystalline waters had returned to their hotels, giving up Hawaii's sea life for its nightlife.

It was now past seven o'clock. For over two hours, Brian had driven around Honolulu, out to Kailua and inland to Wahiawa. He kept backtracking, turning around, looping about. It was easy not to reveal a destination because he did not have one. Finally, he found the Hanauma parking lot.

He was confident no one had followed him this far but knew they would find him again. Whoever they were.

Brian was thinking, desperately trying to analyze the facts and align them with the possibilities. It was a mental test, like so many he had performed as an executive officer on the *John Adams*. Each was designed to test and refine the abilities of a submarine commander to function under stress. The stress that would accompany the potential fact that his boat could be the country's first, or possibly last, military force available.

The commander had to know his details. For a missile launch, he had to know the surface conditions, weather patterns, his ship's depth, speed, and angle. For a torpedo attack, the type of vessel that was in his scope, its speed, and course. Computers took most of the mental work away, but computers were not dependable. So, he had to know.

And then, there was always the unexpected factor. The one thing that always held success at a distance. Was the membrane of the launch tube intact? Is there an enemy submarine in your wake? *These are the things you can't know until the smoke clears*, Fife had told him over and over.

Now, the smoke still stood thick in Brian's mind. He had to assume they knew where he was headed. The question was whether they were simply following him or trying to stop him. Was there really something to find on a forty-year-old battlefield? He remembered what Mills had said about uncut diamonds and national treasures.

They could have their diamonds and fossils. Treasure was not his reason for racing half-way around the world. If the *Mako* was in that lagoon, he was going to find it and clear his father's name.

The wind came up off the bay. The salt smell, that aroma of the plankton and brine, was calming. Near shore, the water darkened as the sun dipped its eye below the hill. Two bronze-skinned teenagers, with beach towels around their necks and masks and fins in their hands, walked up the steep trail from the beach to the parking lot. They gave Brian a side glance as they moved to their rented Jeep.

For the first time, he remembered he was still wearing the same wrinkled clothes he wore boarding the plane from D.C. He rubbed his chin and felt the oncoming beard. He was a man in a trench coat in the middle of a desert.

Brian returned to the Camaro. Popping the trunk, he found what the woman had promised.

There was a set of burgundy suitcases and a matching carry-on. The two cases were full of clothes for various occasions. Mimi had thought of everything, from bathing suits to dress slacks and collared Hawaiian shirts. The small carry-on was empty, suggesting Brian get rid of his flight bag and put its contents into the new one.

As he stuffed his clothes into the new carry-on, he found another envelope with his name. Inside was another note and an airline ticket. *This is getting ridiculous,* he thought.

Dear Commander Bovan,

Is Honolulu not beautiful? I would love to be there and show you all the places your father and I once visited. Of course, I cannot.

The ticket is for your flight to Truk Lagoon. Notice the name is not yours. Brian Bovan is scheduled for the flight the following day. This may or may not buy you 24 hours.

I must stress again it is important to remain anonymous.

Mimi

The letter was simple and to the point. *Here are the means. The way is for you to find.* The first order, he realized, was to get rid of the car and find somewhere to shower, shave and change.

From the suitcase, he pulled out a pair of light brown cotton pants, a white shirt, socks, and a pair of casual shoes. They were deck shoes, the kind wealthy sailors bought for walking around their eternally anchored yachts.

Once he had the new clothes in the old flight bag, Brian returned the suitcases and shoulder bag to the trunk. He slipped several hundred dollars of the cash Mimi had given him into his pocket. Behind the wheel, he headed slowly back to Honolulu.

As the road dove from Diamond Head to the city, it was as if the island and sky had switched places. The lights from the metropolis shined like a million stars framed by the blackness of the ocean.

Along Kalakaua Boulevard, a thick line of high-rise hotels, shopping malls and overpriced seafood restaurants shouldered Waikiki Beach. Amid the concrete sprawl, Brian found what he needed.

He pulled into the self-parking structure of the Outrigger Hotel, maneuvered two floors below ground level and wedged the car between a Ford Taurus and Chevrolet Caprice. If the man who had followed him to the islands was still searching for the Camaro, it would take him days to find it here.

Shouldering his old bag, Brian entered the main lobby of the elegant hotel. Hidden speakers played classical Hawaiian music as beach-clad vacationers were returning from their day on the sand. Everywhere across the island, from people to the tides, it was all in a constant flux.

Brian sauntered to the front desk, his story already in mind.

"Good evening, sir," the balding Hawaiian acknowledged him.

"Do you have a room for two nights?" Brian asked meekly.

"You don't have reservations?" the clerk pressed, as if he had never heard of such a thing. A vacant hotel room in Waikiki? "It may be hard to accommodate you, sir. We're fairly booked."

"Damn. I am here on business and need to stay an extra couple of days."

The clerk scrolled through his computer.

"Really, anything will do," Brian said. "I am always jumping around hotels. You know how the import-export business can be. I usually cover our Europe markets."

The clerk forced a smile as if interested.

"The Pacific region is actually a promotion for me."

"Congratulations," the Hawaiian said without lifting his eyes.

"Thanks. From Sydney to Beijing. It is going to keep me busy," Brian leaned one arm across the counter. "I'll have to look for a long-term hotel suite. Better than renting an apartment. More expensive, but hey, that's a problem for the guys upstairs, right?"

"You'll be coming to Honolulu often, Mr.?"

Anonymous, Mimi had told him. Brian smiled. "Andish. Chuck Andish. If it is as busy as Paris, I'll be here four or five times a month."

"We offer a few select suites at corporate rates, Mr. Andish, if there is a continuing need."

"You do? Excellent."

Turning back to the computer screen, the clerk, now in a more inviting mood, told Brian a corporate suite would be available tomorrow. For the first night, however, a small room overlooking the street was the only thing available.

"I am sure it will be fine," Brian assured him. He noted the name tag. "Daniel. You've more than helpful," he said. He paid for the hotel room in cash and slid an extra fifty-dollar bill to the clerk.

"Room 535, Mr. Andish," he said. He glanced over the counter for Brian's luggage. "Do you need a porter?"

"Unfortunately, that won't be necessary. United lost my bags," Brian said as he swept up the key.

The room was as he expected. Twin double-beds with hibiscus comforters pressed against one wall. A television, a coffeemaker, and a carafe for water. No bathtub, just a shower that forced him to keep his elbows low as he let the cold spray run over his head and down his back.

He stood there, stretching his neck muscles. A long shower was a luxury aboard a submarine, even aboard a nuclear-powered sub with their banks of distillation equipment. It was not the lack of fresh water, but the lack of time that kept such indulgences to a minimum.

Brian took the time to think. Something here was not right. A detail was missing. An unexpected factor, he couldn't see it. A sub in his baffles.

It all banked on what the Chinese woman had told him and how much of it was true. The *Mako*'s mission to Truk might have been secret, but to make it work, others along the Navy's chain of command had to know. The question was how many links up the chain did it go?

Brian dried himself with the large terry cloth towel. Another luxury lost aboard ship.

Getting to distant islands was suddenly the easiest part of his problem. He had read about the famous Gibraltar of the Pacific. A hundred and forty miles of coral reefs surrounded the natural harbor. A battlefield port, the Japanese could not have designed it better. What they had not planned enough for was America's aerial attack. It turned the deep-water lagoon into a graveyard filled with naval freighters similar to the one in the photograph alongside his father's submarine.

That was his edge. The sketch he had taken from the photograph showing the freighter and adjacent shoreline. It would be a starting point, not the best, but at least he was not heading to Truk blind.

Brian slipped on his watch. 9:30 p.m. It was time to find someplace else to stay the night.

As he dressed in his gifted clothes, he was not surprised by how well they fit. He hung his suit in the closet and set his flight bag on the floor. He pulled the bedcovers back and twisted the sheets until they looked properly slept in.

He lifted the phone from the small table between the beds. "Good evening. Is Daniel still at the front desk?" Brian asked.

"I am sorry, sir. Perhaps someone else can help you?" the desk operator asked.

"That is okay. May I order breakfast for tomorrow?" he said.

"I'll connect you with room service, sir."

From room service, Brian ordered a large breakfast of bacon, eggs and toast, coffee, and orange juice. "At 9:30 a.m. Room 535." He hung up, thinking it was too bad it would go to waste.

Exiting the elevator, Brian veered away from the front desk. Daniel was not there to see him leave, nor would anyone else notice. He was just another guest leaving the hotel for a few hours.

Brian entered the parking structure through the side stairs he had noted earlier. The Taurus and Caprice were still shouldering the Camaro.

Pulling the luggage from the trunk, he tossed the car keys inside and closed the lid. He dropped down the stairs to the street. In front of the hotel next door, he found a lingering cab.

"Airport?" Brian spoke through the passenger window.

"Yeah, brah, no problem," the young driver said as he waved Brian into the back seat. "What airline you go?"

"TWA," he said.

"Easy drop." He tapped the mileage counter and pulled into the headlights of Kalakaua Boulevard's traffic.

"Could you find me a pay phone?" Brian asked as he leaned between the front seats. "I forgot to make a call."

"No worries for me. Clock's ticking." He found a bank of phones along the sidewalk.

It took calls to four hotels before he found a vacancy. Every other clerk said the same thing. Height of the tourist season.

"Change of plans. Drop me at the Hilton," Brian instructed as he returned to the car.

"No sweat off my cheeks," the driver said. "Happy service."

The porter at the huge, monolithic hotel was a young native girl with triangular tattoos on her biceps. She muscled Brian's bags effortlessly to the front desk.

She offered a pleasant smile as she passed him to the evening clerk, another young woman, a girl with shaggy blond hair and skin the color of mocha. "Reservations, Mr. huh?" she asked.

"Janson. And no, no reservations. I just phoned. They said you had a cancellation."

Her fingers skated over a computer keyboard. "Got it. I am sorry it is not an ocean view." Her apology was sincere.

"That's fine. I'll take it for two days," Brian said. As he signed the registration, he mistakenly printed his real name. He scratched it out, signed the made-up name, and paid for two nights with cash.

"Enjoy your stay at the Hilton Hawaiian Village, Mr. Janson."

"Thank you," Brian said as he picked up his shoulder bag and followed the porter and his suitcases to the elevators.

The room was probably one of the smallest in the hotel, but it was massive by submarine standards. The bed was firm, as he preferred. He always slept better on a hard bunk.

Room service was at his door in twenty minutes. A tropical salad, seared Ahi with blistered tomatoes, garlic, and lemon butter sauce. A dry martini on the menu tempted him but he decided on a half-bottle of Chardonnay from California.

The next morning, he would barely remember his meal as the sleepless hours between Washington and Honolulu finally caught up to him as he fell into bed.

15

PEARL HARBOR, HAWAII, 1944

ALTHOUGH THE RAIN had stopped, the gray clouds over Honolulu remained. Backlit by a full moon, they cast the harbor in charcoal shades of onyx, wrought iron and whale gray. The bay itself was a black slate of stone with hardly a ripple to crack its surface.

Douglas had covered a half a mile to the submarine docks from where Captain Yates had dropped him. The walk gave him time to think. Time to assess. He thought about national treasures. The Japs. Five million in diamonds. Truk. The Liberty Bell. And about Mimi.

Her face kept coming to him with tears perched on the edges of those beautiful eyes. He crossed the unsteady gangplank to the *Mako*'s deck and climbed the steel rungs of the conning tower.

"Good evening, Captain," the youthful voice called from the Cigarette Deck.

Douglas tossed a nod to the silhouette of a crewman. He could see the man raise a salute. "Anything to report tonight, Mr. ...?" he asked, trying to remember his name.

"Hawthorne, sir. Machinist's mate, 2nd class," he said, his voice so crisp Douglas knew it was heard across the harbor.

"That's right, Mr. Hawthorne. You transferred over from a tender," Douglas remembered.

"Yes sir. From the *Sperry*. After resupplying subs for six months, I was feeling left out of war, sir. So, I put in for the transfer."

Douglas laughed. "Good to hear. Most guys sign on for the extra pay."

"No sir, I'm here to sink some Jap ship," he said.

"That's the job," Douglas said. "First thing to know, Mr. Hawthorne, you don't need to salute aboard a sub."

"Sir?"

"There's never enough room."

"Oh right. Sorry, sir."

Douglas patted Hawthorne on the shoulder. "Welcome aboard the *Mako*, Mr. Hawthorne. I'll do my best to help you sink those Japs." Grabbing the hatch rail, Douglas lowered himself into the circular hatchway.

Even before his eyes adjusted from the outside darkness to the bright lights in the submarine, Douglas slipped easily through the narrow interior of the tower. The *Mako* had been home for two and a half years. He knew every inch of the undersea vessel.

Down the next ladder to the control room, he shouldered his way through a half dozen hatchways to the forward engine room.

"I want to hear good news," Douglas said into the narrow cavern before he saw anyone. A huge Fairbanks Morse diesel engine, gunmetal gray and oily, shared the space with a mist of burning oil and fumes.

"Up late tonight, huh, Skipper?" Clancy said, without looking from his work. He was crammed between the bulkhead and the motor working a comically large wrench. He swept his face with a stained rag.

The Scotsman hated the Navy, or so he said every time he reenlisted. But the food was better than his wife's, as was the company.

"You too?" Douglas asked. He could feel the heat of the still engine. "Find the problem?"

"Not yet. I re-plumbed the water jackets with larger intakes, but she is still heating like a teakettle," he said, eyeing the mass of iron and rubber, steel, and wire.

"Water ports all clear?" Douglas asked.

"Flushed those first off," the mechanic said with a wry glance. Of course, Clancy checked the intake ports first. It was clear the Scot didn't think the engine room was the place for the captain.

"Well, Clanc, she's your baby. I'll leave you to get her running," Douglas said.

"Thanks, Skipper," Clancy said, dropped the heavy wrench into the tool chest at his feet. The clatter echoed through the submarine.

Douglas changed from his dress uniform into his browns. He left his captain's hat in the center of his bunk and headed for the galley. He passed through the crew quarters, noting only a few bunks were occupied with sleeping men.

For the most part, the *Mako* was deserted. While the Pacific subs were in Pearl for resupply or repairs, it was the services' practice to allow their crews to take their leave at the Pink Palace, the lavish Royal Hawaiian Hotel that dominated the western stretch of Waikiki Beach.

Tomorrow they would return and if Clancy was satisfied with his repairs to the big diesel, they would run the boat out of Pearl for an afternoon of shakedown dives.

Pouring himself a cup of coffee, Douglas settled behind one of the small dining tables and thought about the night. If Tendrey reported the gambling, Douglas' career was over and if the men at the ranch knew he had turned down the money for his debts, they might carry out their threats.

An admiral, a flyboy or a man on the street, it didn't matter. When you owe them money, they said, you pay it back or forfeit a part of your body.

"Skipper?" Hawthorne's head appeared in the galley doorway. "There's someone on the dock wanting to speak to you, sir. He wouldn't give his name and he's in civilian clothes," the machinist's mate said. "He asked to come aboard."

"You did right," Douglas said as he laid the coffee cup in the sink. "I'll be right up."

Returning to his quarters, Douglas withdrew his issued Colt .45 automatic from the small, waterproof safe built into the bulkhead. He slipped the gun into the back of his pants and headed toward the conning tower hatch.

"He's alone, sir," Hawthorne whispered as Douglas emerged.

"All right. Watch your post." Douglas slid down the stern ladder and crossed the gangplank to the dock.

"Commander Bovan," the man said as he approached. He was stocky, thick in the shoulders and neck, thick in the chin with a broad nose. His fedora sat so far back on his head; it should not have held. His overcoat was still wet from the rain that had passed an hour before.

"That's right," Douglas answered without meeting the outstretched hand. "Kind of late for a visit."

"Not if you are just getting back from a party," he said in a monotone voice. He flipped his wallet open. "Wagner. Office of Special Services."

"What can I help you with?"

Wagner shifted his hip, scrutinized the crewman on the conning tower above them. "Let's walk, Commander." He did not wait for a response as he started down the dock.

Douglas followed.

"I'll not bore you with what I know, Captain. I want to go home and go to bed, and I am sure you'd rather be doing whatever you do. But my boss is screaming at me to find out about a black-market operation he's heard about."

"You should head over to the mess hall, Mr. Wagner. I am sure you'll uncover enough illicit deals to keep him happy."

"I'm not talking the usual samurai swords and bootlegged liquor, Captain. This crawls up a bit higher. Into the command level of CINCPAC."

"Someone in my command? And you expect me to know?"

Wagner stopped at the end of the dock. He tapped a Camel cigarette from a pack. He offered one to Douglas, who waved it off. "We don't have a clear picture. We know there's a lot of money involved and the need for a submarine."

"There are a lot of subs in Pearl."

Wagner gripped the cigarette in his teeth and struck a match. "Yeah, but not all of their captains are in debt with the local dregs," the OSS officer said. "We know about your off-base excursions." He paused. "Not a good position to be in."

"Are you here to arrest me?"

"Hell no," Wagner laughed. "It's more fun to squeeze your balls."

"What do you want, Wagner?"

"There's a certain admiral who's under our surveillance," he said between pulls at the cigarette. "A slimy guy we can never corner."

"You expect me to blow the whistle on a fellow serviceman?"

"I expect your alliance lies with the United States Government, Captain. That's where mine lie," Wagner said, his voice chilled.

"You got a name?"

"Rear Admiral Joseph Tendrey, and if I'm not mistaken, you've already spoken with him."

Douglas tried not to react.

Wagner grinned. "Then he told you?"

Douglas held his response.

"I want him, Bovan. I don't care if he's an admiral. He's crooked. He's got friends in places you and I don't even know about, and he uses them for his own gains. Not for the country. Not for the war effort. For himself."

"Friends in the OSS?" the sub captain asked.

"If he does, it doesn't matter me," Wagner said. "My CO wants to see him dragged in front of a court martial board."

Douglas stepped closer. "How about that cigarette?"

"Sure." Wagner offered a struck match.

Douglas leaned into the flame, sucked the stick until it glowed. "He's working with the Chinese," he said in a hushed voice.

"Details?"

"They're trying to work the Japanese black market to get some sort of national treasure."

"Why go to you?"

"They need a sub," Douglas pointed over his shoulder.

"And you told them no?"

"Damn right I did." Douglas pinched a loose piece of tobacco from his lip. "But he threatened me the same as you."

"Gambling debts are easy to exploit."

"I get it."

"He didn't tell you anything?"

"I didn't say that."

Wagner waited. "Well?"

"Like you said, gambling debts are easy to exploit."

The OSS man nodded. "I'm not sure I can make those disappear."

"Just keep them out of my file."

"That I can do."

Douglas took a long draw of the bitter smoke and told Wagner all they had discussed in the library. He told of uncut diamonds, the ambassador's assertion that bones were worth risking Douglas' crew, the plan about booby traps and radio calls. The suggestion if it was not his submarine, it would be someone else's. The significance of Truk Lagoon and its dangers. What he did not mention was Mimi and her part in the scheme.

"Jesus Christ," Wagner said when Douglas finished.

"They're paying him," Douglas said flatly.

"Of course, they are," Wagner agreed.

The angry clouds had finally parted, and the two men stood huddling under a starlit night. A light sea breeze carried their smoke-filled breaths away from them.

"We'll need proof. Otherwise, it's just a captain's word against a rear admiral who happen to hate each other."

"Arrest the ambassador. He'll confirm it."

"He's a diplomat of one of our allies," Wagner said. "No one else in the room," the officer pressed.

"No," Douglas lied.

"Really? Not a woman perhaps? A Chinese woman?"

Douglas stared into Wagner's hard face.

"Save your breath, Captain. She's got immunity as well."

"She's not a part of this," Douglas stressed.

"Like hell. Up to her cute ass in it," Wagner said. "You might have already blown the whole thing by walking out. But I tell you what, I'll keep your record clean and your China Doll out of my report."

"And keep her safe. You watch over her until I get back."

Wagner mulled over what he was asking. "As long as you convince that bastard that you're in."

Douglas felt the intensity of Wagner's voice and, suddenly, knew its source. "The bad torpedo. It's not your CO who wants Tendrey."

Wagner's shoulders fell. "My kid was aboard the Sargo off Borneo. They went after a freighter. Sent off a spread of four Mark 14 torpedoes. Three misfired and one circled back and detonated just under the sub's stern. She survived, but three crewmen died in the ensuing fire. My son was one of them." The OSS man spit into the bay. "Their own torpedo," he hissed.

Douglas searched for something to say, the words of comfort captains were expected to know. Praise the dead, console the living. "I'll tell her I had a change of heart. I'll get you your proof."

"Be careful, Captain. If they doubt you, you become a threat."

The statement took Douglas by surprise.

"Five million in uncut diamonds? Not the scuttlebutt you'd want getting around," the OSS officer said and then, as he turned away. "I'll be in touch."

Douglas watched his silhouette disappear into the thick shadows of the pier-side warehouse.

•   •   •

Wagner pulled his black Ford sedan into the empty dirt lot, turned off the engine, slouched down in the seat, and waited. Through the front windshield, he watched the small street on the far side of the lot. At three o'clock in the morning, it was void of life.

He tilted the rearview mirror so he could see anyone approach the car from behind. For thirty minutes, there was no one. It was as though the short length of the avenue was quarantined by military order.

Another ten minutes passed when he finally opened the driver's door and stepped out. He closed it quietly, across the dirt lot to the row of silent shops. He headed for the last one.

The double glass doors were set back a few feet from the sidewalk. The space used for small tables set out daily and filled with decorative seashells and dried sponges.

Wagner used a single key to unlock the doors. He slipped silently into the store. The room immediately exploded with an ear-piercing screech. "Shut up, Macbeth," the OSS officer snapped as he spun around and closed the doors.

The screeching subsided to a string of whistles and chirps. With the help of its powerful beak, the blue Hyacinth macaw scaled the steel rods to reach his wooden perch. As Wagner passed, he slapped the cage, causing the noisy bird to slip back to the bottom.

"I wish you wouldn't do that, Duare," said the slender man standing in the doorway at the rear of the shop. He held an M3 submachine gun under his left arm.

"I hate that damn bird." He pushed past the man and entered the narrow hallway behind him.

"He's better than a watchdog."

"I'm feeding him red peppers next time. That'll shut him up."

"Gosline is waiting for you in the decoding room," the guard said, ignoring the officer's comment.

A few minutes later, field agent Duare, or Wagner, as he had told Douglas, was standing in the middle of the windowless room that contained nothing but a steel desk and two chairs. The room's only other feature was a second door Duare remembered leading to a side alley and allowed the OSS officers to slip out unseen.

Colonel Jim Gosline, the head of the Honolulu branch, leaned over the desk, skimming the sub captain's files. "These fossils are a big deal to the Chinese," he said as he closed the file jacket.

"That's what Bovan said."

"What do you think, Major?" Gosline asked Duare.

"In all honesty, sir, if Tendrey passes something tangible to the commander, some sort of hard evidence we can use against him, that's when we'll have him, sir," Duare said with a cocked smile.

Gosline rose from his desk and paced the room with his hands behind his back. The thin physique of the colonel reminded Duare of the Oklahoma farmers he had worked beside during the dust bowl days. He could see the farmer was worried.

"The Peking Man," Gosline mumbled. "That's a prize Washington would be happy to have on hand. It'd look good returning them to the Chinese at the end of the war," the colonel said. "We lost them, you know."

"Yes, sir," Duare said.

"He didn't tell you how they were going to do it?" the farmer asked.

"He didn't have details, sir. I don't think the captain believes it can be done."

Gosline grunted. "Maybe. What do you think? Is he the right man to try?"

Duare measured his commanding officer, his brow raising. "I couldn't say, sir. I've read his file. There's nothing that says he wouldn't carry out a direct order. The Navy considers him one of their best sub captains. He's smart, seasoned, and confident."

The colonel stared at the vacant walls of the small room. His mouth twitched as he chewed his decision. "Contact him again. Inform Captain Bovan he is now under secret orders issued by the OSS field office of Honolulu to carry out this mission of Admiral Tendrey's. The opportunity to recover these fossils is too important to forgo," Gosline said. "I promise, Duare, when the admiral greets the returning captain to claim his prize, you'll be at the docks as well with a handful of military police officers."

"That's a day I look forward to, sir."

"As do I," Gosline said. "Keep me posted on Bovan. Directly."

"Yes, sir," Duare said. He exited the door that led back through the storefront.

Gosline heard Macbeth screech twice. When the bird was quiet again, he knew Duare was gone. He stepped to the secondary door and opened it.

The Naval officer on the other side was still wearing his formal uniform. He stepped into the room. "That sounded like it went well," Admiral Tendrey said with satisfaction.

"Better than expected."

"I hate leaving things to chance."

"Duare's a good man. He'll carry out his orders without question."

"It'll be bad for us all if he doesn't," Tendrey said as he slipped through the door.

16

HONOMU, HAWAII. 1986

TENDREY'S SECRETARY saw the headlights of the limousine as they swept the estate's front gate. He hurried out and down the polished steps of the mansion, taming his pace to reach the car's rear door as it stopped.

"Good morning, sir," Marks said.

"Morning," said the man in a heavy baritone voice as he hoisted himself from the rear seat. It was the same voice Marks had heard across the private line without ever knowing the owner's name. The man fit the mental picture he had developed. Tall, broad-shouldered, rod-iron jaw. A supereminent presence, Marks always assumed Tendrey also had carried in his prime.

What he had not expected was the man's lack of hair. Not just from his head, but his face as well. He had no eyebrows.

"The admiral is in his study, sir," the secretary said as he followed the man up the stairs and into the open entry hall. "Is there anything I can get you from the kitchen, sir? Coffee? Ice water?"

"Just show me in."

"Right through here," Marks knocked lightly on the double koa doors. They heard Tendrey's voice summon. Marks closed the doors from the outside.

"You made good time, Tom," Tendrey said, as he wheeled himself from behind the desk. He stretched out his hand to his old friend.

"You made it sound as though the end of the world was coming."

"It is."

Mills continued past the old man and out the open sliding glass doors. The cool morning air greeted him as he strode onto the broad lanai overlooking the estate's lush grounds. "We're letting ourselves get worked up over nothing," Mills said. He examined the line of the distant horizon.

"Nothing?" Tendrey parked himself beside the Navy man. "Do you know what happens if the kid gets to Truk?"

"Yes," Mills said. "He'll swim around the lagoon for a week or two until he realizes it's pointless. There are too many wrecks. He's looking for a needle in a stack of needles." Mills glanced down. "Don't you think I would have stopped him if I thought he'd find anything?"

"He'll find the sub?" Tendrey grunted.

"We tried for years, Joe. Like I've said a million times over, Doug got out before she sank." It was an argument neither wanted to start again.

"The Jap was on to something," Tendrey said quietly.

"Who?"

"Maetani. The history professor."

"Who the hell are you talking about?"

"He knew. He knew the *Kuma Maru* was there," Tendrey defended.

"Jesus Christ. What did you do?"

"What you would have done, I hope. I had it taken care of."

"Ah, Christ," Mills' entire body slouched.

"Don't worry, it was an accident," he half-smiled.

Mills' eyes narrowed. "If anything happens to Brian, it'll be on your hands."

"He'll find the orders," Tendrey countered.

"Orders? Are you kidding? All that's left of the *Mako* is a pile of rust on the bottom of the South China Sea, Joe. There are no ghosts coming for us."

Tendrey rubbed his face with his gangly fingers. "He'll find them. The sonofabitch is as dead set as his father was. You can't let him get to Truk. It is as simple as that."

"And if I can't stop him?"

Tendrey's lips twitched, sucked in and out as if he was trying to form an order he could not bring himself to bark. Before he could answer, the phone rang in the next room. It stopped quickly.

The double doors opened, and Marks entered.

Tendrey pivoted the wheelchair. "Well, well?" he asked impatiently. "Did they find him?"

"Not yet," the secretary stated. "They're still searching for the car. We have the license number, so it won't take long."

"Then why the call? What did they say?"

Marks glanced at Mills, hesitant to share the news beyond his boss.

"Just tell us," Tendrey snapped.

"The agent from Los Angeles. He overreacted to our friends."

"Jesus," Mills breathed, as if knowing what was coming.

"And?"

"They nullified the problem, sir."

"How the hell…" Tendrey screamed. "Son-of-a-bitch! You said these people knew what they were doing."

"I am sorry, Admiral. The agent turned on them. He was armed."

"He was a field agent, for god's sake," Mills said. "What did they expect? I hope your people were smart enough to cover themselves."

"Of course," the secretary said.

"Of course," Mills mocked. "Tell me you have more to report. Something positive," he said, taking control of the conversation.

Marks turned to Tendrey for direction. The old man was staring at the Hawaiian quilt across his lap. The secretary was not sure if he was still listening.

"We don't know where your guy is at, but there is only one flight to Micronesia, to this Truk Lagoon place. The flight departs at 6:20 a.m. every morning. Bovan is on the flight day after tomorrow."

"Put your people there," Tendrey said.

Mills stepped close to Marks. "Get someone there tomorrow. He almost made it to Honolulu without us knowing. He's not letting his guard down now."

"Tom is right," Tendrey said. "Send them tomorrow."

Marks backed out of the room.

Tendrey rolled to the back of his desk. "I am telling you; it's her."

Mills remembered the elegant Chinese woman that had brought them all together. She had to be dead. She was part of the ambassador's entourage who had been aboard the plane with the mechanical malfunction. Or so concluded the official investigation.

Mills knew better. Tendrey had a small explosive placed aboard the C-47 taking them to Washington D.C. The plane was lost over the Pacific. When the *Mako* did not return, he made sure there would be no way the ill-fated exchange would come back to haunt them. And it had not, until now.

"There is someone," Mills agreed. He eased himself into the rattan chair next to the bookshelf. "The rental car proves that," he said as uncertainty swirled about his gut like a maelstrom.

"He could have faked the logbook. It got him what he needed, didn't it?"

Mills ran his palm over his non-existent eyebrows. "It's not in his makeup to lie."

"Given a reason, everyone lies. And she's given him a good reason."

At once, Mills felt the weight of the Pacific Ocean crushing him. It was what he imagined it felt like when a submarine dove beyond its maximum depth and imploded.

"This isn't about diamonds and bones. If young Bovan finds his father's submarine, it will ruin our careers." Tendrey leaned forward, laced his fingers, and pyramided his thumbs under his chin. "I've spent too much time and money making sure mine remains impeccable. There is no way in hell I am going to let this bastard tarnish it now."

17

HONOLULU, HAWAII, 1986

BRIAN LEANED OVER THE SINK and splashed chilled water onto his face twice. He rubbed his chin and felt the stubble. The hotel's operator had woken him at 4:35 a.m., five minutes later than he had requested. It was the last person he spoke with the night before that worried him.

The ticket agent informed him there were no later flights from Honolulu to his destination. Continental Airlines was the only carrier that flew to Micronesia from Hawaii and the flights departed at 0620 once a day.

The airport would be empty, Brian thought. No way around it. The man who had trailed him across the Pacific would spot him. And if not him, it would be someone else.

Somehow, Brian had to pass through the entire airport without being seen. As he lathered up the shaving soap and patted it into his cheeks, he stared into the bathroom mirror. He grinned at himself. Being seen was not the problem. It was being recognized.

He called the airline desk a second time.

•   •   •

It took the doorman ten minutes to gather a taxi that early in the morning. Brian noted the time as the driver pushed his suitcases and carry-on bag into the trunk.

Brian closed the rear door and passed the driver a hundred-dollar bill.

"It's too early, brah. I can't break this," he said across the rearview mirror.

"It's all yours. Just don't say anything when we get to the terminal. There will be an airline porter waiting. Give him my suitcases. If he asks, you picked me up at the hospital."

"The hospital?" the driver cocked his head. "No need to say more," he said, his face broadened as he slipped the bill into his pocket. "Shoots, I tell them maternity ward if you want."

The streets of the island metropolis were quiet in the minutes before dawn, but not empty. The city's energy was re-surging as the day promised fresh waves of tourists. Storekeepers were on the sidewalks washing their store fronts. At the beachfront hotels, the maintenance staff were busy raking the shore and sweeping walkways that webbed through their vast complexes, each a city within the city.

The talkative taxi driver made good time to the airport, although Brian now knew more about Hawaiian life than he thought possible. "Those two people. Stop in front of them." Brian directed the driver toward the porter and a young woman in a powder blue airline uniform.

Brian rolled down the window of the cab. "I hope you're here for me," he said, working to make his voice sound hoarse and weak.

"Mr. Brock?" the young Hawaiian woman asked as she reached for the door.

"Yes," Brian responded. The driver was already out of the car and opening the trunk.

"One moment, please." She rushed into the terminal and returned, pushing an airport wheelchair. Maneuvering it against the cab, she locked its wheels.

Brian used both hands to lift himself slowly from the cab. The woman, as attentive as a nurse, guided him to the chair. Brian winced just enough for the charade.

"I am sorry for the trouble," Brian said to her.

"The airline is more than happy to help its passengers when we can. I'm just sorry you had to spend your vacation in the hospital," she said as she took his carry-on bag from the driver. "The porter will have your bags on your flight."

"You feel better, ya?" the driver said with a smile. He flashed the girl the shaka wave, then disappeared into the taxi.

"Nice guy," Brian mumbled.

"Is there anything you need before your flight, Mr. Brock?"

"No. I just can't get over how lucky I was to be in Honolulu when my appendix acted up. I'm not sure what I would have done on Kwajalein."

"You're headed to Kwajalein? My mother's family was from those islands. It is beautiful." She wheeled Brian into the terminal and down the long, empty corridor. "We visited once when I was a little girl."

Although he nodded, Brian did not listen to her story of her childhood adventure to the atoll. He was scanning the main terminal that spread out like a hand with long, narrow fingers. Thankfully, it was more crowded than he had expected.

The small coffee shop and the bar on the opposite side of the gates were bustling with passengers awaiting their boarding calls.

The woman from Continental rolled Brian directly to the check-in counter. "Frank," she said to the heavy-set Hawaiian in khaki slacks and white shoes. "Mr. Brock is on Flight 4. Have you called for boarding?"

"Six more minutes, but you can get him aboard," he said. "Do you have your ticket, Mr. Brock?"

As Brian fished it from his pocket, he casually scanned the faces of the nearby passengers. No one seemed out of place.

Frank returned his ticket. "Hope you feel better, Mr. Brock. Enjoy your flight."

The attendant pushed him toward the gate. A few more feet and he would be aboard. They moved into the enclosed ramp, down its length and onto the small Boeing 727.

If there were people trying to stop him, they had either not recognized him or hesitated to stop him with an airline escort at his side.

At the plane's door, Brian thanked her again as she passed him to the flight attendant, another exuberant young Hawaiian girl with a waterfall of black hair down her back.

With a hand floating in the swell of his back, she helped him to his seat over the wing. "We'll be boarding in a few minutes," the attendant said. She dropped the overhead bin and set his carry-on inside.

"I'd rather hold on to that," he blurted.

"Of course. Call if you need anything, Mr. Brock," she smiled with perfect teeth and returned to the front of the plane.

•　　　•　　　•

Brian watched the faces of the passengers as they shuffled down the center aisle. He sat about a third of the way back from the entrance, giving him a clear view. Of all the faces, none were that of the man who had followed him from Los Angeles and into the Honolulu parking lot.

They were simply the excited faces of tourists leaving one paradise for another, more exotic location. Loud Hawaiian print shirts and shorts, wicker bags and suntanned smiles.

"Excuse me," said the young Asian woman standing over him.

Brian tilted his head, hesitant to look away from the next group of passengers. "I am sorry," he said honestly as he stood.

"That's okay," she said squeezing into the window seat. She leaned forward shoving her small bag and purse next to her feet. Struggling out of her cream-colored linen coat, she revealed deeply tanned shoulders holding the thin straps of her pink cotton blouse. "Do you mind putting this in the overhead?" she asked.

"What?" Brian continued to watch the incoming travelers.

"My coat. Up there?"

"Sure." He reached the drop-down cabinet and pushed her coat inside.

"And I was worried about wrinkles," she said, more to herself than to him.

But Brian caught it. "I'm sorry. I wasn't thinking."

"That's okay." She smiled and he saw her bright cinnamon eyes were edged with flecks of green. They sparkled in the plane's fluorescent lights. "Nervous to fly?" she asked as she swept her dark hair aside.

"Not usually," he said. "Just having a hard time relaxing."

"Me too. That's why I came a couple of days early."

"You're not from here?" He glanced toward the entrance as the attendant closed the hatchway and swung the large orange handle to secure it.

"New York."

"That would make this a long flight."

"And painful."

Brian smiled. He offered his hand.

"Leslie Maetani."

The Continental jet lurched as it rolled from the terminal. By the time the pilot lined up the 727 with the departing runway, the attendants had double-checked the overhead bins and made sure their passengers' seatbelts were secure.

The Hawaiian flight attendant who had initially helped Brian to his seat stopped to check on him. "If you need, Mr. Brock, I can get you extra pillows."

Brian thanked her.

The attendant turned to Leslie. "Anything for you, Doctor?"

"I'm fine, thank you."

"The snack cart will be out as soon as the pilot turns off the seatbelt sign," she promised and moved to the next set of passengers.

"Doctor?" Brian lifted a brow. "As in a medical doctor?"

"Afraid so."

"Wow."

"Why the surprise?" she asked, with the tilt of her head.

Brian saw a growing look of indignation in her face. "I was just thinking, I've never seen a doctor without a white coat. But then, you do have a white coat."

She laughed lightly. "Nice dodge."

"Thanks," he grinned. "For a second, I thought I was going to need a new seat."

"I wouldn't do that to you. This airline is terrible with reservations. I was supposed to be on this flight yesterday. I am lucky I got a seat at all," she said.

After a brief hesitation, the 727's engines spooled higher until their thrust matched the pilot's intentions. He eased his feet off the brakes and the jet started its race down the runway.

Within seconds, the nose wheel left terra firma, joined quickly by those under the wings. The plane banked left and found its heading westward. The line of tall coconut palms that normally waved to all departing visitors were hidden in the pre-dawn darkness.

Once they leveled off, Leslie shuffled through her small bag and retrieved a stack of brochures held together by a rubber band. She pulled the top one out and opened it.

Brian glanced at the large bold type across the top of the pamphlet: TRUK LAGOON UNDERWATER TOURS.

"You've come prepared," he said.

Her nose wrinkled like a cute bunny. "I probably grabbed more than I needed."

"I was going to find a guide at the hotel."

"You're flying through to Truk?"

"This isn't a direct flight?"

"Umm, no. We stop on three other islands," she said.

"This trip was last minute for me," Brian explained.

"Here." She handed him the next pamphlet from her lap. "Clearly, I have plenty to share."

Brian opened the brochure: WAR & PEACE: TRUK LAGOON TOURS. The colorful, tri-folded pamphlet was brimming with idyllic photographs and picturesque descriptions. It told of untouched beaches, pristine reefs, and where all the history touched the atoll.

There were underwater snapshots of submerged ships, deserted bunkers on the shore, and of the forgotten relics of war that were quickly falling to a thriving jungle. One inside photo was of a bikini-clad girl sitting in the cockpit of a sunken Japanese fighter plane. Another showed the same young woman in the same bikini running into the waves of an unspoiled, sugary beach.

"Are you on vacation?" Leslie asked.

"No," Brian said, flipping through the pages. "I mean yes. Yes and no." His efforts to correct himself only made his mistake worse. "You?"

"Kind of yes and no too," she said. "I'm visiting my dad. He is there for research."

Brian sat up slightly. "Fish?" he ventured.

"No, he's a history professor. He has tenure at the University of Hawaii."

"Hard to visit from New York."

Leslie nodded. "It's not always the geography."

"I'm sorry. I shouldn't have…"

She touched his forearm thoughtlessly. "That's okay. It's not a raw nerve or anything. It's just how we turned out."

Brian might not have touched a nerve, but she did. The warmth of her hand radiated across his skin so unexpectedly, it caused him to catch his breath.

"My dad has always had an infatuation with the place," she said, with a rise of her shoulders and, for the first time, Brian noticed how thin she was. "He was there during the war, so I get it."

"Your father was at Truk?

"Morbid, right? That he keeps going back."

"Not really," Brian said. "They say, once you're in the service, you're always in."

She flashed her smile. "Well, I think that deserves another brochure." She passed it to him.

Brian flipped through it. "How often does your dad go out there?"

"I thought it was just a few weeks each summer, but his assistant said he's been on sabbatical for three months," she said. "I guess he's been there the whole time."

"He must have found something interesting."

"He only goes for one thing," Leslie said. "To look for his ship."

Brian felt his breath catch. He dropped the seat back tray and spread the brochure. He unfolded the center page, revealing a simple chart of the atoll. Scattered across the image were little red flags, revealing the best wrecks to explore. "There's a list," he said flipping the page to a two-column tally of Japanese ships and planes. "Do you know the name?"

"Oh yeah. But I don't think it would be on a list. It was just a freighter or something," she said. "Growing up, I heard all the war tales. And every February, we had to go to the Buddhist church to make offerings for his friends."

"February 17th?"

She looked to him with surprise. "How did you know?"

Brian turned the pamphlet and pointed to the description. In bold lettering, it revealed the American Navy's attack on Truk Lagoon started on February 17, 1944.

"He said it was to respect the friends who were still there. Still on his *Kuma Maru*."

Someone poured iced sea water down Brian's back. Or so it felt. It took a moment for the shock to subside, and he could breathe again.

"You said your flight reservations were mixed up. Did they say why?" he asked.

"I didn't ask. Honestly, I was a little relieved to get an extra day to prepare."

"For?"

"Seeing my dad," she flashed the guilty smile of a twelve-year-old caught in a lie. "Oh, that sounded worse than it was meant." She squeezed his arm again. Another bolt across his nervous system.

"I won't tell," he promised. And he wouldn't. He had other things to discuss with this woman's father.

For the next several hours, as the flight attendants brought coffee and a barely digestible lunch, they talked. Leslie told him about New York and her dancing career, though she made her work sound unremarkable. Brian, on the other hand, spoke mostly of his mother and made no reference to the twenty-year career he had just given up. When Leslie's questions were more detailed, he avoided direct answers.

Occasionally, he wondered if she was part of what he was trying to avoid from Washington. He hoped not.

The plane landed on Johnston Island for an uneven exchange of passengers and luggage. Next, they flew to Majuro and emptied more seats. Fifteen minutes later, the 727 put down on the single runway of Kwajalein Island.

"We'll be refueling here," the attendant announced to the passengers she passed. "If anyone feels like stretching their legs, there are some cute shops across the road. We will be here for about 45 minutes."

"Let's go shopping," Leslie said, putting her hand on Brian's.

"Sure," he said, following her from the plane.

They descended the mobile staircase pressed against the fuselage from the back of an old Chevy pickup truck. From the size of the one-story terminal, Brian guessed it never hosted more than two or three jets at any one time. Unlike Honolulu, Kwajalein's horizon was dominated by swaying palm trees.

Leslie took the lead, heading through the terminal building and out the other side. As promised, there was a line of three-sided shops huddled along the street.

Calling them shops, however, was an exaggeration. They were made of second-hand slates of plywood nailed haphazardly together, bringing to mind a full-scale house of cards. If the wind blew strongly, that would be the end of them.

A few yards behind the huts, a rocky shore swept east and west, encircling the calm crystal waters of the island's bay.

Leslie grabbed Brian's hand as she dashed across the street. They barely outran the bulbous front end of a speeding green bus. Reaching the gravel curb, she turned and laughed. "You look terrified."

"You forgot to mention you were suicidal."

"I thought you would be quicker." She moved to explore the tables of hand-crafted wood carvings and seashells glued to make animal shapes for the tourists. Everything from T-shirts with Kwajalein printed across the front to sun-bleached grass skirts hanging on lines strung through the tiny shops.

Brian watched her intently as her delicate fingers drifted over the offerings. "Different from Madison Avenue," he joked.

"I may never go back," she said. She held a string of small white shells to her neck. "What do you think?"

"You buy," the squat woman with swirling black tattoos on her plump forearms appeared from the cool shadows of the hut. She nodded approvingly. "For your beautiful wife. I'll do you a deal. Ten dollars. American."

"She's, ummm, we're not married," Brian said.

"Could be," the woman grinned. "You buy. She marries you tomorrow." The woman wrapped a thick arm around Leslie's waist. "Beautiful puka shells for beautiful girl. Come, you buy. Eight dollars."

"Six," Brian countered.

Leslie's eyebrows perked. "You think I'm going to marry you for a six-dollar necklace?"

Brian frowned. "You're right. Seven dollars," he said to the shopkeeper.

"Deal," the woman took his cash straightaway. "What about a palm frond hat? Beautiful hat for beautiful girl. She gives you sons she wear this hat."

"One step at a time," Leslie said, taking Brian's arm and leading him away. "At this rate, we'll be grandparents before we get back to the plane."

"She'd make a killing on Madison Avenue."

"Thank you for the necklace," Leslie said.

"Beautiful puka shells for beautiful girl," he teased.

"Look, they have mango," she said, eyeing the next hut. The long front table was filled with a brilliant palette of native fruits. "I wonder if he will cut it for us." She squeeze-tested several yellow-green mangos, chose one of the largest and carried it inside. A moment later, she returned cradling two dripping halves, each skewered with a bamboo stick and wrapped in a paper napkin. "Let's sit by the water," she said, handing Brian his half.

A few yards down the beach, she found an alcove in the mangrove hedges where someone had stacked volcanic stones to create a rough bench. This was a secret place most everyone knew about, but as the strip of sand between the trees and lagoon was less than a foot wide, it could be reached only at low tide.

Brian and Leslie were just in time. He sat with her. Although they had sat like this for the last ten hours, being next to her felt uncomfortably intimate. He watched with amusement as she delicately bit into the sweet, pulpy meat of the mango. Somehow, she finished her portion with little drama, while he drenched himself with mango juice as it cascaded over his hand and down his arm.

"There is a trick to this, right?"

"You're trying to eat it like an apple. There is too much juice for that. You drink as you bite."

"Got it." He tried again, and again the mango won.

She laughed. A flickering chuckle that shook her entire body. It made him laugh as well.

Finally, he gave up and tossed the remnants of mango into the hedge. He dipped his hands in the water and shook them dry. He surveyed the far side of the lagoon, where the sea swells crashed over the outside reef. "It's beautiful out here, isn't it?" he asked. "Almost surreal."

Leslie moved to the edge of the sand. She slipped off her shoes and walked a step into the warm water. "Why surreal?"

"Forty years ago, this was a war zone," he said with a hint of disbelief. "Before the fleet hit Truk Lagoon, they hit here. In three days, they leveled the Japanese base and killed over 5,000 men. Look around now, and you can hardly tell they were ever here."

"I missed that in the brochures."

"Just stuff I read as a kid."

"My father is going to like you," she said as she exited the water. "You talk about the same things in the same way. And you have his habit of avoiding straight answers."

As they walked back toward the airport, their shoulders brushed, an intimate gesture not lost on the island shopkeeper. Leslie saw her point to the puka necklace and flash a 'thumbs-up.'

The 727-airliner climbed into a sky once dominated by American Hellcat fighters and the black soot of anti-aircraft fire. It pitched west toward Truk. The route that once took the U.S. Navy three years and thousands of lives to complete was now achieved by a passenger plane in less than eleven hours.

18

HONOLULU, HAWAII, 1986

"T HIS THE GUY?"

"No."

"The description fits."

"Not him," JP said flatly.

The sergeant from Hawaii police department shrugged. "If you say so."

"This guy's too old," JP inspected the gaping slash that started under the left ear, down into the jugular and out through the larynx. Gummy blood matted his chest hairs.

The sergeant waved to the young man in the white coat holding the sheet off the body. "Bag and freeze him, Doc. We'll keep rotating his picture," the sergeant said as he and JP stepped away.

"What happened to the guy?" JP asked, trying to sound casual.

"Typical thing. The locals just want to roll a mainlander for his cash and the guy thinks he's Magnum P.I. For a couple hundred bucks, he ends up here. Happens all the time," the sergeant shook his head. "People think this is paradise. It's Chicago with palm trees and suntan oil."

"I'll remember that." JP offered his hand. "Thanks again for your time, Sergeant."

Fuck, JP thought as he exited the refrigerated air of the morgue and stepped into the steam bath of the tropical day. He saw the brown Dodge the Honolulu sector had given him against the curb. He headed for it.

"Well?" Karen asked as JP opened the passenger's door.

"It was Cranken. I don't know who filleted him, but it wasn't for his wallet."

"What now?"

"Back to the airport. I'm going to make a house call," he said, staring out the windshield, trying to put the puzzle together.

•　　　•　　　•

It took the Bell 222 Twin Executive helicopter only 45-minutes to fly from Honolulu International Airport to the Big Island. The pilot knew where JP wanted to go. He had never landed there himself, but he had flown the admiral's guests from Honolulu to Hilo plenty of times.

JP watched out the window of the jet chopper as it sped along the coast of the youngest Hawaiian island. Yet, he did not see the providential beauty in the lush green hills of the Kohala Forest or the drastic change of colors of the sea where the turquoise shallows ended, and the abyss began.

All that JP saw was the surgical pink gash in the CIA man's neck. It was a surveillance job. An old-fashioned stand-back and take notes affair. Jesus, an agent he had never met or spoken with, was now laying in the morgue as a John Doe because JP had made assumptions.

"They tell you where I should land?" the pilot asked.

"I think he said the north side of the house," JP said. Below, the red-tiled roof of Tendrey's isolated estate came into view. It was larger than JP imagined.

The helicopter touched the trimmed green lawn gently and before its blades slowed, JP was out the door.

"Mr. Powell," Marks said as he leaned into his charm. "John Marks. Admiral Tendrey's personal secretary. I hope your flight was comfortable. We use this charter now and then." He extended a hand.

"Where is he?"

"To be honest, he's a little put off by your visit. The admiral is not used to drop-ins."

"Well, I was in the neighborhood," he said.

"Of course," Marks said. "He asked me to show you to the grand lanai. He'll join you momentarily."

They walked across the gravel driveway and passed a marble fountain, its water jetting high into the breeze, the spray falling cool against JP's face. On the other side, the chauffeur was washing a blue limousine in the shade.

The lanai overlooked more trimmed lawns and the cliffs where, far below, the sea came ashore in a rage.

A young Hawaiian girl with short black hair was clearing the glass patio table of lunch dishes when the men stepped out. Marks glared at her. He immediately turned to JP. "Please, have a seat, Mr. Powell. She'll finish in a moment. I'll let the admiral know you are here. If you'd like something to drink, I'll have the butler come."

"Nothing," JP said, as he continued to the edge of the balcony. As soon as Marks left, the agent turned to the girl as she stacked the dishes. Two cups, one with a ring of coffee in the bottom, the other with a tea bag hanging from it. Two food dishes, two sets of silverware. And a tumbler of a small amount of gold liquid on the bottom. *Who's the guest?* JP wondered.

"Ah, Mr. Powell," the admiral reached out his hand as Marks maneuvered the wheelchair through the double glass doors. "Your phone call was a surprise. I assume that was your intent."

"Not at all, Admiral. But circumstances as they are."

"Yes. The agent in Honolulu." The admiral signaled Marks away. "It was a mugging?"

"That's the police report."

"You have doubts?"

"He was too smart to let a street punk open his throat."

"No one is immortal, Mr. Powell."

"That's what I've heard," the agent said. "My superiors asked me to run surveillance on a Navy officer as a favor to you, Admiral. I did not ask enough questions, which has turned into a deadly mistake. I don't like making mistakes."

"I assume you read his file. A nuclear submarine commander has a lot of knowledge, Mr. Powell. Particularly important knowledge,"

Tendrey said as he wheeled himself to the edge of the lanai. He focused on the distant sea. "I'm sure you understand the concern."

"Oh, I understand the concern. I just don't understand your place in it."

Tendrey pivoted. "I have my own reasons, Mr. Powell."

JP stared into his watery red eyes. "Where is Bovan now?"

"The last I heard, he was on Maui enjoying the sun," the admiral said.

"You have people on him?"

"Of course."

"Where on Maui?"

"As I stated over the phone, Commander Bovan is no longer your concern. I'm sure you will receive instructions to return to Washington." Tendrey turned in his wheelchair. "I am sorry about your man, but thank you again for your help," he said with the same gesture of dismissal he had given his secretary.

As if on cue, Marks stepped from the house to escort the agent back to his helicopter. JP glared at the back of Tendrey's head. It took all his effort not to respond.

JP followed Marks toward the front door. "Do you mind if I use the bathroom?" JP asked politely. "It's a long flight back to Honolulu."

Marks studied him. "Through here," he said. He took him through the kitchen and past the pantry and linen rooms. Entering a narrow hall, the secretary pointed toward a set of double doors. "Through there, go right, second door on the left," he said.

"Thank you," JP said as he followed his directions. But once through the double doors, the agent went left instead.

Just down the hall, a different door opened as a butler rushed out, balancing a small tray in his right hand. On the tray, JP noted a tumbler of gold liquid and ice. He smiled innocently as the butler hurried by.

Staying a few paces back, JP followed the butler as he wove his way through a maze of halls and corridors. Finally, the butler entered a narrow door and before he could close it, the agent leaned inside.

The large man with the powerful face and bald head stood next to a high bookshelf, casually considering the cover of a thick, leather-bound tome. As if acutely aware, the man's head snapped up. His eyes met JP's and for an instant, the agent recognized panic.

JP crossed the rear driveway toward the helicopter at a quick pace. His mind was reeling so quickly, he did not see the small suitcase set beside the rear bumper of the limousine until he stumbled over it.

"Sorry," he said, as the chauffeur helped him to his feet.

"My fault, sir. I didn't see you come out of the house.

JP noticed the suitcases in the car's trunk, the chauffeur, and again the suitcases. He turned and ran to the helicopter.

•   •   •

"Can you hide this thing behind the hills? I want to see where that limo goes," JP said as the helicopter left Tendrey's estate behind. "Just be sure it looks like we're headed for Honolulu first, before you loop back."

"Whatever you say, man. It's your bill," the pilot said. "They'll have to go south along Mamalahoa Highway. It's the only way to Hilo."

"Can you follow them without being spotted?"

"Cake, man, a piece of cake. We'll drop behind the trees and, when they leave, pop out. Just like 'Nam."

Great, JP thought, *just like 'Nam*. He remembered fighting the Vietnam war from a musty disinformation office in Hong Kong. He watched as the red-tiled roof of Tendrey's mansion fell behind the tops of the green palm trees.

•   •   •

"He saw me!"

"Goddamnit, how?" Tendrey said as he glared up at Mills.

"Who let him wander around the house?" Mills shot. He felt himself wet under his arms. He didn't like the CIA. They always thought of themselves apart from every other arm of the government and, worse, they never followed orders. This JP was a prime example. "Now what?" Mills was pacing the lanai.

"You get to your plane. I'll take care of Mr. Powell," Tendrey said.

"What are you going to do, kill another CIA agent?" Mills asked, as he hurried into the house.

"John!" Tendrey screamed. It made him cough in spasms. "John!"

•   •   •

The Nam pilot was right. He held his chopper below the tree line until the limousine passed. Engaging the throttle levers, they lifted high into the cloudless sky and fell in behind it.

"Like I said, man. They're headed to Hilo. I bet to the airport," the pilot said. The sleek Bell helicopter felt uncomfortable pacing the slow-moving car below. It was designed to speed executives from boardroom to boardroom over the tops of skyscrapers.

JP said nothing. He simply watched the car travel the nearly deserted highway, past downtown and directly toward the airport.

"I told you, man," the pilot smirked.

"You got binoculars in this thing?"

"Behind the seat."

JP grabbed the Zeiss binoculars from the small elastic pocket on the seat back. "Get us closer," he said as he raised the glasses to his face.

"I've gotta get clearance from the tower."

"Do what you need," JP said without looking away from the limousine.

Tendrey's car wound its way past the visitor's parking and through two airport gates. It stopped at a third with a guard and passed unimpeded. Turning left, the limousine drove onto the airfield apron.

It stopped next to a small Learjet, its white fuselage and hawk-sharp wings glistened in the sun. The rear of the limousine opened, and JP saw the man step out.

He knew who Tendrey's guest was. Admiral Thomas Mills. JP had run a check on the name after the yeoman had contacted Bovan at the hotel suite. And now he was in Hawaii meeting Tendrey. *Oh, no coincidence here*, JP thought.

"Get me closer. I've got to get the tail numbers off that jet."

"Sorry, man. This is as close as I can get. The heliport is on the other side of the runways."

JP reached into his breast pocket and pulled his wallet. He flipped open his CIA identification. "Closer. Until I get the numbers."

"Shit. You're going to pay for the fines, right?" the pilot protested as he dropped his craft toward the tarmac.

Through the binoculars, JP picked up the first letter and five numbers from the jet's tail. "Let's get out of here," JP said, hoping they hadn't been spotted. "I need to get to a phone."

"No worries. There's one in the back between the rear seats," the pilot grinned. "Remember, man, this is an executive chopper."

JP unclipped his seatbelt and pulled the headphones off his head. Crouched over, he moved to the rear section of the helicopter.

"Where to?"

"Back to Honolulu," JP hollered. He felt the pilot lift the helicopter briskly into the sky. Its nose dipped slightly as the war vet ran his blades to full.

JP picked up the black telephone and dialed the Honolulu sector's special number. The operator connected him to the wrong office twice. Finally, Karen picked up the line.

"They shoved me in a closet. This office is smaller than my car. And it's hotter than hell in here," she complained.

"Yeah, yeah, I'll take care of it," he promised. She was not used to the heat, and it was getting to her. "Listen, find out the flight plan for a Learjet, number N18349. It took off from Hilo airport about fifteen minutes ago. I am betting it is a charter out of D.C."

"Got it."

"Run Bovan's name through the computers again," JP told her. "And, Karen, search Admiral Thomas Mills while you are at it. Do it on the down low."

The helicopter was only ten minutes out of Honolulu International when Karen called back on the executive phone.

"The computer came up with Bovan's name on a Continental flight leaving tomorrow morning," she told him. "But I wouldn't trust the asshole to make it."

"Going where?" JP was anxious.

"Caroline Islands. It's a hopper with several stops."

"And what about Admiral Mills?"

"Nothing on Mills. What made you ask?"

"Did you get the flight plan for the Lear?" JP was trying to think.

"You were right. It was a charter out of D.C. Landed on the Big Island with a single passenger."

"Flight plan out?"

There was silence for a minute as Karen worked her computer. "Nothing," she said. "No flight plan beyond Hilo."

"It went somewhere," JP said in frustration. "Get me a seat on Bovan's flight. Don't say anything to anyone. Do it from a phone outside the building."

"What about me?"

"Meet me at the hotel in forty-five minutes," he said as he hung up.

JP leaned against the cushy leather backseat of the corporate chopper. Out the side window, he could see the peak of Diamond Head growing across the aircraft's windshield and the line of monolithic hotels standing over Waikiki Beach like a defensive front line.

The helicopter dropped smoothly as the pilot approached his designated landing spot. "We're home," the pilot announced as he flipped switches to shut down the engine.

JP did not hear him. He was revisiting the serpentine gash down Cranken's throat, the look Mills' eyes and the dismissive wave of a wheelchair-bound admiral who expected unquestioning loyalty from his subordinates.

"Commander Bovan is no longer your concern, Mr. Powell. You will be issued new orders this afternoon instructing you to return to Washington." That's what the old man had said with his wave.

Too bad, JP thought as he thanked the pilot and hurried across the tarmac to meet Karen. Simply too bad he did not have the chance to remind Admiral Tendrey that the CIA does not take orders from the military.

19

HONOLULU, HAWAII, 1944

THE SLEEK, TWENTY-FOOT TORPEDO dangled precariously over the sub's narrow deck by a single cable. As the dock crane lowered the weapon, two crewmen muscled the munition into the loading cradle that stood at a forty-five-degree angle over the forward loading hatch. With heavy ropes fed through block and tackle, they eased the dagger into its sheath.

"That's fish number twenty-four, Skipper," Alberts called out.

Douglas watched the procedure from where he stood on the gun-deck. Over his shoulder, the long barrel of the 20mm Oerlikon anti-aircraft gun stood watch. Waving his XO over, he reached between the bars of the safety rail and took the clipboard from Alberts' outstretched hand.

Leveraging the bottom rung, Alberts pulled himself up. "We're close to ready. The crew is all accounted for and, I'll tell you, they are all more than eager to get underway."

Douglas hoisted himself into the port seat of the big gun and swept Alberts' checklist. "What are we missing?"

Alberts lowered his cap slightly to shade his eyes. "Frank's scouring the supply depot for green food coloring. Says he's going to bake a cake for St. Patrick's Day."

"Great, we'll all be pissing turquoise for a week. What else?"

"The provisions are topped off. Batteries are pegging their charge and we're scheduled for fueling just after 1200. The *Bonefish* is getting her fuel now. The *Herring* is next," Alberts said. "The only thing holding us back, Skipper, is Clancy's blessing."

"Still that number two engine?"

"He promised it'd be running by eleven hundred. I checked about thirty-minutes ago. All I heard was a lot of banging and cussing coming from the lower flat."

Douglas checked his watch. "I'll give him more time," he said, handing back the clipboard.

"Aye, Skipper."

Douglas climbed to the bridge, acknowledged the crewman polishing the gyrocompass, and continued down into the conning tower. Inside, another man was putting extra effort to a polishing cloth. It was a seaman ritual, reaching back for centuries. Swab the deck, toe the line, shipshape and Bristol fashion. While it was Navy fashion to keep a vessel neat and orderly, aboard a submarine, the compulsion could mean the difference between returning from patrol on time or not returning at all. If a piece of equipment failed while submerged, there would be no tugboat to tow you in for repairs.

While every inch of the *Mako* herself was scrubbed and clean, the air within her watertight hull reeked of men and machines. It could be eye-tearing bitterness: battery acid, fumes of motor oil and hydraulic fluid, and the intimate aromas of seventy-seven men who could only bathe once every two weeks. After her time at Pearl, the submarine still held its odorous identity.

Douglas never got used to the stench, but like all submariners, he learned to ignore its perpetual assault. In the control room, he greeted his Chief Officer Fenton, the short Californian who convinced the recruitment office he was perfect for sub duty. He never had to duck the hatches.

Heading aft, Douglas leaned into the narrow radio room. "Everything checking out, Danny?" The young radio man with only a patch of soft blond hair on his cheeks turned in his chair. "Yes, sir. We're set, Skipper," Danny said.

"See if you can find some music. Pipe it through the ship," Douglas instructed.

"Aye, sir. I could use a little of that."

"We all could," Douglas said.

Passing the small mess hall, he joked with the men playing cards—watch out for Riley, he told them. He's too good. Mendez never bluffs. Carrillo laughs when he has anything better than a pair.

Douglas continued aft toward the upper engine room. Throughout her length, he noted his crew scurried with last minute duties, securing stores, double-checking equipment, and then checking it again.

It was a symphonic clatter with a distinct purpose, like a thousand chaotic ants laboring individually yet ultimately achieving the same goal. Douglas knew, however, these tasks, even the simplest, had another aim.

They were the remedy for fear. It is said there are no atheists in foxholes, but there are fewer still in a submarine sliding across the murky abyss under a shower of depth charges.

Every man aboard understood the enemy could make a lucky strike or something within the complex craft could malfunction, and the *Mako* would descend into the depths until her hull cracked and shattered, and her crew was delivered to the numbing darkness of the sea.

No one aboard ever talked of it. That was bad luck. Only the captains knew of the official losses. Of every five submarines that slipped out of Pearl Harbor, only four would return to see her shores again.

As Douglas reached the forward engine room, he wondered if he should have requested the base's repair crew work the sub for an extra day. They had been aboard, upgrading several pieces of equipment to the level of the new *Balao-class* boats, but add what they might, the new submarines had an advantage that could not be bolted to his boat.

They built the newer subs with thicker hulls of high tensile steel which extended their depth. That was something every commander would trade a year's pay and maybe a few good men for. The ability to lay a spread of torpedoes into an enemy ship and slip away at four-hundred feet instead of three hundred would be a godsend.

But as Douglas tucked his shoulder and dipped his head through the low hatchway leading into the engine room, he realized he trusted

Clancy's work and his word. If the mechanic did not think the diesel would get them through the patrol, he would be the first to say.

"Clanc…?" Douglas called as he walked the length of the massive sixteen-piston diesel engine. Unlike the rest of the sub, the power plant had not received a fresh coat of paint. It remained blistered and burnt as the chief mechanic and his men worked around the clock to bring her operating temperature within reason.

The four monstrous diesels were the heart of the *Mako*, although they did not drive the sub through the water. Their purpose was to generate the electricity to charge the forward and aft battery banks, the true silent force behind the propellers, the actual means of attack, the actual means of escape.

Douglas held his hand near the iron block of the diesel and felt the radiant heat. "Clancy," he called again.

"Here. Goddamnit," the voice came from the crammed space between the engine and the hull. There was grunting, a clang of tools and Clancy's grease covered face appeared. "Skipper? Sorry, I thought you were Peter. I sent him for a four-inch elbow an hour ago."

"Are we going to have four engines tonight, Clanc, or three?"

"Four. Another hour and I'll have all four of these beasts running in top condition."

"Never had a doubt."

Clancy cocked his head, wanting to believe him. "Thank you, Skipper."

As Douglas headed back toward the crew's mess, a whiny rattle leapt from the squawky PA system. Slowly, as Danny adjusted the volume, the angelic voices of The Andrews Sisters singing "Here Comes the Navy" rose above the background racket of the ship. Douglas laughed at the kid's choice.

"Skipper!" Alberts yelled from above as Douglas walked back through the control room.

"Yeah?" Douglas saw his face framed by the conning tower hatch.

"A truck just pulled up to the gangplank, Skipper. Driver is asking for you."

When he reached the bridge, they heard the forward diesel belch and saw a hiccup of black exhaust. "Make sure he gets what he needs," Douglas instructed. "I don't want any doubts when we cast off."

Alberts bobbed his head.

Douglas transitioned effortlessly from the ship to the dock where a Navy ensign was standing at the fender of dull, olive-green Willys jeep. He snapped a salute.

"Admiral Tendrey requests you report to his office, sir. I am to take you," he said.

Bingo. The proof Wagner wanted was being served. "Let me grab a clean shirt," Douglas said as he returned to the boat.

"What's up?" Alberts asked as he followed Douglas into his cabin.

"Tendrey wants to see me."

"Is he coming aboard to check on our torpedoes?" Alberts asked, brow furrowed.

Douglas slipped on a clean khaki shirt. Buttoned it in the six-by-six-inch polished square of stainless steel mounted to the cabinet door of his quarters. "Won't know until he tells me."

"I don't like coincidences," Alberts said, pressing his shoulder to the bulkhead.

"What do you mean?"

"Tendrey. He pushed that new kid on to us. Seaman 2 Class."

"Hawthorne?"

"Yeah. The talkative one."

Douglas shook his head. "I looked at his file. I didn't see that."

"It wasn't there. I talked to Springer, the XO on the *Sperry*, the sub tender Hawthorne was assigned to. He told me Tendrey made a personal request. I wonder why Stein would allow a last-minute transfer?"

Douglas knew exactly why Hawthorne was there. Tendrey now had a pair of eyes aboard the *Mako*. Yet, he was surprised Captain Stein, the squadron commander, would grant the request blindly. He and Tendrey were friends, Douglas remembered. They had served on the old K-boats together after the first war. Maybe that is all it took.

"No disrespect, but I don't trust Tendrey."

"I got a secret for you. No one does."

Alberts chuckled.

"The Chief say anything more?" Douglas asked.

"Only that the kid performed well during their test runs."

"Just keep an eye on him," Douglas said as he brushed down his shirt. From the cabinet above his bunk, he pulled a stressed leather satchel. He stepped from his cabin. Alberts followed him up the ladder.

"You going to mention him? Hawthorne?"

"What do you think the old man will say?"

"He'll show you the stripes on his sleeve and tell you not to question his orders."

•　　•　　•

With his satchel under his arm, Douglas paced in the small office waiting for Rear Admiral Tendrey. It was only worth six steps. The absence of pictures on the walls and the few books on the shelves showed this was not going to be the admiral's permanent niche.

Douglas could guess why. It was an old office in an old building, hot and humid, and the air was stagnant because the fan in the corner did not work. He could imagine Tendrey's rage when he found out where HQ had stuck him.

The office's only door squeaked open and Tendrey stepped in.

"Sorry to keep you waiting, Commander," he said, with unexpected pleasantry.

"You wanted to see me, sir?" Douglas said directly.

"You left the party before we finished our conversation," the admiral said as he moved behind his comically small steel desk.

"I was finished."

Tendrey grinned with his crooked lips. He pulled two envelopes from the top drawer, one letter-sized, the other a thick manila package. "As promised." He pushed the letter across the desk.

Douglas studied the unmarked envelope without touching it.

"It's your supplemental orders," Tendrey pointed. "You're assigned reconnaissance off Truk. Those justify slipping inside. I must admit, they'd fool me."

Douglas opened the envelope and offered the single page a brief, half-hearted glance. In truth, his scan of the forged document was word-for-word. He fought the smile growing on his face. In his hand were falsified orders from a man he hated. A man who had avoided accountability, until now.

"I take these, I just signed up as a traitor."

"You think I am a traitor, Doug? Don't be naive. This isn't aiding the enemy. This is supporting an ally," Tendrey pointed a knobby finger at him. "I don't care for the Chinks any more than I do the Japs, but one problem at a time."

"If this is so important, why false orders?"

"Those are for your XO. You don't think he's going to wonder where you got these?" The admiral swept the larger package off the desk and shoved them into Douglas' hands. "The charts for the lagoon. They show the underwater break in the reef and where the freighter's anchored. They're from the ambassador's staff, so they're difficult to read, but you'll manage."

"I haven't agreed."

"We both know your options. You've got none. Not if you want to keep your command." He drew his chair and leaned back on two legs. "You're scheduled to head out zero-hundred. At 2345 hours, a Navy truck will deliver a small wooden crate. Inside, the uncut diamonds and a small timer and detonator. The Marine Ensign will show you how to activate it and how to defuse it." The admiral said. "Remember, the explosives are your ticket out of the lagoon."

"You really think we're going to pull this off?" Douglas asked.

"I figure a ten percent chance."

"It doesn't matter to you either way, does it?"

"I don't want to see the Navy lose a good sub or a good crew, but no, not really. I've done my part," Tendrey said.

Douglas opened his satchel and pushed the two envelopes inside. *Two solid packages of proof,* he thought.

"Oh, Commander," the southerner said as Douglas pivoted toward the exit. "You'll have to be in and out of Truk by the 16th. Stein will brief you."

Douglas crossed the spread of grass outside the building to where the Willys had dropped him off. It and the ensign were gone.

CINCPAC Headquarters was a mile up the road. Swinging his satchel over his shoulder, Douglas started towards the command buildings. The Hawaiian sun was already beating down on the black pavement and the wind off the coral blue sea was just enough to move the palm leaves gently overhead. But he felt neither the sun nor the breeze. His mind was on last night and what she had said to him. "No matter what, you'll stay with me."

The 'no matter what' was too much. She had set her hook deep, reeled him in, and used him for shark bait.

The sharp metallic beep of a Willys horn startled him. The open vehicle skidded to the curb. "A ride, Commander?" the driver called.

Douglas glanced at the shoulder marks and saw the rank of lieutenant junior grade, but as he thanked him, he saw the man filling the uniform was Wagner.

The OSS man acknowledged Douglas' recognition of him. He crammed the Willys into gear and popped the clutch.

"You're a lieutenant now?"

"I am what I need to be," the agent told him as they drove to the base. "At the moment, I'm the bearer of bad news."

"Well, I've got great news. Tendrey just handed me his ass." He patted the satchel.

"Falsified orders to infiltrate the base at Truk. Signed, sealed, and delivered by him personally," the agent called Wagner said.

"How did you know?"

Now Wagner gave him a sidelong smirk. "You're kidding, right?"

"Oh yeah. It's your job."

"And it is also my job to tell you to hang on to those. You're going to need them."

"The hell I do. This is what you said you needed to hang the bastard. You needed proof. Shit, it is practically a signed affidavit," Douglas said.

Wagner slowed for two WACs crossing the street. He shifted, sped up, shifted, and sped up again. He was driving nowhere. Simply circling the base to talk without being overheard.

"It's not what I want, Commander, believe me," Wagner said.

"They expect me to put my crew in jeopardy?"

"Isn't that your job?"

"These don't tell me to attack the enemy. They tell me to deal with him."

"War is nothing if it is not a contradiction. The enemy of my enemy is my friend. Didn't George Washington say that?"

"I don't think so."

"Doesn't matter. What I've been told is that retrieving the package for the Chinese has become extremely important," Wagner said. "Look, we have the forgeries from Tendrey. The rope is secure around his neck. Whether we pull it tight now or when you return, it doesn't matter."

They drove a few blocks in silence until Douglas finally said, "Tendrey transferred a crewman to my boat. What do you suggest I do about him?"

"He did?" Wagner chuckled. "I am sure he's just there to keep tabs on you." The OSS agent pulled to the curb. "What time do you set sail, Commander?"

Douglas suddenly realized they were in front of CINCPAC Headquarters. "Midnight?"

"I'll be there before you shove off. What do you need? An ensign? A petty officer?" he asked.

"You're not kidding," Douglas said, figuring that the agent could arrange any transfer orders he needed and with any rank he wanted. "My boat has a complete crew."

"How about a Naval Observer assigned directly by Washington? The old boys at the State Department want to know exactly how their Silent Service is operating," he said.

"Thanks for the ride, Lieutenant."

"See you tonight, Skipper," he said as he snapped a salute.

Douglas watched as the OSS man pulled from the curb. He wondered if it was necessary to have the agent aboard. What more could Tendrey's man be there for than to observe? *Pawn for pawn*, Douglas thought. Still, he did not like the game being played aboard his submarine.

•   •   •

"Kwajalein is on its knees, Commander. The Japs never saw us coming," Captain Linus Stein said, slapping his hands together and rubbing them palm against palm as though he were trying to set them on fire. "The first reports came in this morning."

Stein was a short, square man, carrying fifty pounds of excess at the belt line. A grey-haired veteran easily excited by the battle reports. He moved around his desk with the spring in his walk of a new father.

He pulled out his ever-present checkered handkerchief, blew his nose and pushed the crumbled cloth back into his pocket. "We'll flatten the place by dusk," he said, rubbing his hands again.

"That's good to hear, sir," Douglas said as he stood stiff-backed in the center of the squadron commander's office.

"It's great news, Douglas, but I have better," Stein said. "They're pushing Operation Hailstone up by eight weeks. They hit on the 16th."

"Sir?"

"Truk Lagoon. The bastards think it's invincible. We'll see."

"Yes sir. I've heard the scuttlebutt. But no one thought we could move so fast."

"Exactly. No one here believes it. That means the Imperial Navy won't expect it either. ComSubPac is issuing orders. As soon as we secure the Marshalls, the task force will head directly towards the atoll," Stein said. "I'm aware you've been having trouble with one of your engines, Doug, but we need the *Mako* at Truk before the operation starts.

"The *Searaven* and the *Darter* are going to be on lifeguard duty just to the north and south of Truk. They want the *Mako* east of the lagoon. Our flyboys are going to run into a lot of Zeros coming off those islands," Stein said.

"It's going to be tight, sir," Douglas said. His mind was figuring at least twelve days to travel the four thousand miles across the Pacific.

"I know. That's why the orders are specific. You are not to engage any enemy vessels with anti-submarine capabilities. Don't get me wrong, if it's easy prey, take it, but Operation Hailstone outweighs everything on this patrol. If we can take Truk, the rest of the Pacific is only a matter of time," he said, still grinning. "Here," he scooped the patrol orders off his desk. "Good luck, Commander."

"Thank you, sir. You can be sure we'll have the *Mako* on station by the sixteenth," Douglas promised. He tucked the package under his arm, saluted, and briskly headed out of the office.

In the waiting room, Douglas stopped and set his satchel on the edge of one of the secretary's desks. He opened it and shoved his patrol orders inside.

"Oh, Commander Bovan," a slender, brown-haired secretary called to him from down the hallway.

"Yes, ma'am?"

"Margaret was looking for you. I think she's outside," the woman said, keeping her face down, too shy in front of the tall lieutenant commander with the heart-stopping eyes.

"Thank you," Douglas said. *What the hell did O'Tullie want*, he wondered.

The yellow Packard rested at the curb, its engine crackling. Margaret sat alone in the driver's seat, taking in the sun. Wearing thick sunglasses, a pink scarf covered her hair and her thin right arm dangled lazily over the door.

"Oh," she said, startled when Douglas touched her shoulder.

"Looking for me?"

The surprise turned to a frown. "You're a jerk."

"That's common knowledge."

"I mean it. She's at my house crying her head off, Douglas," Margaret said directly.

"She has reason to," he said, leaning against the long swooping fender.

"She wouldn't tell me what went on between you two, but you have to talk to her." Margaret put her hand on his arm. "Please, Doug. She knows you're leaving tonight."

Douglas glared at Nimitz's secretary wondering how much she knew. But he realized her kinship with the Chinese assistant to the ambassador went only so far. Margaret might think they were kindred spirits, but Mimi was here with a surreptitious purpose.

"Please."

1130 hours by his watch. He tried to remember when his boat was supposed to get fuel. Alberts could take care of it, of course, so there was no excuse there. "All right," he said, finally.

"Oh, I knew you would," Margaret sparkled. "You drive. I need to get back to the office."

Doug circled the car's long hood as Margaret slid across the bench seat.

"She'll be so happy."

Douglas had his doubts. He set his satchel between them and climbed behind the banjo-sized wheel. He had several things to ask Lai Ming. The first was about Machinist's mate Hawthorne.

20

MOEN ISLAND, TRUK LAGOON, 1986

BRIAN FOUND HIS SUITCASES on the long wooden table at the back of the cinderblock terminal building. The two-man ground crew had piled them there along with everyone else's luggage, a dozen cargo boxes and three wire cages of domestic chickens.

He joined Leslie in the center of the terminal where two young airport attendants nearly came to blows trying to be the first to gather the American woman's suitcases and offer any other aid she might need during her stay on the island.

Leslie, however, focused on the flow of people in and out of the building's doors. Rising onto her toes, she scanned the faces as she clutched her hands nervously.

"See him?" Brian asked. He set his bags with hers.

"Not yet." She worked a corner of her lip.

"Are you sure he knew you changed your flight?"

"I sent a telegram," she said. "Maybe he didn't get it?"

"I imagine things work slower out here," he said with a shrug. He felt the need to ease her worry. "Let's grab a taxi. If he doesn't show before we leave, you can call from your hotel."

"I guess so," she said as she drew her carry-on to her shoulder.

"Miss Maetani?" a voice rose from across the terminal.

Two police officers approached. The one who had called out was tall and awkwardly thin, so much so his blue uniform looked to hang on wired bones, like a medical school skeleton standing in the corner. Brian half expected to hear the clatter.

He was followed by a second officer, who was a head-snapping contrast. Several inches shorter, the man was as broad as a truck with a thick face and a neck of rolled muscle. His forearms were a canvas for tribal tattoos.

"Yes?" she swirled around as if performing.

"Good afternoon, ma'am. I am Captain Honma, with the Truk District Police. Will you come with us, please?" He said solemnly. "The sergeant will gather your luggage."

Leslie stiffened. "Is there a problem?"

"Better we discuss things at the station, ma'am. It'll be more comfortable."

Brian saw she was searching. Not for answers, but for questions. It was in the way she stiffened her back and planted her heels. She could not fathom the idea of a police officer wanting her to go with him.

Brian noticed the second officer gathering her suitcases. "Hold on," he told the sergeant. He stepped closer to Leslie. "I am sorry, Captain. We're just coming off an eleven-hour flight. Can this wait until tomorrow?" Brian asked.

"You are?"

"Brian Brock. And this is *Doctor* Maetani," he corrected the officer.

"Oh," Honma apologized. "I am sorry, Doctor. I didn't realize."

"It doesn't matter. Is there something wrong?"

Honma's manner softened, and for the first time, Brian recognized despair in his hollowed face.

"Better to talk somewhere else," he said. He turned to his sergeant. "Ty, find us an empty office. Anyone's office. We just need a few minutes."

Leslie looked to Brian nervously. He smiled for her. It might have taken the sergeant forty seconds or forty minutes to find the small, closet-sized office with a wobbly table, and a yellowing chart of the lagoon pinned to the wall, Brian did not know. All he remembered was how dread had stiffened Leslie's joints as they followed the captain.

"What's happened?" she asked directly as Brian lowered her into a steel chair.

Honma glanced at his second. "Sergeant. Gather their bags into the truck, please."

The muscular officer hesitated. Brian noticed he was staring, not at Leslie, but at him. A hard glare of frustration.

"There was an accident" the captain was saying. "A diving accident."

"My father?"

"I am sorry for your loss," the captain said honestly.

"No. Oh God, no." She put her delicate hand to her mouth, muffling a cry. She closed her eyes and pressed her face into Brian's shoulder.

"We found your address at Henry's house. I sent a telegram," the captain said.

Leslie nodded automatically, barely registering the conversation.

"She stopped in Hawaii for a few days," Brian told him. "You said it was a diving accident?"

"On one of the deeper wrecks," Honma confirmed. "We think he became disoriented and couldn't find the dropline to his decompression air tanks. If you stay too long on the bottom, you can get sick. It is like getting drunk."

"Nitrogen narcosis. I know the effects."

"You dive?"

Deeper than you can imagine, Brian thought, but said simply. "Yeah, I have."

Outside, Honma led them to a tan Land Rover with the powder blue flag of Micronesia on the driver's and front passenger's door. The sergeant slouched behind the wheel, an unlit cigarette in his lips, watching them approach.

The captain leaned in. "Take them to the house."

Before he climbed in, Brian lowered his voice and asked, "Do you know the wreck he was diving?"

"We know nearly all the wrecks, Mr. Brock. We know their names. Where they rest," the captain said with a shrug. "When you live amongst gravestones, you get to know the residents." Honma glanced into the truck, making sure Leslie was not listening. "No one had seen Henry for several days until we found his body washed up on the west side of Uman."

"You do know the wreck?"

"There are several off the reef," Honma said. "Everyone liked Henry. I liked him," he pressed. "He was not only interested in the lagoon but also our people. I think that is why they granted him permits no one else could get."

"For collecting artifacts?"

"Anything he wanted," Honma nodded. "My lagoon is a very tranquil place, Mr. Brock. An accident like this is upsetting for everyone." He held the door as Brian climbed in. "Come to my office when you are ready. Unfortunately, there are papers to sign," he said, then tapped the truck's roof.

As the sergeant drove, Leslie rested her shoulder against Brian's. By the time they reached the main two-lane road that circled the island, he could feel her shaking as she cried quietly. He gently set his hand on hers.

A fifteen-minute drive south and the sergeant turned onto a dirt road leading to the water. It wound through a thicket of mangroves and palm trees. At the end, it became a broad sandy beach sprinkled over the top of an ancient reef. He turned left, maneuvered the Land Rover's narrow tires over the natural roadway.

A hundred yards down, on the opposite side of a crooked finger of land, a small white, tin-roofed house appeared. Wedged tightly into the thick foliage, it stood out of place, as if a storm surge had swept it ashore.

"Here," the sergeant stopped at the sun-bleached stairs that dropped into the sand from a raised patio deck.

Leslie climbed from the truck and, without a word, drifted toward the house.

"You have the keys?" Brian asked the officer.

"Keys?" The sergeant laughed. "That's mainland talk. No need to lock anything in the lagoon," he said as he pulled the suitcases from the truck. He dropped them into the sand. "Americans built this place. The army corps in the 1970s," he told Brian. "Not many big houses like this."

Brian moved Leslie's luggage next to the sliding glass door that separated the patio from the interior of the house. On a better day, he would have appreciated the view, but in the moment, his focus was on the girl.

"I'm sorry, I should help." Leslie turned from the patio's railing.

"I've got this. Why don't you go inside," he told her as he tugged open the glass door.

"Shame about Henry," the sergeant said as he slammed the tailgate closed and handed Brian his flight bag. "The bends can be very painful. A terrible way to die."

"I can't imagine a good way," he said.

"Why did she come?"

"He sent for her," Brian said casually.

The officer's brow deepened. "Bad timing," he said. "The captain's wife brought food when she heard the daughter was coming. It's inside."

Brian walked him to the driver's door. "I'm sorry, but I never caught your name, Sergeant."

"Wuun. It is an old, native name. A pure name." He slipped behind the wheel.

"Can you tell me, Sergeant Wuun, is there a place to rent a boat and maybe some diving gear?" Brian asked as he leaned on the truck door.

The sergeant studied him for a moment, as if weighing his response. "Henry had a small skiff he rented with the house. There is an old Jeep too. It's parked around back. The boat is docked at the end of the green pier. Look for George. He will help you." Wuun cranked over the Land Rover and pulled away with a kick of sand.

Brian watched the truck snake its way down the beach. It turned into the grove and disappeared.

Mounting the steps, Brian took in the lagoon. The cool aqua-blue of the shallows darkened quickly as the sandy bottom fell away. Beyond, he saw a line of seething whitewash where the swells confronted an inner reef of staghorn coral. After that, the palette of deepening blues revealed the increasing depths of the lagoon.

"Leslie," he called, as he stepped into the house. Moving first through the kitchen, he ambled further along the hallway.

The first door on the right was a bedroom converted to a workroom. Inside, Leslie's father had installed a long workbench, a vice and shelves for power tools. Lining the other side were several scuba tanks stacked like a core of fireplace logs. Near the bench, Brian saw an underwater oxyacetylene cutting torch. It was a portable system with two stubby tanks, one for oxygen and the other for acetylene gas, and a six-foot hose and brass nozzle.

He found Leslie in the next room. Another converted bedroom, this one a study, although it looked more like a cluttered deposit for books and cardboard boxes. Against one wall was a floor to ceiling shelving unit filled with more books and various artifacts from the lagoon: pressure wheels, levers from ships' helms, an empty cannon shell, and broken dishes of fine China. Each had a crust of dried coral covering it.

The center of the room was dominated by a large metal desk. Behind it, a second sliding glass door opened onto a second wooden patio deck. This one was much smaller and stretched into the mangrove trees.

"Are you okay?" Brian asked her gently.

She nodded unconvincingly as she circled the room looking at the alien objects scattered about. Leaning against the wall were several fishing poles and Hawaiian spears with trident barbs.

Leslie picked one up, thoughtlessly tapped her finger to the needle-sharp point. She grimaced at the prick of pain. Seeing a small picture frame on the desk, she sat down and drew her knees to her chest.

"The only picture on his desk," she said passing it to him.

It was a black-and-white photograph of Leslie and her father at her college graduation. In the photo, a younger Leslie had her arms wrapped around her father. His face was small and round and already creased with age. An unyielding sort of man, Brian guessed as he saw Henry Maetani staring directly into the camera without a smile. No, there was a smile, a subtle turn at the edges of his mouth revealing his pride.

"I should have flown straight through. I don't know why I stopped in Hawaii."

"It wouldn't have mattered."

"It might have. The captain sent me a telegraph. He didn't know I had left New York. If I had come straight, I would have been here."

"The accident happened before, Leslie. Before you left the mainland."

She shook her head, tears welling. "You can't know…"

"They didn't find him right away."

She closed her eyes and let her head fall back against the chair. "I don't know why I waited for him to ask me to come here. I should've just showed up."

"My mom died last week," Brian said, and was immediately sorry he had, as it sounded self-serving. "I don't know why I am telling you. It's just that, I guess—" He stumbled. "I mean, I got to spend a few weeks with her, but it wasn't enough. He knew you were coming to see him, and he had this." He handed her the picture. "The only photo he kept around. That matters."

Leslie took the frame and wandered to the sliding glass door. She walked onto the deck. He followed.

"You're welcome to..." she began, shyly. "I mean, you don't mind. I'd rather not be here alone."

"Well, you're in luck. I don't have a hotel reservation."

"Good." She stared at him, then her lip quivered, and she cried again.

"Why don't you lay down? The captain's wife left food. I'll see what I can put together."

"You can cook?" Leslie asked, as if desperate to find a new subject.

"If I am starving," he said as he walked her to the bedroom at the end of the hall.

From the ceiling, a white gossamer bug net hung like a misty cloud.. She slipped through it and fell into the rumpled sheets.

"Door open or closed?"

"Open, please," she said, her voice just above a whisper.

•   •   •

On the single burner of a battered Army-issued propane stove, Brian fried four thick slices of Spam in an iron skillet. He discovered a large cache of the gelatinous canned meat in a flimsy cupboard in the kitchen. He remembered the small gooey bricks from his childhood when his mother had invented a thousand ways to serve the pinkish pork by-product for breakfast, lunch, and Sunday dinner.

On the low table by the front door, he found the two wicker baskets left by the captain's wife. She had filled one with fresh yams, mangos, star fruit and papaya. The second included a small bag of dry white rice, some unfamiliar spices, and a half-loaf of American Wonder bread. She had also left several jugs of fresh water and, to his pleasure, four squat bottles of Primo beer.

Once he had seared the Spam, Brian turned off the flame and stepped quietly to the bedroom.

Leslie was asleep under the whispery veil. She had changed into a cotton tee-shirt and white shorts and laid across the bed like a Persian cat enjoying the luxuries of its kingdom.

She had stacked her suitcases on the floor between the bed and the wall. Over a chair, she had tossed the dress she wore on the plane. Brian eased the door shut.

He made a white bread sandwich, sprinkled the meat with some peppery spice, opened a beer and carried his dinner into the makeshift study.

He flipped on the desk lamp and perused the dusty bookshelf. The array of American paperbacks lay across the shelf in a chaotic jumble. Amongst them were books in Japanese and a few written in Filipino. He assumed the subjects were all the same.

Across the wide desk, Leslie's father had erected stacks of textbooks about the Second World War with several specific to the Pacific theater. These too, were in English and Japanese.

Brian sat where Leslie had been, took a bite of his sandwich, and glanced around the room.

Across from the chaotic shelves, there were two cheaply framed posters on the wall. One was an advertisement for Pan Am Airways, the other a picture of a mountain that was either in Wyoming or Germany. The large wall directly across from the desk, however, was empty. Except, he noticed, a large nail hammered into the center.

Brian sipped the Primo. *Something was off,* he thought. He held the last corner of his sandwich in his teeth and yanked open the lower drawer of the desk. Empty.

"Find anything interesting?" Leslie asked as she leaned against the door.

"Just this." He held up the beer bottle. "Your dad must have had connections. Alcohol is only sold in restaurants."

"No alcohol?"

"You read the brochures."

"Not well enough, I guess."

"Did you sleep?" he asked.

She shook her head.

"You hungry?"

"Maybe a little. I'm not sure."

"There's Spam?"

"Please, anything but that."

Brian laughed. "Fresh fruit."

"Perfect."

Brian stepped past her as he circled the desk. "You said your dad was doing research?"

"That was his passion," she said, following him to the kitchen. "Actually, more of an obsession. He came here every summer."

In the shallow sink, Brian washed the mangos. "Maybe it's nothing, but the study only has generic books."

"What do you mean?"

He found a paring knife in the drawer. "Here," he said, passing her a papaya and the blade. "Don't cut yourself," he said.

With a smirk, she took the knife and expertly removed the fruit's thick, rubbery skin.

"They're basic history books on the war. Where are specific ones? The scientific papers and official reports? For that matter, where are his charts and notes? If he's been doing research here for years, then where is all his work?"

•　　　•　　　•

At the Blue Lagoon, a one-room restaurant with three tables and a bar hammered together with splintering driftwood, Wuun sat engulfed in his own cigarette cloud. A three-bladed fan, caged like a cockatiel, hummed in the corner.

The sergeant stretched his back and shoulders in boredom as he eyed the dried shark jaws hanging over the bar's mirror like a line of barbed portholes. Blacktip. Reef. Grey. Another Reef. Another Grey and a pair of much larger jaws that were once owned by a pair of Tiger sharks. He was certain of those because he had speared them himself.

Was it time? Wuun glanced at the wall clock. Almost. He double-checked the payphone in the back room near the rancid bathroom with the missing door handle. No one was using it, and no one would. He was the last patron in the bar. He dropped his cigarette into the ring of gold at the bottom of his glass and sauntered to the telephone.

"Tendrey," Wuun barked. He did not like the assistant who had picked up the other end. He was always snide and abrupt. Wuun could hear the passing of the phone, a shuffle of papers and a wet, sickly cough.

"Yes," the old man answered sharply.

"Your man is here. And he has brought the daughter."

"Daughter? Whose daughter?" Tendrey switched the phone to his better ear.

"The Professor's daughter. The diver's daughter."

"Jesus Christ," the admiral spat. "Where the hell did she come from? My god," the old man howled through the phone line.

"I don't know but they arrived together and are staying at Henry's house."

There was a long pause on the other end of the line.

"What do you want me to do?" the sergeant asked.

"No. Don't do anything. Not yet. Just watch them and let me know what they do."

"I understand," Wuun said.

"Mother fuc…" Was that the last thing the sergeant heard before the line went dead.

21

MOEN ISLAND, TRUK LAGOON, 1986

L ESLIE WAS QUIET all morning. Brian understood. Yesterday was devastating. She had come to the lagoon with expectations. With hopes of reuniting with her father. To ask what had happened to them and reverse course. Leslie had flown across the world to find common ground and mend their wounds. Now she would bury him here.

She went to bed at midnight, no longer able to fight off the day. Brian took up the rattan lounger in the corner of the front living room. The tropical evening was warm with a breeze that ebbed back and forth, carrying a scent of sweet hibiscus. In the distance, the ever-present drums of the surf were soothing.

Still, he laid awake listening to the squeak of the steel spring bed as Leslie tossed from one side to the other. He knew it was partly his fault. He had foolishly brought up her father's missing notes. She did not need questions that might never find answers.

Now, under the midmorning sun, they drove toward the town in the old gray Jeep with the missing right fender. Brian had found the keys on a nail in the workroom.

He brushed away the fallen palms from the seats, sat down and twisted the ignition key. The little engine took its time to start, but it finally relented and chugged to life. As Brian steered the Jeep out of the soft sand at the back of the house, and to the hardened path between the beach and mangroves, chips of rust fell from the undercarriage.

"It's nice today," Leslie said as they headed along the narrow brown road lined by the lush jungle on one side and the lagoon on the other. There were fishing skiffs drifting outside the reef, their crew swinging small nets over their heads like cowboys with their lassos.

With the sweep of her hand, she unwound the loose twist in her hair and let it billow over her shoulder. She wore a simple white blouse buttoned low and tailored lime-green shorts that fell mid-thigh on her muscular legs. He tried not to stare.

Brian wore what he found in his supplied suitcases: khaki slacks, a light tan shirt, mahogany brown belt and matching deck shoes. Mimi's taste was probably Vogue Magazine perfect, but he felt as if he was Hemingway on safari. "We'll have to find the local store or the fish market," he said. "Otherwise, it's mouthwatering Spam."

She wrinkled her nose as she kept her windswept hair from her face. "You've been like a knight in shining armor, you know. And I've been the useless damsel in distress. I'm not normally like this."

"Don't worry. This is hardly *normal*," he said as he slowed for a wobbly pickup truck ahead of them.

"I guess not," she agreed. "But it's not an excuse to ruin your vacation."

"You're not," he said, suddenly regretting he had not told her more. His gallantry, he realized, was self-serving.

"Yes, I am, and I feel horrible. You don't have to come to the police station. I can go."

"Are you sure?"

"Honestly? No," she said with a nervous chuckle. "But I can't ask you for that too. I really can't."

He looked at her through the corner of his eye. "Tell you what, let's grab breakfast. Your treat," he said. "Then you can decide."

Leslie nodded, seemingly happy to put off the decision.

As they neared the town center, more thatched houses appeared on the inland side of the road. Many stood on thick pillars like spider crabs, ready to walk into the surf.

As the road widened to a distinct two-lane street, Brian slowed the Jeep. The town was smaller than Brian had imagined. He knew the dozens of war ships scattered throughout the lagoon made Truk an epicenter for sport and wreck diving. He expected to see diving shops lining the roadway along with fancy hotels and expensive restaurants, all feeding off the hordes of smiling tourists.

Instead, the main road arching toward the harbor was edged with small one- and two-story buildings painted in creamy whites and pastel blues. Most of the two-stories had small balconies overhanging the street and the calm bay.

Seeing a small roadside sign announce a hotel restaurant, Brian pulled to the curb in front of the Truk Stop Hotel. The white three-story building with the red-trimmed roof sat on the edge of the lagoon directly opposite a small fishing pier. Painted on the wall next to the open lobby was the word 'Vacancy' and next to that, a small wooden sign that said simply, 'Today.'

Entering the lobby, Brian had not realized how bright the tropical sun had been until he felt the cool air of the dimly lit interior. Leslie lifted her sunglasses and rested them on her head.

A robust woman with thick curly hair, lowered her magazine and grinned. "You need a room?"

"Thank you, no. Is the restaurant open?" Brian asked as he glanced toward the single large room across the lobby. There were several tables, most of them empty.

"Sure, sure, go in. Boggy!" she called over their heads and a young boy dressed in tattered jeans and a starched white shirt appeared at the entrance, menus in hand.

"Two?" he said, his eyes locking onto hers.

Leslie nodded. "Please."

The boy's smile widened. "Let me seat you outside. It's always much nicer outside with the breeze," he said, leading them through the tables, out a narrow door and onto the wooden veranda. "This good?" he asked.

"Fine, thank you," Brian said.

Boggy opened a menu for Leslie. "Anything to drink? Beer? Coffee?"

"Do you have orange juice?" Leslie asked.

"We have fresh papaya."

"That sounds good," Leslie said and Boggy nodded, happy that she had taken his suggestion.

"Coffee, please," Brian asked.

When the boy left the table, Brian laughed. "I am not getting my coffee."

"He's cute." She smiled, and for a moment, it was the smile he had seen on the plane, before they landed, before the police captain called to her.

Brian watched the scatter of anchored boats bobbing in the slow rolling swells that had eased past the distant reefs. On a large ketch moored near shore, a bikini-clad girl scaled the aft mast, walked gingerly to the end of the boom and dove into the lagoon. It was a beautiful sight. The dive itself was awkward, but the act radiated with playful foolishness.

North from the restaurant's deck, Brian could see the cluster of buildings along the thoroughfare of the central harbor. A three-hundred-foot length of splintering oil-soaked timber and unsure pylons, Baker's Pier, jutted from the beach.

Along its length, both expensive yachts and shabby local fishing boats shared cleats and fuel lines. He could just make out the busy figures of the fisherman emptying their morning catch of shark and stingray into wheelbarrows to be hurried to the local markets and restaurants.

"How many do you think died here?" Leslie asked suddenly.

"What?"

"On all these wrecks? How many soldiers do you think were killed?"

"At the height of the war, there were forty thousand men here. The lagoon was Japan's primary base beyond the home islands. I don't think anyone knows how many men were lost here."

"What about the survivors?"

"Most starved," he said solemnly. "Along with a large portion of the islanders."

Leslie looked across the beach. "He never talked about it," she said. "I remember he had nightmares. That's what made him drink and kept him angry. By the time I was a teenager, we hardly spoke. I never thought about this and what he went through."

"You said it yourself. You were a teenager. Tell me what teenager thinks their parents had a life before they showed up?"

She managed a weak smile. "It's nobody's fault. Certainly not his," she said, trying to smile. "I have to go to the police station and get that over with," she said, as if there was strength and resolve in her words.

"Are you sure you don't want me to come?"

"I was feeling pretty sure about it earlier."

"I don't mind."

"A visit to the morgue," she said, tears welling. "Bet you didn't see that in the tourist brochure." She pulled the paper napkin from under the cheap silverware, rubbed her nose.

"No," he said softly.

"I can't ruin any more of your vacation."

"You're not because this really isn't a vacation. It's more like…" he hesitated. "Research."

She turned to him, her head tilted slightly. "Fish?"

"No. Not fish." He did not want to deceive her, but he hesitated to say too much. First her father's death, then a confession that his own father was tied to the *Kuma Maru*, as well. That was too much for breakfast conversation.

Suddenly, Boggy appeared at the table with juice and coffee. The young boy took their orders for the house specialty, a tropical omelet with coconut, papaya and pineapple and a few minutes later, he brought it out. After they finished, he swept the plates from the table, lining them expertly along one arm. "My sister is the cook," he said, taking the last plate from in front of Brian.

"Please tell her she is an exceptional chef," Leslie said. "And you're an exceptional waiter."

"Thank you, thank you," he kept smiling ear-to-ear as he disappeared through the door.

Boggy's mother came out, pulled a chair from the next table and sat beside Leslie. "I'm very sorry about your father," she said. "Good man. Always polite."

"How did you know who I was?"

A grin crept onto the woman's face. "These islands not very big," she said. "He also come here a lot. Sometimes his friends stay in the hotel," she pointed over her head. "Your father was good to so many people around the island. We all liked when he came. Such a shame."

Boggy came back with the check, but his mother sent him away.

"Please, let me," Brian insisted.

She shook her head adamantly. "Your money is worth nothing here."

"Thank you," Leslie said.

"Anytime you come, you leave your wallet in the truck." She motioned to the Jeep. "And if you need anything, you ask for me, Rota."

"Thank you, Rota," Leslie said as they stood to leave.

"Sergeant Wuun said to find someone named George. Any idea where I might find him?" Brian asked.

"George. You find him in only two places, on top of the pier fishing or under the pier asleep."

As Brian inserted the ignition keys into the Jeep, he glanced at Leslie. "Are you ready?"

She nodded. "I promise, after this, I will leave you alone."

•   •   •

"Your father's personal belongings from the boat," Honma said as he set a cardboard box on the desk between them. "And my file for the accident."

Leslie reached out, but the captain held back. "Let Mr. Brock look. Please."

"I can handle it," she said, trying to sound firm, although it did not.

"There are photographs," the captain said as gently as he could.

Leslie shuddered. "Do I need to identify…"

Honma shook his head. "Henry has been coming to the lagoon for many years. There is no doubt," he said.

Leslie stared at the folder as if spellbound.

"Why don't you wait in the Jeep?" Brian said.

"Shouldn't I…?"

"I'll let you know if there is something," he said. He waited until she left the room before opening the folder. He immediately realized Honma had been right not to let her see its contents.

The black-and-white photograph showed the deformed figure of a man twisted from a painful death. His skin was bleach white and with the texture of toothpaste.

Scavengers of the reef had ripped away bits of his flesh. Blue damsels or butterfly fish or any of the hundreds of other species of fish had taken their share. No food source would be untouched. It could not be if the creatures of the lagoon were to ensure their own survival. *The sea is a vicious and beautiful place*, Brian thought.

"We found his body about ten feet up the beach in the mangroves. The night before, the tide was high. The wreck he anchored above is in about two hundred and seventy feet of water. My guess is that he was dead long before he reached the surface."

"How long was he missing?" Brian asked.

"About three days. He always dove alone, so no one can say when he went into the water."

Brian read over the report:

Hiro 'Henry' Maetani

Japanese - United States Citizen. Age. 62

Cause of death: Diving accident; air embolism. Buried at Moen Cemetery.

"You buried him?"

"This is the tropics, Mr. Brock," Honma shrugged apologetically. If Miss Maetani wishes to make other arrangements, we can exhume the body."

"I'll ask," he said as he closed the folder. He opened the box and took out a dive mask, a single fin, what remained of his wetsuit jacket and from a smaller envelope, his diver's watch, and a simple gold wedding ring.

"That's everything," Honma said.

"What about the rest of his gear?"

"His diving equipment is on his boat. We've kept it moored at the end of the pier."

"Did anyone go through his things at the house?"

Honma frowned. "There was no reason. And when I found the telegram that his daughter was coming, I assumed she would make arrangements," the captain said.

Brian dropped the diving gear back into the box. He slipped her father's watch and ring into his shirt pocket. "Thank you, Captain."

"Of course," the officer said as he held open the office door.

Brian stopped. "How do we get to the cemetery?"

"Our tradition is to bury our dead near our homes. We didn't know what Henry would have wanted, so we placed him up the mountain where his spirit could watch the lagoon for his friends."

Outside, Leslie sat in the Jeep, her head bowed staring at the cheap sandals she purchased at the Moana gift shop. *Why didn't I get the blue ones with the flowers,* she wondered, her thoughts purposely skipping about like a stone flung across a lake trying not to sink.

She did not hear the old man approach from the back of the Jeep, although he made a distinct effort to be heard, and to hear. He tapped the gravel lot of the police station with his bamboo cane as he neared. He hit the tire with the tip, heard the dull thud and stopped.

"Your father was Henry?" he asked, his voice low, but thick with the sound of slushy rocks.

Leslie was startled, both by his suddenly being next to her and by his shocking appearance. Hunched over slightly, the left sleeve of his frayed khaki shirt was rolled and pinned, hiding his missing left arm. His face was a frightening mosaic of scars that ran down his neck and disappeared beneath his collar. But most horrifying, was that his eyes too, had been the victims of his misfortune. From where they had once viewed the world, now only rutted lumps of sinewy flesh remained.

She gasped.

"Oh dear," the scarred man said with a half-hearted laugh. "I didn't mean to startle you."

"You didn't," she said. "I am sorry. My mind was elsewhere."

"Who could blame you finding out about your father as you have. I am so very sorry."

"You knew him?"

"Everyone knew Henry," the blind man said, his voice warm and caring. "But over the years, and a few warm bottles of beer, I like to think he and I became good friends."

The tears she had been trying to keep back suddenly rushed forward like a deluge of sorrow and regrets.

Hearing her, the man found her shoulder and squeezed it. "You should know, he spoke of you often. He was proud of his daughter the doctor." He patted her shoulder again, then slowly, he made his way down the street, tapping the sandy ground as he went.

•   •   •

At the island cemetery wedged in the green hills high above the lagoon, Leslie bowed head toward the weathered plank wood that stood at the grave's edge. Between her fingers, she held his watch and wedding ring. After several minutes, she moved to the plank and ran her hand over the two Japanese kanji symbols burnt into the wood.

Brian watched her sadly as he leaned against the Jeep where it was missing the fender. Turning, he scanned the lush valley that poured down the mountain and into the blue swirling waters. Truk had finally claimed a soul that had eluded it for forty years. He wondered if it had taken his father's or if the *Mako* had managed to slip out of the lagoon to start her eternal patrol somewhere else in the Pacific.

22

HONOLULU, HAWAII, 1944

MIMI HEARD the distinctive squeak of the Packard's brakes as it pulled into the driveway. She had been flipping the pages of the Evening Post, not reading, not seeing the photos. She noticed the cover art when she pulled the magazine from the dining table. A dalmatian mother sitting with her litter of puppies longingly watching a firetruck race away from the firehouse. Responsibility was the cover line along the bottom.

Was she being responsible? She wondered as she stared at the sketch. Was she honestly battling the enemy from the comforts of an American territory and in the trenches of cocktail parties wearing the battle fatigues of a Claire McCardell evening gown?

It did not seem so. With the car's return, she remembered the pains of duty. It was past two o'clock in the afternoon and she was still in her cotton nightdress. Breakfast and lunch were combined into a cup of coffee and a single piece of toast. Beyond that, she had put little effort into the day.

She would have to apologize to Margaret. Her new friend had sat up with her all night, trying to comfort her tears. It was easy for the Naval secretary to guess it had everything to do with Douglas, but Mimi could not say why.

She set the magazine aside, wiped her puffy red eyes and rushed to the door. She would take Margaret to dinner in the mountains, Mimi decided. And she would explain what had happened the night before. Or at least, what she could.

God, she thought. *This was supposed to be an official mission.* What had happened? How could she have let herself become involved with one of the primary objectives? How could she fall for him so quickly, so easily?

Instead of Margaret flinging open the door, Mimi was met by a sharp insistent knock.

"Why is he on my submarine?" Douglas demanded as he stepped inside.

"Douglas?" She moved to hug her arms around him.

He held her off and closed the door. "Who is he? And why is he on my boat?"

She saw the darkness in his face her delight to see him vanished in a breath. "I don't know what you're talking about."

"I got a new crewman yesterday. Tendrey transferred him over," he snapped. "Did you put a spy on my sub?"

"No," she gasped, tears rising. "I don't know anything about him, Douglas, honest."

"Honest? What's honest? What have you told me since we met that is honest?" He marched further into the house. "Has it all been a setup?"

"No." She fell onto the couch, her face in her hands.

Douglas let out his breath. He sat beside her. "You really didn't know?"

"I met the admiral only twice before and the ambassador, he does not tell me all his plans."

Douglas sat rubbing his hands together. "You should have told me."

Mimi dried her eyes with the back of her hand. "I don't wear a uniform, but my duties are just as clear as yours. I was supposed to find an American submarine captain I thought would help us. To get to know him, and judge if he can be trusted to do what we were asking." She forced a smile. "I am glad you told them no." She caught his face in her hands. "I cannot bear the thought of losing you."

Douglas bolted upright. "They are sending someone else," he said. "Who?"

"I am not sure," she said. "I heard Admiral Tendrey mentioned the *Shark*."

"Burkie? Jesus. He can't handle something like this. It'll be a suicide run, for sure."

"Aren't they all?" She said as she fiddled with the fold of her nightdress. "I made a promise to Doctor Zdansky. I would get his fossils back. They were his life's work."

"Tell him it's impossible. They're gone. Just like everything in this war, they're lost.

"I wish I could," she said softly. "But he died a few days after hearing we lost them to the enemy."

Douglas walked to the window that overlooked the backyard. It was a sea of roses, red and pink and white. Another contradiction to his assessment of Margaret O'Tullie. "I don't know how your boss managed it, but my orders already send me to Truk."

"But you said…" Her eyes darted across his face.

"I am not stepping aside so they can send Burk. I'll get your national treasure." Douglas said. "But you promise me one thing. You don't leave Honolulu until I get back."

"I don't understand."

"Not a word to anyone, not your ambassador and especially not Tendrey. But promise me."

"You won't tell me why?"

"No," Douglas said sternly.

"I promise," she said. "But what about the man on your submarine?"

"I'll worry about him once we're at sea."

"When we planned the rendezvous, and the ambassador was receiving the secret communications, I never thought about the men who would actually have to go," she said, her voice low.

He eased into her, his arms slipping around her body. "We'll be in and out of the lagoon before anyone realize it."

She leaned into him, her delicate shoulder fitting into his chest like the second piece of a precise puzzle. Pieces meant to fit. She turned his face and kissed him.

Rising slightly, she pushed him back onto the couch, their lips never parting. Hands fumbling, she released the buttons of his shirt. Her heart thundered, matching the pounding in his.

His shirt disappeared and her fingers swept across the soft hairs of his chest. Slowly, gently, she kissed his sun-darkened skin of his neck and felt the catch in his breath.

She unclasped his leather belt as she felt his hands at the edge of her cotton nightdress. He lifted the veneer over her head, and she closed her eyes.

Suddenly, he stopped. "Wait," he breathed.

"You don't want?" she whispered.

"Oh, I want," Douglas said honestly as he eased himself from beneath her. "I want very much, but I can't. I..."

Mimi straightened her nightshirt, suddenly feeling the heat of shame in her cheeks. "You don't think I was told to..." she shuttered.

"No," he twisted around. "I don't think that at all. It's just that, I mean. I haven't been a great guy in the past."

"You mean your extramarital affairs?"

"You know about those?"

"I know of four of them. But I suspect your file is not complete."

"Four? I can live with that."

Mimi frowned.

"My marriage, it's not much of a marriage. Just so you know," he admitted. "It's just that you're... It is not like you're a local girl, or one of the nurses, or a..."

"No need for comparisons, thank you."

He chuckled. "I want you to know you're not them. And you are definitely not her. You're, I don't know..."

"Different? Exotic?" she smiled slyly.

"Those things, yeah, but you also make me think about after the war. For the longest time I've tried not to. It's not healthy."

"You think you are going to die?" she asked, sadly.

"It makes it easier to accept," he said. "I'd rather be pleasantly surprised if I don't. But now you, you throw that all out of wake."

Mimi laughed. "Are you really sorry I involved you?"

"Not really. This mission or another, if it is my final patrol, at least I got time with you. And for that, I'd swim into Truk."

She laughed again, a sweet song of silver bells. "I made you a promise. Now make me one," she said. "Come back to me."

Douglas swept a loose web of hair behind her ear. This was the moment she would remember most distinctly. His eyes held her with the warmth of a sunrise, swept her up and made her safe. "That's my plan," he whispered.

"Let's make sure," she said, her voice deep with purpose. She rose from the cushion, pushing him into the couch with both hands and a sudden boldness. Her mouth absorbed his. This time, as she reached for his leather belt, she would not be discouraged.

•   •   •

Seaman Lewis stared at the sparkling yellow Packard with envy. "Fucking Japs," he mumbled. He did not care that Admiral Tendrey had told him Lai Ming was the assistant to the Chinese Ambassador. Chinese or Japanese, they were all the same. And the thought that a Navy man was banging the woman disgusted him.

Lewis watched the house from down the street, crouched uncomfortably in the bench seat of his father's Ford pickup truck.

The admiral had assigned him to the commander because he knew Honolulu better than most locals, all the back streets, all the dirt paths, all the one-way alleys. Growing up on a small dairy farm, he had accompanied his father's delivery runs since he was six years old.

Lewis knew Honolulu all right, and now he was planning the quickest route back to the base. Tendrey would not only be interested in how Bovan was spending his time, but of his extended ride in a Jeep driven by an ancient-looking Lieutenant Junior Grade.

•   •   •

Douglas traced the line of her backbone with his index finger, stopping at the dimple above her bottom. He kissed her there, causing her to giggle. It made him laugh.

"Oh, you're laughing at me," Mimi said, pouting. As she rolled across the double bed, her long hair unraveled over the pillows like a bolt of silk.

"Yes, I'm laughing," Douglas said, slipping his arm around her waist and pulling her back. He uncovered her breast and kissed her there.

"I've changed my mind," Mimi said as she snuggled against him, her left arm across his chest, their legs intertwined. "You can't go."

"Too late," he said.

She studied him for a moment and sensed he was not telling her something. "There is more, isn't there? Something you are not saying."

Douglas kissed the top of her head. "All that matters is that we keep our promises."

She held him tight. "Okay," she said, breathing in the natural fragrance of his body. It stirred her inside. "My mother used to read me poems when I was a little girl." She turned to him. "I remember my favorite. 'The white crane on the highest branch spreads his wings wide. Below, the mountain is still. Both wait for sunset.'"

"What's it mean?" Douglas asked.

"That some things are inevitable. Whether you stand to the side and watch or try with all your heart to change them," she said, sitting up on her elbows. "I have spent my life studying the Peking Man. What he ate, what he drank, if he used fire or made tools. They suspect he was a cannibal." she grinned as if humored by the idea. "I don't think he was."

"They're that important to you?"

"The fossils are my country's history. They are a part of everyone's history, if the world would only stop killing each other and recognize it," she said. "Now, you are all that is important to me."

As he kissed the tip of her nose, her cheek, her neck, her shoulder, she wrapped her arms about him and drew him closer. She lifted her hips as she used her legs to guide him to her, to welcome him again.

Through the delicate curtains that hung across the open window, the tropical scents drifted in from the early afternoon. The sun followed the breeze inside, lighting the white sheets of the bed as they made love.

"I cannot fall for you, Douglas," Mimi whispered in his ear in a moment they were catching their breath.

"No," Douglas turned to her. "And I can't fall for you," he said. He kissed her right cheek, kissed her on the left. The tip of her nose. Her forehead and chin. "But when I return, I won't be able to help myself."

Mimi took a deep breath and smiled contently.

Douglas looked to the window and saw the softening light. "What time does Margaret come home?"

"Not until late afternoon."

He lifted his wristwatch from the nightstand. "Damn, it's almost 1500. Three o'clock."

"No. It can't be," Mimi twisted to see.

"Come on," he said, swinging his legs off the bed and working his pants up his legs. "You have to drive me back."

Panic suddenly shot through her. "I'm not going to see you again."

"Not for a while." He swooped into his shirt. "You stay in touch with O'Tullie, and she'll let you know when I am back at Pearl."

Mimi slid off the bed and pressed her naked body against him. On her tippy toes, she kissed him again. She helped him dress before she put on a simple red sundress and high heel shoes.

"Don't you wear anything under that?" Douglas asked.

"Are you in a rush or not?"

"I am but…"

"You'll just have to remember how you left me. And what I won't be wearing when you get back," she teased.

Neither of them noticed the Ford truck as its engine started the same time Mimi turned over the Packard's straight eight-cylinder. Nor did they see it pull away from the curb and follow them down the street and onto the main highway.

The Packard glided up to the submarine dock accompanied by the usual stares from hard stomached crewmen and dock workers. To Douglas, the Detroit convertible did not compare to the elegance of the three-hundred-foot war ship from Portsmouth Naval Yard.

The *Mako* lay beside the main dock, her skin covered in fresh coats of dull black paint. Gone were the abrasions of depth charges and machine gun fire. They had to replace the rear platform rail but had not yet painted it. Instead, its iron-red undercoating would attest to one of their close calls.

Only a few men were on her deck when they arrived. A gun crew was loading the magazines for the 20mm on the stern platform. Others were lowering the last stores through the forward hatch. She was ready. Douglas could sense it in the way she sat in the water. Her diesel tanks were topped, her batteries at full charge.

As Douglas climbed from the car, he reached for his coat and satchel behind the seat. Mimi put her hand on his. "Promise me again that you'll come back. Make me believe it."

"A thousand depth charges won't stop me," he said.

She drew him back into the car. She would not let him go without a last, lingering kiss.

"The next time I see you, I'll bring you a box of bones," he promised. As he lifted his satchel, neither of them noticed his small logbook fall from its inside pocket and drop behind the seat. Douglas pressed the door, stepped back and watched Mimi slowly drive away.

"Tell me something good, Mike," Douglas said to his XO as he climbed into upper bridge of the conning tower. He knew the answer. The dock lines were singled up with two of its three mooring lines stored below deck. The warship now hung by a pair of threads, ready to cast off with a nod from her captain.

Alberts scanned his ever-present clipboard. Satisfied, he turned to Douglas. "Give the command, skipper. We're seaworthy and battle ready."

Douglas took in the length of his ship, scanning her from bow to stern. "We've got a helluva patrol ahead of us. Let's take her out and shake her down a bit," Douglas said as he moved toward the hatch. "You got the con."

"Aye, skipper," Alberts said. He gave the orders to take away the gangplank and to cast off the dock lines. A crewman at each cleat caught the line being thrown by a corresponding dock handler. "Port. Back one-third. Mind the rudder," Alberts ordered.

Douglas turned one last time toward the roadway leading away from the submarine docks. The Packard was gone. He felt a hole in his stomach as he watched the oil-tainted water of Pearl sweep the side of the *Mako*'s dark hull.

Crouching, he handed his satchel and coat to a crewman inside the conning tower. "Put these in my cabin," he said.

The *Mako* glided through the calm harbor, around Hospital Point and toward the broadening channel that welcomed the open sea. There was the usual group of patients on the Point, taking in the last rays of the afternoon and watching the ships pass. The bright colors of plumeria, ti plants, and hibiscus flowers along the shore defying the ugliness of war that had come to Pearl only a few short years before.

As the submarine cleared the first set of black and red channel buoys, Alberts sent lookouts onto the small platforms alongside the periscope shears. Bent elbows and binoculars locked against their eyes, they scanned the sky. Two more lookouts stood on the cigarette deck, watching the sea and the horizon.

The vintage minesweeper that guarded the harbor maneuvered out of their way. Several of the sweeper's crew waved as they assumed the submarine was heading out on patrol.

With the palm of his hand, Alberts switched on the press-to-talk button on the waterproof bridge speaker. "Conn, rig for diving," he ordered.

"Aye, bridge," came the response from the conning tower. And a moment later, "Bridge. Rigged for dive."

Douglas stood between Alberts and Quartermaster Dustin Blare. "Let's head out to Barber's Point and push her to full speed on the top."

"Aye, skipper," Alberts said. He leaned toward the bridge speaker. "Answer bells on four engines. All ahead full."

"This should give Clancy a heart attack," Douglas chuckled.

"Yes, sir."

Douglas did not say as much, but alongside the problems with the forward diesel, the *Mako* had undergone extensive repairs to her hull, and he wanted the crew confident she could handle a deep run when needed. Better to remove any doubts now, he figured.

For twenty minutes, as the submarine pushed effortlessly through the thick rolling swells and the island fell away, Douglas waited for Clancy's call that the troublesome Fairbank was overheating. The message never came. Finally, it was time. He turned to his XO. "Okay, Mike, I got her from here," Douglas said.

"Aye, the con is yours, sir," Alberts confirmed.

"Let's give her a little shakedown," Douglas said.

Alberts nodded. "Lookouts below, clear the bridge!" he called and instantly the men standing on the narrow platforms scampered to the bridge and down the circular hatchway. The other two crewmen followed directly behind as if they were connected. Alberts followed.

Douglas heard the distinct gulp and thud of the main induction valve as the hydraulic system slammed closed, cutting off the air to the diesel engines. Now the submarine's power was solely drawn from her battery banks.

He leaned on the button for the Klaxon, sending the alarm's grinding screech throughout the ship. Pressing the bridge speaker, he gave his orders. "Take us down, periscope depth."

A last glance forward as the *Mako*'s bow planes spread like wings from her dagger form to catch the whitewash and drive her into the depths. Douglas dropped through the bridge hatchway into the conning tower. The quartermaster pulled the wire lanyard attached to the circular door and brought his full weight against it.

Alberts immediately reached over the captain and spun the small brass hand wheel. The steel dog-leg latches extended across the hatch's ring as it sealed.

The downward angle of the submarine's deck would have unnerved any other Navy man, but to the sixty hardened souls aboard the *Mako*, their plunge toward the abyss was as natural as waves crashing across a surface ship's bow.

From the control room directly beneath the conning tower, familiar noises rose. The venting air whistled like a soft breeze in a cave, the popping and gurgling of rushing water as the sea swept across the false deck and across the open bridge.

"Pressure in the boat, green across the board, sir," came the report that the *Mako* was sound, all hatches sealed, and the hull airtight.

At Douglas' order, the periscope rose smoothly out of its greased sleeve. He spread the handles and fixed his right eye against the scope. "Ahead fifteen hundred a side," he ordered. Turning slowly, he swept the horizon.

He shot Alberts a side glance. "Ready to give her a shake?"

His executive officer nodded. "She'll hold," he promised.

"Let's be sure," Douglas said. "Bring us to heading one-seven-zero. Planes down twelve degrees. Make depth two-zero-zero feet." He folded the scope's handles, and the instrument dropped into the floor.

"Aye, Skipper. Depth two-zero-zero," Alberts relayed the commands to the control room beneath their feet.

As they descended further into the hull, Alberts assisted the quartermaster in securing the secondary hatch.

"Seven-five feet and steady, sir," the helmsman reported as the submarine slipped further from the ocean surface.

The new air-conditioning unit clicked on as the internal temperature rose in the small space of the conning tower. The air was still sweet from just being pumped in from the surface, but that would not last as the sharp bitter smell of men would soon become apparent.

"One hundred and twenty feet. Heading one-seven-zero."

"Rudder amidship. Straighten us out, Bill," Douglas spoke to the helmsman.

"Aye, rudder amidship, skipper," Bill made the change.

"One hundred and sixty feet."

The command crew watched their controls in silence, although there was never true silence. There was the hum of the air-cooling system, the distant whirl of the huge propellers pushing them forward and the sheer mass of machinery required to operate the warship. Only under attack, when silence was their last defense against an unrelenting enemy, did the submarine become a ghost in the water.

"Depth two-zero-zero. Leveling out."

The men rode the deck as it rose under their feet. Douglas nodded contently. "Not a sound," he said.

"Not a whimper," Alberts agreed.

"Let's see what three hundred sounds like," he said.

The first moan from the intense pressure surrounding the submarine's hull came at the two hundred-and-thirty-five-foot mark. It sounded like a large man's stomach turning from too many spicy foods.

The sounds increased as the *Mako* pierced the two-hundred-and-eighty-foot depth of the murky sea. Like a voracious monster, the weight of the water was trying to find a way into the steel eggshell.

"Speed through the water?" Douglas asked.

First Class Electrician's Mate David Casey scanned the voltmeter panel, the ampere meters and the motor shaft-revolution indicators. "Seven knots, skipper," he answered.

"Level off at three hundred feet," Douglas ordered as the men in the conning tower watched the needle sweep around the depth gauge.

The helmsman made the correct adjustments. "Aye. Three-zero-zero feet."

As the hull groaned from the strain, Douglas noticed a bead of sweat form on the helmsman's thin upper lip. He imagined it was the same for most of his men. Although every submariner knew the dangers, no one could expect them to disregard the reality that even a shakedown dive off a friendly harbor could send them on a final patrol.

"Still as tough as they come," Douglas said aloud. "Good job, gentleman," he said to his officers. "Mike, you have the con. Take us back to Pearl."

"Aye, skipper," Alberts said. He barked the orders to return them to the surface.

Douglas swept the curtain door aside and stepped into his cabin. His leather satchel was on his bunk, his coat hung on a bulkhead hook.

He closed the curtain carefully, making sure no one walking by could see inside. He pulled both sets of orders from the case, Tendrey's and the real ones. At some point during their patrol, Douglas would have to show one of them to his XO. The idea gutted him. Beyond the falsified orders, he would not involve his officers or crew. Except Seaman Hawthorne.

As he returned the envelope to the case and stored it in the wide locker over his bunk, he wondered if Wagner was going to show up on the docks. Maybe he would pass himself off as a machinist's mate or a steward. He just hoped it would not be a critical crewmember.

Leaning into his bunk, he thought about Mimi, and how she felt stretched over him with her soft breasts pressed against his skin. Douglas suddenly worried she would be with the ambassador and the diamonds when they docked. He hoped not. He was not sure how he could bear seeing her slip away again.

23

MOEN ISLAND, TRUK LAGOON, 1986

"EXCUSE ME," Brian said to the man sleeping inside the remains of a splintered rowboat that was half-filled with coral sand. The fragment of the hull created a perfect windbreak against the noon breeze.

The man, his heavy left arm arched over his face, made no sign of waking. He wore pants that were once white or khaki but were now a stained variation. One pant leg was torn above the ankle, the other just below the knee. His mis-buttoned shirt, stretched over a mountainous stomach, documented motor oil and fish blood.

"George?" Brian nudged his bare foot.

Leslie peered at the man, her arms folded. "You sure this is the guy?"

"It's where Rota said we'd find him."

"Rota knows nothing," the voice from under the arm grunted. "Busybody."

The man rolled to his feet like a wallowing buffalo. He wiped his face, yawned wide, revealing sparse teeth. His bloodshot eyes bulged as if he had been reeled in too quickly from deep water. He paid no attention to Brian, but focused his broad, crooked smile on Leslie. "But she knows I am the best guide in the lagoon. So, you tell me. Where can I take you?"

"Where they found Henry," Brian announced and watched the islander's face turn somber.

Twenty minutes later, they rode the midmorning chop in the rented runabout, an American-made Owens with a cabin and galley and a wide rear deck designed for big game fishing.

"It's always bad for everyone," George said, absorbing the kick of the waves with his legs. The bow split the swells, leaving a wake of white frosting.

Brian took the punching as well as he stood beside the open helm. He watched as George maneuvered the craft along the dim outline of the submerged reef. Leslie sat in the boat's stern on thick cushions, staring silently at the white beach passing them on the left.

"A diver dies here, and nobody wants to come to the lagoon for a time. They say the wrecks are too dangerous, that you will get trapped or blown up from the ammunition," George said. He pressed his lips together, popped them open, and mimicked an explosion. He laughed. "All the divers go to Tahiti or Fiji with their big hotels and little reefs."

With the gesture of outspread arms, he said seriously, "Truk is the most beautiful lagoon in the world, and though the war was hard for us, it made our home more wonderful. You dive once and you will agree."

"I already agree."

"No," George smiled. "You think this is a lovely place to visit? Lots of history? But it will take hold of you here." He tapped the center of his flabby chest. "You will see."

Brian turned to Leslie and saw the speed of the boat was lifting her hair like a spinnaker running before the wind. She tilted her sunglasses to focus on a break in the trees. She caught him staring.

"Why do you make her come?" George said, absorbing another wave.

"She wanted to," Brian countered.

"You want, not her," he grunted.

Brian ignored him. From the corner of his eye, he saw Leslie rise from the bench seat and mistakenly let go of the seat back. She took one step toward them when the boat hit the back of a steep wave. The sudden jolt sent her reeling.

Two strides and Brian had his arms tight around her waist, his bare feet clamped to the deck. "Careful," he said. "Don't want to lose you over the side."

"No, that wouldn't be good."

"First rule in seamanship; one hand for yourself, one for the boat," he told her. "Always hold on to something."

"Right," she said, her lips pursed in embarrassment, as she unlaced herself from him. "What island is this?" she asked as the boat rounded the sandy point and continued toward the next low-lying sweep of land.

"George," he yelled over the wind. "What island is that?"

"Fefan," he said. "Many of the original buildings from the Japanese are still there."

The land rose steeply out of the blue water, yet it reached only nine hundred feet into the sky, falling short of touching the cotton ball clouds that were sprinkled above.

Brian stared into the green carpet of the jungle, trying to see the army's rusting turrets and pillboxes. In his mind, he saw the armaments teaming with infantry dashing into doorways, rushing to man their anti-aircraft guns as American Hellcats roiled across the like hornets buzzing their nest. He saw the bombs dropping, heard their stabilizing fins roar in the wind, and felt the air jolt from their explosions.

Red fiery flames poured through the thick greasy black smoke that blinded the soldiers and burned holes into their lungs. Yet they still fought for their Emperor as blue wings blocked out the morning sun. Fighting hour after hour until Truk became a burning wreckage of steel, jungle, and flesh.

"Much further?" Leslie asked.

She brought him back to the present. "What? No," he said. "I think it's the next island." He pointed to the long green arm laying across the blue waters. There was no war here now. Only the wind and the sun and the sea.

Like all the islands of Truk, it was an emerald gem in the middle of a sapphire sea. Laying across the waters, it was long and narrow, with a single hill in the center rising only seventy feet above the waves. Its narrow band of beach was identical to all the other island shores of the lagoon, a white neutral zone between a volatile sea and a patient tropical jungle.

George maneuvered the skiff to the southwest side. He slipped the boat gingerly into the shallows until he nudged the bow onto the coral sand.

Brian jumped from the bow with a mooring line trailing from his shoulder. He lashed the line to a palm tree whose base was as thick as an elephant's leg. George secured the other end to the skiff's bow cleat.

Leslie slid over the gunwale and dropped into the cool water. The breeze was warm and carried the sweet scents of yiang-yiang flowers. With her sandals in hand, she followed Brian and George up the beach.

"How far off is the wreck?" Brian asked.

"About two hundred meters," he pointed. "We crossed over her when we came in."

"You head that way, and we'll cover the beach up here," Brian said.

George nodded. "What am I looking for?"

Brian realized he did not know how to answer him. "Anything that doesn't seem to fit here."

George waved and headed off.

Brian walked along the beach just above the lapping waves. Higher along the sandy slope, he could see where the tides and wind chop had tossed driftwood and debris.

Leslie strolled in front of him, zigzagging from the water's edge to the sand and clearly uninterested in their search. She picked up a palm frond, still vividly green and stiff as though it had fallen only moments ago.

In a grand gesture, she swept it across the blue sky, executed a perfect pirouette and turned the frond into a sword, thrusting it into Brian's heart. "Good king of cats, nothing but one of your nine lives."

Brian stood still, the plant against this chest. His brow rose.

"Romeo and Juliet," she stated, her shoulders dropping in disappointment.

"I must have stepped out for popcorn during that scene," he admitted.

"Why did you ask George to bring us here?" she asked as she lowered her frond sword.

"This is the beach they found your father."

"I know. But why are we here?"

"You don't want to know what happened?"

"I know what happened. He drowned. Horribly," she said, a catch in her throat. "He was doing his research because that is what he always did. He couldn't let go of the past. I understand it a little bit better now, but what I want to know is why do *you* want to know?"

Brian turned as he tried to avoid her stare.

"You said you came to do research. Is it like my father's?" she asked.

"Not exactly," he said.

"I don't understand."

Brian lowered himself to the sand. Leslie sat beside him, but with a clear neutral zone between them.

He realized his options were narrowing. "Your father's ship. The *Kuma Maru*. It's the one I came to find."

"Oh my god," Distrust spread quickly across her face. "Did you know him? Did you know my father?"

"No," Brian said quickly.

"On the plane? Our seats?"

"I didn't plan it," he said firmly

"But it *was* planned?" She stood up. "Goddamnit." She marched a few paces up the beach, then spun back. "What the hell is going on?"

"The truth?"

"That'd be a nice."

"My name's Bovan. Not Brock."

"Shit," she huffed. "I am so stupid."

"It wasn't to trick you," Brian rose, his hands open as if in surrender.

"That makes me feel better. I just found out my dad died and now this?" Tears started swelling again. "Take me back. Now."

"Let me explain," he pleaded.

"I don't want to hear any more. I just want to go home. My dad is where he'd want to be." She was staring at the beach, processing, wiping tears. "I just want to pack my things and get out of here." She started for the boat, not caring if Brian followed.

"My father died here too," Brian said abruptly. "Because of your father."

She froze. She turned and stared with disbelief and growing fury.

He stepped up and put out his hand. "Lieutenant Commander Brian Bovan, United States Navy, second in command of the nuclear attack submarine, *John Adams*. At least, that was my rank until they kicked me out."

They sat again on the high berm with Leslie keeping a boundary of distrust between them.

Although his military instincts told him to remain guarded and his years in the submarine service demanded secrecy, Brian told her everything he knew about a forty-year-old conspiracy that he sensed had brought them together.

He spoke of classified documents, of secret missions, of the war. He told her about fossils and diamonds. The man in Hawaii following him. The surprise of her sitting next to him on the plane. Watching her face twist as he told his tale, Brian had to admit it was sounding farfetched.

"And you didn't think twice about accepting a plane ticket from a strange woman?" Leslie asked. "Not even for a second?"

"Maybe for a second. But between the logbook and his record." Brian stood up. "I researched what she told me. When the Marines were overrun and lost the fossils, they never got a shot off. They just surrendered. It doesn't matter now, but then, it was an embarrassment."

"Honestly, you don't think all this sounds farfetched?"

"All I know is that I grew up believing my father was supposed to be a war hero." Brian dug a chip of coral from the sand and sent it skimming across the water. "Now I'm told he was a traitor."

"You said there were forty thousand men here. How could my dad have anything to do with yours?"

"The fossils were aboard the *Kuma Maru*."

Leslie shifted uncomfortably in the sand. She tossed her palm sword aside and stared at the waves rolling steadily up the beach. "My dad never talked about what happened here. Only about the friends he lost. Never about fossils. I would have remembered that."

"But if he spoke English, they would have used him as an interpreter," Brian pressed. "He had to have known. Why else would he keep coming back?"

She turned. "You don't believe it was an accident."

Brian let out a slow breath. "I'm not sure, but I am going to find out."

•　　•　　•

George was already at the boat waiting for them. Stretched out across the foredeck, he was asleep.

"George." Brian slapped his shoulder.

The native lifted his head. "You find anything?"

"Nothing," Leslie said.

"Me either." He hopped off the bow. "I don't know why you wanted to come here. Anything Henry lost out here would be in New Guinea by now."

"What do you mean?"

"Things from this side of the island go straight out the south pass. The current runs that way. It can be strong when the tide shifts."

Brian stopped. "What about all this driftwood?"

"That's from inside the little reef. The wrecks are a hundred meters out."

Leslie was listening intently. "But the police said they found my father here."

George shook his finger. "This isn't where Henry would go."

"Do you know where he dove?"

"Not exactly. But it was not here," George said firmly. "Look. Today, the fuel tank was almost full." George moved to the rear of the Owens and pulled the red fuel tank from under the rear bench that filled the back side of the deck. "You see. It is half empty. We have to switch to the secondary gas tank to get back to the harbor."

"It was full when we left," Brian said, understanding. "This is the wrong spot."

George nodded.

Leslie stared at Brian. "They lied."

"Come on," he said as he helped George push the skiff into the water. "You need to be on the next plane out."

24

HONOLULU, HAWAII, 1944

WAGNER WRAPPED his German Walther pistol in an old shirt and shoved it into the bottom of his canvas bag. On the bed, he laid out the clothes he assumed he would need. He had never been aboard a submarine, but he had plenty of assignments on Naval warships. The difference, he figured, was that there was no going outside for a smoke.

His second-story apartment was comfortably quiet through the night, with only the light tap of a midnight shower against his window. It was an odd thing, the rain in Hawaii. It came and went with little concern from anyone. He wondered if there was an umbrella anywhere on the island. People just kept moving, letting themselves dry in the salty breeze.

While he packed, Wagner indulged himself with his latest acquisition: a slightly used LP of Carmen Melis singing the opera *Tosca*. He had found the thick, raven-black record sandwiched between discarded jazz albums on a second-hand shelf of a feed store in Wahiawa. How the thirty-five-year-old shellac disk ended up in Hawaii, he had no idea, but for sixteen cents, he was not about to pass it up.

As the agent set the needle of the Zenith phonograph into the record's spiraling groove, he closed his eyes, lifted his hands like a marionette and lead Carmen's voice through the room. *I should have studied music,* he thought as he returned to his preparations.

He inspected the neat piles of clothes laid out across his bed. Khaki pants, khaki shorts, white shirts, underwear, khaki jacket, white sailor's cap. Moving into the bathroom, he cleaned out the drawer next to the sink. Straight razor, shaving soap, toothbrush, and a comb. Taking a small pocketknife from his pillow, he rolled it with his comb in a face towel and dropped it next to his underwear.

Last, he pulled out the single sheet letter from the envelope that rested on the top of his dresser. Typed on CINCPAC letterhead, the orders were perfect down to Nimitz's signature. It explained the need for Washington to review first-hand how the Submarine Corp was fairing under the intense pressure of 50-day patrols in enemy waters.

Wagner snickered to himself, knowing Bovan's executive officer would not question them. No one would. He refolded the letter, slipped it into the envelope and packed it tightly in the thick oilskin pouch. He tossed the package on the bed. Now he was ready, or at least his tools were gathered.

Still, there was something else. A missing component that had been gnawing at the back of his mind all day. Something nudging him, whispering in an unclear voice that was causing him misgivings. It made his agent's mind mumble; reevaluate, rethink, be careful.

He had approached Gosline with his idea of joining Bovan's crew to make sure Tendrey's went as planned. At first, the OSS colonel was against the idea. One of his agents on a submarine? But when Wagner briefed him on the mysterious crewman the admiral had inexplicitly transferred, he reluctantly agreed to the fake Nimitz letter.

"Perhaps you are right, Major," Gosline said. "I don't like the idea of some low-ranking machinist's mate suddenly being put aboard. Who knows what this bastard admiral has in mind?"

Wagner kept going over that conversation. He did not know why. His head just would not let it go.

His packing done, he returned to the bathroom, cranked open the brass spigot and splashed his face with lukewarm water. "Goddamnit," he cursed his reflection in the oval mirror. "What the hell is missing?"

He snatched the terrycloth towel, padded his face, wiped his hands, stared in the mirror, and watched his smile grow. "Machinist's mate?" he said out loud. "Well, fuck me," Wagner said with sudden realization. He remembered he had only referred to the mystery sailor as a crewman, not as a machinist's mate. "He's in on it," the OSS agent hissed as he felt a chunk of lava in his gut. He was at once sorry and furious.

In the other room, Carmen Melis's voice suddenly grew louder and louder. Wagner dropped his towel into the sink. The old Zenith was always going haywire.

As he leaned through the door, he felt the thin wire noose drop over his face and slip under his chin. He didn't have time to react. The tension on it was immediate. It jerked against his throat with a vise-like grip, snapping his head forward.

Wagner struggled to turn and grab his attacker. Arm flinging, he reached back to gouge at the eyes, but his hands found nothing. Dropping low, he went for the groin. Again, there was no one to grab. In desperation, he launched himself backwards, yet all he managed was to slam himself against the apartment wall.

The wire slipped tighter around his neck. He reached for it, digging his thumbs into his own flesh. Still, the wire tightened.

Blackness came finally with a wave of intense pain. Death was slow for the OSS officer named both Wagner and Duare. It was a combination of lack of oxygen and blood to the brain as the line sliced the carotid artery and crushed his trachea.

The body slouched against the wall and slid to the floor. After a moment, the small, elderly man with sun-rumpled skin stepped off the sofa that sat beside the bathroom door. Releasing his grip on the wire, the slip knot loosened at the opposite end of the five-foot steel pole. He had seen the device used to capture gazelle in Africa and was amazed at the leverage it gave its user against his prey.

Satisfied, he pulled the wire over the wobbling head. *A job well done,* he thought. Simple, silent and effective and worth half the money they had paid him. As he walked from the room, he lifted the Zenith's needle from the record. Personally, he preferred Emmy Destinn's *Tosca* to Melis'.

•　　　•　　　•

Douglas leaned against the cold rail of the cigarette deck as he watched the small crowd of well-wishers on the dock. Only a handful of his crew had anyone in Honolulu beyond the bar girls they fell deeply in love with the night before. Still, Douglas made sure the Marines at the gate would let them come to the dock to say their goodbyes.

A glance at his watch. 2331 on the illuminated dial. In a half an hour, the *Mako* would cast her lines and slip off to war again.

"Skipper." Alberts crossed the gangplank and leapt to the first rung of the tower ladder. "Just got this pushed into my hands," he said as he passed a folded piece of paper to the bridge.

Douglas angled himself to catch the light from the dock. He saw his name penciled across the front. He opened the handwritten note.

Captain,

Sorry I won't be able to make it aboard. I have received new orders. Good luck with yours. I'm sure you will carry them out to the fullest. I will see you upon your return to Pearl.

Wagner

Douglas felt his shoulders tighten. He did not know the agent, but a small handwritten note was odd. "Who gave you this?" he asked.

"A marine on the dock."

"What did he look like? Young, old, tall, short, what?" he snapped.

Alberts raised his hands. "Young, I guess. I didn't get a good look at him."

Douglas saw the worry in his officer's face. It was handwritten, but that didn't mean a thing. He had never seen Wagner's writing.

"What is it, Skipper?" Alberts climbed the tower.

"Nothing," he said. The squeak of truck brakes pulled his attention to the dock. Two men and the driver stepped out and circled to the tailgate.

Douglas shoved the paper into his jacket pocket. He crossed the gangplank.

"Good evening, sir," the Ensign said as he and the two men came to full attention.

Douglas returned the salute. They were young, all three boys just out of bootcamp. The ensign was fresh out of officer's school.

"I have orders to turn this over to you, sir," said the ensign as he dropped the tailgate. "And to brief you with several instructions, Commander," he said, adding. "In private, sir."

"Charlie, grab that end," he said, and the two men lifted the narrow, footlocker-sized crate by its rope handles.

"Set it down," Douglas ordered.

The two men did as they were told.

"My orders, Commander, are to be sure this is placed aboard your vessel," the ensign pressed.

"I'm not questioning your orders, Ensign. But I am not about to let unauthorized personnel aboard my boat. With you, I'm forced to make an exception. Only with you," Douglas said flatly. He turned toward the small gathering of crewmen enjoying their last minutes of land.

"Epstein, Shear," he called over two crewmen spitting tobacco. They hurried to Douglas' side. "Take that and put it in my cabin." He pointed at the crate.

They immediately elbowed the landlubbers out of the way and hoisted the box.

"After you." Douglas waved the ensign toward the sub. The two officers followed the crewmen as they maneuvered the crate through the tight opening of the forward hatch, with Epstein easing it down the ladder as Shear held it to his shoulder.

"Make room," Shear called to the cluster of men standing between him and the captain's quarters. They scurried. "On the floor, sir?"

"Yes, next to the bunk. And that will be all," Douglas said.

"Yes, sir." They nodded to the ensign as they disappeared.

Douglas reached over the ensign's shoulder and pulled the thick doorway curtain closed. "How much of this do you know?" Douglas asked as he knelt beside the box.

"I am an explosives expert, Captain. I was the one who assembled the detonation mechanism. I was told to explain how to set it and how to disarm it. Now, to why the Navy would bring this aboard a submarine is beyond my need-to-know, sir."

Douglas nodded. "Okay, explain."

The Ensign unlatched the flip-locks. He lifted the lid slowly, revealing several layers of waxed canvas. Peeling them away, he exposed a dozen brick-sized blocks of brownish clay pressed against the inner wall. A rope of color-coded wire linked the bricks to a small brass clock in the left corner.

Filling the center of the footlocker was another wrapping of waxed canvas. This piece, however, was stitched together like the burial shroud of a dead sailor ready to be committed to the depths. It kept the contents of the locker safe and hidden.

"These are it," the ensign said, pointing to the brown cubes. "Plastic explosives. The Army developed it over the last two years. Extremely stable and extremely effective. You could leave these suckers in saltwater for a year with no effect. The best part is the detonator. Uses the same stuff, but it's sealed." The ensign grinned like an adolescent. "This goes off inside your sub, Captain. It'll rip her open like a tin can. Kablooey."

Douglas chewed his inner lip. He did not like his sub being referred to as a tin can. Still, he understood the man's emphasis.

The ensign reached for the clock set in the corner. "Now this thing, I wired it to give you options. You can set the timer from a minute to twelve hours. So, they can't open it too soon."

"And if they try?" Douglas asked.

A broad smile crossed the ensign's face. "That is something I am really proud of. See the three latches? Normally, you'd think to undo all three to open the lid. But that'll set off the charge. To open the lid without arming the plastic, you leave the center latch closed and just open the ones on the end."

"How do I set the clock?" Douglas asked.

"The hands work like a combination lock," he continued, showing Douglas how to unscrew the clock face and remove the glass. "Turn the hands counterclockwise to how long you want the timer to last. It detonates at 12 o'clock. Set it at eleven fifty-nine and that gives you a minute. At two o'clock, you get ten hours and so on. Simple as that." he said, standing.

Simple as that, Douglas thought. *The only hard part was delivering it.*

He followed the ensign out of the forward hatch. As they reached the dock, the young officer turned and saluted him. "Good luck, Commander. I don't know where the hell you're headed, but I suspect you'll need as much as you can get."

Douglas returned his salute without a word. He watched as the Ensign and the two other men climbed into their truck and drove off.

"What was that all about?" Alberts asked as he stepped up.

"Are we ready to shove off?" he asked as he turned to the long, black silhouette. "Crew accounted for?"

"Yes, sir," Alberts said, understanding he was asking the wrong questions at the wrong time. "Just give the order, Skipper."

"What's the time?"

"Five minutes till midnight."

Douglas sighed. "You think Stein is going to see us off?"

"I've never known him not to be dockside when one of his boats leaves for patrol," Alberts said.

"We'll wait," Douglas said, turning on his heels for the gangplank.

As if on cue, the sound of an approaching car and its cat-eyed headlamps stopped them both. Captain Linus Stein stepped from the olive-green Ford before his driver had brought them to a stop.

"Line them up, Mike. Let's give our squadron commander what he deserves," Douglas ordered as he stepped to meet Stein. A salute and handshake. "Thank you for coming, sir."

"I haven't missed a single departure. The least I can do is to show my gratitude and respect for your boys," Stein said.

"Thank you, sir. It's appreciated by every one of them."

"I know your orders don't make your patrol simple. Get to Truk as soon as possible," Stein said, as if he felt there was a need to remind him.

On the deck of the *Mako*, her crew lined up at attention. Douglas heard his XO give the orders to single up on the dock lines.

"Understood, sir," Douglas said, snapping a final salute.

"Good luck, Commander," Stein smiled.

Douglas was the last across the gangplank. He climbed the steel ladder to the bridge. "Mike. Let's take her out."

Orders given; the aft diesels grunted to life. The sub's propellers bit into the harbor's calm waters as the motors swirled. The lines fell from their iron cleats and the sub pulled with determination away from the dock.

Along the deck, the men waved to their well-wishers as the linemen joined them.

Stein stiffened and saluted the crew and ship. He was sending another crew to war and, as he did with them all, he prayed silently for their safe return.

As the warship pivoted in the middle of the bay and made her way out of the naval base, a slim figure watched from the shadowy corner of a nearby warehouse. She desperately wanted to walk out onto the dock and wish them well, but she could not. A tear rolled down Mimi's cheek as the man on the bridge became only a silhouette against the evening sky that was growing dark over Pearl Harbor.

•   •   •

They were fourteen hours across the Pacific when Douglas confronted his new machinist's mate. Alberts escorted him through the control room into officers' country.

"Skipper?" Alberts rapped the bulkhead. "Machinist's Mate Hawthorne to see you."

"Ah, Hawthorne," Douglas said, turning from his tiny desk.

"Sir." Hawthorne was at full attention.

"So, I understand you transferred from a tender at the request of Admiral Tendrey," Douglas said, coming right to the point. "I'd like to know why."

Hawthorne's eyes darted between the two officers. "I.., I thought you knew, sir," the machinist's mate said nervously.

Douglas wondered if he needed to dismiss Alberts. "Remind me," Douglas said, his voice firming.

"I was told to explain, sir, on the third day out. To brief you on my specialties."

"Specialties?"

"Yes, sir." Hawthorne glanced at Alberts. "I am sorry, sir, but the admiral was explicit that I speak with you in private."

"You're standing on my boat, Ensign. Guess who you answer to now," Douglas pressed. He could see the sweat forming on the side of Hawthorne's brow.

"I am a graduate student of anthropology, Skipper. From Berkeley. My specialty was with *pithecanthropus erectus*."

"Pith cat what?" Alberts' grimace was comical.

"*Pithecanthropus erectus*, sir. I specialize in identification," Hawthorne said. "Number two in my class."

"And what the hell is...whatever you said?"

"Java man, sir. He lived about a million years ago," Hawthorne spoke with a growing excitement about his subject. "I think he is a direct relation to the Peking Man. Of course, Zdansky's theories of *Sinanthropus pekinensis* being three million years old? No way, sir. I think he is off by a million, maybe two. There's also the theory that…"

"Stop," Douglas shot.

Alberts' face was wrinkled again.

"You're here to verify the package?"

"Yes, sir. I can tell you then and there if they're bupkis," Hawthorne said proudly.

Douglas took a deep breath. "And your other specialty?"

He eyed Alberts again. "When I was part of an excavation team in Utah, sir. I was part of the explosives team," he said.

Douglas nodded. "Thank you, Hawthorne. I understand. You can return to your station."

"Yes, sir," Hawthorne said. He slipped past Alberts' shoulder and out of the cabin.

"Well?" Douglas said, feeling his XO's stare. "Ask."

"All right." Alberts leaned on the bulkhead. "What the hell was that about?"

Douglas pulled his satchel from the overhead cabinet. He stripped the oilcloth from the envelope and handed it over.

Alberts made a quick read of Tendrey's mission.

From his expressions, Douglas knew his XO understood their instructions. He wished he could tell him about the OSS but there was no need. In his officer's mind, the orders, even from Tendrey, were real.

"This is crazy," he said in a slow voice.

"Those were my words," Douglas said. "But we've got charts of the lagoon no one else has."

"Are they accurate?"

"We'll find out. Once this part is done, we get out as fast as possible. I don't want our flyboys mistaking us for an enemy boat."

Alberts handed him back the letter. "We're not supposed to question orders, but…"

"No, we're not," Douglas agreed. He folded the papers and carefully replaced them in the oilskin wrap. "I know what you are saying."

"If the Japs give us this Peking Man thing? What do we give them?" Alberts asked.

Douglas reached under his bunk and pulled out the heavy crate. He flipped back the lid and the canvas covers.

"And that's?"

"Just a torpedoes' worth of explosives and five million dollars in uncut diamonds."

"You expect to sleep with that under your bunk?"

"I don't expect to sleep until we're back at Pearl." Douglas closed the lid and returned it to its hiding place.

"What happens if a patrol catches us inside the lagoon?"

"We've got twenty-four tin fish to make the most of our position."

"Tell me, Skipper," Alberts said. "Do you think caveman bones are worth the lives of our crew?"

Douglas swept his hat off his pillow as he stood up. "We're a warship, Mr. Alberts. We carry out our orders, we don't get to pick the ones we like."

Alberts stiffened. "Yes, sir."

"To answer your question. I don't," he said. "And I'll promise you this, after we make this trade, we're not slipping out quietly. Those bastards are going to know we were there."

"I hope you're right, Skipper," the XO said, following him toward the control room. "I hope to God you're right."

Douglas did not say more, but he hoped the same thing.

25

WUUN RAN HIS HANDS quickly along the suitcase, one on the inside, one on the outside. He felt only lining between his fingers. This was the last of Leslie's luggage and he was satisfied she had nothing hidden. He took a last, slow look around the bedroom.

In the study, he rifled Brian's suitcases in the same manner. Quick, thorough, and indifferent that his trespass would be discovered. He popped open the cases, rifled through each, tossing the clothes aside as he pulled through them. Nothing.

Now he got angry. They wouldn't be happy unless he found something. They would accuse him of being careless. He kept searching behind every book, in every box and through all the pieces of junk Henry had pulled from the lagoon.

He hated this sneaking about, this slinking through the jungle. It would be better to come when the daughter and the American were here. He would simply demand to search the house. What could they say? He was the police.

Stepping from the study, he tromped back to the makeshift workroom. He had already bulldozed the tiny space. Searched the toolboxes, around the stack of steel scuba tanks and through the dive gear closet. *There was nothing to be found here,* he thought. It was that simple. They were wrong. The house held no more secrets.

If there were charts of the wreck, the daughter had them. And the only way to get them would be a face-to-face confrontation with the American. Wuun smiled at the thought.

Turning to leave, he realized there was one more place. The tiny bathroom was lit by a naked bulb in the center of the ceiling. Wuun lifted the toilet's tank lid but found only the normal assembly. He poked his head under the sink, around the counter and behind the bathtub made from a tin watering trough.

He grabbed Leslie's cosmetic case from the countertop and cracked it open. Woman's makeup. *What a surprise,* he thought. In frustration, he threw the case into the tub. He slammed his fist into the wall. Wuun's violent outburst shook the flimsy door, causing it to close. He then saw Brian's travel case hanging from a small copper hook.

•   •   •

"I need a chart of the lagoon," Brian said, as he leaned on the warped counter. It was hot inside the old Quonset hut that housed the Truk Trading Company. The metal building, with its dull white and rusting finish, kept heat in better than an oven.

The thick native with earlobes that drooped off his shaved head like droplets of honey didn't seem to notice the heat. He studied the wall behind him where a small sample of the diving charts were fanned out on display. "Which one you want?" he grunted.

"The whole lagoon."

The man fetched a rickety footstool, put a barefoot to it and hoisted his bulk upward. He reached into the overhead storage. He handed Brian the chart. "That shows everything, all the islands and outer reef. You want more detail, you need the others," he told him as he sauntered to an antique brass cash register that was wildly out of place. "Anything more?"

"That will do it."

"Wait," Leslie said as she dropped an arm full of cans and groceries in front of him. She set several tomatoes and a fresh pineapple she had snagged from the table out front. "And these." She opened a small basket of eggs, showing the cashier what she had picked.

"What's all this?" Brian corralled the cans.

"Dinner," Leslie said.

The shop owner laughed. "Don't argue. My wife cooks the same thing every night. Guess what?"

Brian stared. "Fish?"

"Pork," the man said with a shake of his head. "Always pork."

Leslie laughed, realized he was not joking, covered her mouth with her fingers.

"You want fish?" he asked her.

"Fresh?"

"Look where you at. Of course, fresh," he said, reaching into a portable ice chest behind the counter. "Triggerfish. Nice size. Two for you." He wrapped them in newspaper before either could argue. He dropped the fish and groceries into a cardboard box.

"You have beer?" Brian asked.

"Oh no. Our island is dry. You can drink at the hotel bar, but you can't buy in the store."

"That's a shame. You have Pepsi?"

"Coke?"

A few minutes later, Brian carried the box out to the Jeep. Leslie walked with him swinging a six-pack of Coke-a-Cola. They set the food on the back floor under George's legs.

The islander had spread himself across the rear seat, his feet hanging over one fender. A white hat that had not been there before rested low on his head.

"Where did the hat come from?" Leslie asked as she jumped into the passenger seat.

"Rota," George said, his face hidden. "She wants to marry me. I have to be on guard."

"That's silly," Leslie huffed.

Brian pulled onto the street, slowed for a young boy, still wet from the sea, his spear perched on his shoulder, as he crossed from the beach with his afternoon's catch of grouper and purple parrotfish.

The sun was falling fast, yet the warmth of the day was holding. That was the way of the lagoon. One beautiful day evolving into another. Even during the stormy season, when the waters within the reef foamed like an angry beast slashing at the islands, there was beauty in it.

By the time they pulled up to the house, the wind off the lagoon had settled to an evening breeze. Brian steered the Jeep along the front of the deck.

George rolled lazily out of the back and headed inside. Brian handed the chart to Leslie. He grabbed the cardboard box, and they climbed the steps close together.

"Do you have enough food?" Brian tilted his head toward George. "I figured he'd be staying."

George was ten paces ahead. He stopped at the door and glanced at Brian. "You are messy people," he said.

"What?" Leslie was through the door.

"Shit," Brian said as he stepped inside and saw the chaos.

The intruder had not tried to conceal his time at the house. Every drawer askew, every surface disrupted, every book tossed to the floor.

"Why would anyone do this?" Leslie said, as she frantically gathered the pots from the kitchen floor. George helped her.

Brian dropped the grocery box and rushed into the hall.

"Brian," Leslie called out after him.

The study was now modeled after the kitchen, a whirlwind of destruction. Brian reached under the desk and thankfully felt the smooth cover of his father's logbook still crammed into the gap behind the drawer. Another thought shot through him, and he hurried into the bathroom.

Leslie walked into her bedroom, saw the mess, and cursed. "Shit. My clothes." She righted her suitcase and started tossing her things inside.

Brian stepped into the room and slumped on the edge of the bed.

Leslie waved at the room. "Can you believe this?" She looked at what he was holding and the stiffness of his jaw. "What is that?"

"My toothbrush holder," he said. "I had hid a drawing in it. Something I thought would help us find the *Kuma Maru*."

"That's what they wanted?"

Brian shook his head. "Maybe."

She sat beside him. "You don't think it was an accident? My father's drowning?"

"I think he was close to finding something he wasn't supposed to. Or maybe he had found it."

"What are we going to do?" she asked, her eyes filling.

"I'm going to find out what I can. You? You're getting on the next plane to Honolulu."

With the back of her hand, she wiped back the first tear. Took a substantial deep breath and said, "The hell I am."

Before Brian could argue, George leaned in the doorway. "I will start in the kitchen."

"Give us a minute," Brian said.

Leslie stood. "I know you think you're looking out for me. It's sweet, honestly. But you forget, Commander, I am a New Yorker. I'm not running again."

George had the kitchen drawers back and was sorting the utensils. Leslie took up the job and sent him to help in the study.

"Did they take anything important?" George asked as he stacked the tossed books onto the study's shelf.

"No, I don't think so," Brian lied. He collected several pushpins from the floor. Over the vacant wall, he spread the chart of the lagoon and tagged the corners. "How much fuel did you need to top off the tanks this morning?"

"About two gallons, maybe a little more."

Brian measured the chart. "Two gallons to get somewhere. So how far would that much fuel take him?"

George stared at the chart as well. "If the currents are gentle. Ten miles."

Brian found a fist of string, stretched one end across the chart's mileage scale until he had a length that matched ten miles. He tagged one end into the island harbor with another pin. Keeping the sting taut, he swung 360 degrees about the chart, noting each island that fell within a ten-mile radius.

"You've done this before," George said, watching him intently.

"A few times."

The circle filled up a larger part of the lagoon than Brian liked to think about. It contained Moen, Dublon, Param islands, Fefan, Tsis, a dozen smaller islets and hundreds of outcroppings of reef. The worst area were the waters between Fefan and Dublon. This was the highest concentration of Japanese wrecks, both identified and unidentified. So many, in fact, the United States Defense Mapping Agency had a note on the side of the chart that said the channel was a danger to navigation.

"That's a big area," George said, tapping the circle.

"How many sunken ships are there, do you think?"

"Too many to guess which Henry chose."

"We'll dive all of them," Leslie said as she entered. She carried three glasses of iced tea on a bamboo tray. She handed them to the men.

The islander pushed his cap back and scratched his forehead. "It will take weeks," he said.

"Maybe we can narrow it down. Most of these wrecks are known," Brian noted. "Their names and how deep they are."

George nodded.

"When you serviced the boat, how much equipment did her father take with him?"

George thought for a second. "A set of twin tanks with the backpack. And two singles with regulators to set on the hang line."

"Two singles for decompression stops."

"Yes," George remembered. "That is what he told me."

"Maybe the wreck isn't deep," Leslie ventured. She folded her long legs under herself. "Maybe the two tanks were for two dives."

Brian shook his head. "They each had a regulator. You switch out regulators, you don't have separate ones."

"And too many dives in one day can curl you like a pretzel," George said.

Brian shot a sidelong glare at the islander. He did not want Leslie imagining the details of her father's death. "You are more likely to get the bends from repetitive dives," he said in a matter-of-fact tone. "Your body needs time on the surface to release the nitrogen that builds up in the blood stream."

Leslie let her eyes drop to her glass. Brian noticed her hand shaking.

"Henry was a nice man," George said, his voice suddenly hushed. "He knew the lagoon is a place of ghosts. It is beautiful, but they guard their secrets."

Leslie's gaze moved between the men. "I have to know what happened."

The islander frowned. "The dangers here are not only in the water."

"We know."

George sighed. "Most of the wrecks are on Dublon's west side. Not so many in the north." He pointed at the area inside Brian's circle above Moen. "I have friends who might know different. They are fishermen. They know the fish and fish know the wrecks better than anyone."

Forty minutes later, Brian had finished replacing most of what the intruder had tossed about the study. He scanned the wall chart again, trying to compare the beaches of each island to the mental picture he had of the aerial photograph. With growing aggravation, he realized the more he stared at the drawing, the more every beach was the same from the belly of a Hellcat.

Stepping into the hall, he could hear George explaining how to prepare a local fish soup. Brian had offered to help, but after admitting his culinary expertise beyond Spam meals extended only to a one-pan pasta dish, Leslie decided his efforts were best left cleaning the study.

With the kitchen still in a state of chaos, George joined her, which, Leslie would later confess, was a savior. She had no idea how to cook fish, let alone gut and clean one as particularly thick-skinned as this.

Brian entered the workshop and flipped on the light. The same human hurricane had hit this room as well. The intruder was either searching for something or, more brashly, leaving a message. Hand tools and scuba gear swept from the bench were scattered across the wooden floor. Most of it had been purposely damaged.

The stack of a half-dozen canary yellow scuba tanks next to the far wall reminded Brian of miniature torpedoes. He carefully eased the air valve of one, but found the black knob already twisted open. It was the same for the remaining tanks. The intruder's work.

"Henry had an air compressor." George suddenly filled the doorway. He pointed to an empty corner. "It is in Guam for repairs."

"I think our visitor emptied all of them."

"We can refill them at the harbor dive shop," he said.

Brian pulled a set of twin tanks from under the work bench and set them near the door. He lifted a single cylinder and leaned it against the first.

"I would like to find who did this," George said as he picked up a broken dive mask.

"Me too," Brian said as he revealed a dive regulator and pressure gauge hoses that had been cut.

"Maybe better to get all new equipment," he suggested as he reached for a single dive cylinder pushed far beneath the bench. Grabbing the tank's valve, he yanked it hard.

Suddenly, something snapped, and George toppled backwards against the hardwood floor. With his legs straight out in front of him, he looked up at Brian, dazed.

"You okay?"

George rubbed the back of his head as he opened his hand. To their surprise, he held the tank valve and a sizable chunk of the steel tank's domed top, except the piece was not steel. It was clay but painted to match the air tank.

On their hands and knees, both men slowly pressed their faces to the floor and investigated the cavity of the cylinder half. The dim ceiling light revealed something inside.

Brian stretched his arm into the cylinder. He felt something, grabbed hold and pulled out a tightly rolled tube of paper. Inside the roll was a small, spiral notebook.

"He knew," George said as the two men sat on the floor with the contents between them. "He knew someone would search the house."

Brian unrolled a few inches of the stiff paper revealing the edges of a chart marked with penciled notes. "I think you are right," he said.

In the study, Brian yanked away the chart he had just hung and replaced it with Henry's. They quickly push-pinned the corners.

Unlike the diving map Brian had purchased, this was an official color-coded nautical chart with bottom contour, notations for actual bottom depths and shipping channels.

There were a dozen penciled marks between Param and Fefan islands. Henry had scratched in crosses and circles, small flags and five-pointed stars. Next to each, he had added notes that were almost too small to read. Written in kanji, the Japanese ideograms, Brian realized they were going to be of little help.

Brian opened the notebook and found the same. "Damn." He passed the book to George. "This won't be much help."

The islander flipped through the wrinkled pages. "I can ask Kenji. He reads this," George offered.

"No," Brian shot. "Small island, remember? This is what they came looking for. Let's not give them a reason to come back."

"What reason?" Leslie stood in the door. She had changed into a cool white cotton dress with shoestring straps over her slender shoulders.

"See," George said excitedly. "We found your father's chart and notebook."

Leslie stepped into the room and tentatively took the thin book from the islander's hand. Without opening it, she held it to her chest.

"At least these narrow our search," Brian said. He tapped at the handwritten notes on the chart. "It's one of these."

"It is better than diving the entire lagoon," George nodded.

"The *Shotan Maru*, the *Aikoko*," Leslie ran her finger over the wall. She stopped at each point and read her father's note.

"You can read that?"

Leslie smirked. "While my friends were at Sunday school, I was learning Japanese." She opened the notebook. "Never thought I'd used it."

Brian saw her face tighten as she skimmed the page.

"Entered the bridge of the *Gosei Maru*," she read softly. "The ship rests to port in shallow water and in silence. Against the bulkhead I found three skulls. I think one is Tashima-san. My brave friend still stands his watch." Leslie slowly closed the book.

"This can wait," Brian stressed.

"I'm okay." She moved to the chart and scanned the islands and reefs like a weary sea bird searching for a place to land. Finally, she set her finger on a kanji mark next to Falo Island.

She turned to Brian, tears rising. "The *Kuma Maru*," she whispered.

26

MOEN ISLAND, TRUK LAGOON, 1986

T HE BREEZE THAT SPRINKLED moonlit sequins across the lagoon had faded with the dawn, leaving the earthen smell of the nearby mangroves. It was prevailing, but not entirely unpleasant. It was the scent of stagnate salt and sand, of organics being overturned from one form to the next. The pungent reminder of nature's constant drive to keep moving on a microbial scale.

The sun had barely let go of the horizon, but without the breeze, the early warmth already had Brian's t-shirt wet as he hoisted the last pair of scuba tanks into the rear of the Jeep.

The night before, after Leslie had found the wreck's location on the chart, the three of them had moved out to the front deck. George served his fish soup in mismatched bowls. They ate under a bosun's lamp with Leslie reading from her father's notebook.

It took her a few minutes to separate the carefully printed notes from the hand that had set them down. After a time, her eyes cleared, and she could relay the passages without a squeeze in her throat.

From the pages, it was clear Henry had surveyed over a dozen wrecks throughout the lagoon. He wrote with an intimate familiarity about each ship and their crews and how it was likely they were still aboard. He wrote about watching black billowing clouds rise from their decks and the fires. Fires everywhere. On the ships, on the water, across the jungle. The world was on fire and crying with ashen tears.

Brian had sat on the steps of the porch, watching the peaceful lagoon, listening to her. It was a three-quarter moon and the slice of sea it illuminated reflected up onto the deck and filled the shadows the bosun's lamp didn't reach.

George became restless. He tried to angle his wicker chair closer to the railing to set his head against it, but after several scoots left and right, he concluded there was no comfortable position for him. He stood up suddenly. "I will be at the pier in the morning," he announced as he stepped around Brian and descended to the sand. "Thank you for the dinner."

"Thanks for cooking," Brian said.

"You don't want to stay?" Leslie asked.

George pointed at the book and shook his head with an expression of disdain. "I liked your father, but I do not care to hear their names," he said.

"You want a ride to town?" Brian asked. He was beginning to understand George a little better.

"I will walk to clear my head. At the pier tomorrow. I will have the boat ready."

Brian watched him until he was only a white hat drifting over the sand.

"I am sorry about all this," he said. "Sorry you got involved."

She crossed the deck and, with feline ease, sat beside him on the steps, her slender toes dipping into the sand. She leaned into him, shoulder to shoulder. "Our dads got us involved."

Brian stared across the lagoon's shimmering waters that sparkled like a fractured mirror under the celestial spotlight. "The sins of the father are to be laid upon the children."

"If you're going to start quoting Shakespeare, I going to bed," she said as she rose to her feet. She touched his shoulder. "Goodnight."

"Night," he said and after a time, he moved to the lounge and stretched himself across the stiff pad. At the back of the house, he could hear Leslie climb into the spring bed. When he finally fell asleep, her light was still on.

In the morning, with two cups of instant coffee waiting for the kettle to boil, he diced the remaining fruit into a passable breakfast platter. But he found Leslie door was still closed with silence behind it. He decided to let her sleep until he had the Jeep packed.

Brian lined the back of the truck with as many air tanks as he could fit. On top of those, he set a canvas gear bag filled with dive masks and fins. But of the two regulators he managed to salvage from spare parts, he took extra care and slipped them under the Jeep's front seat.

Returning to workroom, Brian found the phony tank top and valve still on the bench. The thought of someone rifling the house again while they were on the water was not a pleasant one. If he and George found the wreck, losing the chart might not matter, but her father's notebook? That he was not willing to give up.

As he reached under the bench and freed the lower half of the phony tank, he heard something it slide to the bottom. Brian tipped it over.

A black handgun dropped onto the floor. Brian immediately recognized the Colt .45 caliber automatic. He slipped the heavy weapon into his hand and instinctively checked its readiness. He released the magazine into his palm and noted the copper rounds filling its length. He checked the barrel and found another round perched inside.

He grabbed a piece of cloth from the table and wrapped the gun. From under the desk in the study, he recovered his father's black logbook.

Stepping through the sliding glass door, he found a nook under the raised deck and stuffed the bundle inside. It was not the best hiding place, but it certainly wasn't the first place someone would search.

Finally, he tapped on the bedroom door. "Leslie? Are you up?" He pushed slightly and peeked in. The bed was empty. He stepped in. "Leslie?"

He dashed to the kitchen. "Leslie." The pot was still on the stove, only his cup on the table.

"Leslie!" he called from the edge of the deck. He ran out to the water and looked up and down the deserted beach. "Leslie!" He went to the side of the house. "Leslie!" he called into the mangrove.

"Here," her voice carried to him as she stepped out of the thick jungle. She had her father's notebook in her hand.

"Jesus!"

"What? I went for a walk," she said innocently.

"You have to tell me."

"I didn't want to wake you."

"Please, wake me."

"Okay," she smiled at him.

"It's just that…"

"I get it. I am sorry," she said honestly.

"I don't know what we are dealing with, Les," he said, wanting her to understand but not wanting to scare her.

She touched him on the cheek. "I get it. Honest. You don't have to worry." Her hand slipped into his, squeezed it, and pulled him toward the house.

•   •   •

The doctor from New York City never saw the man in the mangroves. He started watching the house just after sunset when he could make his way silently through the thicket and press himself into the shadows of the patio deck.

He heard her reading to the ex-commander and the islander as they ate. What she read meant nothing to him, but he made mental notes of Brian's response.

And when the girl left the house in the morning as Brian slept on the outdoor couch, he followed her. Making her way through the mangroves, she became disoriented twice. She stopped, backtracked, and once almost walked right into him. The sound of the surf hitting the coral rocks led her back toward the beach where she corrected her bearings and she continued along.

Why the hell was the commander was sleeping outside? The man could not understand. *Jesus, make a move, Commander,* he thought. Although rail thin women with unimpressive breasts normally repulsed JP, he had to admit, the Maetani girl was a stunning woman.

Hidden by the thick foliage, he had gotten close enough to appreciate the distinct pleat of her thigh muscles as they stretched from the cuff of peach-colored shorts. Long legs, long torso, long arms, long hair. *Goddamnit,* he thought, *she is half my age, maybe younger.* Still, he could not help wondering about her breasts under the light material of her white blouse.

The CIA man pushed those thoughts from his mind and got himself back to work. He watched the pair as they climbed the deck stairs and disappeared into the beach house. He saw they had loaded the Jeep with dive equipment.

JP had expected that. He had read all about this isolated end of the world on his flight. If he gleaned anything from the stack of tourist brochures, it was that you come to the ghost ship lagoon to get in the water and not for the nightlife or cuisine.

He rented a small fishing boat from a local woman. For her exorbitant price, she tossed in fishing gear and a floppy canvas hat. It was all under-the-table, cash-in-hand. Exactly what he needed.

Darting back through the mangroves, JP returned to the dirt road and the particularly dense thicket where his Honda scooter lay hidden. Unfortunately, the motor scooter was not a rental. The teenager straddling it at the airport would only turn it over for an outright sale. No doubt for twice its worth, but JP had little choice. Pay the kid or try hitchhiking across this primitive hump of sand.

•   •   •

"We need to go," Brian said as he gulped the last of his coffee. It was cold and bitter. "I have a feeling George is going to change his mind about helping us."

She was staring at her father's book. "Listen to this," she said, following him from the house.

"Save it," he said, plodding down the stairs.

"No listen," Leslie persisted as they climbed into the Jeep. "Forward and stern holds sound," she read. "Midship where torpedo struck, best way in."

Brian stopped as he was about to turn the ignition key. "In?"

•   •   •

When the braided anchor line went taut, George leaned over the skiff's bow and gave it a two-handed tug. The line ran low into a whirlpool of its own making before disappearing into the depths. He signaled with a fist raised above his head and the engine fell silent. Two wraps and a twist across the forward cleat, and George had the Owens secured off the island's western beach.

"Do you think we're above her?" Brian asked.

"We hooked something solid."

Tucked into a natural arch of the beach, the surge was light and the waves gentle, like a Georges Seurat painting. The runabout settled against the line.

Leslie sat on the boat's cabin with her legs swinging freely over the companionway. She grasped the bottom of her cotton blouse, twisted it over her head, revealing her purple string bikini. Balling the shirt, she dropped it below.

George was watching with a smile and when her eyes caught his, he grinned wider with his crooked teeth. "The day is turning beautiful," he said.

Crouched over the scuba tanks, Brian was busy attaching the regulators with meticulous care. "Maybe some help?" He tapped George on the knee.

"Of course. That is what I am for."

Brian shared his eye roll with Leslie, who laughed lightly.

"Can I do anything?" she asked, leaping to the deck with ease.

"In a few minutes, you can help us get over the side," Brian said as he passed the last regulator to George.

As she watched them prepare, Brian's fervent attention to detail and how it annoyed George's easy-going manner amused her. "It's all good. You got it," the islander kept telling Brian as he triple-checked their equipment. "I have dived these waters for thirty years," George proclaimed. "I know what we're doing."

Brian glared at him, was sure Leslie could not hear him, and whispered. "And the last guy you helped?"

"That is not right. He did not want my help in the water."

"Fair enough," Brian conceded. "In my old job, there was no margin for error. Old habits."

George stared down his nose and grunted.

With the same weighted rope Henry had used, they lowered two sets of life-saving air tanks into the crystal-blue water. Strategically spaced, the extra tanks afforded the divers the time they needed to release the deadly nitrogen molecules that would accumulate in their bloodstreams.

Brian checked the rope's depth by the plastic markers woven into its strands. Satisfied, he secured the line to the stern cleat.

With the decompression tanks set, Brian snaked his arms into a thin, well-abused, wetsuit jacket borrowed from the dive shop. Torn at the elbows and with an obstinate front zipper, it would, nevertheless, keep his upper body warm against the chill of the deep water.

He helped George hoist the cumbersome twin-tanks to the gunwale and checked his regulator one more time. He loosened the shoulder straps for the islander to wiggle into.

Brian sat beside him and did the same.

Leslie hurried to hand the men their face masks and fins. She winced as they spit into the plate glass and rubbed the saliva with their fingers. "What should I do while you're gone?"

Brian squinted up at her. Framed by a brilliant blue sky, her hair flickered like a hallow. "I hate to ask, but anything more you might find in your father's book would help."

"Me? I think you get a better suntan," George suggested. "You are too pale."

"You ready?" Brian asked as he tested his dive lamp. The bulb was dim in the sunlight.

The islander pushed his thick feet into his swim fins, hooked the strap over his heel and stared reluctantly over the side. "How deep?"

"The chart says a hundred and sixty," Brian told him. "You said you've been doing this for thirty years."

"I never gone inside."

"Don't worry. We're just taking a peek," Brian promised. He slipped on his fins, double-checked his harnesses and weight belt.

"Be careful, okay," Leslie said. She squeezed Brian's hand as if suddenly hit by what they were doing.

"We'll be up in an hour and ten minutes," he assured her. He pointed to a small coil of nylon rope. "Hand me that?"

"You have enough air?" she asked.

George squirmed. "Good question?"

"You said…"

"Never this deep either," George admitted.

Brian frowned. "Just stay close." He pushed the nylon rope under his dive jacket.

George nodded woefully. He lowered his face mask, put the regulator between his teeth, and flashed Brian a thumbs up. Lifting his feet, he disappeared over the side.

"Please be careful," Leslie frowned as she saw the unfamiliar strangle of nylon straps and high-pressure hoses.

"An hour and ten minutes," Brian reassured her.

As he pulled his mask over his face, she abruptly leaned down and kissed him. She eased away slowly, smiling shyly, as if she had surprised herself more than she had surprised him.

"An hour and ten." She tapped her wrist. "Don't make me come get you, Commander."

The clear water enveloped Brian with an effervescent explosion. The water was cooler than he expected, a crisp counter to the warm day. He let himself drift beneath the boat's hull.

George was waiting a few feet below him. His silvery bubbles flowed from the regulator with a smooth, calm rhythm.

Brian flashed the 'okay' sign, and the islander returned the same. In unison, they swam to the decompression line and started their descent.

·   ·   ·

Through the pair of Nikon binoculars, JP watched the men disappear under the water. He had followed them at a distance in his rented outboard, which was now hidden on the opposite side of the island.

Perched behind a natural fence of palm trees, he turned his attention on Leslie as she spread a white beach towel over the Owen's cabin. Peeling off her shorts, she revealed the bottom half of a purple bikini. The sharp vee of cloth that cut tight between her legs seemed to be held magically in place with impossibly thin pieces of string.

JP swallowed hard as he watched her straighten the towel and settled herself against the sloping foredeck. Suntan lotion applied on slender legs and arms. Big Audrey Hepburn sunglasses. A plastic sun visor. A small book. He felt a tinge of guilt for his voyeurism.

Then again, he remembered that was ninety percent of the job. Sit and watch people. Take notes and watch some more. He would not apologize for his work. Through the binoculars, he could see the shimmer of the tropical sun on her skin.

"The lagoon is beautiful here," the soft voice behind him came like an electric shock. Sudden and unexpected.

JP spun, his right hand instantly drawing his revolver from its belt holster, his thumb automatically cocking the hammer.

But the elderly Asian woman with a long braid of gray hair simply smiled down at him. She stood beside a coconut palm, her sandals dangling from her fingers. "But there are prettier waters off Pata. The water is so blue there. Blue like a robin's egg."

"Who the fuck…?" JP said, his voice too loud. Shock was still vibrating through his chest. "You almost got yourself shot, lady." He eased the hammer with his thumb and lowered the revolver to its leather sleeve.

"I was not worried, Mr. Powell," she chuckled. "You are a professional."

A new surprise. He thumbed the gun's hammer. "You have the advantage. You know me. I don't know you."

She laughed. "I always have the advantage," she said pleasantly, like a patient grandmother watching a grandchild. She carried herself to a fallen tree trunk half buried in the sand. She brushed it off and sat down. "You'll excuse me if I sit. These old legs can't cross the sand like they used to."

"How the hell did you follow me?" JP asked, both surprised and disturbed an elderly woman could track him.

"Oh no, Mr. Powell," she told him. "I've been here waiting for you. You see, I am also a friend of the Vicar."

JP could not help himself. His brow lifted at still another surprise from the woman. The Vicar. The most recent code phrase for field agents to acknowledge each other's alliances. It changed on random days and at random times. It was a First World War throwback, but it worked well when other means of verification were impossible.

JP had received this one on a paper napkin passed to him along with a ginger ale and bag of peanuts by an indifferent stewardess on his flight from Honolulu.

"You're in…"

"Shocked that a woman my age would be in the profession?" she chuckled. "Your surprise is the point?"

JP was surprised. He also felt duped, and it was a feeling he did not like.

The woman continued. "How many old spies do you know, Mr. Powell? Ones that are honestly retired? It's a rhetorical question, of course. We either die off or we are put on hold."

The agent studied her for a moment. There was no menace in her voice, no violence. "Are we here for the same reasons? Or is this just a coincidence?"

"Do you believe in coincidence?"

"Not for a second." He pocketed his sidearm.

She laughed. "I am Lai Ming. To friends, just Mimi," she said, rocking back and forth as she enjoyed the sun's warmth. She glanced through the palms toward the Owens. "I wish I could tell you everything, Mr. Powell, to ease your concerns. But all I can say is Commander Bovan is not a security threat."

"I was starting to believe that, but there have been other developments."

"Your man in Hawaii?"

"That has to be accounted for."

"Of course, it does." Mimi leaned against the course bark of the palm tree. She let her head fall back as she was simply enjoying the intense blue dome above. "Maybe I should tell you a little more. It might help."

"Help?"

She gave him the sidelong smile. "Come and sit, Mr. Powell." She beckoned to the spot beside her.

•　　•　　•

At thirty feet below the surface, Brian checked the first set of decompression tanks. He took a breath from each regulator. He did the same with the next set of tanks dangling at eighty feet. Satisfied, he signaled George, and the two men continued their descent. Sunrays followed them, slicing the ocean like a blue velvet theater curtain swinging across the stage.

As they neared a hundred feet, the colors of their masks, and fins became muted, everything a shade of gray and black against the depth's haze.

The divers continued with the line, side-by-side, their exhaust bubbles shooting up like silvery signal flares. George's eyes, encircled by the facemask, were wide. He kept staring between his fins and at the void below.

Brian was comfortable here. In the sea. In its growing darkness. He had grown up at the edge of the Atlantic where the beach and surf were the only forms of entertainment a widow could offer her son.

Had Brian never known his father was a Navy man, he would still have gravitated toward the sea. "You have saltwater for blood," his mother would say. "Fish scales under your skin and, I betcha, one day, kiddo, your feet will turn into fins."

Once again, Brian waved the 'okay' signal in front of George's mask and got an enthusiastic nod. A moment later, the islander pointed excitedly toward the bottom.

In the wavering shadows, an eerie silhouette appeared at the end of the weighted decompression line. It was a murky figure, huge and foreboding, like a pre-historic leviathan lying in wait for its next meal.

Brian felt a chill squirm down his back. It was a mixture of excitement and dread. This was a military ship and though they were once the enemy, they were navy men who perished in the service of their country.

Brian flipped on the dive lamp, creating a cone of light beneath his fins. Illuminating a portion of the massive ship, it revealed how she had settled at a steep angle on her starboard side.

Covered with a fine layer of silt and a blanket of soft corals that exploded with brilliant colors under his sweeping light, it was clear the harsh sea was gradually devouring the *Kuma Maru*.

A hundred feet of her port railing had broken free, either fallen from corrosion or torn by American bombs. Regardless of how, it now laid like a twisted vines across the lower levels of the superstructure.

Brian aimed his lamp into the bridge where her windows had been there was now a schooling wall of silvery sardines.

Moving toward the bow, the men descended into the yawning hatch of the forward hold. Inside, they could see a three-man army tank that had never reached the island it was supposed to defend. Now, it was camouflaged with orange and purple sponges.

A quick search and Brian saw there was no way through the forward hold into the midship chambers. Henry's notes were proving to be accurate.

Returning to the bridge, Brian and George drifted into the open window. Inside the oddly angled room, years of fallen debris had accumulated against the far corners of the deck and bulkhead. Although they knew to be careful, every kick of their fins stirred the snowy silt, making their lamps nearly useless.

Brian continued past the ship's shattered wheel and the toppled compass binnacle. At the rear, an open hatchway led them into the inner passages.

The room directly behind the bridge was surprisingly large. It stretched from the port bulkhead to the starboard. Knowing ships were designed with standard conventions, Brian suspected it was the navigation room and would have been lined with cabinets and drawers filled with sextants and spreaders, paper charts and brass time pieces.

The bulkheads where cabinets once stood was now a complex of coral encrusted homes. Damsel fish, snails and barrel sponges took residence within weeks of the freighter's arrival on the sea bottom. Given she would never leave this last port, it was fitting her new occupants were indifferent to the state of her navigational tools.

Brian checked his watch. They had been down for fourteen minutes. He checked his air supply, then pulled George close and inspected the air pressure gauge dangling from his tank.

Brian knew that a man's breathing rate would increase under stress or when he was forced into an unfamiliar environment. None was more stressful or unfamiliar than diving a deep-water wreck.

George did what Brian expected. He had consumed almost half his air while Brian still had three-fourths of a tank. To stay within their safety margins, they would have to shorten their dive by several minutes. Brian flashed an okay signal. The islander nodded.

In his light, Brian caught another doorway further down the corridor. He tapped George on the shoulder and signaled him to follow.

The open companionway revealed a ladder descending to the next deck. And to their surprise, secured at the entrance was a length of line. Not a relic, but a modern three-braid nylon safety line. Knowing it was Henry's, Brian took hold and headed downward.

The line ended in the ship's engine room. Sweeping their lights from side to side, the divers carefully made their way through the maze of lopsided catwalks that once hung over the freighter's engines.

Brian swam purposely toward the far bulkhead where he hoped to find a way into the midship hold. *There would be one there,* he thought. Like

American shipbuilders, the Japanese would certainly have incorporated small passageways through the freighter for its repair crews to move easily from one section to another.

He found it in the lower corner. A small maintenance crawl tunnel with a thick, water-tight door.

As the divers drifted to it, Brian immediately saw the fresh scrap marks at the base of one of the four dogleg latches. Then, in silt near his feet, he uncovered Henry's iron crowbar.

Brian felt George pull at his arm. For the first time, excitement replaced the islander's nervousness as he pointed to the rusting latches. Clearly, Leslie's father had reached the door, but he had not gotten farther.

Brian glanced at his watch. Twenty-three minutes in the wreck. They were pushing their limits, but he could not leave. Not without knowing what Leslie's father had given up his life for.

Grabbing the crowbar, Brian shoved the forked end under the edge of the door and began to lift.

George grabbed Brian's wrist and shook his head.

Brian ignored him as he continued to fight the hatch. The strain was making him light-headed as the muscles in his neck knotted.

George took hold of the bar as well and added strength to Brian's efforts.

Still, the hatch resisted, until finally it began to yield inch by inch. They pushed the bar deeper. The door gave more, yawning ever so slowly. Again, they shifted the crowbar and fought against the hinges.

A ten-inch gap opened. *Just enough*, Brian thought.

He motioned George to hold the bar tight. The islander shook his head frantically, trying to scream through his mouthpiece.

Brian knelt against the muddy deck, twisted himself over and squeezed his head past the door and into the blackness. He snaked his right arm and dive lamp inside.

The bright beam drew back a curtain of darkness that had not been parted in four decades. Brian swept it across the steel ribs of the port side of the hull. They were red with corrosion yet void of the musky silt that covered every other inch of the freighter.

Along the ship's starboard side, Brian could see the massive breach that had been ripped open by the American torpedo bomber. It ran the entire length of the midship bay, its jagged edge curling inward like the teeth of an enormous shark.

Then, just beyond the reach of his light, an odd shape came into view. The twin cannons of an unknown weapon stood as though it was about to rise from the cargo bay and challenge the incoming enemy. A fight it never joined.

Shifting his dive beam, Brian tried desperately to add more details to his vision. But above him, he heard the screech of the crowbar as it began to slip.

Brian yanked himself back, pulling his arm from the falling door as it slammed shut. It caught his dive lamp, popping the bulb and smashing its dense plastic casing with the sickening sound of cracking bones.

George hauled Brian off the floor by his shoulder straps, held him at arm's length and checked for damage. Seeing none, he glared at him, face mask to face mask.

Brian flashed the 'okay' sign. The islander shook his head with dismay.

Following the nylon line from the engine room to the bridge, the divers started their slow climb to the surface.

27

S ECOND LIEUTENANT HIRO MAETANI ran the tip of his pencil along the edge of the ship's log. In the shifting light of the candle that burned with a greasy tail of black smoke, he scratched off the freighter's cargo deliveries. The crew had transferred everything requested by the supply sergeant on Dublon. Everything but that wretched tank.

It remained in the forward hold, waiting for repairs. The colonel in charge of the island's armaments would not accept the vehicle unless it was in fighting condition. *Empty-headed man*, Maetani thought.

The Army mechanics would have its engine sorted out in a day, but the colonel blamed the damage on Maetani's crew. They had quarreled, but still, the tank remained.

Now, Maetani had to locate a willing mechanic from one of the other Army battalions. Otherwise, there would be no delivery and no returning to Japan. Briefly, he entertained the idea of dropping the damn thing on one of the lagoon's deserted islets.

But the war was not going well, and every piece of weaponry was desperately needed. There was that sense across the island and amongst the freighter's crew. The Solomons. Tarawa. Kwajalein and Majura. They had each fallen over the last few months to the American forces, and it did not take a navigational master to draw a line directly through those losses to Tokyo itself.

Watching Admiral Koga's fleet of carriers and destroyers leave the safety of Truk and head out to sea early yesterday morning did not help. It was a bad omen strengthened by the merchant fleet's orders to unload their cargo and leave the lagoon as soon as possible.

"Maetani-san," the voice came from the other side of the door.

"Yes," Maetani leapt to his feet. The deep voice of Captain Kiyohara was unique to no one else. Maetani yanked the door open and stood at attention.

"Evening, Maetani-san," Kiyohara said with an unfamiliar smile. He was a big man with a pot belly and a closely shaven head. The crew referred to him as Captain Buddha. They meant it to be insulting, but the captain took it as reverence.

"You are still working?" Kiyohara glanced at the open book.

"Making sure all is in order, sir." Maetani remained at attention, his broad chest firm against his sleeveless undershirt. "The tank…"

"Yes, the tank," Kiyohara nodded with disappointment. "The Army is always a headache. They forget they are on an island, and they need us far more than we need them."

Maetani grinned. "Yes, sir."

"Come, Lieutenant," the captain said. "We have something to talk about."

Maetani snatched his uniform shirt from his bunk and followed the large man as he wobbled down the companionway.

"The army tank does not worry me, Maetani-san. I like this lagoon. It is a paradise and there are no torpedoes tearing into my ship."

"Our orders…"

"Our orders, Lieutenant, are to deliver equipment and supplies. After, we return to Sasebo. An extra day or two will not change the world," Kiyohara joked.

"I hear our fleet left because an American plane was sighted," the lieutenant ventured.

Kiyohara laughed; it echoed through the quiet ship. "A thousand planes could not chase away Admiral Koga."

For a moment, Maetani felt foolish at his assumption. The captain was right. A thousand planes would not send the admiral running. He would stay and fight to the last man. But the single American plane that had flown high over the islands was not a bomber, it was a reconnaissance plane. And the fact was, the Americans had more than a thousand warplanes.

Koga was not running in the face of an attack. He was avoiding it. After so many recent losses, Maetani understood the admiral had no other option. Their weakened fleet had to withdraw. Suddenly, the lieutenant realized what Kiyohara did not. An American attack was imminent.

"How long did you live in America, Maetani-san?" Kiyohara asked over his shoulder as they continued to the stairway that led to the bridge.

"Twelve years," Maetani said, reluctantly.

"Ah!" Kiyohara nodded. "A long time. You must know how they think?"

"That is difficult to say with any man, Captain."

"Yes, yes, but you can judge better than I," Kiyohara said as they entered the open bridge of the *Kuma Maru*.

The two men on watch saluted the captain and second officer as they walked through.

Kiyohara turned to Maetani and raised his hand. "Wait, I need to get something from my cabin," he said, disappearing down the companionway.

Maetani glanced at the crewmen watching him. "All well tonight?"

"Quiet as always, sir."

"Let us hope it remains that way."

"Yes, sir."

"Come, Lieutenant," Kiyohara reappeared. In his hands, he carried a gray flask of sake and two palm-sized drinking cups.

The men on the bridge saluted their officers again as they passed.

"The Americans are strange people, Maetani-san, very strange people," Kiyohara stepped outside onto the open passageway. He walked along the upper deck through the moonless night.

Neither man needed the railings to guide them. They had walked miles on the *Kuma Maru* and instinct told them where to step.

"They think they rule the entire world," Kiyohara spat. He led Maetani to the lower decks, down several stairways and back inside the ship. They walked down a series of catwalks and into the engine room.

The three sailors working on a generator unit and covered with thick brown grease stood quickly and saluted. Kiyohara asked them how the repairs were coming.

"It will be finished by morning, sir," the dirtiest promised.

The dismantled generator was spread across the steel deck like a shattered toy, but Maetani knew the man would keep his word.

The captain shuffled through the wooden bucket that held the mechanic's tools. He took one of the claw hammers and continued through the ship.

Maetani followed his captain, uncertain where he was leading them. At the far end of the engine room, Kiyohara handed him the flask and cups. He removed a kerosene lamp where it hung on the wall and, with a striker, lit the moist wick.

"Are Americans trustworthy, Maetani-san?" he asked as he kicked open the dogleg latches of a small maintenance hatch and wiggled his bulk through.

The lieutenant hugged the flask and cups as he ducked through the doorway. On the other side, he found himself at the bottom of the midship hold. With the upper hatches sealed closed, only the small pool of light cast by Kiyohara's lamp gave him reference.

"So, do you think they can be trusted?" the captain asked again, impatience rising in his voice.

"I would not trust one with a pistol to my head, if that is what you are asking."

"It is not," he grunted. Kiyohara headed deeper into the hold, the glowing lamp leading their way. He paused, turned, and leaned into his lieutenant. "What I want to know is whether or not an American will keep his word."

Maetani stared into the narrow eyes of his captain and saw red in the corners. "I believe so."

"They are not animals, are they? Not like we've been told?" Kiyohara asked, although he clearly knew the answer.

"Not at all."

Satisfied, Kiyohara lowered the lamp until it illuminated a green tarp piled against the hold's forward bulkhead. The captain handed the lamp to Maetani. He pulled the heavy canvas, revealing a large wooden crate.

Maetani took a step closer. He had never seen this crate before. It had no markings or tags on the lid to tell its destination. "This isn't in the logs," the lieutenant stated.

Kiyohara laughed, "I should hope not," he said. Using the hooked claw of the hammer, he pried open the lid. The first nails cried like an alley cat, its screams echoing through the cargo bay.

With the crate's lid removed, Maetani saw two smaller wooden boxes packed tightly with straw. The writing on the top of both struck him with horror.

"These are from the Americans," he gasped.

"You can read and speak English, can't you," Kiyohara said with delight.

"What do they hold?"

Kiyohara smiled widely. "Our fortune, Maetani-san," he said as he grabbed the rope handle at one end. He pointed at the other end. "Lift," he ordered.

Together, the men hoisted it to the deck. The captain quickly unclipped the latch and pulled it open.

In the light, Maetani saw the dozens of newspaper-wrapped objects. The paper was old and brittle and tore easily as he unraveled it. Suddenly, he was holding a mahogany-colored bone embedded with reddish dirt. "What is this?"

"A fossil. Very old and very important," Kiyohara said. He took the sake bottle, twisted the cork free. He filled the cups with the clear liquid. "I took the sake from a case going to that Army colonel who left us with the broken tank. We will drink to the emperor, but we will thank the colonel," he laughed.

Maetani felt the rough surface of the bone under his fingers, enthralled with the artifact. He took the sake cup.

"Kampai," the captain raised his cup. Maetani did the same, and the men drank.

As he studied the bone in the lamplight, Maetani asked. "What do you intend to do with these?"

The captain filled their cups once again. "That is all taken care of. We are just a step in a much greater plan." He lifted his cup, and they drank again.

Still, Maetani was unsure.

Kiyohara saw. He snatched another oddly shaped bone from the crate. "Do you know what this is worth, Maetani-san?"

Maetani shook his head. He honestly did not know.

"It is worthless. You would care about the bones of dead men? Not even men, of monkeys," he laughed as he leaned forward. He lowered his voice to a whisper. "Unless they were the bones of your family, of your ancestors. Those bones would be precious, don't you think?"

Maetani inspected the fossil. "Americans don't care about their ancestors."

"But think who does," he toyed.

Maetani slowly looked at his captain. "The Chinese."

"Yes," he laughed harshly. "And they are eager for their ancestors to return home. Four-hundred-million-yen worth of eagerness."

Maetani stared. "That is not possible. They are an appropriation of war. They are the property of the emperor, not the Chinese."

"The problem with that is the emperor will never agree to our price."

"You can't take these into China, anyway," Maetani said. "There is no way into the country."

"We do not need to. The Chinese are sending us a submarine. An American submarine."

Maetani tensed. "What you are saying is treasonous."

Kiyohara waved his hand dismissingly as he poured more sake. "The war is over, Maetani-san. You know that fact as well as I do. What matters is what we will become after. I do not plan to be a beggar in a conquered Japan."

Maetani ran his hand over the footlocker. "You are bargaining with our enemy?" He could not conceive of it.

"Today, he is the enemy. Tomorrow," Kiyohara shrugged. "I promise you, Lieutenant, I will make sure you are paid for your assistance."

"No!" Maetani dropped the fossil and clambered to his feet. "These must be reported to Tokyo and given to command."

The captain winced. "There will be no report," he said calmly. "And when the Americans arrive, you will translate for me."

Maetani shook his head in defiance as he backed away from the captain. Slipping into the darkness of the vast cargo hold, the lieutenant was suddenly aware he and the captain were not alone.

28

A S BRIAN MANEUVERED the *Owens* alongside the low pier, George took a broad leap from the bow onto its bleached planks. Bowline in hand, the islander hurried to the first cleat, wrapped the line around its rusty base and hitched it tight.

Brian shut off the motor. "Now," he told Leslie.

She tossed George the stern line as the boat drifted into the old tires that hung from the pier's oily pylons. Half-submerged, they wore green beards of algae from their worn treads.

"I'll check with Ramon about filling the acetylene tank," the islander said, his voice an octave higher than normal.

"George," Brian grabbed his arm. "Don't forget, if anyone asks, we're using the torch to fix the Jeep frame."

"The cutting torch for the Jeep," he nodded. "Okay."

"Good. We'll meet you at the truck," he told him.

He watched George walk the length of the pier toward the Quonset hut of the Truk Trading Co. A handful of men, dressed in stained pants and unbuttoned shirts, sat near the entrance talking. They all nodded to the islander as he passed.

They would believe him, Brian knew. So far, everyone believed Leslie's father's death was an accident. Just another diver who did not understand the dangers of the wrecks and ignored their ghosts. But someone on the island knew otherwise, and there was no fooling him.

It was quiet around the harbor. With dusk less than an hour away, the usual activity of Moen was already winding down.

Brian could hear the dinner music coming across the harbor from the Truk Stop Hotel. Rota would be working in the kitchen with her daughter, Brian guessed, while Boggy set the tables, hoping for large tips from the wealthy tourists who came from places he knew little about.

Tomorrow, the tourists would swarm the lagoon in rented boats or set out on motor scooters to search for the remains of Imperial Japan still scattered through the jungle and the hillsides. All they would discover would be the fierce armaments of righteous men that were now little more than rusted monuments covered by twisted tree roots and spiders' webs.

"Leslie," Brian called into the skiff.

"Coming," she said over her shoulder as she heard him step down the companionway. She slid the charts from the table and rolled them tight. Dropping them into the phony diving tank, she set the dome top in place.

"The notebook too."

"I was going to read it on the drive back," she said.

"Better to do it at the house."

"Do you think someone is watching us?"

"I always think it's better to be cautious."

She set her hands on his chest, tapping. "You're scaring me," Leslie admitted.

He touched her chin. "Scared enough to get on a plane and go back to Honolulu?"

"Not even close."

"Just don't let your guard down. For anyone," he pressed.

"Even you?" she smiled sheepishly.

Brian laughed. "I think I lied enough to you."

"That's true."

"I am never going to live that down," Brian said as he hoisted the phony tank to his shoulder and climbed to the pier.

"Nope," she said as she casually slipped her hand into his.

•   •   •

"Ramon said we can pick the cutter up in the morning," George said as he climbed into the rear of the Jeep. "He'll also have the scuba tanks filled."

"Good," Brian said, shifting into gear. As he pulled out onto the street, he saw Boggy running toward them waving his hands.

The boy stepped around the jeep to the passenger side. "My mother asked for you to come to dinner," he said to Leslie. "We have three lobsters, all giants." Boggy held out his arms as far as they would go.

"Please tell your mother thank you, but we need to get back to the house," Brian said.

"Not right away." Leslie put her hand on Brian's leg. She leaned into his ear and whispered. "If we are being watched, let them think we are just tourists." She kissed his ear.

"Rota makes the best lobster in the islands," George said as he sat up. "And the hotel has a good bar. Good stuff she locks up in the back. She'll open it for you," he grinned. "Drinks with kick."

They won him over. "But we're not staying late," Brian said. He turned to George. "Or drinking too much."

"Oh no, just one." George held up three fingers and laughed.

"Come on, Boggy," Leslie slid herself closer to Brian, giving the boy half her seat. Boggy beamed as he jumped in.

Brian parked in the same place they had the day before. Boggy dashed inside, announcing their arrival.

Leslie laced her arm through Brian's as they entered the restaurant. George trailed behind.

"On the veranda," Rota pointed as she came out of the kitchen, rubbing a dish towel between her hands. "Boggy, set a table outside for you two."

"What about me?" George protested.

Rota turned and said in a stern voice, "Shhh. You eat in the kitchen with me."

"I'm sure all four of us can eat together," Leslie said politely, but her eyes conveyed what Rota understood.

"Good," George said as he pulled a chair from a nearby table and edged against the one set for two tucked into the corner of the veranda.

"We leave them on their own," Rota told him. "Besides, I have something special for you."

George frowned as he backed away. "She is trying to confuse me with food," he whispered to Leslie.

"We'll talk later," Brian told him as the islander followed Rota through the double-swing doors.

"This is nice of her," Leslie said as she sat down. Brian held her chair. "Oh, and a gentleman too."

"We're a rare breed."

"Not really," she toyed.

As Brian sat down, he glanced at the Jeep. He could see their diving gear stacked behind the rear seat. The phony tank was safe beneath it all.

He found Leslie staring at him. She turned to the golden dish of the sun resting on the horizon, the silhouette of a moored sailboat etched into it. "Too bad people found this place. Can you imagine what it must have been like a thousand years ago?"

Brian looked out at the broad stretch of beach to the south, and the harbor to the north. With the coming dusk, he could see the flashing red lights of the airport in the distance.

Although he tried, he could not picture the lagoon without people. In fact, to his regret, all he saw were the dark waters on that February evening before the American attack. He could imagine the Japanese aboard their ships, resting their bunks, smoking, writing letters, and dreaming of going home as all soldiers did. But with the rising sun, they would wake to the chainsaw buzz of warplanes sweeping across the horizon.

"It is hard to imagine," he admitted.

Boggy came with a bottle wrapped in a napkin. "My mom said you might like this," he said in a gentle voice. He showed them the label. It was a white wine from New Zealand.

"That is perfect."

Boggy topped their glass. He lit a small candle, pushed it to the center of the table and then disappeared into the kitchen.

"He's enthralled with you," Brian said.

"He's cute," she lifted her glass. "To finding what you are looking for."

Brian reached across the table with his.

"Do you think we were supposed to sit together on the plane?" she asked. "That your Chinese woman arranged it?"

"I'd put money on it."

"And my father? Could she have arranged that?"

Brian felt himself tense, as if her questioning stare touched every nerve across his skin. "I hope not."

"But maybe?"

Brian would not lie to her. "Maybe."

"Only one way to know," Leslie said, with a subtle rise of her delicate shoulders. "We find what she sent you to find."

Boggy was suddenly at the edge of the table, his hands filled with dishes of fresh broad-leafed salad sprinkled with native fruits and shreds of coconut. The salty night air was immediately swept aside by the seasoned aroma of the broiled lobster centered on palm fronds and spicy Surimi curry.

As they ate, the night tried to cling to the heat of the day, but slowly it relented with the easterly breeze. In the distance, the riggings of sailboats chattered against their masts like broken metronomes.

In the restaurant and at the other tables on the veranda, tourists came in large and small groups. They ate and laughed at Rota's cloth-covered tables and spoke about their day's adventure.

"When George held the hatch, and I got a quick look," Brian said over his fork. "There was something in there." His brow curled.

"Like what?"

Brian shook his head. "Some kind of deck gun. Like a cannon, but not really. I don't know."

"You won't let me talk you out of going back, will you?"

Brian did not answer.

"People get lost inside the wrecks, Brian. George told me it happens all the time. They go in and they disappear."

"That's not going to happen."

"I bet my father said the same thing," she said, her eyes holding his.

By the time they finished, both Leslie and Brian felt as if they could hardly move. Boggy cleared the dishes and brought black Bamikele coffee and let them sit in the veranda's corner alone.

Leslie brought her cup of coffee to the edge of her lips. "What do you think you would've done?"

"About what?"

"If you were your father. If it was your submarine tied against a ship that was under attack? What would you have done?"

Brian stared at her. What would he have done? He had not thought of that. Every time he looked out at the lagoon, he tried to picture the attack on Truk, but all his mind could play was a jittery, black & white newsreel of propeller driven warplanes dropping from the clouds, their wing guns blazing.

"My stomach is full, and I am happy," George said as he stepped to the table. Rota was beside him, her shoulder under his heavy arm. "This woman is the best cook on the islands," he said.

Rota giggled. A schoolgirl with her star quarterback. "He is always so happy after he eats," she said.

Brian could see George had had an excess of wine.

"George, do you want some coffee?" Leslie asked.

"No, no. It will ruin the lobster," he said.

On the way back to the house, George slept over the uncomfortable pile of equipment, his snoring a mysterious sound chasing animals away from the truck's headlights.

To Brian's surprise, he was wide awake by the time they reached the house. "It will be safer to cut the hinges off," Brian said, as he set the false tank in the corner of Henry's study.

"Quicker to prop it," George said.

Leslie sat in one of the swivel chairs, listening. "What if it fell while you were inside?" she asked.

"She's right. The extra time is worth being safe. Plus, we can both get into the hold."

"Both?" the islander winced.

"We'll use a lift bag to get the cutting torch through," Brian said.

"And to take the treasure out."

"Don't get your hopes up."

"If not inside here, someplace on this wreck," George said. He turned to Leslie. "Your father was a very smart man. He knew more about the lagoon than anybody."

Leslie nodded sadly. "He was. He was a very smart man."

"I want to be in the water early tomorrow. That way, we can make another dive in the afternoon."

"I'll tell Ramon. He'll set the air tanks outside the shop for us,"

"You're welcome to sleep here tonight, George," Leslie said.

Brian glanced at her, wondering where he was supposed to sleep if George stayed.

"I told Rota I would come by." He smiled sheepishly. "She is a good woman. A wonderful cook and a good woman."

"At least let me drive you back," Brian offered.

The big man shook his head and disappeared out the door.

29

"SKIPPER, SORRY TO INTERRUPT, SIR," Mouse said, as he leaned into the officer's mess. "We've got a concern."

Douglas sat alone at the small, square table, a steaming cup of coffee in hand, and yesterday's edition of the *Stars and Stripes* newspaper spread in front of him. "A concern?"

"Clancy's word, sir."

Douglas folded the paper, pulled himself from the bench seat, and followed Mouse out of what the crew considered officer's territory.

Mouse was a small man, with wiry arms, noodle legs and an oddly shaped face that, well, clearly was the reason for his nickname.

As they passed through the control room, Douglas stopped at the ladder leading up to the control room. He glimpsed his XO. "Mike," he called. "How is it topside?"

Alberts leaned over the hatch, a face staring into a wishing well. "An easy swell from the north, and the skies are clear, Skipper. We're running smooth at fifteen knots."

"Very well," Douglas acknowledged. He waved to Mouse to continue.

In the forward engine room, Clancy stood staring at the starboard engine panel while wiping his hands on a fresh rag. He was frowning, making his face into a raisin.

"Chief?" Douglas saddled next to him.

The mechanic barely acknowledged him. He tapped the black-faced dial on the panel. "The temp is inching up again." He shook his head. "She was a hundred percent yesterday, Skipper."

"You are going to have to figure it out, Clanc. They've got us on a schedule, and I am afraid, where we're headed, I am going to need all the speed you can find."

"Charging the batteries won't be a problem. The other three can manage that without a hiccup. As for topside speed, you'll have it, Skipper."

"Good to hear," Douglas clapped his chief on the shoulder. He made a nod to Mouse and headed forward.

Returning to the control room, he found the shift had just changed, and he was met by a wave of good morning and good day greetings from his eager crew. If they were disappointed to leave Pearl or reluctant to head back to war, he could not see it in their youthful faces. They were men resolute in their duties and what was being asked of them. None of them complained, ever.

Grabbing his leather coat and hat from his stateroom, Douglas returned to the ladder and climbed through the lower conning tower hatch. He heard Alberts above take command of the bridge. "You're relieved, Mr. Fenton," he said sharply.

"Thank you, sir. You have the con," Fenton confirmed.

As Fenton descended the ladder from the bridge to the conning tower, Douglas stepped aside and let his officer pass. "Morning, Skipper," Fenton greeted him.

"Good morning, Mr. Fenton."

"Heading topside, sir?"

"I think I'll give Mr. Alberts some trouble."

"Very good, sir," Fenton said as he descended into the control room.

The crest of the morning sun was revealing itself, its rays of gold over the calm sea already brushing back the black night with lavender strokes. On the bridge, behind the chest high barrier of thick steel, it was still dark and cold.

Douglas buttoned his coat and flipped the collar up around his neck as he stepped onto the edge. "Morning, Mike," he said. He lifted an extra pair of binoculars from the hidden shelf.

"I saw the report on the number two diesel."

"The chief says he can work around it," Douglas said as he swept the binoculars across the horizon from the bow to the starboard quarter.

"It's going to push the remaining three hard."

"We'll be okay. And if the charts are right, we get in and out with plenty of time left over."

"And if they're not?"

"If they're not, we'll find another way in," Douglas said.

Alberts said nothing more. He lifted his binoculars and watched the portside horizon.

Three days later, Douglas was the officer of the deck with command of the bridge. It was late afternoon, the sun not yet on the horizon, but the eastern sky was already shifting from a cloudless blue to a new evening of lavender and diamonds. Not to be forgotten, the Pacific was throwing jabs at the sub as a brisk sea and a following wind that, as they held their westerly course, brought the choking fumes of the diesels over the aft deck.

The junior officer, Mr. Parker, assigned to stern watch over the cigarette deck, was trying not to cough out his lungs. It was a fight. The lookouts posted on the windswept mast, however, were spared most of the emissions.

Still, until the wind shifted, or the *Mako* changed course, their watch would feel unbearably long. Douglas glanced at the bridge compass. *A few degrees to port would carry the fumes away*, he thought.

As he reached for the telephone to order the course change, the explosive voice of the radar man met him.

"Bridge! Contact. Aircraft. Incoming. Bearing oh-ate-niner. Range fi-yiv oh double-oh."

Douglas knew immediately the enemy aircraft was coming in fast and low and would try to keep the sun directly behind its tail. A perfect execution of attack into the lookout's blind spot. With or without their sun filters, they could not stare directly into it.

He acknowledged the emergency call, followed by his own high-pitched call, "Clear the bridge! Dive! Dive!"

Instantly, the lookouts dropped from their perch and scrambled through the hatch into the conning tower. Inside the sub, Douglas heard the Klaxon alarm roaring. Throughout her length, his men were scrambling to their battle stations.

From under the false deck, he heard the induction valves slam closed as they choked off the air to its massive diesel motors. Under his feet, the deck fell steeply.

Douglas dashed to the bridge hatch when he saw Parker frozen with his binoculars against his face. "Mr. Parker, with or without you," he called. The sea was racing quickly over the submarine's bow.

"It's a lone Val, Skipper. Nothing hanging under her belly." He called, his voice high like a siren. "We could get off a few shots, sir. Before she radioes our location."

Douglas glanced east into the sun. "Don't make me regret this, Parker," he snapped. "Con," he blurted. "Belay depth. Level us at two seven feet."

At twenty-seven feet, most of the *Mako* rode beneath the waves with only the conning tower and the cigarette deck seen above. Douglas and Parker would get a shower of ocean spray, but there would be less of a target for the Jap to focus on.

"One pass, Parker. That is all you get."

The officer flashed a grin as he dropped his binoculars and hoisted himself over the backside of the bridge. He landed awkwardly on the cigarette deck and stumbled into the shoulder purchases of the Oerlikon anti-aircraft gun. He slapped down the safety, pulled the breach.

From his breast pocket, he drew a pair of sunglasses and slipped them over his eyes almost casually. The thunderclap of the 20mm rounds jack-hammered through the single-barrel gun pounding the air as Parker fired into the rising sun.

"Con. Prepare to crash dive," Douglas ordered.

He heard Alberts in the chamber directly below acknowledge his call.

Looking over Parker's head, Douglas still could not find the incoming plane, but now he could hear it. A gut-wrenching buzz of hornet growing as it neared. The next thing he heard was the tang of enemy bullets ripping along the stern like the footsteps of a ghost running up the submarine's spine.

Parker did not seem to care. He simply continued to fire the savage Oerlikon into the golden ball while discharged copper shells bounced off the platform and danced into the sea.

Suddenly, the black silhouette of the dive-bomber split the disk of the sun in half as he roared toward them fifty feet above the waves. Amazingly, red and blue flames engulfed the plane's entire fuselage. Yet, while he was certainly dead, the Japanese pilot was still on the attack.

Douglas screamed into the conning tower hatch. "Con, right full rudder."

"Right full rudder," came the response.

Douglas dove at the hatch between the bridge and the conning tower. He kicked it closed as the plane swooped toward the turning submarine.

It passed within feet of the periscope tower, so close Douglas felt the heat of the burning plane cross his back.

The Val's left wing hit the sea first, just fifty feet to starboard. It sent the plane cartwheeling across the waves like a child's toy. There was no following explosion. It simply disintegrated into an oily black cloud. The tail lifted steeply, and the plane and pilot vanished within seconds.

Douglas peered over the bridge rail. The Oerlikon was vacant. "Parker," he called.

"Down here, Skipper," the junior officer scrambled for cover as well. He stood up, his sunglasses askew. "Got the bastard."

Douglas lifted the conning hatch. He called directly into the chamber. "Secure from general quarters. Standby to surface."

"Secure from general quarters. Standby to surface," Alberts responded.

"Surface, surface, surface," Douglas commanded.

The call was repeated to the helm. "Surface, surface, surface."

"Bring us back on course. All ahead, standard."

Alberts repeated the orders.

The lookouts hurried back to their positions. "We could take on the entire Japanese Air Force, Skipper," Parker said with a smirk.

Douglas gave him a halfhearted laugh. "I'd rather not have to, Mr. Parker," he said. "One other thing. When I say clear the bridge, it is an order, not a suggestion."

Parker's smile faded. "Yes, sir."

Douglas turned to the open hatch. "Chief, will you take the bridge for a minute?"

"Of course, Skipper," the chief said as he climbed the ladder.

A few minutes later, Douglas and Alberts sat in the officer's mess. The doorway curtain closed.

"That class of fighter-bomber has a range of 850 miles," Alberts informed him. "We are supposed to control the skies between here and Truk. That base is still a thousand miles west."

Douglas leaned back into the bench cushions. "She was off an aircraft carrier."

"Or a base the Marines haven't taken yet."

"This is one time I'll bet the leathernecks have done their job," he said, rubbing his forehead with his fingers. "We're still running slow."

"By about eighteen hours."

Douglas nodded slightly, agreeing with Alberts' estimation. "The rendezvous is going to be tight," he said.

"We have to go inside?" Alberts asked.

Douglas did not face his XO. "Those are our orders."

30

MOEN ISLAND, TRUK LAGOON, 1986

LESLIE MOVED SILENTLY from the bedroom to the deck, a white cotton coverup trailing her like a mist. The moon was bright again and the breeze warm. She slipped behind Brian as he leaned back in a chair, two legs for balance, and jiggled him slightly. "You are so vulnerable." She held the chair back, a breath from toppling.

Brian held his hands up, fighting for balance. "At the moment, definitely."

She laughed as she moved to the railing. Leaning on it, she arched like a cat, her body long and sinewy.

"I'm sorry about all this," he said, setting his elbow to hers.

A sigh, deep and slow. "I keep thinking, two days. If I had come just two days earlier. Maybe he wouldn't have gone into that wreck."

"He would have eventually."

"But I would have been here to watch over him."

They stood quietly together, shoulder pressed to shoulder, hip against hip, while a few yards away, small waves tippytoed up the beach and disappeared in the gritty sand.

"You never asked me why," she said quietly.

"Why?"

"Why I haven't spoken to my father in over six years."

"I didn't think it was something to bring up."

"I told him it was his fault," she said quickly as if thrusting a weight from her chest. "The picture on his desk was taken at my graduation. We had gone out to dinner to celebrate, and as usual, he drank. One, two, three, until I lost count, and he was drunk again. I stormed out of the restaurant but not without telling him the accident was all his fault. That he killed mother and little brother."

Brian turned to her, surprised.

"I knew it wasn't really his fault. But he was supposed to take my brother to his scout meeting. Instead, my mom had to drive. They never got there." Leslie set her elbows on the railing and rested her chin on her thumbs. "I don't know why I said it to him. I guess I was just mad. Now that I think about it, I was always mad at him for one thing or another."

Brian tried to think of something to say, but there was nothing soothing enough to say. He leaned it her instead, pressing his shoulder against hers.

"Want to go for a swim," she suggested.

"A swim?"

"Why not?" she said, letting the coverup fall from her shoulders. She wore a black one-piece strapless bathing suit. It cut high along her slender legs and low down her back. Brian was still in his swimming trunks. Leslie helped him pull the t-shirt over his head as they walked down to the water.

The lagoon was bathwater warm compared to the cool night air. They walked in to their knees; the water swirling around them. Without hesitation, she playfully kissed the corner of his mouth, then she was gone. A pixie dashing into the waves and disappearing.

Brian searched. She was everywhere and nowhere, a dance of shadows as the waves played with the dying light.

She rose a few feet away. Splashed and called. "Come on, Commander. You are not afraid of dark water, are you?"

Brian dove after her as she headed further into the lagoon. The water was exhilarating, as if it was cleansing her, releasing her, healing her. She wanted Brian badly; she had since the first time his shoulder touched hers. A spark? She did not believe in such things. A need? Definitely. But too much had happened in the last two days for her to let her feelings surface. Until now.

In two powerful strokes, Brian had caught up with her. With his outstretched hand, he grabbed her ankle and pulled her back. She felt the power of him, the strength of his body. She shivered inside.

They were in deeper water now. Brian could barely touch the coral bottom and Leslie could not. She wrapped herself around Brian, her legs twisting around his. They laughed like two children who had snuck away from a camp counselor.

Slowly, their laughter subsided. She ran the back of her fingers across his cheek, saw the moonlight in the wet tangle of his hair, and felt a growing hunger for him.

She hoped his passion would rise with hers, but she sensed his hesitancy. *No more waiting,* she thought and pulled herself tight against his chest, her arms locked about his neck. She kissed him deeply, kissed him with promise. Leaning away, she leered with eyes hidden by a growing grin.

"I see evil thoughts in that smile," he said.

"You have no idea, Commander," she said, slipping away and disappearing beneath the opaque waters.

Brian frowned. "Again?"

She popped up to his right, giggled playfully, and swam back. She wrapped herself about him. This time, her bathing suit was gone.

She was liquid, legs and arms flowing like currents about his body, washing over him like warm, shimmering silk. A kiss to his neck, a kiss to his ear, a breast pressed to a gentle palm.

He kissed her ever so gently and her body responded with an animal's shudder. Parted lips and she felt his tongue search for hers. She pressed herself hard against him, feeling herself meld.

With her free hand, she slipped his swim trunks from his hips, gripped the waistband with her toes, and shoved them down his legs.

She felt him laugh at her flexibilities, knew he would appreciate them, and kissed him deeper.

Twisting her legs around him, she drew him to her. Feeling him eager, she arched and welcomed him.

Brian held her, the only thing in the world, the only thing that mattered in the moment. The lagoon faded, the islands vanished, the moon eclipsed by her, by the inner warmth absorbing him, slow at first, then complete.

Their movements churned the surrounding water. Possibly piquing the interests of the creatures nearby.

Her head fell to his shoulder as her body shuddered. She buried her fingers into the muscles of his back as the rhythmic quakes rose and rose, lightning bolts in her legs. Gradually, they subsided.

She gazed at him again, saw a look of want and growing need in his eyes. Then, they clamped tight, as if crashing headfirst into a tidal wave. His jaw flexed and he moaned from the back of his throat. He shivered and she felt it like ripple dancing across her body.

She could not help herself. She giggled, kissed him again, on the lips, the nose, the cheek, the ear. "Let's go inside," she said, her voice still heavy. She lifted herself away and swam toward the beach.

They melted into each other again. This time with the bed turned down and the window open to the breeze and the sound of the wind in the palms. He glided over her body with tiny kisses from the nape of her neck to her toes. The touch of his lips jolted her like sparks on her skin.

Catching her breath, Leslie pulled him to her. She was a powerful animal who was hungry again.

Brian yielded to her, let her take him this time, absorb him. She covered his mouth with hers. They loved until they could not. After, they simply slept, side by side, no longer strangers.

●　　　●　　　●

Their passion had not gone unnoticed. The open window had let the breeze in and the sounds of their pleasures out. Finally, the man at the edge of the mangrove trees heard nothing from inside, so he moved closer.

He wore only a wrap, a tight-fitting white cloth tied high about his waist, a flat of material across his groin, and a twisted length snug between his buttocks. It was the traditional dress of the men of a warrior, the dress of a once mighty island tribe.

The charcoal black swirls and geometric shapes across his face were driven into the skin with bone needles and the soot of roasted ama nuts.

The terrifying patterns arched over his brow and across his cheeks. An image of a stingray hugged his chest, the center of the animal's black wings, the thick browed face of Gora-Daileng, the Micronesian god of judgement.

In his hands, he carried a polished club skillfully carved from the dense branch of a koa tree. Only a few inches smaller than a modern tennis racket, its paddle-like end encircled by a row of white tiger shark teeth, each natural razor lashed in place with olona fibers. The weapon was both ancient and barbaric.

Careful to move with the rustling of the palm trees, the warrior slipped from the edge of the grove to the house. With quick steps, he slid to the kitchen door. He found it locked. The sliding glass door on the deck was locked as well, but not as secure.

Silently, he worked one of the club's angular teeth into the gap of the aluminum frame. It caught the latch and popped it free.

•   •   •

Leslie opened her eyes. The room was cool and shadowy, and she could just make out the paint peels across the ceiling. It reminded her of the wind waves on the lagoon. She felt herself tucked into the awning of Brian's left arm, his biceps under her neck, his arm over her shoulder. His hand rested on her left breast. She wanted to laugh. *Men,* she thought. With her cheek melted to the side of his chest, she could hear his deep, gentle breathing. She smiled.

She hated to wake him, steal him from the deep place he had gone, but she needed to get up. Lifting his hand slowly, she contorted herself beneath it, slinking away and off the edge of the bed and to the floor in an ungraceful manner. She tippytoed silently through the door.

"Hurry back," Brian said, his voice a sleepy growl.

"Right back," she whispered. Through the louvered window shades of the bathroom, she could see the purple blue of the night sky and a drizzle of lingering stars. Sunrise was still an hour away. *An hour. Not much time,* she thought, as a renewed need warmed inside her. She would just have to wake him up, she mused.

As Leslie glided back to the bedroom, she did not hear the man slip behind her, she did not see his wide-eyed determination or his shark-toothed club high over his head.

279

"Leslie!" Brian yelled as he stepped into the hall.

She immediately realized he was looking past her at something terrifying. Instinctively, she dropped. *À terre*—the swift ballet move she learned as a young girl that now saved her life.

The savage weapon's strike did not go unfulfilled. The shark bit, ripping across Leslie's flawless shoulder. Her scream pierced the morning calm.

Brian rushed the assassin like a defensive tackle; shoulder down, head tucked. He hit him full force, driving him backwards slamming into the wall. The man was unfazed.

With both hands, he smashed the club's blunt handle into the back of Brian's neck. A knee to his face popped Brian's head up. Another knee. A swing with the club.

Brian stumbled, eyes watering. He bobbed low as the assassin swung his weapon. The teeth crashed into the wall. Stuck. The shark biting into the wood. A bare foot caught Brian in the stomach. The blow sent him backwards.

The assassin gained time to yank his weapon free. He lunged at Brian again. The rows of shark teeth hissed as the man swung the club inches from Brian's face.

Brian ducked left, pivoted right, the shark forcing his retreat. Inch by inch down the hall, the shark dove at him.

The assassin heard Leslie's cry from the dark study. He lunged at Brian again, then he turned to the girl.

Leslie had fallen to the floor just inside the doorway. She lay naked and bleeding, her legs tight to her chest, one arm around her knees, the other stretched to her shoulder, blood gushing between her fingers.

The assassin made a single mistake. He underestimated the American's reaction to a deadly threat. Brian was trained to act decisively. No hesitation, no second thoughts. He rushed the assassin before he could draw the club against Leslie again.

Their collision sent them both sprawling across the floor. The assassin leapt to his feet as Brian struggled. The man torqued his body and swung the weapon. This time, Brian could not escape the teeth of the shark.

"Commander!" a voice roared from the other end of the hall behind the man. "Down," it screamed.

The first round from JP's revolver barely missed Brian as he dove to the floor. The hollow-point bullet was a tumbling mushroom of lead, having just passed through the throat of the assassin. On its path, it pierced the jugular, the right thyroid lobe, his larynx and tore away the man's vocal fold.

JP's second round was for good measure. It hit the assassin just to the right of the sternum. The agent was aiming for centerline, but the secondary points of entry are dedicated by the body's response to the previous hit. Later, upon inspection of the target, JP would still be pleased with his results.

Brian snapped to his feet, pulled the club from dead hands, and turned to JP with uncertainty.

The agent held his gun at gut level.

They stared at each other. "Check on the girl," JP told him as he knelt beside the body and felt for a pulse. There was none.

Brian found Leslie behind the desk, her shoulder a cascade of blood. He inspected the gash, found it shallow but long. "Jesus. Come, we've got to get you to the hospital," he said, lifting her to her feet.

JP was at the study door. He had tucked his gun away and covered the intruder's body with a bedsheet. He also had Leslie's beach wrap and a t-shirt and swim shorts for Brian. For the first time, they both realized they were still naked.

"Who the fuck are you?" Brian asked as he punched himself into the shirt.

"At the moment, Commander, your best friend," JP said. He pressed a rolled bath towel to Leslie's wound, causing her to cry out. "Keep the pressure on," he whispered as he helped her into the wrap. As best he could, he tried not to look at more than her injury.

"You have to get her to the hospital," he told Brian. "It's not bad, but she'll need stitches."

As they stepped from the study, Leslie glanced at the body sprawled across the floor and the fling of blood along the wall. She turned and shuddered.

"Don't worry," JP promised. "He won't be swinging that thing at anyone again."

"Call the police," Brian told him as they walked from the house.

JP laughed. "Not me, Commander. I'm not here."

Together, the men eased her in the Jeep. As Brian twisted the key, he asked JP. "You're not coming?"

"Like I said. Not here."

"I've got questions," Brian shot.

"So do I."

Brian turned to Leslie and saw the tears cascading. "It's going to be okay," he promised, and she nodded weakly.

Cramming the Jeep into gear, he fired a glare at the stranger who had saved their lives and launched the Jeep down the beach toward town.

•　　　•　　　•

Rota came from her room behind the check-in counter at the shrieking pulse of the door buzzer. "What! What?"

The heavy woman was still rubbing her face when she saw the blood. "My God. Come, come," she took Leslie into the kitchen. "What happened?" the woman asked as she turned on the lights. She pulled a stool and set Leslie near the prepping table.

A furrowed brow and tight white lips told of the pain Leslie was holding in, but she barely uttered a sound as Rota helped lift her blouse from the bloodied shoulder. The moist fibers pulled at her skin, drawing a lock-jawed gasp.

She handed Leslie a kitchen towel to hold to her chest as she hurried to a kitchen drawer where there were a few medical supplies; band aids, aspirin, and several rolls of gauze whose wrapping looked vintage.

"Someone attacked us at the house," Leslie said, her lip shaking. She turned to Brian. "He really tried to hurt us," she said, wide-eyed, tears growing. The reality of it was catching up. She lived in a bubble, she realized. Even in the middle of New York City, she lived charmed.

Brian lifted her chin. "It's over," he told her.

Leslie stared at Brian, her face blank. "This really hurts," she said, with a swallow. She was processing the events of the last hour, remembering. The fog was there but lifting.

"It's going to be okay."

"You have to go to the hospital," Rota said as filled a pan of water and put it on the stove.

"We went. It was closed," Brian said, incredulous.

"That is the clinic. It is not good. You must take her to Guam. The mail plane comes early. You go with them."

As the woman dabbed the wound, the pain felt like splinters of glass were being pressed further into her arm.

"She's right," Brian pressed.

"No," she whispered as she bit the inside of her lip.

"It is easy to get infected," the woman warned.

Rota dipped the gauze into the warming water and dabbed it around the shark tooth gash. She wiped the drying blood as gently as she could.

Boggy plodded through the door. "What's the matter?" He was still in the tentacles of sleep, rubbing his face.

"Go back to bed," his mother told him.

"What happened?" he asked, his eyes widening as he saw the blood.

"I said go!" Rota rinsed the gauze and continued. "This is going to sting," she whispered. She squeezed the roll above the cut and let the warm water run through the slash.

Leslie pulled Brian closer, pressed her face into his ribs and fought her tears.

Boggy receded into the doorway to watch. He did not want to see the blood or to see the beautiful woman cry, but he could not pull himself away.

Outside the kitchen, Brian heard the front door open. Instinctively, he scanned the cutting table for a weapon. A heavy cleaver stood out amongst the caving knives and readied himself to leap for it, but the boy made no move away from approaching silhouettes.

Honma entered with another man in tow. He was young with a sage brush beard. Long, oily brown hair dangled over round-framed glasses. From the sunburn of his face and the tatter of his clothes, Brian was certain he had washed up on the reefs, tossed overboard by a passing freighter.

"Whoya," the disheveled man gulped as he eyed Leslie's gashes from the door. "What do we have here?"

Brian instinctively put his body between them.

"Let him help," Honma told him. "Paul's a doctor."

"Medical practitioner, actually," he said, sidestepping Brian. "Oh, that is nasty." He winced. "Take a tumble across the coral?"

The captain pulled Brian aside. "He's been teaching at the grade school for the last six months and helping where he can. Always saying he wants to give back. Why he thinks that I don't know. I don't care. I am happy to have someone like him here."

"How did you know to bring him?"

"A phone call woke me. The woman said you were attacked at the house and Henry's daughter was hurt," he glanced at Leslie, who was now holding Rota's hands tightly as Paul poked at the wound. "I knew you would come here."

"We tried the hospital."

"The clinic?" he grimaced. "An empty building with empty rooms. There is no doctor. That's why I am thankful we have him."

"Wait," Brian was doing his own processing. "Who called you?" he asked.

"A woman," he said. "I don't know who. I was sleeping."

From the table, Leslie cried out as the bohemian poked at her shoulder. "You've treated deep lacerations before?" she asked. "Because I'll need stitches."

Although Brian could hear her pain, her voice had changed. Frightened Leslie was turning back into Doctor Maetani.

"Maybe." Paul prodded the deepest cut again. "Maybe not. We'll see."

She caught her breath. "No. I do," she said firmly as she shifted her chair. "I haven't gotten a good look, but I'm guessing there are at least seven linear incised lacerations across the mid to outer trapezius. I can feel the puncture wounds, but I don't think they reached the deep fascia."

"Are you a nurse or something?"

Leslie eyed him through the pain. "Actually, I am an emergency room surgeon."

Paul pushed back his glasses. "Oh."

"Rota cleansed the wound with hot water, but we'll need a stronger antiseptic. Do you know how to stitch a Lembert suture?"

"Um, yeah, I think so," Paul said, his voice falling.

"Rota," Leslie turned to the woman. "George said you had alcohol with a real kick. Have anything at least 180 proof?"

"Everclear. Sometimes we use it to start the stove fire," Rota told her.

"That'll definitely stop any chance of infection," Paul said. "And sting like hell."

Leslie ignored him. She called to Boggy who was watching from the kitchen door. "You have a fishing box, right? Can you get me the smallest hook you have and the thinnest line?"

"Leslie, this isn't a MASH unit," Brian spoke up. "You need to get to the hospital."

"If I have to go to the hospital, you have to go with me."

Brian stared at her.

"I didn't think so," she said turning back to Paul. "I am going to walk you through this. Step by step."

"I've set a couple of broken arms and helped deliver a few puppies but this" His uncertainty was glaring.

"It's going to be fine."

Brian turned to Honma for help but all he got was a skinny shoulder shrug from the police captain.

Twenty minutes later, Rota's bottle of American vodka was split between what Leslie drank and what was poured over her wounds. Paul closed five deep lacerations using Boggy's number twenty fishhook, with the barb removed, and monofilament line.

To his credit, Paul was surprisingly steady as Brian stood at his shoulder holding a small mirror for Leslie to watch and give directions.

"You still have to go to the hospital," Brian pressed as they finished.

Paul stood behind her holding a clean dressing pad over the stitches as Rota wrapped her in a corset of cotton gauze. Once she was bandaged, Boggy returned from the hotel's gift shop with a lapis blue t-shirt two sizes too big. It was the ubiquitous tourist shirt with an image of a red diver's flag over the left breast pocket and a large image of a sunken wreck on the back; "Truk Lagoon—Dive into Hallowed Water" it hawked.

"I think you just graduated from medical practitioner to resident ER doc," she said. "A good thing too, because now that the adrenaline is wearing off, I am definitely feeling the anesthesia." She reached for the table to steady herself as she sat again. She crossed her arms and dropped her head.

"You need to eat something," Brian said. "And sleep."

"Good," Rota said. "Everyone out. I will make breakfast."

"We need to take a ride," Honma reminded Brian. "You have something to show me?"

"Right," Brian remembered what they had left at the house. "Rota, will you?"

"Don't worry," Rota said, promising she would tuck Leslie into one of the hotel rooms after breakfast.

"Just for a few hours," Brian said, then whispered. "Until I can get her on the plane."

"I am not going," Leslie pipped up.

Rota padded his arm. "I will take care of her."

As Brian followed Honma from the kitchen, Paul flashed two thumbs. "I did great, right? Surprised you, didn't I?"

"You did," Brian nodded. "Now you just have to be sure your patient recovers fully," he said as he left.

•   •   •

Brian lifted the bedsheet from the body slowly as if not wanting to disturb it. A pool of syrupy blood had formed beneath him, dusted with a cloud of tropical flies. The embellished shark-tooth club rested across the sprawl of his legs.

Honma bent close. He eyed the simple entry wound to the chest, and the one that had violently torn open his throat.

"You know him?" Brian asked.

"I have seen him on the docks working," the captain pointed at the tattoos. "He is from the Marquesas. The weapon is Hawaiian," he said casually. "He probably liked the damage it would do."

"It certainly did that," Brian said, thinking of Leslie's tears.

"I was worried about this. Everyone thinks you are searching for Yamashita's gold, the Japanese plunder from the war. They went after Henry, now they come for you, Mr. Brock."

Brian studied the captain for a moment, decided he had to trust him. "It's not Brock. My name is Bovan."

Honma nodded. "I had my suspicions," he acknowledged.

"You never believed her father's death was an accident?"

"Another suspicion," Honma admitted. He gathered the club from the floor. "You didn't shoot the Marquesan?"

"No," Brian said firmly.

"And you don't know who did?"

"Honestly, no."

"Maybe there were two men working together. He was aiming for you but hit his friend. Twice," Honma said as he scanned the hall from the front kitchen to the back bedroom. "You know, the lagoon is usually a very tranquil place."

"So, you've said."

They wrapped the body in the bedsheet and laid it in the back of Honma's police truck. Brian quickly gathered what he thought Leslie would need and stuffed it into her carryon case.

The edge of the sun had just broken away from the sea's surface as they pulled from the house and headed back to town. Honma would put the body in the clinic, he said. At least the building had air conditioning.

Brian thought about Leslie. About the gash in her shoulder and the pain in her face. About the love they had made hours before and how she would only be safe on Guam. He knew people at the Navy base who would take care of her until he arrived.

Honma recognized it first, lying just above the high tide mark, but drove past without a second glance. When Brian saw the white brimmed hat half buried in the sand, his stomach turned.

"Stop."

Honma stomped the brakes.

Brian leapt from the truck. "It's George's," he said, sweeping the hat out of the sand. A few yards away, they found a toiled patch of sand. Dollops of drying blood littered the purity of the beach. And more flies. Two parallel furrows ran up into the jungle.

"Jesus," Honma whispered as Brian knelt beside George's body.

31

SOUTH PACIFIC SEA, TRUK LAGOON, 1944

D OUGLAS DREW BACK from the periscope. "This is it," he said
to his XO standing on the opposite side of the control room.
"Steer course, wun ate six. All, ahead, standard," he ordered.

While the helmsman set the rudder from his controls in the conning
tower, the sub's speed was adjusted at an electrical panel the size of a large
upright piano. Located a hundred feet astern and just ahead of the aft
torpedo room, the men received their orders through the intercom and
immediately worked a series of brass levers to adjust the motors' output
and bring the *Mako* to speed.

From his gauges in front of him, the helmsman verified the request.
"Course wun ate six. All, ahead, standard."

"Time?" Douglas asked, his face pressed against the periscope.

"2207 hours," Alberts said. "We're cutting this close."

"No turning back now. Not if we have the chance to get inside,"
Douglas said.

Alberts nodded, although with less enthusiasm than his skipper
would have wanted. Slipping into the Japanese fortress hours before an

aerial attack was a risk neither of them wanted, but they understood their orders.

Illuminated by a three-quarter moon that threw glitter across the wind chop, Douglas saw the cone peak of Dublon Island. He knew the island held both the Japanese submarine base and their seaplane docks. They would both make perfect targets for stern torpedoes during their departure. At least, that was his plan, but first, they had to find their passage into the lagoon.

As the *Mako* slid through the inky water, Douglas watched for the next shadow. Per the ambassador's charts, he watched for a small islet that rose off the outer reef. It was barely large enough for a few palm trees, but its location against the larger island's silhouette would reveal the underwater opening they were looking for.

After several minutes, he found it. "Ready for a mark?" he called to Alberts.

"Ready for a mark," the XO responded.

"And…… Mark."

"Mark at bearing two seven fo-wer," Alberts said.

Douglas remembered the ambassador's instructions and allowed the *Mako* to continue three more miles northeast. He now scanned the black silhouette of Falo islet looking for two small lights revealing the *Kuma Maru*. Anchored off the small island, the Japanese freighter would dangle the two lamps close to the water, one off the bow and one off the stern. If Douglas could maneuver his submarine along her starboard side, it would hide the Mako from the hilltop lookout towers.

Douglas had little trust in either the Chinese ambassador, Tendrey, or the Japanese captain of the freighter. "Anything on the sonar?"

"I'm still getting a solid wall, Skipper," Tony, the sonarman said.

"Keep chipping at it," Douglas said without lifting his eye from the scope.

Finally, he found them twinkling like small votive candles, two whispers dangling above the mirror waters inside the lagoon. "All stop," Douglas ordered, and felt the sub slow. "Let her drift. Ready for my mark?"

"Aye. Ready for the mark."

Douglas could now see the freighter's outline against the shadow of the island. He immediately recognized the four-hundred-foot freighter as a prize target but reminded himself he was not there to attack her. At least, not yet.

"Mark," Douglas called.

"Bearing mark, two niner six."

Douglas stepped from the periscope. "Care to look," he said, offering Alberts the eyepiece.

Alberts peered into the navigation scope and saw the two dim lights hanging from the freighter. He had read the plans and was more than skeptical. "They expect us to trust the Japs?" he asked. "Sorry, Skipper, I can't."

"Me either," Douglas admitted. "But a fortune in diamonds might outweigh this captain's loyalties."

"You think it's enough?"

"Depends how corrupt this bastard is."

"Would it be enough for you?" he asked pointedly. Before Douglas could answer, he added. "Because it wouldn't be for me."

"If we find this hole in the reef, I want a fish in every torpedo tube, forward and aft. We're not leaving quietly."

That lifted Alberts' spirits and brought him onboard with the idea. They were sneaking into Truk, but they would not slink out.

Alberts worked up an accepting smile. "Your call."

"Let's see if we can find this passage. Sonar? What are you seeing?"

"A stone wall, Skipper," Tony reported.

"Maybe they expect us to fly over it," Alberts said.

Douglas took back the periscope. Maybe the freighter was not exactly in the right spot. "Helm, rudder amidships. All ahead, one-third," he ordered. The helmsman responded, and Douglas felt the submarine ease forward.

A moment later, Tony called out. "Radar! Contact! Target bearing two fo-wer six. Speed, nineteen knots. Twin screws, Skipper. It's a destroyer, sir."

Douglas spun the periscope around. Instantly, he found the owner of the twin screws filling his view. A Kamikaze-class destroyer with the sea foaming at its bow. "Helm! Left full rudder, full dive. Take us to depth one five zero," Douglas snapped as he dropped the periscope. "Rig for silent."

"Left full rudder," the helmsman responded. "Full dive!"

The *Mako* pitched left as it turned away from the reef's ledge. Her nose dropped drastically as she dove deeper into the murky waters of the Pacific. As was the natural geography of a lagoon, the outside shelf fell almost vertically to 3000 feet. It gave the submarine plenty of room to maneuver.

"Is she pinging us?" Douglas whispered.

"Not a blip, Skipper. Don't know why, but her sonar isn't active," Tony reported.

His XO leaned in. "If she's heading for the south passage, we could slip in with her," Alberts offered. "It's been done before."

"And if her sonar man flipped a switch for the hell of it, our patrol would be over."

For a few minutes there was nothing but the natural crackles of the sea, then, the high-pitched whine of the approaching surface ship enveloped the submarine. Douglas held his breath. Alberts did the same as he leaned against the targeting periscope.

Throughout the sub, the crew listened, their eyes turned upward as if they could see through the maze of pipes and wires and the thick, life-saving bulkheads of their vessel, and into the mind of the Japanese captain as he drove his ship over them. Each man wondering if the enemy knew they were there.

Finally, the sounds of the destroyer subsided into the distance.

"Sonar. Target moving off. No change in bearing."

"Sonar, aye," Alberts acknowledged.

"Secure from silent running. Bring us back to periscope depth," Douglas said. "Let's find that hole."

As the *Mako* climbed from the depths, the planesman brought her bow back toward Truk Lagoon.

As the periscope slid upward, Douglas glanced at his watch. 0100. Sunrise in five hours. He dropped the grips and eyed the horizon in every direction. All clear, he focused on the shadowy peak of Falo Island again.

"Helm. Bring us to course two ate fo-wer."

The helmsman responded, turning the submarine to the ordered compass course.

"Skipper," Tony put his hand to his headset as he spun the small brass wheel back and forth. "Something, Skipper."

"Something good or something bad?"

"A hole. An enormous hole, sir," he said, intent on his dials.

"Bearing?"

"Bearing, ze-ro niner-thuh-ree degrees. Depth, nine five feet."

Alberts dropped the periscope as Douglas stepped to the helm. "Down bubble. Make our depth nine five feet. Right rudder three degrees."

Tony spun two dials. He slowly turned the third like a safe cracker breaking into Fort Knox. "Another hundred yards."

"Ahead, one-third."

In the quiet sea, the three-hundred-foot submarine slid toward the ancient reef. A blacktip shark cruising the coral heads for prey felt the presence of the huge intruder. He swung away and darted into the safety of the open water.

"Sonar?" Douglas ventured.

"Definite hole, Skipper," Tony reported. "It's big enough to enter. I just can't tell how far it goes."

Douglas turned to Alberts for his opinion.

The XO shook his head. "It's a big reef, Doug. It could bottleneck and we'd be the cork."

That was something Douglas had already considered. He knew the chances they were taking for a box of bones. He thought about the promise he had made to Mimi, about Wagner's son and about the proof he would show the military court at Tendrey's hearing.

"Skipper!" Tony's voice had that high ring of terror again. "She's coming back, sir. The destroyer. And her sonar is active."

"Range?"

"Eight thousand yards. Speed nine knots. I think she is hugging the reef."

"They're going to run right over us," Alberts said.

"No, they're going to slide right by," Douglas shot. "Helm. Nice and easy, Billy. Ahead, one-third. Mind your rudder. Sonar. Tony. Give me a bearing."

"Aye," Tony responded, feeding the compass course to Douglas, and from Douglas to the helmsman, who repeated it back.

The *Mako*'s twin propellers inched her forward and she silently entered the gaping rift in the reef. It was only twice her width, with jagged walls that rose steeply like the vault ceiling of a medieval church.

"We've got about fifteen feet on each side," Tony reported.

Albert sighed. "It's too tight," he whispered.

"All stop," Douglas said. "Are we in?"

"Aye, Skipper," Tony acknowledged. "By at least fifty feet."

"Where's the patrol?" Alberts asked quickly.

Tony swung the dial. "I can't pick her up from in here."

"If you can't hear her, she can't hear us, right?" Alberts asked.

"I don't think so, sir."

"That also means, if we have to back out, we won't know if she's waiting for us until it is too late," Alberts said to Douglas.

"Then let's not come back this way," Douglas smirked. "Helm, slow ahead."

"The roof is sloping downward, Skipper. We can drop another twenty feet, sir."

Douglas nodded. "Helm, take us down to one ten feet. Hold her steady."

"Depth one ten feet, aye."

The air in the conning tower was becoming unbearably thick, and each man felt it as his shirt stuck to his back. They were four hundred feet into the reef when Tony spoke again.

"There's a wall ahead sir, and it is getting shallow," the sonarman said.

"A dead end?" Alberts turned to Tony. The radar man did not dare take his eyes away from his dials.

"All stop," Douglas ordered.

"Aye, all stop," the helmsman said.

"Well, is it a dead end?"

Tony continued to adjust his dials and knobs as if he hadn't heard Douglas at all. "If we can go another fifty feet, I could get a better reading. I think it opens to starboard, sir."

Alberts shook his head. "We're a three hundred feet steel tube, Skipper. With no hinge in the middle."

"I'll keep that in mind," Douglas said. "I'll give you a peek, Tony. Just a little." He turned to helmsman. "Ahead dead slow."

"Helm. Ahead dead slow."

"It's a bend, sir," Tony said almost immediately. "It'll be tight. I think we can swing around it."

"All stop," Douglas barked. "How much room do we have?"

"Yards."

Douglas wiped the droplets forming on his brow. It was nearing 0200. Time was racing away from them.

"If we get past this, are you sure it doesn't bend again?" Alberts asked.

"Best way to find out," Douglas said. "Helm. Rudder amidship. Port. Ahead, two-thirds. Starboard, back, two-thirds."

For a moment, the submarine remained motionless. The tide was going out, a rush of currents swirling through the undersea cavern, then she pivoted.

"Another two degrees to port," Tony said, as if he had taken the helm.

Douglas did not argue. He simply relayed the message to the helmsman.

"It opens, Skipper, but I don't think..." Tony did not have time to finish his sentence when the bow slammed into the giant outcropping. The impact jolted the sub, sending a nerve-shattering screech down her hull.

"All stop," Douglas yelled, and the *Mako* drifted back away from the coral fist.

Alberts grabbed the microphone. "Forward torpedo room. Report."

"Still watertight and dry, Mr. Alberts. But our ears are ringing," the crewman reported.

Douglas turned to the sonar man, waiting.

"I am getting an ear full of traffic from the other side, Skipper. This has to go through," Tony said.

"We'll take your word for it," Douglas said with a nod. He turned to the helmsman. "Again, Billy. Ease her bow into the reef and give her a hard left rudder."

"Aye," Billy said, easing the controls to set the twenty-four hundred tons of steel into motion.

Tony counted off the feet until impact. "Fifteen, ten, seven, four, now."

Again, the *Mako*'s knife-shaped prow hit the reef hard and again sent a shudder down her keel.

"Port. Ahead full. Starboard, back full."

Douglas imagined his submarine pushing against the living rock. Under his feet, he could feel the bow rise as it pressed forward. The sounds of the calcareous coral shattering came through the hull, cat claws on cold steel.

"There goes the fresh paint," Billy said under his breath as he held onto the wheel. Now everyone was holding on to something as the bow of the ship rose steeply.

A voice came over the speaker. It was Clancy. "Maneuvering room. We're heating the motors fast, Skipper. Water flow is minimum."

"Let me know when it hits critical," Douglas said into the box.

"She's your ship," he said, his voice unmistakably harsh. It was Douglas' command, but they were his motors.

"Skipper," Tony's voice was high again, and it put a knot in Douglas' stomach. "The bow is going to break the surface."

"We are going to fly over the top," Alberts said. He was holding onto the ladder leading to the bridge with both hands.

All at once, the deck fell, throwing the crew forward. A thunderclap railed through the sub as the bow dropped back into the sea.

Tony heard the four-ton outcropping of coral snap from the reef, tumble across the bow and sink to the bottom. The sub lurched as she leveled.

"All stop."

"Helm. All stop," Billy said as he wiped his palms on his pants.

Alberts grabbed the microphone and asked for damage reports. There were none.

"What's our depth?"

"Sixty feet," Billy answered.

"I think we're clear, Skipper," Tony reported. "There is reef to starboard, but it's open to port. We're inside the lagoon, sir." He grinned.

Douglas turned to Alberts. "Remind me not to leave that way." He called to Billy. "Helm. Ahead, two-thirds. Left, five degrees rudder. Bring us up to periscope depth."

Alberts moved close to Douglas and whispered. "How do you plan to get out of here?"

"The sub nets are to keep us out, not keep us in," Douglas told him. "Now let's find that freighter so we can get out of here."

"No arguments from me."

"Sonar. Keep your ears open, Tony. I don't want any surprises."

"Aye Skipper," Tony said as the *Mako* inched her nose out of the coral reef opening and into the clear waters of the expansive lagoon.

32

MOEN ISLAND, TRUK LAGOON, 1986

BRIAN HELD THE CLINIC DOOR as Leslie followed him to the parking lot. With her arm still stiff with bandages, he helped her into the Jeep. He swung himself behind the wheel. They sat in the cool morning on the tropical island saying nothing. She stared at the floor. He stared at the thin black steering wheel with Rota's screams in his ears.

"Was this our fault?" she asked, her voice a whisper.

"No," Brian told her. "This started forty years ago." From the corner of his eye, he saw Honma exit the clinic's dusty glass door.

"They can take you both," the captain said as he approached the Jeep. "They're scheduled to depart in thirty-minutes."

"I am not going," Leslie said.

"Yes, you are," Brian snapped. "We don't know who this guy was."

"He's dead."

"You think he was working alone? I'm not going to bet your life on it."

"And who shot the Marquesan?" Honma added. "You are playing a dangerous game here, Mr. Bovan. Are the answers you came to find worth your lives?"

Brian stared at the police captain. "Put her on the plane."

"You are not getting rid of me."

"I can't protect you."

"I don't want your protection. I want to know who killed my father. I want to know why," Leslie said, her voice dark and determined.

"You are foolish to provoke ghosts, Mr. Bovan. The only thing of value on the bottom of our lagoon, are the wrecks left by the Americans. They bring tourists from all over the world. Anything more valuable would have been discovered by now."

"I am going back," Brian told him.

Honma nodded. "I have no doubt you both are."

•　　　•　　　•

Brian carried the oxyacetylene tanks over his shoulder while he and Leslie pulled the low, two-wheel cart of air tanks down the pier. Her father's boat was still moored to the far end. They loaded gear with Leslie helping the best she could, one-handed, jaw clenched.

"I can get all this," he kept telling her.

"And I can help," she kept repeating.

Gear ready and the fuel topped off, Brian fired up the engine. He pointed Leslie to the stern. "Stand by that line," he told her.

"I got that," said the man, rushing down the dock. He unwound the line from the cleat. "How's that shoulder?" JP asked.

Leslie looked up automatically. Then, under his floppy bucket hat, she saw the round face of the man who had saved them. He now wore a tourist's t-shirt under an open Hawaiian button up and white shorts that just left the rack.

JP turned to Brian standing at the helm. "Bet you could use another hand, Commander?"

Brian glanced down the pier. "It wouldn't hurt," he said.

JP dropped the stern line into the boat, rushed to the bow and, with a nod from Brian, unleashed it.

It was not until they had pulled away from the dock and the runabout jabbed the sea chop that JP made his introduction.

"Name's Powell, or just JP." He stretched a hand to each of them.

"Naval intelligence?" Brian ventured; his voice lifted over the wheeze of the motor.

"Please, no insults. Central Intelligence. Domestic division."

"There's a domestic division?"

"Of course, there is. Just don't tell anybody."

"Or you'll have to kill us?" Brian joked.

"Just you," JP said dryly.

Leslie laughed.

JP smiled at her. "Glad to see your spirits are up."

"Why did you follow me here, Mr. Powell?"

"I wasn't supposed to. I had someone else tailing you. Unfortunately, he's dead."

Brian glanced at Leslie. She was now riding the chop, her good hand clutching the Owens' side rail. "You know I had nothing to do with it."

"I think you had everything to do with it, Commander. As a first officer on a United States nuclear attack submarine, you are a national security risk."

Brian stared at him.

"Yeah," JP emphasized. "Serious risk."

They passed the northern tip of Meno and continued across the open channel. The island, a jagged cut of thick jade-green jungle, rose from the sea to block the morning rays of sun. Brian steered far enough off the beach to stay clear the unfamiliar reefs.

"You don't believe that."

"Why shouldn't I? You'd be surprised how easy it is to be considered a traitor. I've seen it a hundred times." JP peered over the bow, keeping his hat in place with one hand.

"What changed your mind?"

"Someone told me a story. A crazy story. But after I gathered all the pieces in my head, juggled them around and sorted them out I realized it was still a crazy story. Just not impossible," the agent said. "In my business, you consider the impossible and prepare for it."

"This someone? Is she about five-foot-four with gray hair?"

JP laughed. "Long gray hair."

"Then you know why I came."

JP nodded. "And Doctor. My condolences for your father."

Leslie thanked him, her face fighting her lingering sadness.

Brian saw her staring at the horizon as she tried to fight the pain of her wounds. She grimaced at each jolt of the runabout's bow as it punched the waves like a prize fighter working the heavy bag.

He eased off the throttle and found smoother water. They passed two open fishing boats returning with their morning catch. They had gone out early, taking advantage of the night's bright moon.

Finally, Brian swung past the western edge of Falo. He drove along the shadow of the reef that arched along the beach. Watching the foliage that lined the sand, he rolled the throttle down and let the boat drift with the surge.

"How do you know where it is?" Leslie asked as she moved beside him.

"I made mental notes," he said. "Three spots on the beach lined up with three points on the boat and a good guess of the distance from the reef should put us about right." He adjusted their speed. "JP, can you handle the anchor?"

"On it." The agent said as he scrambled along the narrow deck that skirted the cabin. On the bow, he gathered a small Danforth anchor and line.

"Straight off," Brian instructed, and the agent eased the metal wedge into the depths. Once it hit bottom, he secured it to the bow cleat.

By the time Brian was slipping into his diving gear, they had the decompression line and scuba tanks dangling off the stern.

"How long will you be down there?" Leslie asked, as Brian checked his regulator and George's diver's lamp. She held out his mask.

"With the decompression, just over three hours," he said.

"Three hours? That can't be safe."

"Hell no," JP snorted. "And you're taking this?" he asked, inspecting the cutting torch. "Aren't these wrecks full of explosives?"

"I've used one before," Brian countered.

"Where, Commander, in a training pool?"

"Do you want to join me? I could use the help."

"No, thanks." JP shook his head. "I'll leave you to blow yourself up."

"Brian?" Leslie stared anxiously at him.

"Nothing is going to happen," he assured her as he muscled the torch's stubby tanks to the stern. Wrapping the hose and cutting nozzle around the valves, he used a thin piece of rope to attach the scissor-like flint striker. Another length of rope and he secured the torch to the drop ring of the plastic-coated lift bag. "Hand this over when I'm in," he told JP.

"Right," he said, pulling the torch and bag to the edge.

As Brian lifted the twin scuba tanks from the deck, Leslie hurried to help. "You don't have to do this," she said as she held the shoulder strap for him.

"Yeah, I do."

"Not for a minute longer than you have to," she pressed.

"Not a minute," he promised as he slipped on his fins and double checked the underwater lights tied to his weight belt. He motioned to JP. "You ready?"

"When you are," The CIA man said.

As Brian went over the side, JP lifted the tanks and bag and eased them into the water. Leslie leaned against the rail in time to see him clear his mask and wave. Then, in a swirl of bubbles, he was gone.

•   •   •

Into the depths, into the darkness, back in time. As he descended the decompression line, and his distance away from the tropical day increased foot by foot, Brian kept a tight grip on the air-filled lift bag and oxyacetylene tanks dangling below it. He also continued to mull over the question Leslie had raised the day before.

What would he have done had he been in command of a World War II submarine tethered to the side of a ship under attack? Certainly not return fire. Not when the incoming bombers were fellow Americans. No, the only thing to do was evade their assault. And given the circumstance his father had put himself in, there was only one thing he could do.

Realization came as a bone numbing chill that shot through his body. Brian stared into the shadows, past the dancing fingers of sunlight, and searched for the freighter's silhouette.

At a hundred and ten feet, he reached the iron weight at the end of the decompression line. As he hoped, it hung above the shipwreck, but this time he landed above the quarterdeck where a fractured lifeboat still hung from its davits, as if still waiting to save the crew.

With the torch in tow, Brian swam to the wheelhouse. He pulled the bag and cutting equipment through the broken window. He released the torch and let the lift bag float into the ceiling, where it rolled like a child's balloon into the upper corner of the coral encrusted bulkhead.

Now weighted by the oxyacetylene tanks, moving through the wreck became far more difficult, a task he knew would drain his air supply.

Following the white nylon rope he and George had webbed through the wreck the day before, he headed for the engine room. There was no investigating the chart room or officer's cabins this time, and the sea life and artifacts he disturbed as he dragged the cumbersome equipment down the corridors went unnoticed.

Entering the freighter's engine room, he flipped on George's underwater lamp and descended to the maintenance hatch that had kept them at bay. Everything was where they had left it. The crowbar along the floor and the shattered light under the fallen door.

Brian rolled his wrist to check his watch. Ten minutes at depth. He was making good time.

Unwinding the torch hose and nozzle, he opened the valves. Pressing the flint striker to the tip, he ignited the cutter. The flame leapt from the brass tip like a serpent's tongue spitting an orange and blue fire and dusty bubbles. It blinded him for a moment as it illuminated the obscured corners of the dead ship.

Leaning against the bulkhead for stability, Brian set the magma hot torch to the first hinge. Drawing it across the steel knuckles, the cold metal immediately glowed. It sizzled and popped and slowly transformed into lava.

After what seemed a lifetime, the first hinge gave way. A check of his watch revealed only nine minutes had passed, but it was still minutes he needed.

The second hinge should be quicker, he thought, as he saw a hairline crack running along it, possibly the result of George's efforts the day before. Brian was right. The torch easily severed metal. The solid steel door fell hard to the slanted deck, sending a thick cloud of silt into the water column, fogging Brian's cone of light.

Brian closed the torch and set it aside. He twisted himself around, taking extra care not to strike his scuba tanks against the bulkhead as he pulled himself through. With the dive lamp thrust in front of him, he swept the freighter's cavernous midships hold.

It was as if the *Kuma Maru* had sunk yesterday. Her steel ribs and inner skin were crimson red with rust, but there was not the accumulation of silt or debris. Even the sea life was missing from the chamber.

Brian swam further, his light sweeping back and forth until it caught a huge, contorted piece of riveted steel arching upwards like a cresting wave frozen the instance it broke against the beach.

It was a torn slice of the freighter's portside, one of a half-dozen panels rolled inward by the massive explosion from a torpedo delivered by a U.S. Avenger flying fast and low.

As Brian moved closer to the fatal wound and directed his light into its center, his eyes widened, his breathing stopped, and his body shuddered at what he saw inside.

33

SOUTH PACIFIC SEA, TRUK LAGOON, 1944

T HE *MAKO* LAY MOTIONLESS in the predawn darkness with only
five feet of her conning tower out of the water. Douglas cracked
the hatch and stepped slowly out on to the bridge. From below, Alberts
handed him a small flashlight.

Falo Island was a smooth, ink black cone rising from the calm
waters and into a night sky of bright stars. A warm, gentle breeze
brushed Douglas' face as he brought the binoculars to his eyes. He
quickly swept the area, making sure there were no patrol boats waiting.

The *Kuma Maru* lay at anchor only fifty yards off the starboard bow.
She, too, was quiet and still. Douglas covered the flashlight with his hand
and turned it on. He cracked open his fingers and released a sliver of light.

Douglas worried the lamplight would look like flare against the
darkness. After a minute, he released another signal.

This time, the two lights that had drawn the submarine to the
freighter's side went dead. Another light, a narrow band between
fingers, flashed from the bridge. It flashed three more times.

Douglas responded in kind. He handed the light to Alberts, who stood in the bridge hatch with only his shoulders exposed.

"Ahead. Slow," Douglas whispered.

Alberts relayed the command.

"Get Hawthorne up here."

"Aye skipper," Alberts said.

The sub crept through the dead, calm water. "Right full rudder," Douglas ordered into the bridge comm. He felt the response and watched as the bow glided just below the surface. "Starboard. Back one-third." Gently, the three-hundred-foot submarine slipped into the shadow of the Japanese freighter. "Ease the rudder," he whispered as he scanned the looming ship. "All stop."

At first the freighter seemed deserted, then the silhouettes of heads and shoulders of men appeared over the railing.

"Control, bring us up ten feet. No more," Douglas ordered. He hoped to keep as much of the submarine hidden under the surface as he could. He heard the air pumps increase the sub's buoyancy, and she rose until most of her forward deck and a portion of her stern were above the water.

Suddenly, two heavy lines sprung from the deck of the Japanese ship and fell across the submarine.

From the forward and aft hatches, two crewmen clambered onto the deck. Riley was on the bow. "Holy Jesus," he said as he saw the distinct flag with its red rising sun in the center dangling high above him from the ship's superstructure. As ordered, he secured the bowline to the number one cleat and returned below.

Hawthorne climbed up the ladder and stepped onto the bridge next to Douglas. "Mother Mary of God," the crewman whispered.

"Let's hope we don't need her tonight," Douglas said as he led the machinist's mate down the rear ladder to the deck.

As they did, Alberts slipped from the hatch on his hands and knees. He stayed low behind the shoulder-high wall of the bridge. In his hands, he clutched a Thomson machine gun.

A rope ladder suddenly tumbled down the side of the freighter's rusting hull. Grabbing the twisted lines, Douglas glanced back at the *Mako*'s barren deck. From bow to stern, she seemed abandoned, but he knew his XO was poised in the conning tower with five heavily armed men to back him up. And just behind their perspective hatches, the firing crews for the sub's two deck guns were ready and waiting for his command.

Douglas put a second hand to the swaying ladder. "Don't say a thing unless I tell you, understood?"

"Aye, Skipper," Hawthorne said. The machinist's mate was only a shadow beside him.

The two men hoisted themselves upwards as quickly as they could and when they reached the top, four pairs of hands reached over and hauled them to the freighter's main deck.

A broad-shouldered man, as tall as Douglas, pressed him against the cabin bulkhead with one hand on his throat.

Gasping for breath, Douglas grabbed the man's forearm, trying to twist away, but was pinned to the steel wall with no escape. Staring into the Japanese crewman's hateful eyes, Douglas stopped struggling.

Hawthorne was in the same predicament. Held by a man of superior strength.

"Stand down, Mr. Hawthorne," Douglas ordered. He knew they were just putting off the inevitable.

As soon as the machinist's mate lowered his hands, the big man holding Douglas barked several orders. Shadow figures appeared and quickly assaulted them with crawling hands. They padded down their legs, their shirts, the back of their necks, under their arms.

The Colt .45 automatic tucked in Douglas' trousers disappeared. He assumed the same happened to Hawthorne's pistol.

The broad-shouldered man released his grip on Douglas' throat and replaced it with a heavy black pistol pressed against his chest.

The man with the gun stepped away, revealing two more figures. Another big man, not in height but in width, stepped close. The second, much smaller figure, remained at his side.

In the dim yellowish light of a nearby porthole, Douglas could see the wide man's face, fat and wet. He grinned with twisted teeth. "Ohayō Amerika senchō," he said, his voice raspy in the morning air.

"Captain Kiyohara says good morning, Commander," the smaller man said.

"You speak English?" Hawthorne said, surprised.

"Hawthorne," Douglas snapped, not looking away from the man.

"Sorry, sir," the Machinist's mate mumbled.

"Of course. I grew up in Los Angeles. Belmont High School. Class of '36," the crewman told him.

Kiyohara snapped at the smaller man, "Maetani-san. Tell him I want to finish this business quickly. The less time these animals are on my ship, the less the stench will linger."

Maetani stared at Douglas. "My captain thinks it would be best to finish our business quickly."

"I couldn't agree more," Douglas said. It was then he saw the line of Japanese crewmen armed with rifles crouched behind the bulkheads ready to fire on the *Mako*.

"You've made similar preparation aboard your submarine."

Douglas grinned. "What do you think?"

Kiyohara spoke in sharp tones again. Douglas sensed his irritation.

Maetani repeated his captain's instructions. "Please, Commander, this way."

Turning to follow the captain, Douglas saw the small man's hands were bound behind his back. "I take it he is not happy with you."

"I am against this rendezvous," Maetani admitted.

"You are not alone," Douglas told him.

They entered the first cabin, closed the door, and turned on the light. It was the map room and in the center of the floor were two U.S. Marine footlockers.

Kiyohara waved for the lids to be opened. "There is your prize, Commander," he said with a wave.

Maetani translated as Hawthorne knelt beside the small crates. He poked through the dozens of individually wrapped objects, careful not to disturb the sticks of dynamite wired to the lids.

As Hawthorne unwrapped the fossils, Douglas focused on the other objects in the boxes and was sickened by the thought of taking two dynamite-laden crates into his submarine.

Hawthorne whistled to himself as the archeologist turned machinist's mate revealed a peanut brown skull from its paper wrappings. He ran his fingers slowly over the frontal lobe, through the eye socket and over the upper jaw. Using his fingernail, he scraped a clod of dirt from between the first and second molars.

He spat into his palm and mixed his saliva with the dirt. He showed Douglas the gooey red paste. "Iron oxide," Hawthorne said. "Dragon's Tooth Hill is saturated with it." He smiled. "These are the real deal, Skipper," he said excitedly.

"So, you've got no problem with all of it?" Douglas asked, hoping the machinist's mate understood his reference.

Hawthorne shook his head. "Just like Utah."

"Are you satisfied, Commander?" Maetani asked.

"Who's going to inspect your package?"

"My captain."

Douglas judged the man next to him and at his huge, round belly. "He's going to have a hell of a time getting down the ladder."

Maetani shook his head. "You will send the items aboard."

"You expect me to hand over what I brought and then just keep my fingers crossed that you'll do the same?" Douglas asked. "Tell your captain, he can go fuck himself."

Maetani's thin lips turned at the corners. He translated Douglas' suggestion word for word.

The round-bellied man's face went cold. He blurred out an order in sharp grunts and the man with the gun grabbed Douglas again, pushing the barrel up under his chin. Douglas stared into his unblinking eyes.

Kiyohara stepped closer, giving Douglas the unmistakable whiff of sour alcohol. "Tell him to have the diamonds brought aboard or he is dead."

Douglas responded to Maetani's translation. "Remind him the sun is going to be up soon and it is going to bring trouble for both of us," Douglas said. "And let him know, if Mr. Hawthorne and I don't return, the first torpedo will be to your midship."

Again, Maetani translated. This time, Kiyohara's glare softened. His crooked teeth glittered in his face. "Yes," he said to Maetani. "There will be trouble for both of us. You go with this captain to his submarine. Pass me a few diamonds and I will have a look. But this man stays." He motioned to Hawthorne.

Douglas felt the gun barrel withdrawal. He saw Kiyohara draw a small knife from his pocket and cut the twine that bound the translator's hands.

As Maetani rubbed his wrists, he explained Kiyohara's compromise.

"Skipper?" Hawthorne's voice rose in panic. "You can't leave me."

"He goes. I stay," Douglas demanded.

"Don't worry, Commander," Maetani said. "As soon as our business is complete, your crewman will be released. The last thing my captain wants is an American submariner aboard his ship."

"Skipper!" Hawthorne grabbed at Douglas.

"It'll be all right," he promised. "Let's get this done," Douglas said as he swung himself over the railing. Followed closely by Maetani, Douglas dropped to the sub's deck and hurried to its forward hatch. He tapped it twice and the locking wheel spun open from inside.

Maetani saw the man with a machine gun and purpose in his eyes.

"As you figured," Douglas said to him. "Mr. Riley, pass up the crate." There was a scurry of whispers as the crewman disappeared and the narrow box rose through the hatch. As Douglas flipped open the end latches, he hoped the Japanese soldier had not noticed he had purposely left the center one locked. He lifted the lid.

Maetani cut open the center bag containing the stones. Even in the night, the diamonds sparkled with an inherent radiance. Taking a white handkerchief from his breast pocket, he scooped a handful of gems and deposited them in the center. Folding it carefully, he knotted its corners together.

While the Japanese soldier was intent on the stones, Douglas signaled silently to Riley. The crewman passed him his sidearm.

Maetani hurried to the bottom of the rope ladder. "Oi. Kyatchi," he called and tossed the bundle to the rail. Quick, eager hands shot forth to snag it from the air.

"Skipper," it was Alberts' voice coming from the bridge above them. "Sunrise," he warned.

Douglas scanned the horizon and realized the freighter and the *Mako* were both now being illuminated by a royal blue sky and the first slivers of sunlight were reflecting off the cargo booms. "Secure the bridge and the aft hatch," Douglas ordered.

Douglas saw Maetani standing with his hands on his hips, staring at the railing above..

"Does your captain know what he is looking at?"

"It seems, before the war, he specialized in smuggling gems."

"Convenient," Douglas said.

"How much time have you given us, Commander?" Maetani asked.

"Thirty minutes, as we agreed."

"You have followed the agreement?" Maetani asked, a tilt to his head.

"Yes."

Maetani stared at him, thinking. "There must be an element of trust between us," he said.

"My job is to send as many of your ships to the bottom as I can. That's what will win this war. But I gave my word not to sink yours, at least, not today."

Above them, a figure leaned over and called down. "Honmono desu. Torihiki o okonaimasu." Suddenly the footlockers appeared on the edge of the railing. They were strapped together and hoisted over on a heavy line.

Maetani signaled. "It seems you have passed his test."

Douglas moved to the crate with the diamonds. He set the countdown clock, resealed the lid and carefully locked the latches. "It set it for sixty minutes," he told Maetani. "After that, it can be opened."

"Not before?"

"I wouldn't try," Douglas warned as he and Maetani carried the crate to the bottom of the ladder. Taking a step back, they watched as the footlockers were lowered to the *Mako's* deck.

"The blue wire, Commander," Maetani said, beneath his breath.

Douglas turned to him unsure what he heard.

"The timer Captain Kiyohara used cannot be stopped. Unless you cut the blue wire."

"He double-crossed us."

"He may wear soldier's uniform, but he is a criminal. You are a soldier, Captain, as am I. I believe that you will keep to the agreement and not sink my ship."

"At least not today."

"At least not today," Maetani nodded.

As they turned to see the crates dangling above them, an odd sound grew in the distance. It was low at first, like a dull, muted hum. Douglas looked to the lagoon, expecting a Japanese patrol boat to be bearing down on them, but the short horizon to the reef was empty.

Still, the sound persisted. Maetani heard it as well, but as a surface ship crewman, his instinct was to search the sky.

"American fighters," Maetani hissed as he saw the distant formation coming from the south.

"Oh Jesus," Douglas said under his breath.

Suddenly, from the opposite direction, a dozen Japanese Zekes and Tojos fighter planes roared over the freighter as they rose into the morning sky to intercept the incoming forces.

With amazing speed, a handful of incoming Hellcat fighters swooped past the Zekes, came low across the water, and began their attack. Two Navy fighters roared only a dozen feet above the freighter's superstructure, on their way toward Moen's airfield.

Douglas and Maetani instinctively dropped as the warplanes thundered overhead. Around them, the *Mako*'s deck splintered as Kiyohara's crewmen fired down at him. Douglas rolled over, drew the .45, and fired two quick rounds.

Maetani scrambled to his feet and dove at Douglas, grabbing at the gun. With his other hand, he smashed the commander twice in the stomach before Douglas could stop him.

Riley popped open the forward hatch and, like a man in a pillbox, released a barrage from his machine gun into the rail of the freighter.

As others retreated, a solitary crewman fired defiantly at the American. Riley's unrelenting machine gun tore through the man's chest, sending his body over the side and into the lagoon.

Douglas rolled to his knees and twisted his free hand from Maetani's grip. He planted his elbow in the small man's face, followed by the butt of the gun to his forehead. Stunned, Maetani dropped.

More rounds ripped into the deck around them as Riley was reaching for a fresh machine gun. Douglas grabbed Maetani by the collar and pulled him behind the conning tower. He slammed the Japanese officer into the steel and pushed the automatic into his right eye.

"You knew," Maetani said gasping.

"Damn right," Douglas said, his chest heaving. "Just not this early."

Above them, a swarm of blue Hellcat fighters were immediately assaulted by a defensive force of nearly forty Japanese aircraft. Like two clouds of furious hornets bent on mutual destruction, the waring pilots would down one enemy plane every thirty seconds. The clash over Truk Lagoon would become one of the war's most vicious air battles.

From his position in the forward hatch, Riley turned his machine gun on the freighter each time he saw movement. Another man stepped forward and met Riley's onslaught. He fired before realizing it was Hawthorne and that the Japanese had forced him to the railing.

It was too late. The machinist's mate's riddled body fell between the hulls of the freighter and submarine.

Riley screamed with horror. He never heard his own voice. A Japanese bullet ripped through the side of his head, killing him instantly.

"Skipper!" It was Alberts on the bridge. "Incoming," he pointed south.

Douglas saw them. Black spots on the horizon. Fast and low. Avenger torpedo bombers.

"Fate, Commander. They will destroy us both," Maetani spat.

"Not if I can help it." Douglas tucked the gun in his belt, grabbed Maetani by his uniform collar and, with all his strength, threw the man off the deck of the *Mako* and into the lagoon.

"Mike! Emergency dive. Let her vent. Dive. Dive," Douglas screamed.

There was no hesitation in Alberts' response. "Aye! Dive! Dive!" he called to the control room. The submarine shuddered as her valves opened and the sea rushed into her ballast tanks.

Douglas bolted for the conning tower before the upper hatch closed. But as he rushed up the rungs, he heard panicked screams from the bow.

Riley's body had collapsed across the machine gun, which laid wedged under the main hatch. If the crewmen could not get it closed, the forward torpedo room would flood and possibly send the *Mako* into an uncontrollable dive to the bottom.

Douglas hit the water-swept deck, sprinting. He dropped to his knees, grabbed the crewman's lifeless arms, and yanked him upward through the deluge of the incoming sea. "Push!" he screamed to the men below.

As Douglas pulled, Riley's body rose as if on its own. His legs cleared the opening, and the hatch jerked closed. The locking wheel spun tight.

Without a thought, the Commander left Riley's body to the white foam and swirling sea. He dashed toward the conning tower, but it was too late. He knew the entry hatch would be closed and secure.

As the *Mako* sank beneath him, Douglas leapt for the rope ladder still dangling from the freighter's hull. He grabbed hold and pulled himself a few feet out of the water just in time to hear the sharp snap of the sub breaking its mooring lines.

Douglas hung against the side waiting for rifle bullets to rip into his body, but none came. The Japanese crew had forgotten him as they turned their guns skyward.

The last thirty seconds had taken a lifetime, but with relief, he saw the *Mako*'s twin periscopes disappear beneath the surface. His crew would make it. Douglas' solace was brief as he eyed the pair of blue warbirds coming across the eastern edge of the reef directly toward him.

•   •   •

The pilot of the lead TBF Avenger torpedo-bomber saw his four-hundred-foot target resting in perfect position. The freighter would be the veteran's fifteenth victim in the last six months and the first of the day. Still anchored and close to the beach, she was an easy kill.

Swooping low, the pilot set his hand on the release lever of the thirteen-foot torpedo that lay tucked under his fuselage. At fifty feet above the water and doing two hundred miles an hour, he dropped it at a hundred yards off the freighter.

The pilot never felt or heard the impotent rifle fire coming from the deck of the enemy ship, but as he pulled back on the Avenger's control stick and rose safely into the sky, he looked out the side of his canopy.

The white line of his torpedo streaking through the water was distinct and straight. A heartbeat later, with a flash of gold flame, it hit its mark. The blast opened the port side of the *Kuma Maru* and sent her to the bottom in less than two minutes.

34

FALO ISLAND, TRUK LAGOON, 1986

B RIAN DID NOT FEEL HIMSELF sinking until his knees thumped against the freighter's port bulkhead. He froze as he stared at the familiar structure rising through the torpedo hole.

Finally, with labored breaths and a heart ricocheting across his ribcage like a pinball, he swam toward the apparition illuminated by his dive lamp.

What he thought were the twin barrels of a bizarre weapon, were the periscopes and radar mast of his father's submarine. Now he could see the open bridge and the rear portion of the conning tower filling the gaping hole in the side of the *Kuma Maru*.

He understood the reason the *Mako* had never found in the lagoon. His father had done exactly what he expected. He had taken his sub straight to the bottom to avoid the attacking warplanes, but in a vicious twist of fate, or simple bad luck, the Avenger's torpedo sank the freighter directly on top of them.

Brian pulled himself over the cigarette deck and saw the 20mm deck gun still standing on the open platform as if awaiting the crewmen to unbolt its barrel and swing it into action.

The light moved further along the tower, as if leading Brian along. He reached out and grabbed the warped handrail that encircled the deck. A thin piece of steel his father had certainly touched.

The small deck area of the bridge was clear except for a piece of the lookout platform. It had fallen across the hatch leading into the conning tower, the small, pressurized chamber housing the periscopes and main controls. It was still sealed closed.

As 52 American submarines lost to the Pacific War did, the *Mako* hugged her crew like a doting mother, unwilling to let them go. She had become their tomb, a steel crypt that was crushed beneath the weight of the Japanese freighter.

It was just as well, Brian thought. Had the men below gotten the conning hatch open, the first man out would have carried a knife to cut away any obstacles to give the rest of the men a clear path to the surface. But encapsuled by the freighter, they would have escaped from one coffin into another.

Brian peered where the forward section of the sub disappeared below the torpedo hole and under the freighter. For a second, he imagined the Pacific washing across her bow as his father barked orders to dive.

The *Mako*, however, would never surface again. Over the coming millennium, corals and algae would take residence along with the lagoon's sea life, while on a chemical level, the salt water would seek the demise of both the freighter and sub until there was nothing left of their steel structures but red dust for the tides to wash away.

Brian shook the thoughts from his brain. He drifted away from the bridge, making his way back to the maintenance hatch. Midway across the hold, he turned back to the conning tower.

She was one of the most successful submarines out of Honolulu, with over twenty kills to her credit. The *Mako*'s crew should have been decorated, but instead they rested in oblivion, their war records carrying the minimum acknowledgement.

"Those orders may still be aboard," Mimi's words came back to him. Doubtful, but maybe. Just maybe.

With two powerful kicks, Brian swam back to the bridge. *They'll forgive me*, he thought as he reached down and moved the piece of wreckage that lay over the hatch.

Bracing his legs against the deck, Brian tugged at the corroded, 10-inch wheel latch. At first, it resisted his efforts, then, as if someone inside was putting their muscle to it as well, the wheel broke loose and spun open.

The steel rods and pivots of the inner mechanism eased the thick dog latches away from the seal. For the first time in forty years, the hatch was free, and instantly, it exploded.

The heavy door slammed against the deck inches from Brian's foot as air entrapped in the submarine for decades burst from the interior like a volcano spewing silvery lava.

The force of the rising bubbles ripped Brian's regulator and dive mask from his face. As he recoiled from the onslaught, he quickly managed to find his mask and regain his mouthpiece.

Brian huddled into the corner of the bridge as he watched several lifejackets pop out of the hatch in rapid succession and race upward. They clustered like bats in the shimmering pool of air that was swelling in the uppermost corner of the sealed hold.

With the eruption came a snowstorm of debris. Something fluttered past Brian's face like a falling leaf. He reached for it and discovered a portion of a navigation chart in his hand.

It was for Midway Island, but more astonishing was that he could still see the pencil marks the *Mako*'s navigator had set across its compass rose. He tore the edge of the chart, and it ripped cleanly into two pieces instead of dissolving in hand as he expected.

Somehow, the air pocket of the conning tower had kept it dry. But charts were kept in the control room directly below it. Brian realized the hatch between the two internal chambers had to be open. And if this piece of paper was preserved, what else might he find inside?

He let the paper slip from his hand and peered over the bridge. Aiming his lamp toward the bow, he could see through the murky water that the opening in the freighter's hull stretched another fifty feet forward. If the control room was intact, there was a good possibility the cabins just beyond had escaped the *Kuma Maru*'s crushing weight.

That section of the sub, he knew, was officers' country. The officers' cabins. His father's cabin.

As Brian swept the light beam across the planks of the false deck that topped the submarine's pressurized hull, he spotted an odd rectangular shape wedged against a port side cleat. Something in the back of his mind flickered. Something the Chinese woman had said.

Brian kicked away from the bridge and drifted to the main deck. Brushing the silt away, he uncovered the military crate. Saltwater and worms had made their mark, but the lead-based, olive-green paint had held them at bay.

He ran his hand along the front edge of the lid and found the three corroded latches. He knew they would break open easily, but they had waited forty years. A few more hours would not matter.

Brian glanced at his watch. Thirty minutes on the bottom. Twenty left. It did not really matter. Nothing did, except getting inside the *Mako*.

Returning to the bridge, he saw only a trickle of escaping bubbles. They'll forgive me, he told himself again as he swam toward the hatchway and leaned into the dim cavern.

Swimming into the opening, Brian forgot the diameter of the hatch was only that of a man's shoulders. His scuba tanks banged into the rim. Unbuckling the waist, he slipped the shoulder straps and removed the twin tanks.

Keeping the regulator tight between his teeth, he pushed the tanks through the hatch first as he dropped through the circular opening.

A blizzard of floating particles and debris cramped and darkened the conning tower. He saw the two large brass wheels of the helm in front of him, the sub's two periscope stations split the room in half. He touched one. Gently. Thoughtfully. He wondered how many times his father had stood in this chamber, his face pressed to this scope and calling out orders.

He turned his light to the diamond plate floor and found the hatchway leading deeper into the sub. As he hoped, it was open. What he had not expected was the round, cup like object sitting beside it.

The skull was blackish; the crown covered with thin white hair. Trapped in the air-tight hull, decay would take its toll, but the bodies' decomposition would not be complete. He fought away the visions of the man this might have been.

Pushing further down, he crawled along the descending ladder and entered the control room which was much larger than the conning tower. He wondered if Leslie's father would have fought off the sickening claustrophobia that was creeping into his own brain. It screamed at him to stop and turn around. He was tempting death in a place where it certainly had the upper hand.

The point driven further by the litter of pale bones laying across the deck beneath him. The abrupt rush of the incoming sea had swept them from their resting place and scattered them like a child's game of pickup sticks.

Brian found the large oval hatch leading to the officer's quarters. The oval hatch was open, its door yawning wide. He swam through and as he entered the hallway; he felt the unexpected. His head broke the surface of the water.

The angle of the sunken submarine had created larger air pockets that defied the surge of salt water. Brian stood up awkwardly, his fins bending under his feet and keeping him from gaining his balance. His dive light illuminated a fog-like mist filling the air pocket.

Keeping his regulator in place, he lifted his mask. Instantly, his eyes burned and teared. The air, now condensed into the upper half of the hull, was thick with the sulfuric acid vapors released by the *Mako*'s shattered batteries. It explained the bronze color of the skeletons.

He dropped into the water, replaced the mask over his face, and cleared it. He surfaced again and, weaving his left arm through one of the tank's shoulder straps, lifted them to his back.

Coming to a doorway, he flashed his light inside, knowing it was the executive officer's stateroom. A jolt shot through him as bile rose in his throat. He spun away. He took a deep breath and forced himself to look again.

The skeleton, draped with sloppy black skin, laid on the upper bunk wearing a white dress uniform. A black, leather-bound book lay pyramided over his chest.

Michael Alberts. Twenty-three years old. Single. From Detroit, Michigan. The only son of a clergyman and a schoolteacher. Brian remembered the details he studied about his father's men.

How long had the air lasted? Brian wondered. *Hours? Days?* A week until the air turned bitter and heavy with the stench of battery acid. Which of them had screamed for mercy and who, like Mr. Alberts, had come to his quarters, quietly changed into his best uniform, and patiently waited for the end?

Brian moved back to the companionway and stared at the entry of the next cabin. The captain's stateroom on the starboard side, just past the sub's office. The canvas curtains that would have granted the skipper a small amount of privacy were gone.

Brian knew he had no time to hesitate. That he had come this far and if he discovered his father as he had discovered Mr. Alberts, that was their fate.

He pushed forward down the hall, his dive light leading. The water swirled as he peered inside. Unlike the junior officer's stateroom, there was no upper bunk. If Brian's father had done the same as his XO, the water would have covered his single bunk. Brian lowered himself into the water to look.

Suddenly, two flailing arms reached for him.

He jerked backwards. Back, back, back, his mind screamed. His legs kicking, his chest heaving for more air than the regulator offered. He slammed into the bulkhead, but in the same instance, he recognized the arms were the sleeves of a leather jacket floating out of the room.

He swept the coat aside and scanned the cabin. It was vacant. His heart slowed. He moved to the captain's desk, tore open the cabinet. Pencils, rulers, dividers. A penknife in a ceramic cup. Three packs of Lucky Strike cigarettes floated out, leaving a Zippo lighter.

He rifled the drawers. Navy-issue straight razor, a hairbrush, a bar of shaving cream, soft and foaming. Two toothbrushes. It was the bits and pieces of a man he never knew but whose long shadow he had lived under.

Under the bed, more drawers filled with navy turnouts. Shoes that would never be worn.

A glance at the pressure gauge. Fifteen hundred pounds of air. Fifteen minutes' worth. Just enough to make it out of the wreck if he left now. But he had come too far and risked too much to retreat.

Where else? Alberts's cabin? No, it would not be there. It was here. If the orders still existed, they were here. He would have to come back, Brian realized. He would return tomorrow with more air tanks and search again.

Turing to leave, the dive light revealed what he had come for. Hanging on a hook to the right of the door, and hidden from his view when he entered, was his father's leather satchel.

The embossed lettering on the cover flap was faded, but still readable.

LT. CMDR. DOUGLAS BOVAN
USS MAKO
SS-360

Brian unlatched the brass twist lock, dug under the flap, and drew the oilcloth-wrapped papers. Amazingly, the acidic fumes that had penetrated the submarine had not breached the linseed barrier. The papers were white and pristine. He read the first sentences of the letter and grinned under his regulator.

Brian resealed the oilcloth and hoped it would hold against the sea for a few more hours. He closed the cover flap of the satchel and moved into the passageway. One last look at his father's cabin and he headed toward the surface.

Passing the XO's quarters, he wondered if Mr. Alberts had been waiting for him, waiting for someone to come and find the orders. Brian could make no promises, but there had to be someone in Washington who would care enough to clear the crew of the *Mako*. He hoped it was enough for the XO's ghost to know his watch was over.

Brian dipped below the water and swam into the control room and up through the conning tower and onto the bridge.

As he headed for the machinist's hatch, Brian glanced at the crate still wedged against the port cleat. He thought of the islander who had attacked Leslie and what Honma had said about the treasure of Truk Lagoon.

They would come, he thought. They would breach the midship hold in their search and they would find the *Mako*. They would have no hesitation or remorse in entering sacred ground. That, he could not allow.

As he swam quickly through the freighter, he recalculated his decompression times. He would need more time dangling at the twenty-foot depth, but he had added the extra air tanks. Still, his time underwater would push safety limits.

Reaching the wheelhouse, he carefully wedged his father's satchel in the corner of the bulkhead. He retrieved the lift bag from where it was pinned against the ceiling.

He released the remaining air, rolled it under his arm and, once again, followed the nylon line back to the midship hold.

When Brian finally kicked away from the freighter's slanted deck, he held the satchel in one hand and in the other, the wooden crate that now dangled from the lift bag he had filled with oxygen from the cutting torch.

Reaching the decompression line, he looked down at the lingering shadow of the *Kuma Maru*. Beneath the freighter, the submarine's thick hull had kept the sea at bay. Now, with her hatches open, the sea could finally reach her crew and take them to her breast. *Sailors, rest your oar,* he thought as he began his slow ascent.

35

FOR THE FIRST TWENTY MINUTES after Brian slipped beneath the surface, Leslie sat on the runabout's gunwale with her legs to her chest, her chin on her knees, watching the water.

JP stretched himself across the deck, put his head to a coil of rope, and tipped his hat over his eyes. "So, you're a doctor??" he asked.

Leslie glanced over. "Yes."

"A surgeon, right?"

Leslie ignored him as she watched Brian's bubbles break the surface of the turquoise waters.

"I thought about being a doctor once."

"What changed your mind?"

"Bedside manners," JP confessed. "Not my strong point."

"A lot of doctors could use a class on empathy," she agreed. She had yet to look away from the lagoon.

"So, you came here to see your father." It was a statement and not a question. "You weren't close."

"You're right about your bedside manners."

"Just an observation."

"Out of a file?"

"Didn't need to look. You live in New York. He's in Hawaii."

"Do you have kids?"

JP hiccupped a laugh. "No."

"So, not an educated guess?"

"My job is studying people. I am surprisingly good at it."

"Do I have a government file?" she asked.

"If you pay taxes, you have a file," he said honestly. "Beyond that? No. We had to do some digging to find you, but you did send up some red flags. Traveling to Hawaii? Airline tickets? Hotel? None under your name?"

"My friend made the arrangements," she defended.

"Right, Terry Campton. The big time New York attorney's daughter. Just moved in with her, didn't you? Left that Eric guy?"

Leslie swung her legs around and glared at the man under the hat. "Why do you know that?" she snapped.

With his face still hidden under his hat, JP raised his hands. "Relax," he said. "It's all public information. No one is spying on you."

"My ex-boyfriend?"

"Two weeks back. *The Times*. Society page. He's society guy. You're a respected surgeon at a prominent city hospital. You were the better half of the perfect power couple, Leslie. May I call you Leslie?"

"No," she shot. "And what about Brian?"

"Commander Bovan?" the CIA man pushed his hat back and squinted in her direction. "He is in a whole other category. The files on him probably weighs as much as you do." He set his arms over his chest.

"You suspect him of something?"

"I did," he admitted. "And it cost a man his life."

"But it wasn't Brian's fault?" She knew the answer; she needed the agent to admit it.

JP simply shook his head. "The people you think you know the best you know the least." He covered his face again and settled in for their wait.

Leslie turned back to the spot where Brian had disappeared. "He has to be at the decompression line by now," she said. Paradise, she realized, had its contradictions. The slow pace of time was one. A godsend when rest and relaxation was the intent, but a curse when you needed the clock to move faster.

It was not long after that she heard the rhythmic rattle of JP's snoring. She frowned. That he could engage in such a biennial action was surreal. Had he not just killed a man? Justified or not?

In disbelief, she turned to the sea again. The water around the boat suddenly looked different. Leaning over the stern, she saw the rise of bubbles as they crashed into the hull.

"He's coming up," she said excitedly.

JP's sudden appearance beside her was a jolt as she did not hear him wake or cross the deck.

"He must be at the second stop," she said.

"You can tell?"

"George said to watch the bubbles and how they spread at the surface," she explained.

"That means another hour, right?" JP stared into the water. He could only see the decompression line disappear like a bucket lowered into a wishing well.

"At least."

"Back to my nap," the agent said.

Leslie watched Brian's bubbles rise from the depths and sparkle as they passed into the sunlight as if she were watching a 4th of July fireworks display from a seat in the clouds.

"Now, who the hell is this?" JP said with dismay.

Coming from the east, a speedboat ran along the beach with a Santa Claus beard of white foam under its bow. It headed directly toward them.

Leslie cupped her hands, warding off the glare, but in the corner of her eye, she saw JP reach under his shirt. "I think it's the police captain."

"I wonder what he wants?"

"He told Brian he'd come."

"Did he?" JP asked with suspicion.

Leslie heard a change in the agent's voice and watched as he pulled a towel from the cabin. He slipped his gun into its folds and set it innocently on the skiff's helm console. He slipped back into the cabin and out of sight. "Don't let him aboard."

"He's coming to help."

"Tell him you don't need any," JP said firmly.

As the speedboat swung wide and slowed, she could see the twelve-inch blue letters along its hull announced: POLICE. Honma was not at the helm. It was Sergeant Wuun, and suddenly, she was thankful JP was with her.

"Doctor Maetani. The captain sent me to check on you."

"Please thank him," she called between the boats. There was only a twenty-foot gap now. "We're fine."

"Your friend? He's in the water?"

"He was interested in getting some underwater photos," she said.

"The wrecks on this side of the lagoon are dangerous. They're filled with munitions, you know?"

"He's very careful. And, besides, he should be up in a minute or so."

The sergeant worked the boat like a cowboy sidestepping his horse. Then, before she could stop him, Wuun leaned over the speedboat's gunwale and lassoed the runabout's mid-cleat with a docking line.

"Really, Sergeant. We're fine."

Wuun ignored her, stitching the vessels together at the middle and stern cleats. "After last night, I am surprised photographs would be so important," he said, stepping across the skiff's gunwale. For the first time, she saw he was wearing a thick leather belt supporting a holster and pistol. He peered over the stern to the eruption of bubbles. "Perhaps there was something else on the wreck that caught his attention."

"And what would that be?" JP asked as he emerged from the cabin.

Caught off guard, Wuun reached for his sidearm.

JP lifted his hands in surrender and took a step back. "Hold on."

"He's a friend," Leslie said quickly. She saw JP position himself within reach of the hidden gun.

"I thought it was just you."

"We asked him to help," she lied.

"With photographs?"

"There's a lot of equipment involved."

"You are an expert?" Wuun had not taken his hand off the grip of his pistol.

"You might say that." JP nodded.

Wuun peered over the transom as more bubbles exploded against the bottom of the boat with the hiss of a snake.

• • •

Hanging from the decompression line twenty feet below, Brian was struggling with the lift bag. Even with the crate dangling from it, the canvas balloon was intent on dragging him upward. Twice he tried to squeeze air from it. Even so, the bag fought against him.

Finally, he heard the high-pitched whine of the speedboat's motor and saw its dagger-like silhouette draw alongside the Owens. Honma was now with Leslie and JP. The captain could help them drag the box aboard as he waited to finish his decompression stop.

But before Brian released the bag, he pulled his father's leather satchel from where he had tucked it under the scuba tank's shoulder strap. Using one of the lift bag's free lines, he wove it tightly through the satchel's handle.

Before securing it completely, he acted on a lingering suspicion, relocked the case, and wrapped the line around the entire satchel several more times. Then he tied it to the top of the wooden box.

Brian saw the sleek shadows floating above him. Holding the lift bag at arm's length, he aimed its trajectory to the stern of the Owens. He let go. The water-soaked crate and his father's leather bag drifted slowly, but directly, upwards. All he could do now was hope Leslie was watching his rising bubbles.

• • •

"So, you people actually cook it and eat it?" JP was asking Wuun.

The police sergeant was frowning as he stared into the lagoon. He was quickly tiring of the man's relentless inquiries. "Yes. We call them penichon. In soup, it's good."

"Sea cucumber soup?" JP shook his head with a wince. "No, thank you."

"The Japanese eat it raw," Leslie added. She had not taken her eyes off Brian's bubbles for the last twenty minutes.

"You also eat poisonous puffer fish," he noted.

The lift bag broke the surface with a distinct whoosh. It floated against the stern swim step.

Leslie leapt to her feet. "That's not him."

"It's a lift bag," Wuun was beside her. He leaned over, trying to grab its wobbly edges.

"Here," JP retrieved a fisherman's gaff from under the gunwale. At the end of the six-foot wooden pole, George had lashed a three-inch barbed hook. The agent swept the pole under the bag until it snagged the lines.

Together, they drew it to the stern where, through the crystalline waters, they could see the decaying crate lashed under the bag like a meal in an octopus's tentacles.

With effort, the two men hauled Brian's find aboard the runabout. Salt water flooded the deck as they slid it to the center.

Ignoring the leather satchel that was tangled in the lines, Wuun excitedly yanked it and the lift bag free and tossed them to the side. He ran his hands over the badly eaten wood. The slimy film of green and orange algae was smooth under his fingers. "It seems he was not as interested in photography as you said."

Leslie untangled the satchel from the lines. She saw the embossed lettering on the cover flap. Hugging it in her arms, she turned back to the rising bubbles.

Wuun shot JP a sidelong glance. "Perhaps no one is taking pictures today. Perhaps this is what he went to find?"

JP shrugged. "We'll have to wait and ask him."

Wuun inspected the box's three rusted latches. "I wonder what is so important," he said as he drew a small folding knife from his pocket. He worked it under the lid's corner.

"I wouldn't do that," JP warned.

"You are not curious?"

"I am more worried than curious. What if that is an ammunition box? You might mistakenly blow us up," JP said as he took a casual step toward the helm and the folded towel.

Wuun laughed. "The lagoon is full of old ammunition. You don't need to dive the *Kuma Maru* to find it."

"Well, if it was me, I'd want to be sure there was no trick to opening it."

Leslie turned slowly to the sergeant. She glared at him. "How did you know the name?" she asked. "How did you know the name of my father's ship?"

Wuun's face went harsh as he turned. But it was the movement out of the corner of his eye that made him reach for his sidearm.

JP slipped his weapon from the towel. Although it was an excellent ploy to place something so deadly in a benign location, he had not expected the soft terrycloth folds to hinder his actions. The miscalculation cost the agent his life.

Wuun fired two quick rounds while still hunched over the crate. Before the agent's body collapsed, the officer turned his weapon on Leslie.

She had not moved. Frozen with terror, she clutched the satchel to her chest as though it were a shield against the next shot.

"This is what your father was after, wasn't it? Your father and now him," Wuun glanced over the side. "Except your father was easier to take care of."

Leslie swung the satchel, catching Wuun across the side of the face. As he stumbled, she lunged with surprising speed. Vengeful claws drawn. She slashed at him, her fingernails finding the soft flesh of his cheek.

While she had the agility, she did not have the strength or power of the stocky islander. He countered her assault with a blunt backhanded strike made more devastating by the weight of the gun still in his hand.

She crumbled.

"Fucking bitch." Wuun tested his stinging wounds with his fingers. He leaned over the transom and saw the bubbles. Holstering his gun, he quickly hoisted the water-soaked crate onto the runabout's port gunwale and pushed it across the narrow gap between the two boats.

"Get up," he screamed at Leslie. She stirred, and he kicked at her. "I said, get the fuck up."

"Brian," she cried.

"Two minutes more, he's dead," Wuun hissed. "And so are you if you don't get up." He pulled the Owens' fuel tank from under the back seats, unscrewed the lid and poured the caustic liquid across the deck. He dumped a portion on JP's body.

"What are you doing?" Leslie gagged on the fumes.

"Giving the lagoon another wreck." Wuun drew his cigarette lighter, caught a spark, and threw it into the gasoline drenched cabin. It ignited the boat and instantly sent flames crawling across the deck.

Leslie scrambled to her feet. "Brian," she cried out.

Wuun seized a fist full of hair and dragged her toward the speedboat. At the last second, she grabbed the satchel from where it had dropped. It was the last thing she remembered as she was tossed bodily into the police boat.

By the time Wuun backed the speedboat away from the runabout, it was engulfed in flames. A trail of black smoke swirled over Falo and into the blue dome of the tropical sky.

•　　　•　　　•

Given the physics of how sound travels underwater and with only two dozen feet between him and the surface, Brian heard the bark of the outboard motor coming to life as though it was it directly next to him. He looked up to the two boats wavering in the blue ceiling above him.

Without hesitation, the sleek speedboat suddenly backed from the Owens, pivoted and, with a guttural howl that kicked him in the chest, it lifted its bow and sped away.

Brian's mind raced. Was it a police call? Was Honma radioed about an emergency? Would that pull him away? Or had something else happened on the surface? What about Leslie? The agent?

Fifteen more minutes hanging from the decompression line. Fifteen more sweeps of the second hand before he could exit the water. If he surfaced now, would it kill him or just cripple him? Suddenly, it did not matter. He had to surface and see.

Rising slowly, he held the decompression line loosely in his palm. Then, as if something had yanked it from below, the line dropped through his hand. He grabbed it just before losing the end. To his surprise, he saw its nylon fibers were black and burnt.

His heart raced as he stared at the skiff only ten feet above him. Suddenly, the underwater world froze as if everything beneath the surface of the waves time took a collective gasp. In that fraction of a second, he saw the Owen's wooden hull expand a bit, contract, and expand again in a blindly bright explosion.

The shockwave slapped him with screaming banshees, shattered his facemask and kicked his mind into a black fog. For a moment, he could not tell if he was breathing, although he could feel the regulator was still in his mouth.

Instinctively, he tried to kick toward the surface, but something had wrapped itself around his legs like thick tentacles. He found the decompression line tangled about his fins. As he tugged at the rope to free himself, he saw a massive black object racing toward him.

On the surface, the explosion had severed the skiff's cabin from its stern and engine, and now the rear of the boat was plunging through the water column like an errant torpedo.

What small bit of consciousness he had managed to hold onto was knocked out away as the transom slammed into him. Suddenly, Brian's body was pinned to the splintered hull as it spiraled downward toward the bottom.

36

FALO ISLAND, TRUK LAGOON, 1986

D EATH IS A TERRIBLE PLACE. A painful place, cold and lonely. But it was not dark. Brian expected it to be dark and silent. But there were fireworks and thunder. He had never thought much about death, although once a stranger accused him of being the harbinger of Armageddon. He was in uniform. The stranger wore bell-bottom jeans and a tie dye t-shirt.

"Evasive action, Mr. Bovan," Captain Fife's voice came across the dancing lights.

"Aye, Skipper," Brian heard himself say, but his voice came from far away.

"Depth charges!" another voice screamed and suddenly there was more thunder. Brian felt his body jerk with the charges as they exploded in his mind.

A man screamed suddenly. "No, no," he yelled in broken English. It was George.

"Take her down! Hellcats coming over the horizon! Dive, dive!" a strange husky voice ordered. It was the voice of his father, the one he imagined as a kid.

The roar of a torpedo bomber flew from one ear to the other and Brian's body felt the concussion of its torpedo. Then the scream of a woman. *Leslie!* He woke.

The cool of the deep water threw his senses into hyperdrive. He shook his head and discovered the thunder was a growing bump above his right ear. His eyes burned in the sea water and his left arm was numb.

Immediately, he brought the pressure gauge close to his face. The blurred number showed his air supply near empty. He had been unconscious for only a few minutes. He looked at the depth gauge. Its needle rested somewhere between sixty and seventy feet. He did not know how deep the transom had taken him.

He stared into a green fog. Without his facemask, nothing was clear. He yanked the rope from his legs and kicked upward.

The ascent took forever. But it was more from the lack of wanting to reach the surface than the distance. His body told him to give in and let the sea have its way.

How ironic, he thought, that he would die in the same waters that took his father. It could be some sort of broad scheme to balance the world. Who am I to change such a plan? Let go, just let go and sleep.

But his legs kept moving and he rose steadily toward the surface of the lagoon.

Leslie is dead. No, don't think that. There was a fire, but the other boat saved her. JP and Honma saved her.

At twenty feet, Brian heard the clucking of another outboard engine. A small one. As he tried to find the engine source, his skull exploded with pain, and he felt faint. He stared at his fins until his brain settled.

As he listened to the changing tones of the engine, he could tell that it was circling his bubbles. The tone changed again as the throttle decreased until the only thing he could hear was the hiss of bubbles escaping his regulator.

His decompression was thrown off completely, but now, his only thoughts were seeing her face again.

Finally, he broke the surface, pulled the remains of his mask from his head, and spit the regulator from his mouth. Wiping his face, he tasted the bitterness of blood.

A shadow rose over his shoulder. "Commander." A woman's voice. A familiar voice, but not Leslie's. "Commander."

Brian turned to find a low dory hanging over him and a silhouette leaning over the water. A small hand grabbed the shoulder of his wetsuit and, with surprising strength, pulled him against the boat.

Brian gripped the side of the boat as he let Mimi slide the straps of his scuba tanks off his shoulder. She let the gear drop away. "Help me, Commander. I am too old to lift you out by myself," she said sternly.

Brian kicked as hard as he could as he pulled himself over the narrow gunwale.

Mimi directed his fall onto the dory's center bench. She saw blood trickling from his right ear. "Can you hear me?" She asked.

Brian rolled onto his back. "Where's Leslie?" he asked. There was a pounding within the walls of his skull.

"The police sergeant took her."

"And the agent?"

"No," Mimi said with a shake of her head.

Brian squeezed his forehead with his fingers. He felt pain growing across his shoulders. It was either from the explosion or the bends, he was not sure.

"What did they pull from the water?" the woman asked, her voice high with expectation.

With effort, Brian sat up. "A wooden crate," he said weakly. His head was spinning. "It was on the deck of the sub."

Mimi gasped. "It was there? The submarine?"

"I got in."

"My god." Her hand rose to her lips. "You found them." Her question trailed off.

Brian looked over the gunwale trying to get his bearings. "Where would he take her?"

"The house," she said. "It's the only place."

Brian struggled across the dory's bench to the outboard motor.

Mimi stopped him. "You sit. I know where we can cut across the reefs where it's too shallow for the police boat," she said.

Twenty minutes later, Mimi drove the bow of the dory into the beach, just beyond the mangroves and out of sight. The engine gurgled in the surf until she killed it.

She swung her legs over the gunwale and dropped to the sand. Brian followed her lead, but he was far less steady on his feet.

"You're sick, Commander. You have the bends."

"He has Leslie," he said as he drew a deep breath and waved the Asian woman to lead him through the mangroves. He realized she had been through this jungle before as she followed a lightly traveled path that led directly to the house.

He crouched when she crouched. Ran when she did until they were through the web of trees. Just beyond the front deck, the police speedboat rested high on the beach. It sat like a drunk on its port side, the retreating tide kicking sand around the propellers.

They found the house as he and Leslie had left it only six hours before. Brian signaled Mimi to stay in place as he crept forward. Easing himself through the underbrush, he slipped to the side of the house.

He pressed his back against the plywood wall and waited. He listened. No sound radiated from inside, although the throbbing in his head was intensified by the sharp squawking of two parakeets on the branches above.

He saw the side windows like a pair of giant eyes watching for him. But with their blinds down, they slept. Still, he moved cautiously, ducking under each sill.

Reaching the raised deck just outside the study, he dropped to his hands and knees and crawled painfully beneath it. The package he had stuffed underneath was still there.

Brian drew the Colt automatic from the rag, rewrapped the logbook, and returned it to the nook. As he stood with his back pressed to the plywood wall, he tried to stop the hot irons that were piercing into his elbows and knees.

A deep breath and he eased the Colt's slide back. He injected a round into the gun's chamber.

Circling the house, Brian found the back door kicked in. Brian squeezed the Colt with both hands and stepped inside. Along the hall, the floor squeaked with each step. A peek in the bedroom. Empty. He crept further.

The study was to the left, the door open. With his weapon leveled, Brian charged in.

No one. But on the metal desk, he saw Wuun had placed the algae-encrusted crate. There were tools from the workroom scattered beside it. Resting on top was both the leather satchel and Henry's notebook.

She's not here, he thought, his panic growing. But as he turned to search further, he heard movement. He froze, his heart clenched in a vise. Then, a soft moan.

He found Leslie on the other side of the desk, her feet and hands bound. She was gagged so tightly, her lip was split and bleeding. The bruised left side of her face was swelling, closing against her eye. *But alive,* he thought. She was alive. He could breathe again.

In the rush to save her, however, Brian made a deadly mistake. He set the gun on the desk as he lifted her.

Barely conscious, she recoiled from his touch.

"Leslie," he whispered. "It's me."

She stared at him, unsure at first, as though she could not understand what he was saying. Then she began to cry.

"It's okay. I'm going to get you out," he said, untying the gag.

"Not until I am finished with her," Wuun's heavy voice filled the room.

Brian clenched his jaw as he realized he had foolishly disarmed himself. He turned to the police sergeant standing in the doorway with his revolver pressed into Mimi's throat.

"You are a difficult man to kill, Commander," he said. He pushed Mimi across the room.

As Brian caught the elderly woman, Wuun quickly grabbed the Colt and tucked it into his belt.

Brian felt his anger building. Now his body ached not from the nitrogen in his blood, but from the need to kill this man.

"Did you know it's booby trapped? I am not surprised. The Japanese were never trusting. They did not trust my father or my mother even as they worked them to death building their island fortresses," he said. He leered at Leslie. "But the doctor, she is different. She is very trusting. She even told me what wire to cut to disarm the explosives."

With Mimi's help, Leslie slowly gathered herself and stood up. "Fuck you," she shot.

"You think I am a simple islander? I know how smart you are, Doctor. How easy it is for her to lie. Blue wire," he scoffed. "Open the box, Commander. Or there will be another fire and more bodies."

Mimi grabbed Brian's wrist. Her eyes were warning, but not because of Wuun. Brian stepped around the desk and, for the first time, saw the latches holding the lid. Three latches.

Suddenly, the scribbled note in his father's logbook made sense. *Don't open the middle hatch.* Not *hatch*, he realized. The smudged word was *latch*. Like Leslie's father, Douglas had also written himself a reminder.

Brian dug his fingers into the crust, covering the first latch, and snapped it open. He twisted the second, which felt as if it was about to break off. The third latch, the middle latch, was seized by corrosion. It took the tip of a screwdriver from the desk to break it free.

Pushing the satchel and notebook aside, Brian glanced at Mimi. There was no way to tell the elderly woman what he planned. No way to tell her to grab Leslie and run.

Brian set his hand on the lid. "You want to see? Have at it." He said, squaring his body with Wuun.

"Open it, Commander," Wuun said as he leveled the pistol. "Or they will."

"Enough," the heavy voice came from the hall as the broad-shouldered man with the clean-shaven head stepped into the doorway.

Brian suddenly felt sick, his energy sucked from his body. Anger soon followed, creeping though his veins like venom.

Admiral Mills crossed the room and pushed the sergeant's arms down. "Put it away. He's right. We got what we wanted."

"You knew about this?" Brian squinted. His brain was not focusing.

"I told you not to dig," he stabbed a finger at him. "But you had to have a mission." Mills' glare bore into the old woman. "And you, you should have died forty years ago."

"Sorry, I missed the flight you prepared for us."

"Doesn't matter now," he said as he swept up Douglas' decaying leather satchel. "It's over."

"No," Mimi stepped forward.

Wuun lifted his gun again.

Brian put out his arm, stopping her. "Let him have it."

"Those papers prove your father was tricked," she protested. "We need them to clear his name. Your name."

Mills' face reddened. "If he was tricked, it was by you and the ambassador."

"We were never told of the attack," Mimi said, her voice cracking. She turned to Brian. Her rising tears surprised him. "I wouldn't have let him go," she said, softly.

"It doesn't matter," Brian told her. "Not anymore."

"There is no redemption for any of us," Mills said to Mimi. He turned to Brian and Leslie. "We've hurt enough people," he said.

With the satchel in hand, Mills stepped to the door. He turned back to Brian. "Your father was a good man."

"He just trusted certain friends too much."

Mills frowned. "Let them go," he instructed Wuun.

"I killed two men for you and the admiral," the sergeant snapped. "They know."

"It's their word against yours."

"What about the treasure?"

"I suggest you take that box to the deepest point of the lagoon and let it sink to the bottom."

"No," Wuun spat. "It's mine now."

Mills heaved his big shoulders. "Good luck explaining how you found it."

"You'll do the explaining."

"Like hell I will," the admiral said as he turned toward the door.

Wuun snapped the trigger. He might have killed the admiral had he reacted faster, but the shot only caught Mills in the thick flesh of his upper arm. The grazing round spun him out of the room and brought the groan of a bull elephant. A trail of expletives followed as Mills stumbled down the hall and out of the house.

There was venom in the islander's face. Raging spite he would render on to the American admiral but first, there were witnesses to silence.

Brian might have been a match for the sergeant had he not been weakened by the decompression sickness, his stomach not nauseated, and his elbows and knees not throbbing with the pain of nitrogen bubbles. What he possessed was the need to protect Leslie.

He launched himself with all the strength he had. Catching Wuun's outstretched arm, Brian thrust the gun upward as the hammer dropped against the next round. It exploded next to Brian's ear, but the bullet ripped harmlessly through the plywood ceiling.

Legs pumping, Brian drove him backwards into the wall. The impact ejected the Colt from his waist and sent it wobbling across the floor like a fumbled football.

Jaws clinched, the two men seized each other's wrists, and for a moment, they were frozen in the center of the room. But Wuun, shorter and stronger, had the leverage over the commander.

In a burst of fury, he forced Brian backwards. They crashed into the rickety shelves along the adjacent wall and were at once bombarded by an avalanche of books and artifacts.

Across the cobblestones of text, they stumbled and fell hard to the floor. Brian rolled on top of the islander, pouring his weight onto the sergeant's wrist, pinning the revolver-filled hand to the floor.

Suddenly, Mimi was beside them. "He's going," she screamed as she stomped on Wuun's hand to break his grip from the pistol. Once. Twice. Thump. Thump. A third time and the gun fell from his shattered grip. She grabbed the weapon, but instead of turning it on the sergeant, the Chinese woman dashed out of the room after Mills.

Brian watched her retreat with disbelief. The distraction was all the sergeant needed. He freed his right leg and, like a roundhouse punch, kneed Brian in the side. He broke two ribs, sending Brian gasping for breath.

Wuun rolled to his feet, dashed around the desk, and dove for the Colt handgun. Fighting broken fingers, he grabbed the weapon and turned on the commander.

What the sergeant met, however, was a jolt of pain that threw him backwards. Suddenly, a gush of warm blood was flowing down and across his chest. Reaching up, he discovered the steel shaft of the fishing spear had spontaneously pierced the side of his neck.

Standing on the opposite side of the desk, still pressing her weight against the long shaft, Leslie glared at him. "Severed carotid artery with profuse bleeding into the larynx. Difficult to stop," she sneered. "Even if I wanted to."

Wuun's eyes narrowed. He seized the spear shaft and with vengeance, yanked it away. A new surge of dark fluids hiccupped from his lips as he lifted the handgun.

Brian grabbed the desk with both hands and heaved it over. Wrapping himself around Leslie, he pulled her to the floor.

As the desk toppled, the water-soaked crate crashed onto the islander. The booby-trapped box was rigged to destroy a Maru-class freighter. But forty years of salt water had eaten through the connecting wires and stripped the power from the Americans' primitive arsenal. It was only the waterproof Torpex that exploded.

Still, the old detonator had enough force to shatter the study's sliding glass door and knock the remaining shelves from the walls and fill the room with a cloud of dust and sand.

With his ears screaming from the explosion, Brian turned Leslie's face gently. He sighed when he saw a flicker of her cinnamon eyes. "Are you okay?" he whispered.

She nodded.

Brian peered around the overturned desk, or what was left of it. Wuun's body lay torn open as though he had taken a shotgun blast at close range. But he had. The only difference was that the buckshot that tore into him and riddled the walls and ceiling were uncut diamonds. The desk's thick metal top had acted as a barrier, saving Brian and Leslie from the same fate.

Brian helped Leslie to her feet. Seeing the sergeant, she slipped her arms around Brian and pulled him close.

"You both all right?" Mimi asked as she entered the study. She held the revolver limp at her side.

"Yes," Leslie said. She ran a finger through Brian's matted hair. "We're both fine."

"Seems he got what he wanted," Brian said, with a nod toward Wuun.

Mimi glanced at the body and the sparkling fragments with indifference. "So did Mills," she said bitterly. "He got away." She tossed the gun into the remains of the sergeant's lap.

"Not with what he wanted," Brian said as he unzipped his wetsuit jacket. From inside, he pulled out the oilskin-wrapped documents he had taken from his father's satchel.

37

HONOMU, HAWAII, 1986

T HE LAST AMBER RAYS of the day were warm on his face as he sat on the edge of the paved walkway that snaked around the estate. While the rest of the path was edged with a carpet of grass and swept daily by his army of gardeners, this far end of the cement trail was beyond their commission.

It turned abruptly away from the manicured grounds, as if its sole purpose was to lead unattended children to a haunted jungle. Guarded by only two crossed boards leaning against a rock, the short section the admiral now rested upon lead toward the cliff's edge of the grounds. It was speculation that the estate's previous owners planned to build a hanging deck here that would stretch over the volcanic rocks but could never gain the permits.

"Take me to where the sidewalk ends," he would tell Miss Swanson. He was never sure if she understood the reference to Shel Silverstein's masterpiece, but he did not care.

She would wheel him to the corner of the property, tuck an unnecessary blanket over his frail legs and plop that silly, long-billed hat

343

on his head. Embroidered with red sailboats around the brim, she had bought it for him because his Navy hat did not block enough of the sun. UV rays, she warned.

On his lap, he cradled the cordless phone from the house. The telescoping antenna was still extended, ready for the next call.

"You were right," Mills had told him. "She was there." Over the hum of the Learjet's engines, Tendrey could hear the exhaustion in his friend's voice.

"I told you. Goddamnit, I told you. Now, he's going to go back and find it," Tendrey hissed.

"He did, Joe," Mills said, he winched against the pain in his shoulder. "Everything. Somehow, he found everything."

"Oh, Jesus," Tendrey sighed. The anger that gave him strength for eighty years was leaving him. He was suddenly tired.

Mills did not think there would be an inquiry, not unless the Chinese woman pressed for one. Perhaps the Navy would award Douglas and his crew some posthumous commendations for entering the lagoon during the attack and make sure their records were expunged.

"And the false orders?" Tendrey asked. "Do you think they will let it go?"

There was silence on the other side of the line. "It's a forty-year-old can of worms."

"It is," Tendrey agreed, his voice barely a whisper.

"All the same," Mills confided. "I think I am going to pack my desk."

After a time, Tendrey collapsed the phone antenna and let the handset drop to the ground beside his wheelchair. He pushed his hat back, lifted his chin and welcomed the warmth washing over him. *This was life,* he thought. *Sun and sea.*

"Admiral," Marks called as he approached.

The admiral did not open his eyes but lifted his hand, showing his secretary he was awake and listening.

"There are two men here to see you, Admiral." Marks said.

"Who?"

"They're from the Naval office in Honolulu, sir. Internal Affairs," he said, his words filled with an unexpected level of stress.

Tendrey focused on the reefs. "Tell them I am not having visitors today."

"I told them you weren't to be disturbed. They're being insistent, Admiral. Very insistent."

"Well, the old witch certainly didn't waste any time pressing her point," Tendrey said, though it was more to himself than to Marks.

"Sir?"

Tendrey pulled the blanket tighter. He stared at the horizon as if contemplating the world.

Marks waited patiently, although his nerves were frazzled. The two men were more than insistent. They had been threatening.

"Go in the study and take my memoirs from the safe," the admiral said, finally. "Give the gentlemen chapter seventeen. Tell them it will answer their questions."

"Yes, sir," Marks turned.

"And Marks."

"Yes, Admiral?"

Tendrey cleared his throat. "They are not to take anything with them. Once they finish and leave, I want you to take the papers and the rest of my memoirs and burn them."

"Sir?"

"Do it, Marks," Tendrey turned to him, his gaze stone cold. "A favor to an old man. Burn all of them."

"Yes, Admiral," Marks said and hurried to the house.

Tendrey watched as his secretary retreated across the grounds. Once he disappeared into the garden, the admiral turned back to the sea. It was a beautiful royal blue laced with white cap tips.

Tendrey rolled the collar of his robe and straightened his silly hat. He unlatched the brake lock of his wheelchair and rolled himself forward.

A few feet from the crossed boards, the cement path sloped downward. He had not noticed that before, as he had never been this close to the edge.

As the wheelchair gathered speed, he braced himself for the collision, but the makeshift barrier offered no resistance. On impact, the boards simply swung out of his way.

The newspapers will call it an accident, he thought as he reached the end. The last thing he saw was the welcoming horizon and the rich blue of the deep sea.

38

MOEN ISLAND, TRUK LAGOON, 1986

"IS THAT ONE-HUNDRED percent oxygen?" Leslie said in a high voice as she pointed to the clear tube feeding the plastic mask covering Brian's nose and mouth.

The U.S. Coast Guard medic was on the opposite side of the wheeled gurney pushing it toward an awaiting white Hercules aircraft. With its rear boarding ramp extended to the tarmac like a monstrous tongue, it looked as though they were about to sacrifice Brian, stretcher, and all, to the belly of an angry winged god.

"Yes, ma'am," he confirmed. The chest-thumbing rumble of the plane's four massive engines made it impossible to communicate normally.

Holding Brian's hand, she continued to query the medic. "It has to be one hundred percent O2. And fluids. He needs to be well hydrated before he gets into the hyperbaric chamber."

"Yes, ma'am. We are aware of the procedures," the medic assured her. He had a pleasant southern drawl that emphasized his calm patience.

"Do you have oral Dermerol aboard. I'd suggest we start him with ten milliliters."

"We do, ma'am. And I assure you, every member on the transport is trained for decompression sickness."

Leslie pursed her lips realizing he was right. The red marbling color across Brian's face and the blotchiness of his skin were the classic symptoms of the bends. She knew he was in good hands, but still, her eyes began to well.

Brian lifted the oxygen mask. "I'm going to be fine."

She slapped his hand. "Leave that."

"I assume you're accompanying us, Doctor?" the medic asked.

"Are you going to tell me otherwise?"

"Honestly, ma'am, I don't think the entire Pacific Fleet could tell you otherwise," he said with a grin.

Leslie smiled.

Two more Coast Guard airmen hurried down the ramp as they reached the plane. "How are we doing, Commander?" the airman with the baby face and pencil thin blond mustache asked as he grabbed the front of the stretcher and lifted the front wheels.

"Commander," Honma called as he ran across the tarmac waving.

Brian pressed the airmen to wait. Leslie frowned.

"You're forgetting a few things," the captain said as he handed Leslie both her father's notebook and Douglas' logbook. "Miss Ming wanted to be sure you got these."

"She's not coming?" Brian asked.

"I don't think so. She made a phone call from my office. Gave me these, and she said to say thank you."

"That's it?" Brian asked.

Honma had no answer for him.

"Who'd she call?" Leslie asked.

The captain shrugged. "I don't know exactly, but two minutes later, my phone was ringing nonstop. Seems there are a few people in Washington who are suddenly interested in my lagoon."

Brian smiled under the mask. "I imagine there will be more than a few, Captain."

"There is also the matter of a few uncut diamonds," he told Leslie. "They're the property of the government, of course, but your father's research permits entitled him to a finder's fee. A significant fee. Which, I believe, Doctor, will go to you."

Leslie looked out at the blue expanse of the lagoon. She sighed. "Use it for the clinic," she said.

"Are you sure?"

"Absolutely."

"It would be a waste to have a new clinic without a new doctor?"

A smile slowly grew. "You're right," she said. "I shouldn't leave Paul on his own. At least not in the beginning."

Honma grinned. "He'll be happy to hear it."

She kissed the captain on the cheek. "Thank you. For everything."

The medic leaned in. "Time to go, Commander. Doctor."

Honma reached across the gurney and met Brian's hand. "You know, Commander, people come to Truk for vacation too."

"I'll remember that," he said from under the mask.

As the aircraft engines spooled up eagerly and the medics pulled Brian up the ramp, Leslie remained at his side, never letting go of his hand.

•   •   •

Mimi walked the narrow path that started at the shoreline, weaved through a dense grove of trees, and rose along the mountainside. It was worn in some places, but in others, thick foliage covered it as the jungle continuously tried to heal the gouge of footfalls. Pushing through the green blanket, she knew exactly where she was headed.

Midway up the hill, the path ended on a broad, flat of land. At the far end, a small, single room hutch stood wedged into a wild hedge of breadfruit and banana trees. Three sides were built from palm tree logs and old sheet metal scraps, while the cement remnants of a Japanese gunnery position created the fourth wall.

Mimi stepped into the small clearing, the formal garden, as she liked to call it. At the edges, several noisy chickens announced her arrival as they scattered in separate directions. She stepped around the hand tools and the fishing gear leaning on the three-legged table.

Next to the door, seashell wind chimes played with the breeze. She pulled the canvas flap as quietly as she could and slipped inside.

"Tea?" the man asked in a gruff, strained voice. He was standing at the small petrol stove, his back to her.

"With cream," she said. There was no cream, of course. But that was their private humor.

"And our selection of crumpets and scones, ma'am?" In his tattered khaki shorts and stained shirt, with its left sleeve pinned, he played along.

"Let me," she said, trying to take the kettle from his hand.

"No." He shooed her away. "You sit."

She moved to the low bed built along one wall. "They're gone," she told him.

"The satchel?" He filled two mismatched cups, checking the heat with the tip of his finger. He dipped the tea bag briefly into each.

"He found it," she said.

"He did? I never expected that."

"I knew he would." She took the cup from his scared hand.

He laughed. "No, you didn't." With memorized steps, he moved to the bunk and sat down beside her.

She leaned against him, her shoulder into his.

"Too bad about Henry."

"Yes," she agreed.

"Funny, isn't it? That old enemies can become good friends."

"Time heals," she whispered.

"It's over then."

"Finally."

"It doesn't bring them back."

"No," she agreed. "It doesn't."

"They were good men. Every one of them."

"And now they will be remembered that way," she assured him.

Leaning forward, he set his cup on a low, canvas covered table. He ran his fingers to the cloth's edge and pulled it back. Beneath were two water-stained U.S. Marine footlockers. "You've never asked for them," he said. "Do you want them now?"

Mimi set her cup beside his. She gently took his face in her hands. Thick scars had replaced his dark, beautiful eyes, eyes that had once made her tremble. "I have all I want," she said softly.

Slipping his arm around her, he kissed her gently. They sat together in the small hut listening to the chimes dancing in the warm breeze that swirled up the mountain from the peaceful blue waters of Truk Lagoon.

ABOUT THE AUTHOR

Mitchell Sam Rossi is an American novelist, screenwriter, and journalist. Growing up in the beach culture of Southern California, he spent most of his youth in or on the water. An avid sailor, scuba diver, and mediocre surfer, Mitchell first pursued a career in marine biology, which gave him the opportunity to explore the Caribbean and the South Pacific. But a long-held desire to write became his calling and ultimately led to a thirty-year career as a journalist. He has written about ships, classic cars, outdoor travel, and most recently on environmental issues. When not at the keyboard, or searching for his next excursion, Mitchell is usually sailing the waters of Northern California, where he lives with his wife and daughter.

YOU MIGHT ALSO ENJOY

DANGEROUS INSPIRATION

by Greg Stone

Synesthesia alters detective-turned-novelist Ronan Mezini's perceptions. But can it help him find the killer?

DUE DATE

A SHELBY MCDOUGALL MYSTERY

by Nancy Wood

Surrogate mother Shelby McDougall just fell for the biggest con of all—a scam that risks her life … and the lives of her unborn twins.

THE NAMES OF HEAVEN

by Flavia Idà

In 1511, a Spanish ship sank off the coast of Yucata. These were the first white men ever to set foot on the mainland of the American continent, and the first white men the Maya had ever seen.

Available from Paper Angel Press in
hardcover, trade paperback, and digital editions
paperangelpress.com